Rhinos Sharks & Unicorns

A HERO'S JOURNEY

Vic Feazell

ISBN: 0615974627
ISBN 13: 9780615974620
Library of Congress Control Number: 2014942090
Vic Feazell- Austin, TX

FOREWORD

This is a work of fiction. It is written in the form of a parable. Those who have ears, let them hear.

Chapter 1

ON A HOT TEXAS HIGHWAY

Keys rattle in the dark as a hand reaches for the door. A flash of light! Boom!

Fire. More fire.

Windows shake more than two miles away, broken glass for a hundred yards. Bob Johnson is startled from his bed. He thinks a truck hit his house. Twisted metal, bricks, and other debris land on the highway overpass. Traffic stops in both directions.

In a motel across the side street, seventeen-year-old Abel Patel's first thought is that a bomb exploded. Glass shards cover him in his bed. An eerie reddish glow fills the room. He throws the dislodged curtains from his body and runs in search of his parents. His foot slices open.

Outside, a massive whirlwind of fire dances where the building once stood. Sirens. More sirens. Fire trucks fight the blaze. A TV station van moves in as close as the firemen will allow. Live coverage.

The next morning, at the courthouse and in the coffee shops in Waco, everyone was talking about it.

"Did you hear the explosion?"

"Hell, I felt it."

"Any idea what caused it?"

"News said they pulled a body from the rubble."

"Dead?"

"Probably."

Time passes and questions fade from people's memories.

———

One Year Later:

No one was going to die from heatstroke in Austin today, but unfortunately someone was going to get hurt. God had not chosen to answer Marvin's prayer the way he hoped. He would ultimately have to go through with the plan, like it or not.

"Get me out of this," Marvin prayed. "Get me out of this."

But for now he was stuck, dead still, in a traffic jam on Interstate Highway 35 in the middle of Austin, Texas. Nothing was moving.

Interstate 35 runs north and south through the center of the United States. It stretches from Laredo, Texas, at the U.S./Mexican border all the way to Duluth, Minnesota. It divides the state of Texas in half, separating East Texas from West Texas, like a crisp fold in a large piece of butcher paper.

Depending on one's perspective, IH-35 starts, or ends, abruptly in Laredo, Texas, on the bank of the famous Rio Grande River. Then it extends north through the city of San Antonio, the proud home of the Alamo. After dissecting San Antonio, it continues on to Austin, the state capital, which sits in the heart of the state.

Not only is Austin located in the heart of Texas geographically, but it's the heart in a spiritual sense as well. Austin is the feeling center of Texas, its conscience, its compassion, whereas Dallas and Houston are its business centers. In Austin, a popular bumper sticker is "Keep Austin Weird." In Dallas, a popular bumper sticker is "Keep Dallas Pretentious."

From Austin, the mammoth concrete artery continues north through a town called Waco. A popular bumper sticker in Waco is "Keep Waco Wacko."

The gargantuan ribbon then careens on to the metropolis of Dallas and finally across the Red River and the Oklahoma border, a distance of nearly nine hundred miles in the state of Texas alone.

Every day, huge amounts of traffic travel over the vast landscape, like giant lines of ants carrying their crumbs across a picnic blanket the size of Texas. Commerce depends on the flow of traffic up and down Interstate 35, but on this particular day, in the city of Austin, the traffic wasn't moving at all. A tourniquet was wrapped tight across the middle of Texas's main artery like a python squeezing off the flow of life. Not a car, not a bus, not an eighteen-wheeler was moving. And to make matters worse, it was hot.

Anyone who lives in Austin will admit that the traffic is bad. But on this day in 1995, the traffic was worse than usual. The upper deck of Interstate 35 was at a total standstill. All the frontage roads were clogged. No one could exit the highway. Things were at a crawl. Horns honked. People craned their necks in vain, trying to get a look at what was causing the holdup.

The three young men sitting in the old, two-tone blue Ford Tempo were already anxious.

Marvin, in the back seat, was nervous and still praying.

The driver, Mace Spinella, was fidgeting. He lit a cigarette. He had better things to do today than sit in a traffic jam. He didn't have time for this nonsense. He took a long drag on the cigarette, exhaled, and stared straight ahead with a brooding look on his face.

I don't need this shit, he thought. *Why can't I ever get a fucking break? Why does this crap always happen to me?* Negative, self-defeating thoughts whirled in his head.

Gridlock had set in.

"Damn it," Mace muttered, barely audible to the other two passengers. "Damn it. Damn it."

He took another drag on his cigarette and exhaled. Marvin coughed, showing his displeasure with the driver's secondhand smoke, but he dared not say a word. Mace was in one of his moods. It wouldn't be worth it.

"Damn it," Mace said again, only louder this time.

All across town, selfish, self-absorbed drivers, trying to gain a slight advantage over fellow motorists, had inched and crowded their way into intersections after traffic lights had signaled them to stop. Now everything was clogged. Mace felt his anger building.

"They should know better," he shouted. "Gridlock wouldn't happen if people would follow the fucking rules!"

Mace Spinella had seen this happen before, plenty of times, and he didn't like it. And here he was again, stuck in a traffic jam that wasn't his fault and unable to move—*a prisoner of other people's stupidity.*

Mace rolled the window down and stuck his head out of the car hoping he might be able to see something he couldn't already see through the windshield. The heat from the pavement shot up in a wave and hit him hard in the face. He jerked back into the car and cranked the window up as fast as his arm would move.

All four lanes were blocked, bumper to bumper, as far as he could see.

Gridlock sucks, Mace thought. He scanned the lines of cars, looking for an escape route. Out of frustration, he pounded the horn.

"This sucks, damn it. Fuck...fuck, fuck, fuck, fuck, fuck, fuck!" He said it seven times. His two friends in the car knew what that meant. He was really upset.

Tempers were hot, but the weather was even hotter. Central Texas is usually hot, but this was August, and in Austin, August is hotter than it is anywhere else.

If you compare the weather in Austin to salsa, the favorite condiment of most Austinites, the month of June is the "mild" variety, July is "hot," but August is the "three-alarm extra hot" recipe. Today was that kind of hot. The sun beat down on the stalled cars like a sledgehammer. The pavement steamed and blistered under its rays.

There is never a good time for a car's air conditioner to break down, and August in Austin is especially not a good time, but that is exactly what was about to happen to the air conditioner in the car Mace, Brick, and Marvin were in. The old Ford had been on its last leg for a few years.

"Faith and a prayer is what keeps it going," Mace often said, but that wasn't really true because neither Mace nor Brick had any faith, and they didn't pray either. The only reason their 1982 Ford Tempo even had an up-to-date inspection sticker on the windshield was because Mace bribed a friend who worked at a gas station. "This is the last time," his friend told him. "I'm not doing this next year. Don't even ask. You have to get this thing fixed."

Mace laid hard on the horn again, adding to the crazy cacophony of honks and other traffic noise, but his face didn't change expression. He stared ahead, trying to control himself, trying to appear calm, even though he was getting angrier by the second.

Then, a mushroom cloud of steam and smoke bellowed from under the hood of the car, and the air conditioner fan coughed, wheezed, and stopped blowing.

"Oh, crap, what's that?" Brick said, looking helplessly at Mace.

A drop of sweat on the tip of Brick's nose dripped onto what had been, earlier that morning, his clean, white, starched shirt. But now his shirt was ringed around the armpits with perspiration.

Just a few hours before, Brick had paused to look at himself in the mirror, taking pride in his appearance and winking as he straightened his tie, flexed his sculptured biceps, and took one last glance before glancing back again—and then one more time again.

It was Brick's habit before leaving the apartment to check out his looks in the full-length mirror he had personally installed on the wall next to the front door so it couldn't miss him whenever he walked by. Today had been no exception. Brick wanted to look especially good today because he had big plans. Today was the day he would finally get a client—sort of.

Brick had done his research. He had gathered his materials and planned everything out. Today he was going to show people he was ready for business and ready to start hauling in the dough. But now things weren't working out. And if it didn't happen today, it probably wasn't going to happen. Marvin, in the back seat, was having second thoughts. And Bill at the supermarket; well, Bill was another story.

Brick felt for something in his suit coat pocket. It was still there.

"Do something!" Brick complained to Mace.

The whiney tone in Brick's voice added irritation to the situation. Although unconscious of it, something deep in Mace's psyche made him physically cringe whenever he heard that tone coming out of Brick. It was "like finger nails on a chalk board" he would say – a tired, old analogy, but one that fit.

"I told you not to take the upper deck...I told you," Brick continued, "Now look at me. I'm all wet."

Mace cringed again and shot Brick an icy glare from the corner of his eye, but he didn't say anything.

He wanted to, but he held it in. Mixed with Mace's irritation at Brick was material for a good joke if Mace wanted to take it, but right now he didn't.

I'm all wet, Mace repeated the words in his head, but decided to save the put down for a later time.

Mace was accustomed to Brick's complaining and whining, even though it got on his nerves. The two young men had known each other since childhood. They attended grade school and high school together and had been roommates for almost ten years now. People who knew them joked that they were "as close as two men can be who aren't gay."

In spite of being close friends, Mace would readily acknowledge that Brick was a whiner. Mace accepted that quality about Brick long ago. Although it occasionally took an emotional toll on him, most of the time he didn't consciously notice Brick was doing it.

Over the years Mace had become somewhat desensitized to the whining and complaining, much like a man who lives next to the railroad track and no longer notices the train roaring by every hour, but he's still tired when he wakes up in the morning and he doesn't know why.

Mace ignored him again and continued scanning the long lines of cars hoping for a break in the traffic.

I've got to get off this friggin highway, Mace thought. He surveyed the situation, looking for any option other than sitting stalled.

Earlier that day, the plan had called for Mace to drive Brick and Marvin to the supermarket to do their thing before he headed off to the hospital to hopefully gather some leads. They had to make some money and fast, but now they were going nowhere. Now they were stalled under the blistering sun on the upper deck of IH 35 in a car with no air-conditioning.

"Air conditioner's dead." Mace said. "Roll down the windows, but keep your heads inside."

Brick was the only one complaining, but he was not the only one suffering from the Texas heat and the broken air conditioner. Mace had perspiration rings under his arms too, and his heavily starched dress shirt was getting sticky against his chest.

Mace let loose a big exhale that sounded more like a moan, loosened his tie, and looked in the rearview mirror at Marvin in the backseat, who was keeping quiet but looked like he was ready to pass out.

The splotchy, pale pallor of heat exhaustion was on Marvin's face. It consumed his usually soft brown skin and made him look like a shorter, plumper version of one of those zombie dancers in Michael Jackson's *Thriller* video. Marvin's eyes were glazed over, and tiny beads of sweat formed on his forehead and up into the hairline of his neatly trimmed Afro-style haircut. His breathing was measured and short. Mace had never seen Marvin look so pale. Mace had never seen any black guy look so pale.

Mace took a final drag on his cigarette and flicked it out the window. He watched as it bounced off the hood of a car that had crept within inches of their old Ford. The other driver's mouth dropped open in surprise. He glared angrily at Mace, who pretended not to notice.

Mace looked at the occupants of his own car and mumbled between his teeth, "He's lucky I don't kick his hairy old ass." Then he swung his right arm over the seat and turned his back to the driver of the other car. He looked at Marvin in the backseat. Immediately, his voice and demeanor changed, showing his concern.

"You OK, little buddy?"

Marvin caught Mace's eye and nodded, but the expression on his face said otherwise.

"Well, don't pass out back there. As soon as I get off this highway, you have work to do."

Marvin nodded affirmatively at Mace again, but not very convincingly. He was reluctant. Ever since Brick hatched the plan, Marvin had not felt good about it. Admittedly, he needed the money, but he always considered himself to be an honest person, and Brick's plan called for anything but honesty.

Furthermore, the idea that he could get seriously hurt didn't appeal to him either. Yes, he needed the money, desperately, but he didn't feel right about lying, and he certainly didn't want to injure himself and end up an invalid for the rest of his life. What had he gotten himself into? Maybe this traffic jam was God's way of getting him off the hook and out of a bad situation. Maybe Grandma's daily prayers for her little Marvin's safety were being answered right now. Maybe he wasn't going to have to do this after all, and he wouldn't have to disappoint his friends Brick and Mace by telling them no.

"Lord, please get me out of this, and I promise I'll never do anything like this again, please," Marvin silently prayed.

Sometimes it can get hot enough to kill a person in an old Ford Tempo with a broken air conditioner on a sunny August day in Austin. It can bake you like a turkey.

Earlier that month, in a van on a hot parking lot, a mother had left her baby in the car seat for twenty minutes while she went into the store to shop for makeup. When she came out, her baby was dead. There was a sad story in the newspaper with pictures of the mother crying. There were letters to the editor expressing their sympathy for her and bemoaning the Texas heat. There were also letters blaming her. Mace had read the article and the follow-up articles about the funeral and the letters to the editor with interest.

"Leaving a baby alone—how can people be so stupid?" he had said. Now he found himself in a situation where one of his only friends looked like he might have heatstroke, and people would probably say it was his fault.

Mace's imagination presented him with scenario after scenario, each one worse than the one before. *If anything happens to Marvin, it will be all over the papers. I can see it now: "Black Law Student Dies of Heatstroke."*

I could be investigated. I could get indicted for that bogus inspection sticker. I could get charged with manslaughter! Shit! Why didn't I bring a bottle of water? Another panic attack was threatening to set in.

Just as Brick started another whiny episode of "why me, why me of all days, why me…" Mace saw a sudden

11

break in traffic and heaved the clunky old car across one lane, onto the exit ramp, off the highway, bouncing across another lane of access road, and heading downhill toward the light at Eighth Street, where he turned a quick right and then another. He was off on a side street, heading north, still surrounded by honking automobiles, but at least the old heap was moving forward and the breeze coming through the open windows condensed the perspiration on their bodies and faces, breathing new life into the three young men.

Marvin couldn't help himself. He hung his head out of the window like a dog enjoying the feel of the wind whipping at his face and hair. Brick positioned himself in the front passenger seat, stuck both his arms out the window, and let the newfound and greatly appreciated airflow start drying the dampness from his shirt.

Feeling the exhilaration of finally moving and the relief of the cool condensation on his body, Brick exclaimed happily, "Now we're cooking with gas!" and flashed a toothy, self-satisfied grin at his two companions.

Brick actually thought he had said something intelligent, but Mace didn't agree—not one bit—and he couldn't hold back this time. Mace felt the emotion stirring in his stomach like magma. The pressure boiled and suddenly exploded, and a verbal tirade flowed out of Mace's mouth and straight toward an unsuspecting Brick.

"Cooking with gas?" Mace said, his volume increasing to punctuate the last word. He asked again even louder, "Cooking with gas?"

Brick's eyes widened large and round as the volume and the anger struck him head on. Marvin cringed in the backseat.

"What kind of a fucking, dumb-ass thing to say is that?" Mace kept going. "Cooking with fucking gas? We're out here burning up, and you can't come up with anything better than cooking with gas?" He repeated the phrase with as much contempt as he could muster, "Cooking with gas?"

A wounded and startled Brick thought for an instant that Mace was finished, but he started again.

"Cooking with gas? Makes no fucking sense! Sometimes you're the stupidest goddamn person I've ever met. Frying our asses off out here—finally get some relief, and the best you can say is now we're cooking with fucking gas?"

Brick interrupted, "But..."

"Shut up! We were cooking five minutes ago, you dumb shit! Now we're finally not cooking. What kind of fucking lawyer are you, anyway? You're never going to amount to a damn thing if you can't do better than..." Mace stopped himself in midsentence, all frustrated, and then ended with a half-hearted, "Kiss my ass!"

Brick was emotionally shaken and taken aback by Mace's verbal attack. His muscles stiffened like he had been doused with a bucket of cold water. And as hard as he tried to come up with something, all he could think to say in response was a muffled "fuck you, asshole," which Mace pretended to ignore.

Sullenness overtook Brick, and he started to pout. He crossed his arms and looked at the floorboard, his bottom lip protruding. His feelings were hurt.

Mace was his best friend in all the world, and Mace had rarely lost his temper with him in all the years and all the situations they had been through, although it was not uncommon at all for Mace to lose his temper with others.

Brick knew Mace didn't mean it, but it still hurt his feelings. Mace was typically the nurturer among the two. Sure, he was selfish and sloppy and had no respect for other people's property, but he usually cared about how Brick felt.

The two young men had lived apart once since high school graduation, and that was only for a short period of time about a year after they finished college. It was Brick who lost his temper that time and threw Mace out of the apartment because he was three months behind on his share of the rent and had just wasted all of his meager paycheck vainly trying to get the attention of a girl he was interested in dating. It was Brick who went into the tirade then, stuffing Mace's scant belongings into two plastic trash bags and throwing them into the hall with his last comment to Mace being, "I never want to see you again!"

Brick waited three months for Mace to come back with a contrite attitude before he gave up on that idea, sought him out, and took him back in, abandoning the expectation of Mace ever being current on his rent.

Mace careened the old car around a stalled bus on San Jacinto Street, tires screeching hot, springs squeaking and popping. Steam continued billowing from under the hood. It was a pathetic sight. Mace saw an opportunity and pulled abruptly into a parking space at the curb in front of Scholz's Beer Garten where a black-and-gray ten-year-old Mercedes had just pulled away in a puff of exhaust.

Through the smoke, Mace noticed the bumper sticker on the back of the car. It said, "Don't Be A Pharisee—Pharisees Vote Republican." For an instant, his eyes made direct contact with the eyes of the driver, a medium-build, middle-aged man in a black suit jacket with below-the-collar-length salt-and-pepper hair.

If Mace had been at all aware of the internal dialogue in his head, he would have heard himself saying *old hippy* in a judgmental tone just as their eyes met. But Mace wasn't aware of what he was thinking or even that he had made eye contact with another human being, so he swerved thoughtlessly into the parking space in front of Scholz's where the Mercedes had been, the only vacant space in sight, and prepared to give Brick and Marvin their instructions and get everyone back on task.

Mace and Brick didn't know or appreciate it yet, but the place where they had parked, Scholz's Garten, was more than just a hopping music venue at night; it had become a hangout during the day where old lawyers and Democratic politicians, active and retired, gathered to share war stories. Mace and Brick had no idea that their paths would someday cross with Texas political notables such as Anne Richards, Jim Mattox, Garry Mauro, and Jim Hightower.

Scholz Biergarten, as it was originally called, bills itself as "The Oldest Business in Texas," which may be doubtful, but it is pretty old. It was established by German immigrant and Confederate veteran August Scholz in 1866 at the very spot where it still sits. Back in 1866, it was way out in the country, but by 1995, it was right in the middle of downtown Austin.

In days gone by, before the horseless carriage, the moving picture show, and organized children's sports, Scholz's had been a favorite meeting place for the German population of Austin; families would come to make a day of it, and children would play around the bandstand and later nap on quilts under the old oak trees while their parents listened to music, danced, or shared the latest gossip from town or news from the frontier or from back east.

As time passed and the television set took its toll on people's time, Scholz reinvented itself and became a popular nighttime gathering place for the younger University of Texas crowd to flirt with each other and take in the sound of the latest bands. Now, more than a hundred years and a lot of beer and barbecue later, the day crowd was a bunch of lawyers, mostly retired, mostly liberal Democrats, who met for dominoes, drinks, and political gossip.

Mace put the car in park and turned off the ignition. The old car clanked and grumbled a few more seconds before dying with a hiss and a little jump. Mace rested his arm on the back of the seat and looked at Brick.

"Look at me," Mace said, pointing his finger back toward his own face. "Now look at you," he said, pointing at Brick. "I didn't mean to hurt your feelings, but I'm stressed out, you know, and it's your fault. You're being a whiny butthole, Brick. All you ever talk about is if we don't come up with some real money real soon, we're getting thrown out of our apartment. Right? We're behind on all our bills. Right? This friggin' car is on its last fucking leg. Right? That's all you talk about anymore. We're at the end of our rope. Seriously."

There was an intensity and urgency about Mace's expression that made him seem frightened and despairingly in need of help, any help.

Neither Mace nor Brick, nor Marvin in the backseat, had any idea that the traffic around them wasn't the only thing not flowing like it should. The pipeline to their life energy was cut off too. It was like the story of the little girl watering flowers with a garden hose who cried out in frustration, "Mommy, the water stopped." Her mother, seeing her predicament, answered, "Sweetheart, you're standing on the hose."

Mace, Brick, and Marvin were all standing on the hose, separating themselves from the source of their supply, and they didn't know it. Just like that little girl, the young men in the car had no clue that they were the cause of their own trouble. They were standing on the pipeline of life with the full weight of all their mental and spiritual energy and complaining because nothing was coming out. They were like the people who tried to run the yellow traffic lights that day and then complained because they were stuck in gridlock.

Mace adjusted himself in the seat, narrowed his eyes, and slowed the pace of his words, emphasizing each one. His voice acquired a desperate tone as he continued to almost plead with Brick. "You're right; I don't want to be homeless and broke. I don't want another lousy job either. Do you? We didn't come this far to mess it up now, did we? So lay off with the damn whining for a while. I'm doing the best I…"

Suddenly Mace stopped in midsentence. His ears perked up like a Labrador retriever listening for a bird. He cocked his head sideways trying to hear. Brick and Marvin looked at him curiously, waiting for him to finish what he was saying. Then, faintly, in the distance the sound of a siren could be made out over the other clamor.

To some, the wail of a distant siren carries with it a sudden foreboding that not all is well, that their loved one may be injured or their house might be on fire, but not for Brick and Mace. Their eyes widened round with excited expectation. They knew it could mean business. If they were lucky, it might be an ambulance. If they got to it fast, it might mean a client.

The distant, screaming sound of opportunity appeared to be getting louder, closer. Mace lunged for the old gray police scanner hanging by one screw under the dashboard and flipped the switch to the on position. The power light glowed red, and the banged-up old scanner whistled and crackled until a voice could be made out over the static, "Auto-pedestrian, Eighth and Red River, one adult male injured, ambulance en route, Unit Twelve proceed to Eighth and Red River, over." The radio crackled again and then came the response, "Ten-four, Unit Twelve en route, over."

"That's only a few blocks from here," Mace said excitedly. "I can make it!"

Actually, it was more like eleven blocks, depending on how you count them, but Mace was feeling up to the challenge. Plus, it would double their chances for success and get him away from Brick for a while.

"What do you mean?" Brick asked, trying his best not to sound whiny, but he had a whiny, contorted look on his face.

"What I mean is, you two take the clunker and go on to the supermarket. You and Marvin know what to do. I'll get to the ambulance on foot. Got to leave now. Might beat the cops."

Mace turned his whole body around, putting both knees in the seat while reaching for his briefcase on the back floorboard with one hand and grabbing at his suit coat on the backseat with the other. He lost his balance and fell backward, catching himself on the steering wheel with the full weight of his butt. It caused the horn to go off with a deafening blare.

The high-pitched blast startled a plaid-shirted man walking out of Scholz's, and he jumped, convulsing involuntarily into the air about two inches. He grabbed for his heart, caught his breath, and then cursed at Mace, "Fu-fu-fuck you, asshole!"

Shaking his fist wildly, Mace yelled back, "Sure, why not? Wish I could. That's my second invitation in ten minutes. Get in line, why don't ya!"

Mace smiled at Brick and said, "I think I've been typecast as the fuckee today." It was his way of letting Brick know he had heard him before, and it was his way of trying to apologize.

When the plaid-shirted man saw Mace get out of the car, he turned around and scurried off down the sidewalk at a fast pace. When he thought he was a safe distance away, and hearing no one behind him, he glanced back to see the steaming old car with the squeaky springs and the police scanner commotion pull away from the curb and merge into traffic.

Mace was crossing the street with his back to the man, at a full run, in the middle of the block. His briefcase was in one hand, and the other was stuck up in the air like a traffic cop signaling cars to stop and let him through. He swiftly negotiated his way through the flux of rush-hour vehicles, looking like a quarterback dodging and weaving for the touchdown. Then he jumped the curb and took off running at a full heat, his tie flapping over his shoulder and his briefcase keeping time like a manic pendulum. It was a curious sight.

The startled man from Scholz's Biergarten wiped the sweat from his brow with a handkerchief and, realizing he was safe from the horn-blaring hooligans, continued down the sidewalk at a more relaxed pace.

Mace made it to the corner of Eighth Street and Red River just as the ambulance attendant was closing the big double doors and the ambulance was slowly pulling away. Mace was exhausted—sweat dripped from his face and saturated his clothing—but he kept his pace, running as fast as his legs could carry him. Still on the move, he quickly assessed the situation. A car was in the street between him and the ambulance, blocking his approach. A policeman was standing beside the car, note pad in hand, interviewing the driver.

Mace couldn't let this one get away. Instinct took over. He let his momentum carry him forward as he leaped backward over the hood of the car, legs extended toward the curb. He landed on his butt, making better use of it this time, and swung his briefcase sideways, letting the centrifugal force bring his feet around to the other side of the car, where he slid off and hit the ground running.

The sound of Mace's butt hitting the hood of the car caused a loud thud. The cop's mouth dropped open in surprise. He pointed his pencil at Mace and started to speak, but Mace beat him to the punch. "I'm family!" he yelled without missing a step. He took a graceful flying leap and landed one foot onto the back bumper of the ambulance and then squeezed his body and briefcase through the space between the doors just as the attendant slammed them shut.

"I'm family," Mace wheezed at the ambulance attendant, scooting in and sitting next to him. "I'm family," he said again, trying to catch his breath. The man on the stretcher looked up at Mace with an expression of appreciation and gratitude on his whiskered face.

"Family," the man replied. Then he smiled a toothless grin and passed out.

Before Mace and Brick moved to Austin to go to law school, they had tried their hand in the movie business. They convinced themselves they would strike it rich in Hollywood. They shared a small apartment in Culver City, not in the best part of town, and barely eked out a living selling knockoff perfume on the street, bartending, and trying to run a G-string clad, muscleman, housecleaning service called "Tight & Tidy," while at the same time auditioning with hundreds of other young actors for the rare "featured extra" job.

A couple of times, they got lucky and landed paying gigs with end-crawl credits such as "man with lantern" and "dead cop number two." They even wrote a couple of screenplays together and registered them with the Screen Writers Guild. They dreamed that their screenplays would be bigger hits than *Chinatown* and that producers would beat a path to their door, but nothing ever happened, except occasionally they'd see a line or a gag they had written in someone else's movie, stolen, obviously, and changed just enough to avoid a successful lawsuit. Eventually they gave up on the idea, but Mace never gave up on writing. His imagination was always working.

Thud! Thud! Then another: *thud!* Mace smiled, imagining the sound of three gray-suited lawyers, briefcases in hand, bouncing in succession off the back of the closed ambulance door.

Why not make it four lawyers? Mace thought.

Thud!

He smiled again, satisfied that he had made the leap and his imaginary competition hadn't. A slight chuckle escaped his lips. He looked at the attendant, hoping he hadn't noticed. The cool air in the air-conditioned ambulance condensed in Mace's eyes, and a tear formed. The ambulance attendant had noticed Mace chuckle, but thought he was crying.

"You're a kind man," the ambulance attendant said. "Don't worry. I'm sure he will be all right."

———

The old clunker coasted into the supermarket parking lot. It was a small store with one set of doors and maybe ten or twelve short aisles inside. There was nothing super about it. Bill, the redheaded, pimply faced stock boy, was pacing out front, still wearing his yellow-stained white apron and smoking a Marlboro.

"Where you been? I got off five minutes ago."

"Don't worry about it. Let's go in. We can do it now," Brick said.

He walked past Bill and up to the door of the store. Marvin followed close behind, looking more nervous than a novice shoplifter.

Bill put out his cigarette and joined them. "What about my money, man?"

"Don't worry about your money. Trust me. You'll get your money. Let's go."

"No, you don't," Bill snapped. "I didn't agree to do this on the come. Pay me now, or forget it."

"You'll get your money. Don't worry about it. Trust me."

"I don't trust shit. Give me my money, or I'm out of here."

"I don't have time for this," Brick grumbled. He reached deep into his pants pocket, retrieved a sweaty fifty-dollar bill, and reluctantly handed it to Bill. "You better not fuck this up."

"You better not fuck this up man," Bill said, stiffening up. "If I lose my job over this, I'm telling."

"Right," Brick said sarcastically, "you'd confess to a crime. Are you stupider than you look?"

Bill looked like he was considering the question seriously for an instant and then he said, "Not really."

"Then let's get this over with. Go inside. Stand by the vegetable bin. Look busy."

Bill stuffed the sweaty fifty into his pocket, mumbled something angrily under his breath, and walked through the door. He passed the check-out stand and stopped at the produce section. He glanced from side to side while nervously fingering a wad of turnip greens. There were only a few other people in view. Outside, Brick felt for the plastic ziplock bag in his suit-coat pocket for the hundredth time that day. It was still there.

"Come on, Marvin. Show's on. Just do it like we discussed. Say your lines. It's just like acting. Nothing to it," Brick said.

"I don't know…"

Brick cut him short. "What do you mean, you don't know? You need the money, don't you? You don't want to have to drop out of law school, do you? You promised me, didn't you?"

"Yeah, but…"

"Trust me. The small amount of physical pain you might suffer will be nothing compared to the ecstasy that will envelop you when I put a check in your hand to cover the rest of your law school education." Brick was using his best persuasive voice. "Just do your stunt like we practiced, and say your lines."

Marvin looked down and nodded in submission. Brick headed for the door and toward Bill, who by now was looking guiltier than Nixon during his "I Am Not a Crook" speech. Marvin followed about ten paces behind, sweating profusely.

As Brick walked past Bill, he reached his hand into the plastic bag in his jacket pocket and pulled out the brown banana peel that had been ripening in the sweltering heat all day. He dropped it onto the floor in Marvin's path. Marvin hit it with his heel. His feet went out from under him, and both legs flew wildly into the air. Marvin landed hard on his right shoulder, and his head hit the concrete floor with a whack.

"Oh God, it hurts," Marvin screamed. He grabbed his neck with both hands, curled onto his side in the fetal position, and began whimpering like a hurt pup.

Bill looked shocked.

Brick looked at Marvin with a sense of admiration for a job well done. Then he started directing the situation in his loudest blustering voice.

"Did you see that? He slipped on that banana peel! I just walked past it and was going to ask that stock boy why he hadn't picked it up yet," Brick said, pointing at Bill.

Not expecting the public accusation, Bill grimaced, and his face turned even redder. "Don't shit a brick, man," he yelled back.

By then a small crowd was gathering, wide-eyed and hanging on Brick's every word. Brick stepped onto a two-foot-tall wooden display case half filled with cantaloupes in the middle of the aisle and yelled, "Someone call an ambulance! Where's the manager?"

The manager, a balding, rotund man in khaki pants and a white, short-sleeve shirt, with the tail hanging half out, rounded the corner at a slow trot. He quickly surveyed the situation. "I'll call an ambulance," he said, panting, "What happened here?"

"No need to panic!" Brick said excitedly. He was still perched on the cantaloupe display stand addressing the small crowd. "I'm a lawyer. Everybody look at how brown that banana peel is. That's evidence. It must have been there a long time, and that box boy," he said, pointing an accusing finger at Bill, "was standing right by it. It must have been there a long time," he repeated. "See how brown it is. You're all witnesses. I'll need your names and phone numbers."

Brick climbed down and began recording people's names and phone numbers in a small notebook he had pulled from his back pocket.

The manager headed off to call an ambulance. When he passed Bill, he snarled and said, "Your ass is grass."

Bill stammered, "Don't blame me, man. I didn't see it. Besides, I'm off the clock, man."

Marvin was still curled up on the floor whimpering.

After a few minutes of gathering information from customers and threatening the manager with a lawsuit if he didn't immediately write a check for thirty thousand dollars, Brick made it back around to Marvin. He bent over and whispered in his ear, "Good job, buddy."

Marvin looked up at Brick with tears in his eyes. "I'm really hurt, you butt-wipe."

When the ambulance arrived, the attendants took Marvin's vital signs. He was in pain, but everything else looked good. They placed him on a gurney and rolled him toward the door. A little old lady in her blue church dress, who smelled strongly of lavender, had been holding Marvin's hand and comforting him during the fifteen-minute wait. She accompanied the gurney out the door and to the ambulance.

"Don't worry, little man," she said to Marvin, "you'll be all right. I'll pray for you. I don't have the slightest how that happened." She continued, "I had just walked past for some carrots, and I didn't see it there."

"Did I get your name and phone number?" Brick asked her curtly.

"Yes, twice," she said. Then she patted Marvin on the back of his hand one last time. With a concerned look on her face, she said, "Thank God it wasn't me. I could have broken a hip. I haven't the slightest."

"I'll meet you at the hospital," Brick told Marvin as the ambulance doors were closing. Then he turned and faced the few spectators who were left. "Did I get everybody's name and phone number?"

He handed the manager one of his business cards and said in a disgusted tone, "You'll be hearing from me."

Then Brick noticed a little boy, about five years old, wearing a cast on his ankle. He walked over and abruptly extended his business card. "Here, give this to your mother. Depending on how that happened, you might have a lawsuit. Tell her to call me."

The little boy took the card, then his face contorted, and he began to cry. "Mommy!"

The card in his hand read:
Brick Hawthorne
Spinella and Hawthorne
Attorneys at Law
Suing Folks Since…Whenever
512-555-2469

Chapter 2

CRYING IN THE CHAPEL

Brackenridge Hospital was established around 1912 as a modern-day, forty-five-bed, state-of-the-art hospital to replace the dilapidated old Austin City-County Hospital, which was built way back in 1884. The new hospital was named posthumously in 1929 in honor of Dr. John Brackenridge, an Indiana native who moved to Austin in the late 1800s to practice his chosen profession and art—medicine.

Dr. Brackenridge was instrumental in getting the huge $50,000 bond issue passed so the new hospital could be constructed. That was a lot of money back in 1912, an awful lot. He labored tirelessly around the clock as chairman of the hospital board and worked until his death to improve the quality of medical care in Austin, fighting disease and injury with one hand and constantly raising funds for hospital improvements with the other.

It's too bad the powers that be waited ten long years after he was pushing up daisies in the graveyard before they finally decided to name the hospital after him. Dr.

Brackenridge never really knew how much the local folks appreciated him, but he had an idea that some of the other doctors and a few city officials didn't appreciate him at all. After his death, some of Austin's movers and shakers objected to renaming the hospital after him. The Lions Club even offered a twenty-five-dollar reward, which was also a lot of money back then, to anyone who could come up with a better name, but no one, not even his detractors, could think of a better one. Eventually they gave in, and it was named Brackenridge.

Occasionally, Dr. Brackenridge would enjoy the short stroll over to Scholz Biergarten just southeast of the new hospital facility. There he could finally relax away from the rigors of his medical duties and the politics of hospital administration. He would enjoy a plate of August Scholz's famous barbecue and a bottle of that newfangled drink, Dr. Pepper, a soft drink invented at a pharmacy in Waco, Texas, in 1885. By the time Dr. Brackenridge was visiting Scholz's, Dr. Pepper was in popular demand in Austin and as far away as Chicago and even New York City.

Scholz's sold plenty of Dr. Pepper, known by its slogan as the "King of Beverages." Old Doc, a cartoon country doctor with a monocle and top hat, was Dr. Pepper's trademark character. Today, no one knows whether anyone ever suggested to the Lions Club that they name the hospital after Old Doc Pepper, but if they had, the city council might have done it.

It goes to show you that no matter how hard people work, no matter what they do for the community, and no matter how self-sacrificing they are, they will always have their detractors. That's just the way it is. And the higher up the flagpole you climb, the more little dogs there will be barking at your butt. It is reported in one of the lesser known Gospels that even Jesus of Nazareth was slandered by his critics, the Pharisees, after he was seen walking on water. They started a rumor that he didn't know how to swim. Dr. Brackenridge knew just how that felt.

Long before the day Mace hitched his ride in the ambulance, Brackenridge Hospital had become one of the premiere hospitals in the State of Texas—in the United States even. It fills several city blocks of land near the corner of Fifteenth Street and Red River Street. It borders a beautiful little park called Waterloo Park on the west side. On the east side, it borders the IH-35 frontage road, thus keeping it directly connected with every sick person from Laredo, Texas, to Duluth, Minnesota—unless gridlock sets in.

Mace Spinella's ambulance ride was shorter than his run to the accident scene. If he had strolled leisurely from Scholz's front door over to the front door of the Brackenridge emergency room, he would have beaten the ambulance there.

When Brick Hawthorne finally got to the emergency room, he was jubilant and marching. The automatic doors parted before him, and he entered like a conquering hero. He looked around. The place was crowded. There were snot-nosed kids crying everywhere. One hung onto his mother's skirt, pulling it down past the top of her faded, red thong panties. She was overweight and not pretty, or Brick would have stared a little longer. A roll of belly fat obscured most of the waistband, but you could tell that the old, red thong panties had once been lacy and sexy. Now they just looked sad and tired, like the lady who wore them.

An old Mexican man in work clothes and tattered, dusty boots sat fumbling with a small stack of forms on a clipboard while blood oozed onto the papers from a dirty, makeshift bandage around his hand. He looked around helplessly, frustrated and in pain, but no one offered assistance. Brick looked away. He had other things to do right now, and this wasn't one of them. This guy looked like he didn't even speak English. Obviously a day laborer with no insurance. *Tough luck*, Brick thought as he continued negotiating his way through the crowded waiting room.

A very pregnant woman was standing at the information window rubbing her lower back with both hands and talking to the cute, young nurse on duty. Brick started to approach the nurse's window, but then, through the crowd, he spotted Mace slumped in a lobby chair across the room. His head was leaning back against the wall, and he was staring up at the ceiling. Not noticing the long face or the aura of depression that covered Mace like a wet wool blanket, Brick walked over and interrupted his rest.

"What's up, buddy?" Brick asked enthusiastically. "What's the score on the auto/pedestrian?"

"Where have you been?" Mace asked without sitting up or looking at Brick. "I was about to give up and start walking home." Mace looked weary and noticeably perturbed.

"Damn car wouldn't start. Had to wait for it to cool down and then had to bum water off that idiot store manager. So what happened on your deal? And where's Marvin? He ready to leave yet?"

Mace sighed and exhaled loudly. "My guy turned out to be a drunk homeless dude. Stepped in front of the car. His own fault. But he thinks I'm his long-lost brother." Mace took another deep breath, sighed, and continued. "Marvin got here over an hour ago. They've already seen him. Wasn't this crowded when he got here, so they took him right in. I said I was his friend and went in with him. No broken bones. Just soft tissue injury, sprained neck. But he said he was sick to his stomach, so they're keeping him overnight in case he has a concussion or something."

"That's pretty good," Brick said. "Could have been better—a broken bone would have been better, even a finger maybe—but a concussion, that might pay off."

"I don't know." Mace sighed again. "Marvin told them he thought it was his fault."

"What?"

"Said he wasn't watching where he was going."

"What!"

"They were writing it all down in his medical record."

"Shit!" Brick yelled in disbelief.

The lady in the plus-size, faded thong panties gave Brick a dirty look that meant "don't cuss in front of my innocent love child."

"Shit." Brick whispered the word this time. "What was he thinking?"

"That's not all," Mace said. "He showed them your card. Said you were a lawyer he met at the store when it happened and that you were going to file a lawsuit for him."

"So? Good advertising. Right?"

"No. The admitting lady said since it was an accident and he had a lawyer, the hospital was going to file a lien."

"So?"

"So, the insurance company has to pay the hospital first for all the medical bills—off the top of any settlement—before anybody else gets anything. Anybody. Me. You. Marvin. Anybody. Then they scheduled him for a bunch of tests, an MRI and all sorts of things. That's when they decided he should spend the night."

"What the…" Brick cut it short.

The chubby lady with the love-child hanging off her shot another dirty look in Brick's direction.

"Why didn't you do something?" Brick asked, trying his best to make sure he didn't sound like he was whining.

"Don't be stupid. They already had your business card in their hands. My name is Mace Spinella. It's on your card. Spinella and Hawthorne. Remember? I didn't want to bring any more attention to myself."

"Well, we still might get something out of it."

"I tried to signal him to shut the…" Mace paused and glanced toward the sad, tired lady. He left out the offending word and continued, "…up, but he kept right on talking, eating up the attention."

"We still might get something out of it, right?"

"We might," Mace reluctantly agreed.

"Have you hit the nurse up for leads yet? There could be some other poor, unlawyered accident victims laying around here in need of a lawyer." Brick rubbed his hands together like a hungry man stalking a big plate of buttered pancakes.

"No, I just got back. I've been waiting for the ones that helped Marvin to be out of here first."

"Cheer up, then," Brick said. "Not all is lost. A bush in the hand is worth two birds." Brick thought that was funny. Mace didn't. "I'll go check with nursey-poo and see if we have any new admittances with insurance and room numbers." Brick smiled and took off for the nurse's station.

Mace stayed slumped in the chair with his cheek resting on his hand. He watched Brick through the crowd while he made cute with the attractive young nurse.

"What's happening, Nurse Ratchet?" Mace could hear Brick's booming voice from across the room over the other chatter and moaning.

Mace watched Brick with amusement until, failing any attempt at being inconspicuous, Brick pulled a lonely, wrinkled fifty-dollar bill from his pocket, straightened it out, popped it between his fingers, and handed it, smiling, to the nurse. It was the last money they had. Mace felt a twinge go through his body, partly because it was the last money they had and partly because Brick was being so obvious about it.

Mace had noticed the two men in drab suits and drabber ties on the other side of the room occasionally look at Brick, but he hadn't paid much attention to them until he noticed that they had noticed Brick hand off the fifty-dollar bill. Then he noticed the nurse wink at one of the men and then both of them started moving deliberately through the crowded lobby in Brick's direction.

Brick was so self-absorbed with his own wit and charm that he was oblivious to anything else that was happening. Like a drunk who thinks everyone else thinks he is as charming as he thinks he is, Brick continued to ply the nurse with compliments while the drab suits gained ground on him.

Mace scanned the room quickly. His muscles tensed. He realized what was unfolding before his eyes, and suddenly the panic of the moment set in. A hospital security guard standing on the opposite side of the room saw the two men start in Brick's direction. Mace saw the security guard remove the handcuffs from his belt, nod at the men, and start toward Brick.

Oh my God! Mace thought. He leaned forward in his chair to get up, afraid to take his eyes off Brick and the approaching suits.

Right then, one of the suits bumped chest and shoulders hard into a man who seemed to have appeared from nowhere. For an instant, the man looked familiar to Mace, maybe because he slightly resembled Kris Kristofferson, a singer that Mace liked. They collided hard—so hard that Kristofferson and the suit both staggered. The drab-suited man regained his composure and angrily straightened his jacket. Then Kristofferson was gone. Then the angry suit said something to his companion suit, wiped imaginary dust from the front of his jacket, and they continued to move through the crowded lobby in Brick's direction.

"Oh my God," Mace said. He felt the adrenaline rush through him like a chill, and immediately he was on his feet, moving as fast as he could through the people, head down, trying to get to his partner and do something, anything, to save him. But the security guard was ahead of him, reaching out with the chrome-colored handcuffs toward Brick's unsuspecting wrists.

Mace was close enough to hear the jangle of the metallic chain as the uniformed guard grabbed for Brick's arm. Then he saw Brick's body suddenly jerk around, his face surprised and wide-eyed, and then disappear backward like a streak of light.

At the same instant, Mace heard the click, click, click of the handcuffs as they closed on empty air, and Brick was gone, no longer standing there.

The direction of Brick's disappearance had placed Mace squarely between the guard and where Brick had been standing. Mace saw the shocked look on the guard's face as he stood there speechless, holding his empty handcuffs, staring back at the shocked look on Mace's face.

Mace looked around for Brick. The guard looked around for Brick. Brick had vanished. It was like he had been beamed up by Scotty, only faster, and no dust shadow. David Copperfield would have been impressed.

Mace caught a glimpse of the other two men a few feet away still approaching, unaware that Brick was no longer there.

Mace's mind was spinning. Then he noticed that the double doors, a few feet behind and to the left of where Brick had been standing, were rocking, ever so slightly, back and forth. Maybe it was the wind, a draft, but maybe not. Mace was drawn to the doors.

Hoping the bystanders could not hear the drum-beat pounding in his chest, Mace turned, pretending he was not a part of the situation, and walked, as non-chalantly as he could manage, hoping not to draw any attention to himself, toward the double doors, and he slipped between them. The last thing Mace saw was the two drab suits standing with the security guard at the nurse's station, scratching their heads and look-ing around, trying to make sense of what had just happened.

Mace had been through those double doors ear-lier that day when he accompanied Marvin for his x-rays. He knew that the hallway beyond led to the x-ray room and then to other parts of the hospital that would be deserted that time of evening. He moved as fast as he could down the hallway to the x-ray room, swung the door open, and looked inside. No one was there.

His head spun faster. Where was Brick? Then he ran to the end of the long hall where it teed off at right angles. He looked both ways and saw no one. Then, at the very end of the hallway to his right, he noticed something lying on the floor up against the baseboard. It looked like a shoe.

"Oh my God," Mace said and ran as fast as his tired legs would carry him to the object on the floor, the shoe. He picked it up. It was Brick's, all right. No one else was in sight.

Then, faintly, he heard what sounded like a muffled voice. He thought it came from behind a door about halfway down the next hallway. He ran to the door. It was a single, richly varnished, solid wood door with a long, narrow window above the handle.

He peered through the four-inch-wide window. He saw no one in the room. He saw only maroon carpet, benches, a podium at the front, and some flowers on a table. It looked like a small church. Then he heard the muffled voice again, so, without thinking, he threw the door open and stepped inside. He was in the hospital chapel.

There was Brick, dangling in the back corner of the chapel, his toes barely touching the floor. His arms and legs flailed around pathetically like a mouse caught with its neck in a trap.

Behind Brick, the dark, shadowy figure of a lone man stood motionless, holding Brick helpless by the back of his suit jacket. The jacket was wadded tight in the man's hand and pulled back and up, almost suspending Brick from the floor. The man's other hand was over Brick's mouth. He stood there staring at Mace like a stone statue holding a squirming puppy. It was Kristofferson from the emergency room.

A two-foot shard of frozen fear shot down Mace's spine like he had been stabbed with a cold ice pick. Confusion caused his head to spin. Mace searched for his voice but couldn't find it.

Mace had experienced nightmares before where he dreamed he was in a situation that called for an urgent scream, but wasn't able to make the sound come out of his mouth. This felt like one of those frightening, helpless dreams.

Then, as suddenly as his voice had left him, it came back. A screechy yell wiggled loose and broke free from high in Mace's throat. "What the hell do you think you're doing?" he cried. The weak and unfamiliar sound of his own voice added to the fright he was already feeling.

"We're waiting for you," the man said.

There was something rhythmical and soothing about his voice, but the sight of him standing there with Brick dangling in front of him, and the residual adrenaline rush from the emergency room disappearing act, and the mad dash through the hospital halls, and the eerie, dreamy feeling of it all kept Mace from feeling any comfort.

"Put him down!" Mace screeched.

"You might want to keep it down yourself," the man said. "They're still looking for you."

The statement got Mace's attention and shocked him back into the moment, reminding him of Brick's narrow escape from the emergency room and the fact that the police were still around and probably still looking for him.

"What the hell are you doing?" Mace said in a loud whisper.

Brick kept flailing around, kicking and swinging his arms. The man held him firmly and stared at Mace. Mace was still trying to size up the situation. Obviously, Brick wasn't hurt—physically, anyway. Apparently this stranger had saved him from being arrested—maybe. But he was handling him pretty roughly, and Brick looked pretty helpless, dangling there, one shoe on and the other still in Mace's hand. Mace's adrenaline rush was starting to ease, but the lingering confusion made him feel edgy.

"We're waiting for you," the stranger calmly repeated. "I need for you to help steady this boy down before he brings the whole Austin cop shop in on us. Tell him to get still and shut the fuck up, and I'll set him free."

Mace pondered Kristofferson's words for a few seconds. He felt threatened by the man, even though the man wasn't really doing anything threatening, other than holding Brick like a fish wiggling on a hook.

Mace considered what the man said about bringing the "cop shop" in on them. He knew the men in the emergency room were probably police, and they were probably still looking for Brick. He knew if Brick didn't calm down then the police, if that's who they really were, would find them the same way he had.

Mace knew he had no choice, so he tried to calm his heart, without much success. Then he cautiously approached, leaning his head in toward Brick, who was still suspended in the air and tap-dancing on the floor with the tips of his toes.

"Brick, calm down, man," Mace said. Brick kept squirming. Mace got right up in Brick's face. "Calm down, Brick. He'll let you go."

The words had no effect on Brick. He kept wiggling frantically, making muffled, whining noises through his nose. The man tightened his hand across Brick's mouth. Bubbles of Brick's spit oozed from between the man's fingers.

Mace put his mouth up against the side of Brick's ear and whispered loudly the man's words. "Get still, and shut the fuck up, and he'll set you free."

Mace's warm breath condensed in Brick's ear, and the words finally got his attention. Brick immediately stopped struggling and slumped like a limp, worn pillow. His breathing was heavy.

The man let go of him, and Brick tumbled to the floor before catching his balance and jumping up. Brick doubled his fist and pulled his arm back like he was going to swing at the stranger. But all he did was stand there and breathe hard with his arm cocked. He stared angrily at the man. The man smiled.

It was the first time Brick was able to get a look at him. Brick wiped the spittle from his mouth with his coat sleeve and stood there, shaking, trying to regain his composure. The man was medium in size, late forties or early fifties, a little over six feet tall and dressed in a black suit coat and blue jeans. His longish, salt-and-pepper hair touched his collar. He was wearing black cowboy boots and a T-shirt with a picture of Willie Nelson on it.

"What the hell do you think you're doing?" Brick finally said to him, almost teary-eyed.

"I'm saving you, son," the man replied.

"Thanks, old man, but I think we can take it from here," Mace interrupted. He grabbed Brick by his muscular bicep and tried to pull him toward the door. Brick struggled, not able to take his eyes off the strange man.

Staring an even angrier stare, Brick said, "Don't call me son, you son of a bitch. I'm not your son."

"Don't be so sure, son," the man said. His voice was slow and rhythmic. "You called me a son of a bitch? Really? You might want to ask your mom about that before you go calling my mother—your grandmother—a bitch."

The man looked at the ceiling as if trying to recall a long-lost memory. Then he fixed his eyes back on Brick.

"I remember your mama well. It was the early seventies. Beautiful little Jewish princess. Small little thing, small feet, not very tall. Highlights in her hair. She wore it all teased up. Loved jewelry and loved good wine too. We even smoked a little pot. I bet she never told you that. She had the sweetest voice I've ever heard. We had a good time...*son*."

Brick's head reeled from the confusion. He was even more disoriented. This man had just described his mother to a tee. The questions flooded his mind. *Could this strange man somehow be my father?*

Brick's emotions broke through the fence of reason and ran off over the hill. *What is going on here? This man saved me, somehow, I think, but he's freaky, and he scares me. Besides, I know my father. I even look like my father.* Hundreds of crazy thoughts crowded and then jammed the neuron trails of Brick's brain. Gridlock.

"Calm down, Luke," Mace said sarcastically. "Darth Vader here is just dicking with you. He's not your father, dumb ass. He just described every girl out there. All the girls in the seventies teased their hair, and every boy thinks his mom has a beautiful voice. And you're

Jewish…and you're short…damn it, man. And he's seen your shoe. Size eight and a half, damn it. Of course your mother had small feet. Don't let him get to you."

"So, you're the brains of this outfit, and he's just the pretty face," the man said to Mace, gesturing with his hand like Vanna White on *Wheel of Fortune*.

"Let's go," Mace said to Brick. "I've had enough of this freak."

Mace grabbed Brick and headed for the door, but his pace was not so deliberate. There was something about this man that made him want to find out more, but his fear kept him moving slowly toward the door.

"They're still looking for you, so you might as well sit for a spell," the man said, taking a seat on the back pew.

"I think he's a faggot," Brick said with as much hate in his voice as he could muster.

Mace was about to turn the door handle, when the man said, "Barratry is a crime in this state. Wasn't that on the bar exam?"

The statement stopped Mace in his tracks. The hair on his neck stood up. Brick and Mace looked at each other. *How does he know we're lawyers, and how does he know what barratry is?* They were both thinking the same thing.

The man turned, put his legs up in the pew, and crossed his full-quill, black, ostrich-skin cowboy boots at the ankle. Talking to the ceiling, he said, "Barratry. A lawyer commits a criminal offense if, with intent to obtain an economic benefit, the lawyer pays or offers to pay money or anything of value to solicit employment. That's the short definition, boys."

"He's a cop!" Brick said.

"No, he's not," Mace said.

"Sit down," the man said firmly.

"What if they look in here?" Mace asked.

"Look for fellas like you in a chapel? I doubt it. At most, they'd maybe look through the window," he said, pointing at the slit in the door. "Sit over here, and they can't see you."

Mace and Brick checked out the angle of the window and quickly moved to the back corner and stood there. They didn't trust the man, and Brick didn't want to be within arms' reach again. His neck still hurt from being dragged by the collar down three hallways.

The stranger swiveled in the pew and looked at them.

"Take off your jackets and ties, and give them to me. Roll up your sleeves."

"You're not our boss," Brick said.

Addressing Mace, the man said, "How stupid is this guy?" Then, addressing Brick, he said, "It will make it easier for you to leave. The suits outside are looking for another suit."

"What?" Brick asked.

"Take 'em off, and give 'em to him," Mace said, already handing his jacket to the man and rolling up his sleeves.

"Sit down. If anyone opens the door, just pretend like I'm giving you grief…" he paused a second before finishing the sentence, "counseling."

They both sat down in the pew in front of the man. Mace handed Brick his stray shoe, and he slipped it back on.

"Listen to me," the man said. "Your law license and your freedom depend on this. They're looking for a greenhorn shyster, not a guy with his sleeves rolled up and no jacket or tie."

"Sharks," Brick interrupted. "We're not shysters, we're sharks."

"You're green-banana shysters," the man said firmly. "You don't even deserve the label greenhorn. You're green bananas, both of you, junior shysters."

"Screw you and your insults," Mace said. "We are sharks."

"A real shark would have tipped the nurse a twenty, not a fifty. A real shark wouldn't have been caught doing it. And a real shark can tell the difference between an undercover cop and a nurse."

"Really?" Brick said.

His question was sincere, but his wrinkled brow betrayed what he was thinking. He was trying to calculate in his head how much money they had wasted on "tips" over the past couple weeks. Two weeks, that was all the time it had been since their bar scores came in the mail and they started trying to drum up business. It dawned on Brick that this strange man just might know what he was talking about.

"The nurse was a cop?" Mace asked. "I can't believe this shit."

"Pray with me," the man said suddenly. He said it urgently and a bit sharply, yet the command retained a solemn tone. He put his fists on the back of the pew in front of him and bowed his forehead down onto them.

Mace and Brick were incredulous. "What the…!" They both said it at the same time.

"OK. He's really a nut case. Let's get the hell outta here," Mace said.

"Shut up, and bow your heads," the man snapped, without raising his face from the top of his fists. There was no solemnity in his voice this time, just a stern, quick order.

The sound of the door handle turning got the young men's attention. It clicked, and the door hinges squeaked slowly open.

Instantly, Brick and Mace bowed their heads in unison. Brick snapped into the iconic prayer position with his eyes closed tight and his steeple fingers pointing skyward and tucked under his chin. He looked like an innocent child saying his goodnight prayers with mommy watching.

Mace bowed his head, closed his eyelids into little slits, and glanced nervously back and forth through his eyelashes. Then Mace started mumbling something barely audible under his breath. It sounded vaguely like a chant or like he was saying the Rosary—or something like that.

Then the Kristofferson man, softly, but with a reverend-like tone and purposefully loud enough to be heard by anyone standing in the doorway, said, "Lead us not into temptation, Lord, but deliver us from evil."

Mace and Brick waited for him to say something else, but he didn't. Silence ruled. It seemed like forever. It was at least three seconds.

Then the door squeaked again and clicked closed. Whoever it was, they were gone.

Brick and Mace breathed sighs of relief. The prayer that Mace had been saying to himself, the one that sounded like a chant or the Rosary or something like that, had been answered.

From a purely logical point of view, Mace had prayed to himself. It had to be a prayer directed only to himself because Mace didn't believe in a Higher Power, not any Higher Power.

The prayer Mace prayed to himself, while sitting on a church pew, hiding in a hospital chapel, on a hot August night, in Austin, Texas, with the police searching for him, was simply, "No, no, no, no, no, no, no."

Logically, the prayer was prayed by Mace to Mace. Logically, that is, because Mace sincerely thought that he believed there is no Higher Power whatsoever. None. But not everything that works out works out to be logical.

When Mace heard the chapel door click closed, he felt for an instant that there had been some kind of connection with something outside of himself, like something had heard him, something bigger than himself. For an instant, he felt grateful. Then he shook it off, pushed it down, and forgot about it.

Looking at Mace, the Kristofferson man said, "Smart Boy, you can leave first. Go out through the ER. Find where Pretty Boy left your car. If it'll start, drive it to Scholz's. Wait there for Pretty Boy to show up. He's going to leave here in five minutes. It shouldn't take ten minutes for him to get there...but allow for thirty before you start getting your panties in a wad."

"How do you know about our car problems?" Mace said.

"We'll get there."

Then, looking at Brick, he said, "Pretty Boy, you walk. It's only three blocks. Avoid the emergency room. You're a wanted man there. We'll wait in here for five minutes after Smart Boy leaves."

"Why does he get to be Smart Boy?" Brick asked.

"Do you want me to call him Pretty Boy?" Kristofferson asked.

Brick looked down. The answer was obvious.

Kristofferson continued, "I'll show you how to get to the front door. Leave from there, the visitor's entrance. If you don't get lost, it shouldn't take you five minutes to locate Smart Boy parked in front of Scholz's. If he's not there, don't go looking for him. They'll be checking the parking lot. Just go inside Scholz's and wait."

Kristofferson addressed Mace. "If the car doesn't start, leave it. Walk to Scholz's. Safer to pick it up in the morning. Wait for Pretty Boy in Scholz's. If you need help, it will find you."

Then, addressing both of them, he said, "Come see me at Scholz's tomorrow. I'll give you back your ties and jackets."

"No, just give us our stuff now," Mace said argumentatively. "We can carry it ourselves, and we'll be outta here."

The door clicked again and began to squeak open. They all snapped their heads down simultaneously in mock reverence. Mace started mumbling again. "No, no, no, no, no, no, no."

49

"And forgive us our trespasses…" Kristofferson said. The door closed again, "…as we forgive those who are dumber than shit," he finished in a whisper.

Mace sneered, but Brick didn't notice what Kristofferson had said. Brick's opinion of the man had come around fully since he was dragged down three hallways, made to tap-dance on his tippy-toes, and nearly strangled. Brick wanted to trust the man, at least for now. And he liked his plan for getting them out of there. The sooner the better.

"Let's do what he said," Brick said to Mace.

"I guess we don't have a choice," Mace said. He was reluctant, but logic had kicked in. He dismissed any thought of the silly little prayer, the one that sounded like a chant or the Rosary or something like that, the one that had been answered—twice.

"Noon. Scholz's," the man said. "I'll visit your little friend. They're holding him for observation, you know."

Mace wrinkled his brow and scrunched his eyes. Brick sensed he was about to say something else negative, so he spoke before Mace had a chance. "How do we find you?"

"Just ask for Ike."

Chapter 3

PSYCHOBABBLE

They followed the man's instructions to the letter.

After a desperate third try, the old car finally started, and Mace drove it out of the dark parking lot unnoticed. Brick left through the visitor's entrance and did not get lost on the walk, except in thought. Brick got to Scholz's only a minute or two after Mace did.

As soon as Brick climbed in the old car and closed the squeaky door behind him, Mace started telling him excitedly about seeing the two suits and the security guard again while he was leaving through the emergency room.

"You're not going to believe it! When I left the ER, they were still looking for you, scratching their heads trying to figure out how you got away, dude. One of the suits stopped me, asked if I had seen, get this, a young, smartass muscle guy in a coat and tie."

Mace purposefully excluded the word *short* from his rendition. The suit had actually asked Mace if he had seen a "short, young, smartass muscle guy in a coat and tie." Mace didn't want to bring attention to

Brick's shortness twice in one night. He had already done it with the Kristofferson man, or Ike, or whatever his name was. "I wanted to say something smartass, you know, but shit, man, I was too nervous. I just said no and kept walking. Damn, dude, that was close."

"Coat and tie. See. Coat and tie. That dude was right."

"Fuck that dude."

When they got to their apartment on East Riverside Drive, not the best part of town, they found a yellow note stuck to the door with a red pushpin, reminding them, in capital letters, that they were still behind on their rent. Brick looked dejectedly at the note, put it on the table with the rest of the past-due bills, and collapsed sprawl-legged onto his side of their faded, old, threadbare couch. After a few minutes, Mace joined him, and they began their nightly ritual.

Mace held the dirty, brown-stained bong in one hand and a wrinkled plastic bag containing a small amount of marijuana in the other. He put the bong, a foot-tall plastic one, on the coffee table in front of him and unscrewed the metal bowl from its base. After the small metal receptacle was free, he tapped out the burned contents from the night before—or was it that morning?—into an ashtray shaped like the bottom jawbone of a human skull. Then he scraped out some tar and the remaining ashes with a pipe tool.

When he was satisfied that the pipe bowl was clean enough, he filled it with some of the loose marijuana particles that had collected in the bottom corner of the plastic bag. It looked more like sawdust than it did weed. Then he reconnected the bowl to the base of the bong, took a lighter in one hand, and was about to take the first draw when he noticed the whipped look on Brick's face. Mace handed the bong and lighter to Brick instead of lighting it himself.

"Here, you go first."

"Oh, thank you, dude. You're the best," Brick said. The genuineness in his tone revealed that he meant what he was saying.

Brick took the lighter in one hand, held it over the bowl, and applied flame to the green-brown, mostly brown, substance. His mouth covered the opening at the top, and his vigorous inhale caused the water to bubble and the fire glow red. Smoke filled his lungs. He felt his muscles, and his thoughts, begin to relax.

"Ah, that's sweet," he said, exhaling the words along with the smoke and passing the bong to Mace. Mace put flame to the weed, inhaled, exhaled, and they both sat in silence for a spell.

"Pass it," Brick finally said.

Mace handed Brick the bong, and he took another hit. Inhale, exhale, and smoke filled the room. Then it was Mace's turn again, and when he was through, the bowl was spent, gone. Smoke billowed through the room and began to settle.

Again, they sat in silence for a spell.

"Can you believe this fucking night?" Mace said, breaking the peaceful silence and jolting Brick back into the moment. "Can you believe this fucking night?"

"Who was that dude?" Brick asked. "Can you believe that fucker dragged me down three miles of halls? I thought I was being kidnapped by aliens or something."

"I know. I know."

"Shit! I didn't see anything, man, except those two doors close in front of my face like a vacuum. Shit, man. It was fucking awesome!" Brick said.

"I know, man, you should have seen your face. It was like you'd seen a ghost or something—all dangling there—tap-dancing like a little girl. It was like funny and scary at the same time. And like, he didn't even move, man."

"No kidding, dude."

"And you jiggling all over the place. I thought a fucking vampire had you or something. Scared the shit out of me."

"Me too, man. Scared me shitless, and that fucking praying! Freaked me out, dude. Whoa! Shit!"

"Yeah, man."

"Nut case, man."

"Totally."

"I wonder who the hell is he?"

"Guess we'll find out tomorrow. In the ER when he grabbed you, man, he was, like, invisible or something."

"Yeah, and he quotes the fucking penal code like it's written on his eyeballs?"

"How do he do dat?"

"Beats me, man. My question, the main question, to me, man, is why did he save your sorry ass?"

Brick thought hard for an instant. "You think he might really be my father?" Brick spoke too soon. He should have examined that thought before committing it to words.

"Don't be stupid," Mace said.

Brick thought some more. "Then maybe he's a cop?"

"Maybe he's the mob?" Mace said.

"Maybe he's one of them Branch Davidians from Waco the government warned us about."

"Don't be stupid," Mace said.

"Maybe he's a shyster lawyer, and we were cutting in on his action at the hospital."

"Could be," Mace said, and he meant it.

"I wonder why he wants to see us tomorrow?"

"Who cares, as long as we get our jackets back?"

The questions and the speculation kept coming. Eventually, after the conversation lulled, they sat in silence, staring into space for a half hour or so, and then retired to their rooms and went to dreamless sleep, courtesy of the weed. They never mentioned Marvin. He didn't cross their minds.

———

Morning came too early, with a pounding on the door. Brick's eyes did not want to open. He grabbed the alarm clock and pushed the snooze button. The pounding continued. It wasn't the clock. He put on his robe, stumbled to the front door, and peeped out the peephole. It was Mrs. Chen, the apartment manager.

"I know you in dow," she said. "You betta open dough!"

Brick jerked his head back from the door in disgust. Mrs. Chen was on the other side, wearing a wrinkled, exaggerated frown and a faded, uneven, and way too thin housecoat, with rollers in her hair. Half a smoky cigarette dangled from her lip. She looked the same way she always looked. Brick grimaced hard and almost gagged. He steadied himself, backed away quietly, and slid stealthily into the familiar indentations on his side of the couch.

Brick noticed his reflection in the mirror, the mirror he had personally installed next to the front door so it couldn't miss him whenever he walked by. It worked. It didn't miss him, and the image that was reflected back made him glance away.

At that instant, Brick felt an intense emotional undertow of pity, guilt, and shame stir inside and pull at him. He glanced at himself in the mirror again, and he looked away again. An emotional cocktail swirled in his head and in his gut and depressed his ability to reason, to see things as they are, to devise a plan, to do something.

Instead, he just sat and felt pity for the man he couldn't look at in the mirror. And he felt shame because the man he pitied was himself. And he felt guilty because he had somehow allowed himself to become this pitiful, shameful reflection that now sat looking back at him on his couch.

He felt them all: pity, shame, and guilt. And at that moment, he felt them badly.

To Brick, the man in Brick's mirror looked pathetic, desperate, frightened to open his own door. He was petrified at the prospect of having to face Mrs. Chen, at the prospect of having no place to live. He had no close friends except for Mace, and Mace was in the same sinking boat he was in. And it seemed to Brick that he was the only one trying to bail water. Mace really wasn't much help most of the time.

Brick certainly couldn't move back in with his parents. That was not an option. And he couldn't ask them for another loan either. Brick could never, not under any circumstances, admit to his father that he had failed. Dear ol' Dad was never going to be proud of Brick, or even satisfied. He never had been, even when Brick was a child. Nothing was ever good enough to please Dad. He never congratulated Brick on anything, choosing always to find fault. He didn't even congratulate Brick when Brick told him he had passed the grueling, three-and-a-half-day test called the Texas bar exam. It is an ordeal that can make a disciplined honor student feel like he has died in his sleep and gone to eternal test hell. Brick was sworn in and admitted to the prestigious Texas Bar, and all his father said was, "Couldn't you pass the California bar?"

Brick didn't like what he saw in the mirror. He wondered how he had allowed himself to get into such a dreadful predicament. His dad had never bounced a check in his whole life. Brick was reminded of that many times—especially the few times Brick swallowed his pride and asked him for money. His dad worked his way up from the bottom—started in the mailroom— and never had a setback. Now he was an officer and major shareholder in one of the most prestigious financial firms in Southern California, and all that time he had never been late on a bill.

The man Brick faced in the mirror was always late on his bills, was driving a car that may not start today, and was within hours of being evicted, homeless. He needed a paycheck. He needed it now, but he had worked at so many lousy, degrading jobs, and he hated it. He and Mace promised each other when they graduated from law school that they would never work for anyone else ever again. If he called his dad, all he would get was, "I told you so. You should have gotten your MBA and come to work for me like I told you to. Or at least you could have taken the California bar."

Brick was weary of lying every time Dad asked him why he hadn't gone to law school in California. He couldn't bring himself to confess that he had applied to and been denied admission to every single law school in the state, and not just in California but to almost every law school in the United States—except one; and it was one his father would have scoffed at. It was a little law school in Texas established in the 1950s, in the basement of a private Negro theological seminary.

The school was originally chartered out of desperation and protest because no Negro students were allowed admission to Texas law schools at the time. None. Every black applicant was denied admission. All of them, 100 percent. It was state law: no Negroes in Texas state law schools.

Years later, a civil rights activist named Heman Marion Sweatt, along with help from the NAACP, brought a lawsuit and successfully challenged segregation at the University of Texas School of Law, and black students finally, gradually, began to be admitted. But by then, the Carver-Washington Gospel School of Law was already graduating successful lawyers, lawyers with a knack for oratory, partly because of the graduation requirement that they complete at least two gospel-preaching courses at the adjoining seminary.

If Brick ever confessed to Dad, then he would have to tell Dad that he lied all those years about his grades in undergraduate school too…and that he never really attended UT Law, the school where Heman Marion Sweatt was denied admission because of the color of his skin. Brick had been denied admission because of his grades.

It was no coincidence that the little law school accepted Mace as well. Brick and Mace were the only white people who applied that year. The school administrators felt they needed more diversity on campus, even if it meant accepting these two jugheads. Based on their college transcripts, their LSAT scores, and their performance in class, the admissions committee was pleasantly surprised when both of them passed the bar exam on their first try.

"Two day," Mrs. Chen yelled through the door. Then she yelled it again, "Two day, then I call cop. Throw you bums out."

Brick heard the sound of Mrs. Chen's house shoes shuffle off down the sidewalk.

Desiring to relieve his anxiety, he picked up last night's bong that he had forgotten to remove from the coffee table and, without thinking, tried to light it, but it was too spent to light, and the hot stinky air he inhaled made him cough uncontrollably and contort his face like he had just tasted a dead rat.

He yelled at Mace to get up, but Mace didn't hear him. Mace slept like a baby. Brick put on a pot of coffee and stashed the bong and bag back under the sink in the bathroom. When he finished his second cup of coffee, he heard Mace start to stir.

"Is that coffee I smell, buddy?"

"Yes, it is. Get your ass up. We've got to be at Scholz's by noon to get our jackets back from that...whatever he was."

"Did that really happen? Shit, I thought it was a bad dream," Mace said, stumbling to the bathroom in his boxer shorts.

They got to Scholz's at about a quarter till noon. They were apprehensive about meeting the man again—Ike, if that was his real name. The ten-year-old Mercedes Mace had seen the day before was parked out front. He recognized the bumper sticker.

"I wonder if that's his car," Mace said.

"What's a Pharisee?" Brick asked, looking sideways at the bumper sticker. "Don't Be A Pharisee—Pharisees Vote Republican."

"Your people, dude, your people."

"Then I guess I'm a Republican," Brick said. He swung open the big wooden door, and they both stepped inside Scholz's.

"What are you talking about? You've never voted in your life," Mace said.

"Well, neither have you."

Mace scoped out the big entry room with the Western-style walk-up bar. A bartender was leaning over it propped on both elbows and reading the *Austin American Statesman*. Mace asked the bartender if he knew "a creepy guy named Ike." Without looking up, the bartender pointed to an open doorway.

Beyond the door was another room with ten or twelve tables in it. At one of the tables by the back wall sat the man from last night. He was wearing jeans and the same black suit coat from the night before, but his T-shirt had a different picture of Willie Nelson on it.

Brick and Mace were wearing the same pants from the night before, but they were wearing freshly starched dress shirts, no ties, and no jackets. Since becoming a lawyer, Brick had become a stickler for wearing starched dress shirts, and he imposed the same dress code on Mace, who could have cared less but willingly complied as long as Brick paid the laundry bill from his own money. Mace would have been content to pull his least-dirty shirt out from under the bed and wear it, wrinkles, coffee stains, and all. But Brick was convinced that clean, starched shirts would be good for business.

Other than the ones they had on, they each had one clean shirt left. After tomorrow, they'd be wearing their cleanest dirty shirts. Brick was aware of that fact, and it weighed on him. Mace wasn't, and it didn't.

Ike saw them when they entered the room and motioned for them to join him at the table. Another man was already sitting at Ike's right. Mace immediately recognized him as the plaid-shirted man from yesterday. Normally Mace wouldn't have remembered him, but the plaid-shirted man recognized Mace first and pointed at him. "Th-that's the f-fucker that scared the sh-shit out of me yesterday," he said to Ike. Mace stopped in his tracks.

"It's all right. Come on over," Ike said. "He won't bite."

Brick and Mace pulled a couple of chairs out from the table and cautiously sat down while the stuttering plaid-shirted man continued to talk. He had some little ticks or convulsions going on that made him change facial expressions all the time. Mace was fascinated and thought it was funny, but Brick, who had once suffered from Bell's palsy for nearly a year, felt some initial sympathy.

"Th-th-these are those ho-hooligans I was t-t-t-telling you about," the plaid-shirted man said to Ike. "Bl-bl-blowing their horn and p-peeling out."

"Yep, hooligans," Ike said, nodding in agreement, and then he repeated the word with more emphasis. "Hooligans! I can see that. Greenhorn, green banana, shyster, hooligans," Ike added, punctuating the word *shyster* with his voice. He said it in a joking manner, but there was an undertone that he was serious. Mace immediately took offense.

"I told you we're not shysters," Mace said. His tone was stern. Mace didn't trust Ike and was not so quick to warm up to people as Brick was.

Ike looked at Mace. A warm, wide smile covered his face as he spoke, but his words were cold, and they gave Mace and Brick a shiver. "Son," he said, "you're the kind of lawyer that gives the rest of us a bad name. In my book, that's a shyster."

"O...K..., then," Mace said, stretching out each word. His voice cracked a little, telegraphing that he was nervous. This guy creeped him out. What he wanted most at that moment was to run out of there. "Just give us our jackets, and we'll be out of here," he said.

"Not so fast. I might have a job for you," Ike said.

"We're not looking for a job. We just want our stuff."

Brick was taking it all in without comment, until then. "Wait a minute!" he interjected. "A job wouldn't be so bad. What kind of job?"

Brick was thinking about the past-due notice on the rent and Mrs. Chen's threat, "Two day, then I call cop. Throw you bums out." Besides, there was something about Ike that he was starting to like...and then there was the matter of the shirts—only one clean shirt left.

"What kind of job?" Brick asked again.

Mace looked hard at Brick. "We agreed, didn't we? We're not going to work for anyone again. No more lousy jobs," he said.

"Yeah, but..."

"I'm not offering you a regular job," Ike interrupted. "I just have something you can do. Lawyer stuff."

"What kind of lawyer stuff?" Brick asked. He was feeling up for anything, needed anything, and didn't want Mace to spoil what might turn out to be a good opportunity.

Still skeptical and feeling defensive, Mace tried to relax a little for Brick's benefit. He settled back in his chair to listen, but he crossed his arms. Mace sensed that whatever this guy had in mind, it had to be illegal.

People don't just give away stuff for no reason. People aren't nice for no reason. There's got to be an angle.

"Boys, this is Mr. Tripper," Ike began. "He's a friend of mine, and he's got a problem."

"I'll say," Mace said sarcastically under his breath.

"You want this work or not?" Ike snapped back; his eyes were cold as frozen daggers. Mace felt Ike's energy and knew this was no time to joke. This guy wasn't nice, Mace concluded. He was creepy. Real creepy.

Brick added in quick tempo, "Shut up, Mace. Show some respect, and listen."

"Fu-fuck you, asshole!" Tripper added, but a bit late.

Brick was secretly hoping the job Ike mentioned didn't have anything to do with Mr. Tripper getting fired from a sports announcer job or anything like that. That would be a tough case.

"So what's his problem?" Mace asked. "Did he get fired from his TV news anchor job?"

"Smartass!" Tripper said back to Mace. This time there was no stuttering. Ike let Mace's comment pass and didn't respond.

Mace smiled a self-satisfied grin at Brick.

Brick returned Mace's look with a look of his own, a mixture of admiration and contempt—admiration for sharing his sense of humor and contempt for not being able to keep his mouth shut. Too many times, Mace had messed up a good thing by not being able to keep his thoughts to himself. If Mace thought it, he almost always had to say it. Brick called it "shooting himself in the foot." "Every time things start going good," Brick would say to him, "you shoot yourself in the foot."

But Mace wasn't going to let this Ike fellow tell him what to do. His smart remarks were directed more at Ike than they were at Mr. Tripper. Ike might be able to scare Mace a little, but he wasn't going to control him. Nobody could do that. This was a dominance thing, and Mace always wanted to be the alpha dog in the room. He had a need to control things, to have his way, to get the last say.

Ike continued as though he hadn't heard any of the previous exchange. "Mr. Tripper owns Tripper Tile Works, one of the best and busiest remodeling and tile-installing companies in Austin. Maybe you've heard of them. Their commercials are on all the time."

Neither showed any sign of recognition.

"Seems his most talented and dependable tile layer got into a little jam with the local constabulary and wound himself up in the Travis County jail facing a potentially long sentence for simple marijuana possession. You follow me so far?"

The boys nodded that they understood.

"How much weed?" Brick asked.

"Enough," Ike said. "They've alleged over four ounces. That makes it a felony, ya know. You do know that, don't you? That was on the bar exam, right? And if he's convicted, he'll serve a long time and then he'll be deported and Mr. Tripper here loses his best worker. And Mr. Tripper doesn't want to lose him. Get the picture, boys?"

"Deported?" Brick asked.

"We're not boys," Mace said.

"Yeah, he's not a citizen," Ike said.

"What's his name?" Brick asked, revealing a genuine interest.

"Wilfred Johnson."

Brick was surprised. He expected the answer to be a name that ended in "e-z," like Rodriguez, Hernandez, Gomez, Gonzalez, or something like that, but he tried to put on his best poker face and not show his surprise.

Mace interjected, "Well. That's a surprise. I was expecting a name that ends in 'e-z.'"

Brick shot Mace another dirty look, but Mace didn't notice. He was having too much fun throwing smart remarks in Ike's direction. It was that dominance thing.

"You like pissing in other people's cornflakes, don't you, boy?" Ike said. His voice was calm, even though he punctuated the word *boy*. Mace started to say something, but Brick interrupted him.

"So what do you want us to do?"

"Not us, Pretty Boy. You."

Brick and Mace did a classic comedic double take at each other. It looked like something straight out of a Groucho Marx movie. "Me?" Brick said. "I thought you had a job for *us* to do."

"Naw," Ike drawled, shaking his head in the negative. "I got a different job for Smart Boy to do. I think you two can accomplish a lot less together than you can apart."

Brick had to think about that statement for a moment before he figured out what Ike was saying, but Mace got it immediately and rolled his eyes at Ike, purposefully showing his contempt.

"That OK with you, Mace?" Brick asked with a pleading look.

"Sure, why not?" Mace answered begrudgingly. Then he addressed Ike. "These lawyer things you have for us to do, they going to make us any money?"

"Sure, why not?" Ike answered, parroting Mace's words back at him. "If you'll quit rolling your eyeballs at me like some insolent adolescent, you'll make enough to pay your rent."

"How do you know about that?"

"We'll get there."

Brick moved to the edge of his chair. The prospect of having not one but possibly two clients between him and Mace perked his interest and gave him an anticipation of hope. Just yesterday, they were handing out cards and tips, risking arrest trying to get their first client, and now they might have two. For Brick, it was turning out to be a red-letter day.

"So what do we do first?" Brick asked, not wanting to risk losing the opportunity.

"Come to my office, and we'll look over the files."

"How do you know about our rent? And I thought this was your office," Mace said.

Ike considered Mace's comment a moment. "OK, let's go to my *other* office, and we'll look at the files."

"Where is it?" Brick asked.

"Eighteen hundred Guadalupe," Ike answered. "You'll see a sign out front: Goldstein and Turner, Lawyers."

"I knew he was a lawyer!" Brick said to Mace, excited that he had figured right. Then, addressing Ike, he said, "So you're Goldstein?"

"No, I'm Turner."

"You have got to be shitting me!" Mace exclaimed. "Your name is Ike Turner!" Even Brick let out a snicker.

"D-D-Don't be dissin' Ike!" Tripper added, trying his best to imitate a famous scene from the famous movie, *What's Love Got To Do with It*, about Ike and Tina Turner, the famous former singing couple with one famous pair of legs. Tripper, Brick, and Mace broke into uncontrollable laughter. Ike grinned. He was used to it.

———

The squeaky old Ford with the broken air conditioner pulled out from in front of Scholz's Biergarten and followed the old Mercedes with the "Pharisees Vote Republican" bumper sticker on it. They drove around the north side of the state capitol building over to 1800 Guadalupe, a drive of only about six or seven blocks—depending on how you count them.

During the short drive, Brick kept saying to Mace, "We've got to get a break. This could be our break. Don't mess it up. Don't shoot yourself in the foot."

"Give me a break!" Mace said. "This guy's a crook. I can tell. Why can't you tell he's a crook? We don't need him. He's a fucking crook. A crook, I tell you. He's a crook."

They crossed Guadalupe at Eighteenth Street and pulled onto a tree lined, blacktopped parking lot behind a three-story gray building. At one time in its history, the building had been a boarding house for University of Texas graduate students. After the city's business district began to stretch in that direction, it was remodeled and converted into office space. A few of the offices, the ones that used to be bedroom suites, still had closets, and a couple still had full kitchens attached to them. One or two had private bathrooms. One of the offices on the third floor, it was rumored, had a black hot tub in it big enough for eight people.

On one end of the parking lot, in the back corner, was an enclosed garage that looked like it had once been an old carriage house. A huge padlock hung from the big sliding door. Both sides of the office building had screened-in porches with lounge furniture scattered around. Above the porches on the second floor level were large balconies bordered by elaborate latticework and balustrades. The place had a friendly, turn-of-the-century, Victorian-home look about it.

On the exterior wall next to the ornate, solid wood front door was a placard that listed the names of the other tenants who leased space inside. The tenants included a couple other lawyers, a CPA, and an environmental organization called "Save Our Springs," SOS for short.

SOS had been privately organized and funded to protect the city's natural springs and a beautiful naturally formed swimming pool on the western edge of town called Barton Springs. Turner and Goldstein had given SOS a break on their rent and sometimes helped them with their numerous injunctions and lawsuits against developers and the city.

In the narrow front yard, next to the sidewalk, was a simple sign that read "Goldstein and Turner, Lawyers."

If you take Guadalupe Street south from Goldstein and Turner's three-story gray building at 1800 Guadalupe, you pass the Travis County courthouse between Eleventh and Tenth streets.

In years to come, about a decade after Brick and Mace first encountered Ike, the county courthouse would get renamed in honor of Heman Marion Sweatt, the black man who sued the University of Texas law school because of its racially motivated admission practices. Austin really is the heart of Texas. Sometimes the rest of Texas just doesn't get that.

If you go nine blocks further south—depending on how you count them—you end up on the Guadalupe Street bridge that crosses the Colorado River. Within Austin city limits, the Colorado River is called Town Lake.

Turn left on Cesar Chavez before getting on the bridge, and then turn left again and you are on Congress Avenue, looking in a northerly direction straight at the impressive, pink granite state capitol building. It is a mammoth structure shaped like the United States' capitol building, but Texans are quick to point out that it is actually a few feet taller than the one in Washington, DC. That's because everything really is bigger in Texas. It was planned that way.

Ike and Tripper got to the office first and waited on the back steps for Brick and Mace to join them. The weather was still hot, and the old Ford coughed, hissed, and convulsed before dying like a wounded buffalo.

Ike took a key from his pocket and turned the handle. The back door opened, and the coolness of the air-conditioned room hit them like a welcomed norther. Tripper's bifocals fogged up.

They were inside a kitchen. A fifties' style dinette table sat in the middle of the room surrounded by chrome-legged chairs with blue upholstery reminiscent of the interior of a 1957 Chevy. There were doors at each end of the kitchen with antique-looking handles that had once adorned doors in the state capital building. These doors led into other rooms and were closed. A phone was on the wall by the refrigerator. Another phone, with a long, twisted cord attached, sat across the room on the counter top between a coffeepot and an antique ceramic soup tureen shaped like a mother hen with little yellow chick faces sticking out from under her wings.

After offering everyone something to drink from the refrigerator, Ike popped the top on a can of Diet Dr. Pepper for himself and joined the others at the table. He passed them all a paper napkin from a chicken-shaped napkin holder. Then he proceeded to tell them about Marvin.

"Your little friend was discharged from the hospital this morning. He's not very happy with either of you. His uncle picked him up and took him to his house to recuperate. He doesn't want to see either of you just yet, and I don't recommend you try to contact him."

"So that's it!" Mace said. The tone of his voice was accusatory. "You're trying to cut in on our case! I knew you were up to something."

Brick couldn't believe it. Mace was already shooting himself in the foot. But Ike just smiled at Mace and held his glance. Brick looked nervously back and forth between Mace and Ike.

Tripper got up, making a loud sliding sound with the chair legs on the linoleum floor, and left through one of the kitchen doors. He didn't want any part of what might be coming. As the door was closing behind him, Tripper said, "H-howdy, K-K-Kay."

"Fuck you! Eat shit!" a strangely alien and metallic voice answered, and the door clicked shut.

Brick and Mace did a double take at the door and then whipped their heads around and looked at each other, mirroring the other's shock. Ike showed no reaction. He was used to it.

"What the hell was that?" Brick asked.

Ignoring their surprised looks and Brick's question, Ike asked Mace, "Is that what you really believe? That I've horned in on your little case?"

"Well, it looks like it to me," Mace answered.

"I'm surprised. I thought you were the smart one," Ike said. He turned to Brick and said, "No offense."

"None taken," Brick answered mechanically.

"Do you know what it looks like to me, Mace?" Ike asked.

"Go ahead and tell me. You're going to tell me anyway. What? Might as well. What does it look like to you?"

"We always see and condemn in others what we don't like and deny about ourselves. That's what it looks like to me. Do you really think I'm a *crook*, Mace?"

Mace was taken aback by Ike's directness. "I'm not saying that," he said, "but why did you help us last night? Why would you want to give us work? Why are you talking with Marvin? What's in it for you? People aren't nice for no reason."

Ike stared at Mace without saying anything for several seconds. To Brick and Mace, it seemed like an eternity. Mace felt like he had been caught red-handed because of what he had said to Brick in the car just a few moments earlier about thinking Ike was a crook. His face flushed red, and he felt the impulse to run.

Brick kept repeating the words in his head, *Don't shoot yourself in the foot, Mace. Don't shoot me in the foot. Don't shoot yourself in the foot, Mace. Don't shoot me in the foot.* Brick wanted whatever job Ike was offering, and he didn't want Mace messing things up…again.

"I think that's what you are saying, Mace," Ike continued. "I think you're saying you think I'm a crook because subconsciously that's what you think about yourself, and you don't like that about yourself."

Mace was forced to lie. "That's not true," he said. "But I do think you're the shyster here and you're trying to cut in on our case with Marvin. I think that's what all this bullshit has been about." Mace heard the words coming out of his mouth as if someone else were speaking them. That was the feeling he always got when he was shooting himself in the foot. "You're the shyster," he repeated.

"There's that word you don't like again—shyster. I wonder why you react so strongly to it, Mace," Ike baited him.

Mace answered without thinking, "Because you're the shyster!" He sounded like an angry grade-school kid.

As soon as the words escaped his mouth, he knew he had messed up. Ike crossed his arms, leaned in on the table, and looked Mace square in the eyes. "Could it be that you think I'm a shyster because that's what you think about yourself—and you don't really like that about yourself?"

Before Mace could say anything else, Ike continued, "I'm not asking you to answer me. I'm not asking you to agree with me. All I'm asking is that you think about it…OK?"

"OK," Brick said, not giving Mace a chance to answer. Brick stared at Mace, daring him to say anything else. Brick wanted the work. He wanted to pay the rent. He wanted Mace to shut up.

"OK," Mace reluctantly replied. "But it's not true."

"OK," Ike said. "Now let's talk about Marvin."

Ike explained that Marvin was discharged from the hospital that morning. "He had a big knot on his head, headaches, a sprained finger, and soft tissue injury around the neck and right shoulder. The doctors told Marvin it could take a couple of weeks to heal completely. No permanent injury. They did a lot of tests, and his bills already total over eight thousand dollars."

"That's good, isn't it?" Brick asked. "The supermarket ought to have to pay that, plus pay for pain and suffering."

"How long have you boys been licensed?" Ike asked.

"Two and a half weeks," Brick answered.

"Two and a half weeks. See why I call you green bananas? You got within a hen's tooth of losing your law license after two and a half weeks. Don't you remember how hard it was to get into law school in the first place? Don't you remember how hard it was to finish three years of class study? Don't you remember how hard you had to study to pass the bar? Do you really want to lose it all?" Ike looked at them and waited for their response.

"Not really," Brick answered.

"No," Mace said.

Ike continued, "After all you've been through to get to where you are, nothing, I mean nothing, is worth risking your law license over. If you pull a stunt like that, it's going to bite you in the butt. If you pick a place like Albertsons or Randalls or H-E-B, they are going to have video surveillance. And they take a scorched-earth approach to these kinds of cases. They don't pay unless you drag them kicking and screaming into court and prove every penny of your case to a jury, which is expensive and time-consuming. Most people, even the ones with legitimate claims, give up and quit trying."

Ike was on a roll. He took a breath and continued. "And on the long shot that you win, then the medical providers end up getting all the money. They have the expensive lobbyists over at the legislature, so they have first right to any insurance money. That's the law. That's the reason they run so many tests on accident victims. They own all that expensive equipment, and they want to use it and get it paid for with the insurance money. And you're not going to win with a jury by jumping up on your cantaloupe box and putting on a show that smacks of Elmer Gantry. A blind hog could see through that trick."

"But…" Brick protested.

Ike cut him off. "And it's dishonest and frivolous crap like that that makes it near impossible for people who've really been injured to get compensated at all. Like I said earlier, it gives the rest of us a bad name. Whose harebrained idea was this, anyway? Which one of you Einsteins decided to pull this at Lavensky's Grocery Store?" He emphasized the word *Lavensky's*.

Brick looked at his feet.

"Oh, I see - Mr. Brains here let Mr. Brawn draw up the plan?" Ike said. "You green bananas! Don't you know they're flying naked?"

"What? What's that mean? Flying naked?" Brick asked.

"Flying naked. No insurance," Ike answered. "They're barely keeping the doors open over there. The big corporate chains are running the smaller stores like them out of business, undercutting their prices, offering bigger selections. If it weren't for all the barbecue that old man Lavensky cooks every morning in the pit out back, they'd have been out of business years ago. Even if you got a judgment against them, what are you going to do with it? Frame it and hang it on the wall? Everything they have is mortgaged to the hilt. Couldn't you tell by looking at the place? And with no insurance, there's no recovery. I bet if you take into account everything that snot-nosed box boy steals, he probably makes more than old man Lavensky does."

"You telling us that store is broke?" Mace asked, not believing what Ike was saying. "How would you know?"

"If your inventory is on consignment and you're leasing your building, what do you have? Just your labor. I grew up here. That used to be the only grocery store in central Austin. Didn't you guys do your research? Didn't you learn anything in law school? How did you pass the damn bar?"

"Got lucky, I guess," Brick said.

"Well, at least you're honest about that."

Ike turned his attention back to Mace. "If you want a break in life, you've got to stop wishing for it and do something."

"We are doing something," Mace protested. "We're making things happen. That's why we got Marvin to do this, and it might have worked."

"You ain't gonna make nothing happen by wishing and hoping it. Or by cheating. When you get a true desire, that's when you'll get your butt off the couch and do something—do something real, make that desire become your reality. No shortcuts. You can't create the reality you want by trying to steal or cheat your way into it. If you get it through dishonesty, you'll never be able to keep it. And it'll eventually cost you everything you have."

Brick looked at Mace and said, "He knows about our couch. How does he know that?"

"Shut up," Mace said. "He's just spewing psychobabble. I've read a few self-help books myself, you know, and they all say that same bullshit."

Mace knew Ike was right, but he wasn't ready to accept it or admit it. He didn't even want to think about it. But the seed had been planted.

Brick, on the other hand, was willing to go along with whatever the crazy old lawyer suggested, but only because he might throw them some business and help get them out of their present financial difficulty. *Go along to get along,* Brick thought. *Yeah, why not? Why not?*

"So what do you want us to do, Obi Wan Kenobi?" Mace asked, making a sarcastic reference to another character in Star Wars.

"Stop daydreaming, stop complaining, set some goals, accomplish something, work, get your ass off the couch, hit the books, pay your bills, clean up your apartment, and quit smoking so damn much pot."

Mace and Brick shot each other another classic vaudeville double take, one that revealed their guilt, their surprise, and, to some extent, their admiration.

"So you've got our apartment bugged," Mace said sarcastically.

"I don't need any bugs. The look on your face speaks loud enough."

"But how do you know about our couch and bills and…stuff?" Brick asked.

"We'll get there," Ike said.

Chapter 4

THE BET

Brick and Mace sat for the better part of an hour, going through the two files Ike had previously taken from the kitchen counter and flopped onto the dinette table in front of them, before he left through one of the side doors.

Brick studied the file on Wilfred Johnson's possession of marijuana charge, trying to figure out how to complete the blank forms that were paper-clipped together with a sticky note attached saying it would be needed for the court hearing later that week. Mace read through the police report about an alleged prostitute with the street name Diaeta Pepsi, who was arrested for soliciting sex with an undercover cop.

"Diaeta Pepsi?" Mace exclaimed loudly, breaking the silence and Brick's concentration. "What a name!"

"And what a person," Ike added, swinging the same door open he had left through earlier and entering the room as if on cue. "Just wait till you meet her."

"But Diaeta Pepsi?" Mace asked, scrunching his face.

"Yep, what a name. You boys want anything else to drink?" Ike asked. He opened the refrigerator and popped the top on another Diet Dr. Pepper. Ike loved Diet Dr. Pepper. Dr. Brackenridge never had the opportunity to taste a *Diet* Dr. Pepper. He may have loved it too.

"How about a beer?" Mace said.

Ike took a big swig from the soda can. "Not during business hours."

"You got a Diaeta Pepsi then?" Mace asked.

"Sure, why not?" Ike said, reaching in and retrieving a cold Diet Pepsi and handing it to Mace. "Don't get any on you," Ike added cryptically, raising one eyebrow in Mace's direction.

"I won't," Mace answered, wondering what Ike had meant by the comment. *Does he think I'm going to try to screw her or something?* For an instant, the idea appealed to Mace. *I guess it depends on what she looks like.*

"It's not that I think you're going to try to screw her or anything," Ike said, startling Mace just as he was popping the top on his Diet Pepsi can. It spewed the brown, no-calorie liquid all over his next-to-the-last clean shirt. Brick frowned.

"I told you not to get any on you," Ike said.

Mace lunged for the paper napkins in the chicken napkin holder and started patting his shirt.

"Say, Ike, like…are we going to make any money on these cases this week?" Brick asked, still thinking about Mrs. Chen and the past-due rent.

"Like…you mean before you do the work and before I get paid myself? Like, no," Ike said.

That wasn't the answer Brick was hoping for. He was worried. How were they going to handle these cases if they were living in their car? How could they get to the courthouse if the car wouldn't start? And what were they going to do for food? It seemed that just when things might turn around for them, they were out of time. They were two feet from the goal line, and the referee was about to blow the final whistle. If they didn't have the rent in two days, Mrs. Chen was going to call the cops and throw them out. The tone of Brick's voice and the look on his face revealed his concern.

"But I'll loan you a couple hundred if you're that down-and-out," Ike continued.

"We're not down-and-out!" Mace snapped. "We're doing just fine."

Brick could hardly believe Mace was doing it again—shooting himself in the foot. This Ike guy, whether he was a crook or not, was the only thing, right now, standing between them and homelessness. *A homeless lawyer,* Brick thought, *now that's pathetic.*

"OK, then. I'll keep my couple hundred bucks."

"No!" Brick said, his voice taking on an even more desperate air. "A couple hundred would be good; five hundred would be even better."

Brick heard the words echo in his head like they had come from somewhere else, and he was amazed at his own boldness in upping the figure. All those months of selling knockoff perfume on the street had given him a thick skin when it came to asking other people for their money—thick as a rhino, because a rhino never takes no for an answer, and only a silver bullet can stop a rhino. At least that's what he had been taught. Consequently, Brick had learned how to ask for money from anyone—anyone except his dad. But when he realized he had just asked this stranger, in one unnegotiated leap, for more than double what had been offered, he was afraid he might have gone too far.

"Five hundred it is, then," Ike said, and he left the room again. No sooner than the door closed behind him, the eerie metallic voice on the other side spoke again, "Fuck you. Eat shit!"

"What's going on here? This isn't right," Mace whispered in a breathy, excited tone. "He's gay. He's got to be gay. Why else would he be calling you 'pretty boy' and offering you five hundred dollars? This isn't right, man. And what the hell's in the other room? That fucking robot voice cussing up a fucking storm. It's freaking me out. Somebody's on one of them throat-cancer-talking machine things, or something. This doesn't feel right, damn it!"

"You don't turn down money when you're broke, asshole! I can't believe you! We don't have to do anything we don't want to do—just take the money, and pay our rent. We don't even have to come back if we don't want to," Brick responded quickly, trying not to be heard by Ike or the metallic creature beyond the door. But he was taken aback by the thought that maybe Ike was gay and befriending them for sexual favors. *Maybe Mace is right,* Brick thought. *It does seem strange.*

"What do you mean *we* don't have to do anything?" Mace whispered back, emphasizing the word *we*. "It's you he's coming on to and offering the money to, not me. He hates my ass. Five hundred bucks, man? That's a lot of money to give someone he doesn't even know. He's got the hots for you, dude. I can tell. I finally figured it out. He hates my ass, but he wants your ass, Pretty Boy. Yeah, that's the deal."

"Wait a minute. Wait a minute. Just an hour ago, you were saying he was a crook trying to steal Marvin's case from us. Now you say he's gay. Make up your mind. You just don't like the guy." Brick was conflicted. He wanted to believe Ike was legit, but he knew from experience that "if things seem too good to be true, they probably are."

"Of course I don't like him. He's a gay crook horning in on our Marvin case, and he wants to horn you too," Mace said.

"No, he's not, and no, he doesn't," Brick protested. "And even if he is, let's just take the money, pay some of our rent, and see what happens. Like I said, we don't have to do anything we don't want to."

"For the last time, it's not *we*," Mace said. "It's pretty obvious, Pretty Boy, it's *you* he wants."

Brick was about to say something back when the door was flung open; it was Ike again. "You boys having fun yet?"

Stunned by the sudden entrance, Brick and Mace jerked their attention back to the files on the table and pretended they were working. They fidgeted with the papers. They looked like school kids caught misbehaving when the teacher walked back in. Ike took a chair across from them and slowly counted out five crisp, new, one-hundred-dollar bills.

He pushed them across the table at Brick and sat without saying another word. He just sat and looked at Brick. Brick didn't know what to do. He was uneasy, and it showed. He didn't want Mace to be right, but he had a bad feeling now that he might be.

He glanced at the money. Five hundred dollars is a lot of money even when you're not broke. Then he glanced at Ike and, for the first time, noticed Ike's long brown eyelashes. They were the best eyelashes he had ever seen on a man. They looked good. They looked so good, they had to be gay. Suddenly, feeling even more uncomfortable, Brick glanced quickly back at Mace.

Mace looked at Brick with a look that was all too familiar. It said, "I told you so." Then Mace looked at Ike and asked accusatorially, "Why are you giving us this money?"

"Not giving. Loaning."

"Then why are you loaning us this money?" Mace pressed sternly.

"Not you, him," Ike said, nodding his head toward Brick and giving him a wink.

Brick's face flashed beet-red. *Damn it*, he thought, *Mace was right. This guy is coming on to me.*

"I want something, though," Ike continued, not taking his eyes off Brick.

Brick's stomach sunk to his lap.

"I figured as much," Mace said, all self-satisfied and righteous. "Now tell us—tell him—what you really want," Mace smugly demanded, waiting for Ike to confess some perversion, tell them what he was really up to, and prove Mace right. Then he and Brick could be on

84

their way and leave this crazy fag to run his games on someone less streetwise than them.

Ike took a long, labored breath like he was about to say something he'd rather not have to say. He seemed to be having trouble choosing his words. He looked at the money, and then he looked at Brick. Then he drew another long breath and stared at the ceiling as though still searching for the right words. The tension was thick. Mace was anticipating a confession. It seemed to him that Ike was embarrassed. Mace had been around old fags before. He thought they were pathetic. It usually didn't take him as long to get wise to them, though. Ike was better at hiding it than most, he thought.

Finally Ike smiled and began speaking in his customarily slow, steady drawl. It signaled no hesitation, guilt, or embarrassment. "I want him to do what needs to be done," Ike said.

"What do you mean?" Mace asked impatiently. His expression revealed his irritation and disappointment.

"Pay the rent would be my guess. Am I wrong?"

"No," Brick interjected, almost jumping from his chair. "That's right. That's right."

Mace realized he had been played. Ike must have heard them talking through the door.

"But why give it to *him*?" Mace asked, nodding toward Brick, who was still showing his excitement over the prospect of getting the rent paid.

"Because he asked," Ike replied. "And he's the responsible one, right? I mean, you two live together, right?" Ike was picking up speed and talking faster with each word. "And if you're gay, queer, that's your business. I don't care. I'm open-minded. But he's the one that makes sure the bills get paid, right? You don't pay the bills, do you?"

Ike didn't give Mace a chance to answer. Mace's mind was stuck trying to figure out if he had really heard the word *queer*. "Now you correct me if I say anything wrong." Ike continued increasing the pace almost to a frantic pitch. "You're the butch guy, right? And he's the bottom—the responsible one. If something needs to be paid, he pays it, right? He pays the bills, right? Right?"

"Right!" Brick cried out excitedly, carried away by the rush of the moment. Finally, someone had acknowledged his contribution. He did pay, and often dearly. Mace didn't care. He didn't contribute. He just expected Brick to figure out a way to take care of things and be careful not to whine while doing it. "I pay. I do pay," Brick said with a cathartic look on his face.

"We're not gay," Mace protested. "Where do you get off insinuating we're gay?"

Ike pushed the five one-hundred-dollar bills closer to Brick and said, "I want you to pay your rent and then I want you both to come back here and finish the work—lawyer stuff—I've got you doing. There will be more money in it for you when you finish."

"Wait a minute," Mace interrupted. "Where do you get off thinking we need your fucking rent assistance? We're doing just fine without anybody's help. We don't need your help. We didn't ask for your help. And why do you want our help on these stupid little cases? They're not doc-ument-intensive. They're not rocket science. They're…"

"If these cases were rocket science, I'd call somebody besides you, now wouldn't I? All I need is legwork and somebody who can follow instructions. You can do that, can't you?" Ike said, and then he added, "I know more about you than you think I do."

"So what is it you think you know about us, old man?" Mace inquired sarcastically.

Brick cringed. Mace was doing it again.

"I know you're behind on your rent."

"You could have heard that through the door. What else?"

"I know you lie a lot."

"Don't either."

"That was one."

"What else?"

"You have a nasty mouth. You cuss a lot."

"That's an easy one, if you've been around me more than fifteen minutes."

"I know you smoke pot."

"Most people in Austin smoke pot. Tell me something that's not public knowledge, oh great Carnac."

Ike looked at the ceiling as if he were thinking, trying to recall something. Then he said, "OK. How's this? I know you'll say 'fuck' seven times before you turn the lights out tonight."

"That's an easy bet," Brick chimed in.

Mace speared Brick with a look that said shut up, but after considering Brick's comment for a second, he said, "He's right. That's an easy bet. I say 'fuck' a lot."

"Then I will bet you good money," Ike said, "that you will say 'fuck' seven times in one sentence before you go to bed tonight."

Brick and Mace did another double take. Their eyes got big like saucers. Instinctively, they both relaxed their facial muscles in order to conceal their excitement about the prospect of a mark, a patsy, someone ready to let go of some money. They were like coon dogs alerting on their prey, smelling the money, allowing nature to take over. They couldn't help it.

Brick didn't really want to take advantage of Ike, the guy who had saved him, but a mark's a mark. But Mace did want to take advantage of Ike, and as much as he could.

Mace considered the proposal. "Seven times in one sentence, eh? How much do you want to bet?"

Mace was confident he could win a bet like this. All he had to do was watch his language a little, bite his tongue. If he made it home in the clunker, through the traffic, with no major incident, he would have it made in the shade, like finding money in the parking lot. And besides, if he did screw up, he could always lie about it.

"OK. If you really want to lose your money, I'll take your bet. How much you want to bet?"

"Five hundred dollars," Ike answered. "That five hundred dollars right there," he said, pointing to the five one-hundred-dollar bills lying on the dinette table. "Tell you what," he continued, "don't pay your rent tonight. Instead, Brick, you hold the money till dark to see if Mace here has a cussing fit. If he doesn't, then pay your rent, and you don't owe me the money back. It's yours. If he does have a cussing fit and says the 'f word' seven times in one sentence, then bring back my money, and we're even. But you still have to work the cases, for free. How's that?"

"Deal," Mace said, reaching out instinctively to shake hands with Ike.

"No!" Brick screamed. "You can't do that. That's our rent money!" In a flash, Brick realized he couldn't go along with the bet. They had to pay their rent. They had no choice. They couldn't afford to take a chance, no matter how small. And with his sudden outburst, Brick also realized he had totally validated Ike's assessment of their dismal financial predicament.

"Don't worry, buddy," Mace said, trying to calm Brick with his most soothing salesman's voice. "If you're concerned about the rent, I'll front you your half. No problem. All you have to do ask. I'll write you a check from my personal account. Besides, we're only a day late."

"But, Mace."

"I'll write you a check as soon as we get home, if it will make you feel better," Mace cajoled.

Brick knew it was a lie. Mace didn't have any money. He didn't even have a checking account. But Brick knew the rule. They always supported each other's lies when they were working a mark, and Mace was working Ike.

Ike interrupted, "OK, it's a bet then. Maybe you should leave that money here. You can pay your rent tomorrow night since it's really no emergency…only a day late, I mean."

"What's the matter? Don't you trust me?" Mace said. "A bet's a bet. When we shook on it just now, you said we'd be taking the money home with us and then bring it back if I say 'fuck' seven times in one sentence. Wasn't that our deal?"

"I said Pretty Boy, the responsible one, would be taking it home." Ike looked at Brick. "You keep him honest for me. I'll know if you're lying, and I'm not the kind of guy you want to cross." Ike picked up the five one-hundred-dollar bills and handed them to Brick. "Now, let's talk about these files for a while, then call it a day, and I'll see you back here in the morning."

———

The old clunker choked and coughed itself out of the parking lot and headed south onto Guadalupe Street, leaving behind a cloud of exhaust. Mace was at the wheel; a cigarette hung from his mouth. All the windows were rolled down, and it was hot...still.

"Don't you think I should be driving, Mace? This is a pretty serious bet you got us into. It's our rent money at stake here."

"Don't worry about it. Geez, how dumb are you? It's already our money. First, I'm not stupid enough to say 'fuck' seven times in one fucking sentence before dark, and even if I was, do you think I'd tell that asshole about it?"

"But he said he could tell if we lied."

"Yeah, sure. Like I believe that."

"But he knew we were behind on the rent. He knew we needed work. And somehow he knows we smoke pot and sit on a couch."

"Damn, Brick! That's the same trick he played when he had you convinced that he humped your old lady and he's your pappy. He generally described a stereotype of every Jewish girl in the seventies. Today he generally described a stereotype of every young professional male just out of school. We're behind on the bills, and we like to sit on the couch and smoke pot. That describes everybody our age. What else can we afford to do? Hell, we can smoke pot every night for a month for what one night out with a girl costs, especially some high-maintenance, uppity UT girl. Think about it. It doesn't take a genius to come up with that crap he came up with."

"But he saved me from the hospital cops."

"You got a point there."

"And he knew Bill, the stock boy, was stealing from Lavensky's."

"Still trying to figure that one out."

Right after they got onto Riverside Drive, a stream of the forbidden expletives almost escaped Mace's mouth when a soccer mom talking on her big black car phone in her big black Suburban changed lanes without looking and nearly hit them. Mace managed to catch the deluge of profanity on the edge of his lips just as the second "fuck" was pouring forth, and he sucked it back in. He sighed and experienced a momentary sense of victory and accomplishment. It felt good. They drove in silence the rest of the way home.

The old car squeaked, coughed, and popped as Mace maneuvered it into a parking spot at the Casa Grande apartments and turned off the engine. From their vantage point in the car, Mace and Brick both noticed the note flapping in the wind. It was pinned to their second-floor apartment door.

"Another valentine from Mrs. Chen, I see," Brick moaned, as he opened the car door to get out. Instantly, the door to Mrs. Chen's apartment swung open, and she stepped out onto the walkway, leaned over the railing, and peered down at them. She had the stare of a samurai.

"Quick! Give me the money," Mace said.

"But Ike said…"

"Fuck that. Give me the money."

"No way, dude. Ike said to wait till tomorrow."

"Screw him. He'll never know. Besides, we're going to win this money fair and square."

"But you already said 'fuck' once."

"Did not."

"Did too."

"But not seven times in the same sentence. Come on, man. You want to pay the rent or not? This is going to be our money anyway, right? I mean, shit, man, we're not even going to have to lie to him, if that's what you're worried about. Didn't you see me stop myself back there on Riverside when the MILF tried to run me over?"

"OK," Brick said reluctantly, giving in and handing Mace the money. Mrs. Chen was already halfway down the stairs. She stopped and took another long, dirty drag off her cigarette. Then she readjusted her polyester housecoat, making sure it revealed at least some of her sagging cleavage.

Mace took the money from Brick. He put four of the hundred-dollar bills in his right pocket and stuck the other one in the top of his left sock.

"OK. Let's go," Mace said. He slid out of the car and headed for Mrs. Chen. She was taking anther drag at the bottom of the steps.

"You bums got my money yet, or do I call cop?" she said, blowing a burst of smelly smoke into Mace's face.

"Just calm down," Mace said. "We've got your money."

"Don't tell me calm down. Hand over...'fore I change lock, call cop, throw you bums out."

"We got your money right here, sweetheart. You know we wouldn't cheat you. We've always paid our rent."

Mace dug his hand into his right pocket and retrieved the four one-hundred-dollar bills.

When Mrs. Chen heard the word *sweetheart*, she instantly melted from the flattery and giggled like a little girl. She flashed a big smile at Mace, showing a row of crooked and brown-stained teeth.

Just as quickly as the smile filled her face, suspicion overtook flattery. She pulled her wrinkled lips into a frown, cloaking her wretched teeth like a dusty shroud pulled tight around an ancient, bony monk. Her eyes glared at Mace, and she snapped, "What you mean you always pay rent? You late now."

"Yes, but we..."

"No 'yes, but.' You a yes butt. You pay me now."

"OK, OK," Mace said, handing her the four hundred dollars. "Here's four hundred dollars. It's all we have."

"No, no, no. You owe two month—eight hundred. Pay me now."

"This is all we have, really. This should give us another month to come up with the rest. Wouldn't you say? Right?"

"No right. You wrong. You two month behind. You pay now. Me no bank."

"Ah, come on, Mrs. Chen. It's all we have, really. Show her, Brick." Mace pulled both of his pockets wrong-side out. They stuck up in little white points. He motioned for Brick to do the same.

"All right. All right," Brick said, reluctantly pulling his pockets wrong-side out into two little white points.

"Show me wallet," she said.

Mace turned around, pointing his butt toward Mrs. Chen with an exaggerated motion, and pointed his finger at his butt.

"No wallet. See," he said.

"Oh, all right," Brick said. He frowned and pulled his wallet from his back pocket. Inside were three one-dollar bills he was hoarding for an emergency.

Before Brick knew what happened, Mrs. Chen snatched the bills from his wallet and crammed them down her saggy cleavage, where she already had the four one-hundred-dollar bills stashed.

"That mine now, *pretty boy*. Interest. You got one week to get me rest, or I call cop, throw you bums out.

94

One week!" With that, she pirouetted on her house shoe and started back up the stairs.

"Damn, Mace, that was my last three bucks," Brick said.

"Don't fret it. We still got that other hundred. More than enough for our shopping list—coffee, toilet paper, and weed…and not necessarily in that order."

"Tuna, yeah, we need tuna, and toilet paper, and gas," Brick said.

"And coffee and weed," Mace added.

"And clean shirts."

"That can wait."

Mace took the old metal steps two at a time in his exhilaration over his encounter with Mrs. Chen, but Brick strolled behind. He took one heavy step at a time, looking down, shaking his head from side to side and mumbling. "Pretty boy? Where'd she get that shit?"

"What's up, buddy?" Mace called down from the landing at the top of the stairs right outside their apartment door. He fumbled for the key in his jacket pocket. "You should be happy. The rent is paid. You can check that off your list of things to worry about. Rent paid. Check." Mace found the key and turned it in the lock. The door clicked open.

Unlike tonight, the night before had been an unusually hectic and crazy night. Brick and Mace hadn't made it home until very late that evening. Adrenaline was still pumping from everything that had happened to them at the hospital. The excitement of that night had carried over into their activities and their conversation. Their routine was off-kilter. The very first thing Mace wanted to do the night before was smoke, not pee, not open a beer can, not anything. Just smoke. The instant he walked through the door last night, he turned on the lights and headed straight for the bathroom to retrieve the dirty old bong from under the sink. That's what he had done the night before. And they had sat and smoked and talked about what a crazy night it had been until they realized they were exhausted and went to bed. But that's what they had done the night before when their natural rhythm had been off-kilter. Nothing had been the norm. Maybe that is why Mace had not noticed.

But today they arrived home before the sun went down. Neither of them had been in danger of getting arrested today. Brick had not seen any handcuffs or been dragged down any hallways. Mace didn't have to run down the street chasing any ambulances today, and Brick didn't have to walk anywhere in the dark. All and all, except for Ike and his strange behavior and his strange bet, and the strange metallic voice, it was a normal day. Perhaps it was the normality of the day that suddenly caused Mace to resume his habitual behavior and remember.

As was customary for Mace when he entered the apartment at the end of a day, he turned to place his briefcase on the floor next to the wall between the door-frame and the full-length mirror that Brick had personally installed so it couldn't miss him whenever he walked by. But today when he turned to place his briefcase on the floor, a strange feeling rushed through his body like he had stepped into an elevator shaft and the elevator wasn't there. An electric shock pulsated through his nervous system. His expression changed, and a look of surprise overtook his face. It was in that microsecond, in that frozen image in time, that Mace realized he did not have his briefcase. It wasn't in his hand where it was supposed to be—where it normally was. It was gone, and he didn't know where it was. Panic erupted.

"Oh, fuck, fuck, fuck, fuck, fuck, fuck, fuck!" he screamed.

"Where's my fucking briefcase? Where did it go?" He was freaked, and his voice betrayed any attempt to hide it. His mind started making an inventory of what was in the bag.

"Oh, fuck!"

"What? What?" Brick said. He was instantly caught up in Mace's panic and was dancing around like there were mice or roaches scampering across the floor. "What is it?"

"My briefcase. I always put it right here. I can't remember when I had it last? Shit fire. Fuck me running."

"Wait a minute," Brick said, regaining his composure. "We'll find it. Where were you the last time you saw it?"

"If I knew where I was the last time I saw it, I'd know where it is. What kind of dumb-ass question is that?"

"Well, I'm not the dumb ass that left my briefcase somewhere. I'm just trying to help. What did you have in it?"

"Well, let me think: past-due bills…business cards…"

"Past-due bills? What are you doing with past-due bills in your briefcase? I pay the bills. Why didn't you give me the bills? How much past due?"

"I don't know. I emptied the mailbox one day and forgot to give them to you."

"That's probably why they were past due. You forgot to give them to me. I can't believe you, Mace! What else was in there?"

Mace thought for a moment. "Oh, shit! Weed!"

"Weed? How much weed?"

"Two joints. I rolled them so we could celebrate on the ride home after Marvin's slip and fall."

"Oh, crap, man. Weed and your business cards in the same briefcase. Not cool, man. How could you be so stupid?"

"You wouldn't be saying 'stupid' if things had gone to plan—if we had signed up Marvin's case, if we hadn't run into that fucking Ike, and if we had smoked 'em on the way home like I planned. You wouldn't be saying 'stupid' then. You'd be saying 'thanks, buddy.'"

"Yes, but we didn't smoke 'em on the way home because you lost 'em in the same briefcase with your business cards and our bills with our home address on 'em. Shit, the cops are probably on their way here right now!" Brick cracked open the blinds with one finger and peeped outside. "So you must have had it yesterday," he continued, still peeking through the window. "If you had joints in it that you planned for us to smoke yesterday, you must have had it yesterday."

"Right," Mace said. "Right." Mace was trying to think. "Where was the last place I had it?" Then the air was shattered by Brick screaming at the top of his lungs.

"Oh, crap!" Brick screamed. "You said 'fuck' seven times!"

"I did not!"

"You did too. It's still ringing in my ears. I can count them. 'Fuck, fuck, fuck, fuck, fuck, fuck, fuck.' You did it. You said 'fuck' seven times in the same sentence."

"I did not."

"You did too. Now what are we going to do? You already gave the money to that old bag Chen, and Ike's gonna know we're not telling him the truth. What are we going to do? We have to go get our money—the money, my money—back from Mrs. Chen. I can't believe you lost our rent money." Brick's pitch was reaching whining proportions that would have registered on the Richter scale.

"Are you crazy? We're not getting anything back from Mrs. Chen. And I didn't lose our rent money. And crazy Ike isn't gonna know anything if you don't go all stupid and tell him."

"Will too."

"No, he won't. And besides, I didn't lose the bet."

"Yes, you did. I heard you."

"No, I didn't. Ike said that I had to say seven 'fucks' in the same sentence, right? Well, I didn't say seven 'fucks' in the same sentence."

"Yes, you did. I heard you."

"No, I didn't. I said, 'Fuck!' Then I said, 'Fuck, fuck, fuck, fuck, fuck, fuck.'"

"You said 'fuck' seven times."

"Yes, but not in one sentence. I said 'Fuck—exclamation mark.' Then I said a new sentence, 'Fuck, fuck, fuck, fuck, fuck, fuck.' See, I said 'fuck' seven times, but it was in two sentences."

"I don't know…"

"What do you mean, you don't know? He's the one that came up with the stupid rules for the bet, didn't he? Not me. It was his words: 'seven fucks in the same sentence.' In the *same* sentence. Right? It's his fault, not mine."

"Well, yes, but…"

"Well, he didn't say 'don't say seven fucks in two sentences,' did he?"

"Well, no, but…"

"No buts about it. It was his bet. It's his fault. If the bet was that I couldn't say seven fucks in thirty seconds, well, then, I'd lose. But he didn't say that. Did he? No, he didn't. He said 'seven fucks in one sentence,' so I don't lose."

"Yeah…but…"

"No buts about it. I didn't lose. If he wanted to be more specific, he should have been more specific. We're sharks. We're trained to find the loophole. Well, that's the loophole. It was said in two sentences, not one."

"So are you going to tell him you said 'fuck' seven times in two sentences instead of in one, so we win?"

Mace answered with a weary, sarcastic tone. "No, I'm not going to tell him I said 'fuck' seven times in two sentences, so we win. I'm just going to tell him we won. Period. 'Cause I didn't say 'fuck' seven times in one sentence. Period again. I don't know how many times I said 'fuck' tonight. I say 'fuck' a lot. Fuck. Fuck. Fuck. Fuck. Fuck-ity, fuck. But I didn't say it seven times in one sentence. OK? OK? You got that?"

"OK, then, I guess," Brick answered contritely.

"Fuck, where did I leave my briefcase? We were in traffic. I remember that. It was hot. I remember that. I already had the joints in the briefcase. Marvin was in the backseat. Gridlock set in. I threw my cigarette on that guy's car. I got upset and cussed and said fuck a few times then too. Then we got off the highway in front of Scholz's. We saw crazy Ike's car with the stupid fucking bumper sticker pull away. We pulled in. We saw that stupid, stuttering spaz, Tripper, for the first time. We heard the ambulance…" Mace stopped in midsentence. His head cocked sideways, and he got a faraway look in his eyes. "Oh shit! It's at the hospital."

"At the hospital?"

"Remember, I jumped out of the car to run to where the ambulance was headed. I had the briefcase with me while I was running…and when I jumped in the ambulance, I remember. And I had it with me in the waiting room." The tempo of Mace's speech increased along with the volume. "I left it on the floor next to my chair when I got up to save your sorry ass. It's your fault I don't have my briefcase. Flirting with the nurse, showing off cash to the whole undercover squad, nearly getting us busted. It's your fucking fault, not mine."

"Don't blame me you lost the bet."

"I'm not blaming you that I lost the bet. For the last time, I didn't lose that fucking, stupid bet. I'm blaming you that I lost my briefcase. If I hadn't been trying to save your stupid ass, I'd of had it with me when I left, and we'd of smoked the weed that was in the briefcase instead of spending half the night doing 'Praise Jesus' in the hospital chapel with that fucking lunatic."

Mace concluded his oration with the emotion of a tent revival preacher, sighing heavily with exhaustion, crossing his arms at the wrists, and clutching his chest. It was almost Hitler-esque. Mace did that when he knew his logic was a sham. Lawyers have a saying. "When the facts are with you, pound the facts. When the facts are against you, pound the table." Mace was pounding the table, so to speak.

Brick tried hard to think of what to say next. Nothing came. Mace's runaway emotional freight train had stumped him. Brick took a moment to calm himself and adjust his tie in the mirror, the mirror he had personally installed on the wall next to where Mace used to keep his briefcase.

"We might as well get stoned before the cops show up and arrest you," Brick finally said, "and let's use some of that money in your sock for mass quantities of Mexican food. I'm in need of some comfort."

"OK. Why not?"

Austin is home to some of the best Mexican food in the Southwest, but Mace and Brick hadn't figured that out yet. Good food and good liquor cost money. If you can't pay, you can't play. Mace and Brick hadn't been playing for quite a while. They put their party lifestyle on hold back when they decided to go to law school, knowing that someday the sacrifice might be worth it. But as they got closer to the end of law school, their savings got smaller and smaller, and consequently so did their social circles. Tonight, they found themselves sitting together, stoned again, in a Taco Bell, eating bean burritos and twenty-five-cent tacos and talking about how great it all was.

"This is good, man."

"The best."

They ate and ate, but Mace kept eyeing a young woman waiting for a takeout order. She was slim and vulnerable-looking and beautiful. Something about her demeanor said to Mace that she needed help, and something about her made Mace want to help her. She looked fragile, and caring, and responsible...and good in bed. Mace's mind turned immediately to sexual fantasy.

Mace gorged on another bean burrito in the real world, but in Mace's fantasy world, the young woman's clothes melted off her like chocolate syrup running down a tower of vanilla ice cream. Mace shivered with delight. A wad of refried beans dripped unnoticed onto his shirt. Her breasts were firm and perky and turned up, and her nipples were hard from the cold of the ice cream dream. Mace rubbed his face between her shoulder and her neck and started licking the chocolate from her chest. Never had he been so satisfied, at least for the moment. Food, drugs, and sex. What a life.

Mace's compulsive and addictive character defects were in full bloom. His false and lesser gods were having a field day.

"Are you listening to me?" Brick interrupted.

"Yes, what?" Mace said. He didn't try to hide his irritation over being snatched from his comfortable fantasy cocoon. He loved his fantasy cocoon, where everything was perfect. He didn't like being snatched back into reality, where beans smeared his shirt, and nothing was perfect, or at least nothing seemed to be.

"We've got to figure out what we're going to tell Ike tomorrow," Brick said.

"Don't worry about it. Just watch me tomorrow, and follow my lead…Have you ever seen her around here before?"

"Who?"

"That girl over there?"

"So that's it. That's why you didn't hear me. You're goggling over that girl. We don't have the time or money for that. You know how you are. Every time you get stuck on some girl, you do something stupid and lose all our money or get us fired or in some kind of trouble or something."

"But look at her. She's so, I don't know. She's so… don't you see it?"

"All I see is you making a fool of yourself. You look like a pig."

"What?"

"Roll your tongue back in your head. She's looking at you."

The young woman, in her midtwenties, was dressed in jeans, a Baylor T-shirt, and flip-flops. She glanced at Mace and Brick from the corner of her eye. Mace made her feel uncomfortable and self-conscious. She pretended to read the overhead menu, still pretending not to notice them. Mace was obvious about his attraction. He stared at her and talked loudly to Brick about how she was the most beautiful thing he had ever seen.

"Look at that!" Mace said. "Her cute little toenails are painted red. I love red."

Even to Brick, it seemed Mace was being obnoxious.

"No more for you," Brick said. "You're acting ridiculous."

The boy in the Taco Bell uniform finished sacking the order, handed the paper bag to the young lady, and said, "Four twenty-six." She reached into her purse to retrieve some cash.

"Quick!" Mace said to Brick. "Give me a business card."

Mace had already removed his jacket and tie while he and Brick were back at the apartment taking hits off the bong. Brick left his tie on the couch along with Mace's, but Brick was still wearing his jacket, as usual, and in his jacket pocket was where he kept a stack of Spinella and Hawthorne business cards.

Brick grimaced, but he reached into his pocket anyway and pulled out a card. He handed it to Mace.

"I wish you wouldn't do this," Brick said.

The young lady walked toward the door with her sack. Mace grabbed the card from Brick's hand and bolted from his chair. He reached her as she was reaching for the door handle.

"I haven't seen you around these parts before," Mace said.

As soon as the words left his mouth, he realized how incredibly dumb they must have sounded to her. *Around these parts before…geez…I sound like a hick. What parts? My private parts? Haven't seen you around this neck of the woods before, ma'am? Damn, I blew it.* The thoughts and incriminations stirred in his brain. The young woman in the faded denim jeans that stretched across her little bubble ass so perfectly just stood there and stared at him while he stammered.

"Let me introduce myself," he finally said, gaining his composure and shoving the card at her. "I'm a lawyer, and if you ever need anything…"

She was looking at Mace with half a smile on her face, but when she heard and saw the word *lawyer* on the card in her hand, her expression changed. She interrupted him loudly, "That's all I need is another worthless damn shyster lawyer making worthless promises. Just get out of my way, you shyster creep." She punctuated the word *shyster* with her hot, moist breath, and it was full of venom. Then she pushed past Mace and disappeared into the dark parking lot carrying her Taco Bell bag with her.

Mace stood in the door alone. His mouth hung open in shock and surprise because of the verbal assault from the woman he had already decided was going to be his soul mate, the love of his life.

Brick snickered. "Yep, she loves you all right."

"Yep, she loves me. She loves me."

"Didn't look like it to me," the Taco Bell boy chimed in from behind the cash register. "That was pretty awkward, dude."

There was something different when they got home. There was no "rent past due" notice pinned to the door. Brick breathed a sigh of relief. Even though the reprieve was only temporary, it was one Brick welcomed. Mace and Brick found their familiar indentations on the couch, settled into them, and began passing the bong.

"You know," Mace said, "I've never been called a shyster before in my life and now twice in one day by two different people."

"Maybe the universe is trying to tell you something, Mace," Brick said, choking on the smoke, laughing and trying to exhale at the same time.

"Now you sound like that fucking Ike."

"Oh, shit! That reminds me, what are we going to tell Ike?"

"Who cares? Pass it."

Brick passed the bong to Mace. Mace tried to light it, but it was spent. He began the reloading ritual. He scraped the bowl and filled it with what was almost the last of their meager marijuana supply while he sang,

"Hey, Mary, let me light up your cherry." Mace lit the bowl. It glowed red like a cherry. He inhaled, exhaled, and passed it to Brick.

Brick held the bong in both hands and, doing his best to mimic Mace at the Taco Bell, said, "Haven't seen you around these parts before…" He chuckled the words, barely able to get them out. Then, using a fake Texas drawl, he added, "Are you the new school-marm, ma'am?"

Mace coughed the smoke from his lungs. "Shut up," he said. "Not funny. Do you want fresh water in that? 'Cause if you do, you can change it yourself."

"Guess not. I'm not up to it either…pardner."

"Not funny."

Brick took another big drag and passed it back to Mace.

Mace took another drag, and it was spent again. He unscrewed the metal bowl from the base of the bong and scraped the tar and burned residue from it with the pipe tool. "If anybody finds my briefcase, I'll just say it was stolen. Nothing in there we can't live without." He pulled the plastic bag from under the couch pillow where he had stashed it a few moments earlier.

Ever since studying criminal law at the Carver-Washington Gospel School of Law and learning about the "plain view doctrine," Brick and Mace had made an effort not to leave the bong or the weed out in plain view where anyone could see it, because if a policeman were walking by and saw it, through cracked blinds or an open door, he didn't even need a search warrant. He could just bust right in. That was a frightening prospect, so it had become their habitual practice, most of the time, to stash the weed and paraphernalia out of sight if they weren't presently using it. Better safe than sorry.

"Wish we had that weed back though," Mace said. "We're getting low, buddy, really low. We got to get some more pot, and soon."

"And toilet paper and tuna," Brick said. "...and gas," he added, as an afterthought.

"But especially weed," Mace said. "We need to do some *Good Weed Hunting*...real soon...staring Ben Afflek and that other dude."

"You mean Matt Damon and whoever that dude was you said."

"Whatever."

Then Mace broke into song and Brick joined in on the second line, "Legalize it. I wish they'd legalize it. Legalize it. They've got to legalize it." They were so out of tune, it made them both laugh and cough and grab their sides.

Chapter 5

JUST IN CASE

Morning came too early again. Streaks of sunlight beamed through a slit in the tattered old curtain. Illuminated particles of dust danced, suspended in midair, making a slice of Brick's room look like a miniature galaxy filled with tiny, swirling planets and stars. Warm light caressed Brick's face, teasing him awake, but he didn't want to move. The weight of the stifling, humid air on his body informed his subconscious it was going to be another hot day in Austin, Texas.

Coffee. He needed coffee. His brain felt heavy and thick, either from too much marijuana or from too much salt at Taco Bell the night before. Probably the latter. He pulled the cover up over his head and tried to muffle the noise that was coming from the other side of his door. Half awake and half dreaming, he cursed Mrs. Chen for waking him yet again.

Not again, he thought. Then he smelled the aroma of coffee in the air, and a foggy memory stirred in his sleepy brain, reminding him that Mrs. Chen had already been paid and he probably had at least another week before she started hounding him again.

Coffee! It smells like coffee. Brick jumped to his feet, startled by the realization that he really did smell coffee, and he really was hearing banging noises coming from the next room. It wasn't a dream. He grabbed his robe and stumbled to the living room.

Brick stood stunned, staring in awe and amazement, watching the last few drops of freshly brewed coffee drip slowly into the pot while Mace, dressed only in threadbare boxer shorts, put the last of the dirty dishes into the rusty old dishwasher.

Mace dried his hands on a rag and turned around just in time to see Brick flop lifelessly onto the couch like a limp overcoat someone had just thrown down.

"How 'bout a cup of coffee, little buddy?" Mace asked, flashing Brick a toothy grin.

Wolf in sheep's clothing, was Brick's first thought. He was right.

"What are you doing up so early? I've never seen you up this early," Brick moaned, wiping the rest of the sleep from his eyes.

"We got work to do," Mace said. He handed Brick a steaming cup. "This will wake you up."

"Thanks, dude," Brick said. He was sincerely grateful. Then his demeanor changed. "What's gotten into you?" The question sounded more like an accusation than it did a question.

"Ike said he wanted us there by nine," Mace answered.

"So. Since when do you care what Ike wants?" Brick asked. He blew the steam from the top of his coffee and took a sip without breaking the suspicious stare he was giving Mace. "Ah, that coffee's good," he said, still glaring at Mace, still waiting for an answer.

In all the years Brick had known Mace, there were probably fewer than a handful of days when Mace had gotten out of bed before him...ever. *Mace is up to something. He has to be.* Brick couldn't remember Mace ever, not once, making the morning coffee. *The coffee proves it. He's up to something.*

"I don't care what Ike wants, but I do care what we want," Mace said.

"And?"

"And we want toilet paper and more weed."

"And tuna," Brick added.

"Screw tuna. I don't like tuna."

Brick lowered his eyebrows and scowled, "Tuna."

"OK. Tuna. Whatever."

"And...?" Brick coaxed.

Exasperated, Mace sputtered, "OK, gas too. Whatever."

"That's not what I mean. What I mean is, why are you up so early...and since when do you care what Ike thinks? And why did you clean the kitchen? And why did you make the coffee? And why did you bring me a cup? What did you do? You did something, didn't you? What kind of trouble have you gotten us into this time?"

Mace took in a deep breath, looking for the right words, but Brick interrupted, "And where's my check for half the rent you told Ike you would give me? Asshole!"

"You know I didn't mean that. I don't have any money. I don't even have a checking account."

"I know you don't. And you didn't have a dollar to your name until yesterday. At least I had three bucks."

"So?"

"Well, you lied."

"So?"

"You shouldn't have done that," Brick said. He took another sip of coffee and savored the sensation of his body waking up and his clogged brain starting to unclog. His mind and body welcomed the aromatic stimulant and the relief it brought.

"Since when did a little lie ever bother you?" Mace asked.

"Since yesterday when you made me the brunt of it," Brick snapped. "'Oh, I'll write you a personal check for my half as soon as we get home,'" Brick said. "You made me look like a scared little whiner."

"Well?"

"Well, screw you!" Brick said, and then, in a flash, he remembered the bet, and Ike, and the money. "Oh, fuck, what are we going to tell Ike about the five hundred dollars?"

"That's why I'm up this early. I've already thought it out. We go in on time, we do our work, and when he asks, we just say we won the bet and we paid our rent. It's that simple. Open and shut. Like it's no big deal. And it's our money—free and clear." Mace paused a beat for dramatic effect and looked Brick in the eyes, then he added with a tone of confidence, "I figured something else out last night too. There's more where that came from."

"What do you mean?"

"I was awake half the night thinking about this. We're five hundred ahead right now, right? We didn't have to work a bit for it, right? It's ours. Is that good or what? And this so-called law work he has us doing will mean even more money coming to us, right?" Mace didn't wait for an answer to his rhetorical question before continuing. "Now, don't get me wrong. I don't want a job, and I don't want to work for this guy, but— listen to this—he proved to us yesterday that he's loose with his money, and he's not really all that smart either. He's not—he's not smart—because if he was smart, he wouldn't have trusted us to tell the truth on that stupid bet. And if he's that stupid, then he deserves to be taken for all we can take him for, right?"

"And?" Brick asked, almost humming the word.

"And we finish these cases, and while we're at it, we do a couple more dumb bets with crazy Ike, and before you know it, we have a stake to start our own business and start it off right instead of working out of our damn car. Plus, the people we'll meet can lead us to more clients of our own, right? Networking, man. We haven't been doing so good by ourselves yet, right? So, I bet if I do a good job for this Diaeta Pepsi chick, I'll be representing all the prostitutes before you can say jack shit. And if you do good for Wilfred Johnson, you'll be representing all the weed hookups and maybe getting part of our fee in weed—good weed...hydroponic... not that Mexican shit we're smoking."

"And?" Brick hummed.

"And what, damn it? What's with all the damn 'ands?' Isn't that enough?"

"And why did you bring me coffee, and why did you clean the kitchen? I know it doesn't have anything to do with what you're talking about. That may be the reason you got up early, but it's not the reason you cleaned the kitchen and brought me coffee. I know you, Mace Spinella," Brick said, shaking his finger at Mace. "Now what's really going on?"

"Well, that's another story, buddy," Mace answered sheepishly.

Brick grimaced. He knew there had to be a catch.

"I want to go back to Taco Bell tonight," Mace said. He had a slight hesitancy in his voice and a pleading look all over his face.

"Why?" Brick asked. He was puzzled, which was a feeling Brick was accustomed to, but not comfortable with.

"To see if that girl shows up again."

Mace waited a beat to make sure he wasn't going to have to dodge a flying coffee cup, then he continued, "And if she does show up, I'll need some of that money we have left."

"I knew it. I knew it. I knew it!" Brick said. There was an angry, exasperated twinge in his voice that made him sound like he had a kazoo stuck in his throat. "The only time you ever get motivated for anything—you can

115

bet your ass—it has something to do with pussy." He spat the last word like it tasted bad.

"What you got against pussy, little buddy?"

"Not a damn thing, but you're not getting any of that money to chase it with. We need that money. You know, Ike was right about you. I am the responsible one, and you're the jerk-off. Nothing would ever get paid around here if I didn't do it. Nothing would ever get done around here if I didn't do it."

"I cleaned the kitchen and made coffee for you, didn't I?" Mace said. He flashed Brick his most charming smile.

"See what I mean? You're hopeless. Now give me that money. Now! I don't trust you with it."

"That's not fair," Mace protested.

"Yes, it is," Brick snapped.

"No, it's not. And you know *the rule*." Mace said the words with a certain reverence—*the rule*—as if he were invoking a higher power. "If we can't agree, we have to settle it with ro-sham-bo." He gave the word *ro-sham-bo* equal reverence, like it was a magic word or a name for God. Mace knew if he could get Brick to ro-sham-bo, then he would at least have a chance to hold on to the money. He knew he stood no chance against Brick's whiny, angry, moral superiority. Besides, he knew Brick was right, so ro-sham-bo was his only chance.

"But I'm right on this one, Mace. Our survival could depend on it. This isn't just about Chinese or Mexican tonight. This is about whether we survive or not." Brick's tone was angry yet pleading.

"You know *the rule*. Ro-sham-bo," Mace insisted.

Reluctantly, Brick acquiesced. Mace joined him on the couch, and they prepared to settle their disagreement. Brick and Mace didn't reach an impasse very often, but when they did, they always settled it with ro-sham-bo. It was the law that preserved their relationship. Ro-sham-bo was their arbiter. It had been that way since they were kids. It was a part of their personal code of honor, the same as not contradicting each other's lies when they were working a patsy.

Brick and Mace sat on the couch and faced each other. Each made a fist. Mace did the counting. "One, two, three!" And they began the game that most people call rock-paper-scissors. They pumped their fists up and down by their sides with each count until Mace gave the signal by punctuating the word *three*. Then each revealed his chosen weapon. Paper covers rock. Rock breaks scissors. And scissors cut paper.

Mace had chosen scissors, as indicated by his outstretched index and middle fingers—and so had Brick. It was a tie.

Mace began counting again. Fists pumped. "One, two, three!" Once again, Mace chose scissors—so did Brick. It was another tie.

"One, two, three!" The tension mounted. They pumped their arms faster. Then each revealed his respective weapon with the lightening speed of a Saturday-matinee gunslinger slapping cold steel against tethered leather. They stared at each other's hand. This time, there was a winner.

A few days previously, Mace and Brick had settled a disagreement over what to watch on TV with ro-sham-bo. Mace wanted to watch *Law And Order*, but Brick insisted on watching *Friends*. Now, suddenly, this game to determine the custody of the surviving money was playing out like déjà vu.

Mace remembered the first two rounds had been ties on that day too, with scissors as the chosen weapon each time. Mace had won that day when Brick chose scissors for the third straight time, only to see them broken by a rock, as revealed by Mace's outstretched fist when the count was done.

Mace seized on the opportunity to play a repeat of his previous victory. Brick would surely choose scissors again just like he did the last time. *Brick is a creature of habit. He has his routines. It'll be scissors again. I know it,* Mace thought.

The count was done. Mace's outstretched fist revealed his choice of weapon, the rock that was going to smash Brick's scissors and take managing conservatorship of the last of their cash so he could use it to attract the new love of his life, if he ever saw her again.

Mace was rising to his feet to proclaim victory when suddenly he realized, to his shock and dismay, that Brick's outstretched hand was flat, like a pancake, not a fist, not a scissor, but a flat hand symbolizing the piece of paper that covered the rock that Mace had chosen. Brick had not chosen scissors again but had chosen paper and was victorious this time, the keeper of the money, and the incontestable winner under the rule of the game. Paper covers rock.

"Did I win?" Brick asked.

"Fuck, fuck, fuck, fuck, fuck, fuck, fuck," Mace said uncontrollably. His face and body contorted like he was in the throes of an angry bowel movement.

"See, you're doing it again. You never learn. Now, give me that money."

Mace begrudgingly retrieved what was left of the hundred and handed it to Brick. "If I see her again, though, I'm going to need that money back," Mace grumbled. "Just looking at her makes me feel good all over. She's like a drug, man. I've got to have her. It breaks my heart every time I think about her. If I had an idea where she lives, I'd stand in the rain all day long just hoping she might walk by."

"You're kinda sick, man," Brick answered. "It doesn't rain in Austin, anyway." Then he stretched his coffee cup toward Mace and asked, "Can I have a refill?"

"Get it yourself," Mace growled.

———

An hour and a half later, the old jalopy limped into the parking lot of Goldstein and Turner. Before leaving home, they each grabbed a handful of stale Cheerios and another cup of black coffee, and they drove north from Riverside Drive to IH-35. Mace had to restart the car a couple of times when the traffic slowed to a stop, as it usually does, crossing the Colorado River bridge.

They arrived a few minutes shy of the nine o'clock deadline Ike had imposed on them the day before. "Be here by nine, or I might leave without you," Ike had said, and then added, "Wear suits and ties, just in case."

119

In case of what? Neither of them had asked. Ike hadn't said it in a cryptic sort of way. He said it in a very matter-of-fact sort of way, like he thought they knew what he meant. "Wear suits and ties, just in case." But neither of them knew what he meant; nevertheless, they were wearing their suits and ties, and their last clean shirts, "just in case."

They entered through the back door, as they had been instructed, and found their files from the day before on the kitchen table just as they had left them. But in each of their chairs was a cardboard file box containing stacks of paper, bound depositions, and envelopes labeled "photos."

On top of one of the boxes was a handwritten note in beautiful, perfect, feminine-looking handwriting on lavender-colored paper. Brick read it aloud. "Good morning, boys. Ike wants you to read all this for a potential case. The coffee is fresh. Cups are in the cabinet. Put your dirty dishes in the dishwasher, and we'll get along fine. Kay."

"What you s'pose this is about?" Brick asked Mace, holding the note in one hand and fingering the files in the file box with his other.

"I don't know, but I know I'm not reading this crap until I know how much I'm getting paid for it," Mace said. With that, he snatched the note from Brick's hand, held it to his face, and smelled it.

"If it's about a case, I'm sure he'll work something out with us," Brick said.

"Oh, you're sure, huh? Like you know this guy or something. Why are you so sure? All he's done so far is play divide-and-conquer with us."

"What the hell are you talking about?"

"What am I talking about? 'Ike was right. I'm the responsible one,'" Mace said, sticking his bottom lip out and mimicking Brick's kazoo voice from earlier. "That's what I'm talking about."

Brick ignored the comment. "Look, we can get everything in writing even. But I don't think we should wait to get started on this. I'm ready to get started now. This might be a real case, with real money."

"Says you," Mace snarled. "I'm not reading any of this crap until I know what's in it for me. I resent the hell out of this guy taking us for granted like we're a couple of punks and leaving this pile of crap in our chairs without even an explanation or telling us what to expect." Mace was angry, distrustful, and resentful. "I don't need this shit," he said.

For some reason, a reason from a long time ago, a reason he was no longer even aware of, that note full of instructions flipped a switch in his subconscious mind to the "on" position, and Mace's thinking and behavior went on autopilot. He had no choice; at least, that's what he thought. His free will was momentarily suspended.

Angry words flowed out of him, and there was no stopping them. The fear and insecurity of his life made him feel like a scared little child sometimes, and this was one of those times. And the scared little child inside him had to be protected, so Mace had created an angry little bully to do just that. And today that angry little bully was standing up for the scared little child, and Mace lashed out, disguising his fear with anger—fear of being vulnerable, fear of failure, and fear of not being enough.

Or perhaps Mace lashed out in anger this time because somewhere down deep inside, Mace felt a little guilty for concocting the lie he was going to tell Ike about the bet. Perhaps that was part of it. Either way, for now, his little bully was in control.

"I wonder who Kay is," Brick said, without giving any recognition to Mace's tirade.

Mace pushed the box onto the floor and sat down in the chair. "Have it your way," he said. "But I'm not doing anything until I know what the deal is. Until I know what's in it for me. You know I don't trust this guy."

"I thought you said a while ago he was stupid and you were going to play him along and get his money… well?"

"I don't like being told what to do. This note rubs me the wrong way. It's telling us what to do."

"Rubs you the wrong way? You mean 'put your dirty dishes in the dishwasher' rubs you the wrong way? What a candy ass! I know what this is really about. You're still mad about losing ro-sham-bo and about the money and that girl. That's what you're mad about."

"Am not! I just don't like being disrespected. He calls us shysters, and boys, and stupid, and gay—that one really pisses me off. Us? Gay? How the hell did he come up with that?"

"Well, you thought he was gay."

"I still do. And I still think he's some kind of con-man too. You just wait. I'll bet you before…"

One of the side doors swung open with a loud squeak, startling Mace and stopping him in midsentence. His head jerked around, and he expected to see Ike, but instead a beautiful, tall, woman stepped into the kitchen, coffee cup in hand. Her pinky finger was extended in a most polite and feminine fashion. She appeared to be in her early forties, and the way she looked was breathtaking. She wore a blue polka-dotted, pleated skirt, a white blouse, and black high heel shoes. She was reminiscent of the 1950's TV wives, like Harriet Nelson or Donna Reed. Her red lipstick matched her fingernails, but other than that, her makeup was modest. She was a natural beauty.

Her black high heels clicked across the linoleum floor as she walked toward the cabinet where the coffee pot sat next to the ceramic soup tureen with the little chicks sticking their heads out from under mama's wings. The bottom of her skirt swished around the tops of her knees. Nylon hose accented the back of her beautifully proportioned calves. They cast a candlelight sheen that caught Brick's attention and made him swallow hard. It reminded him of his second-grade schoolteacher and his first boner. She poured a cup of coffee from the pot without saying a word and then turned and smiled at them. The hem of her skirt turned a fraction of a second after she did. It swayed gently back and forth across the tops of her gorgeous knees until it gradually found its resting place.

"Hi, I'm Kay," she said, smiling. "Did you boys find the reading material Ike left you?"

Mace cleared his throat and tried to answer, but nothing came out. Other than the young woman at Taco Bell, Mace couldn't remember if he had ever seen such a classy-looking woman. This was a beautiful woman. She was perfectly proportioned—flat stomach, long, smooth legs, and pointy boobs to die for. She looked like she could have been a Barbie doll's older sister. She smiled again and waited for Mace's response. Her smile convinced both young men that she was warm, caring, nurturing…and, of course, good in bed.

"I'm sorry. What did you say?" Brick finally said, rescuing both of them from their stupor.

"Hi, I'm Kay," she repeated. "Did you boys find the reading material Ike left for you?" She took another sip from her coffee cup. It left a smudgy, sexy lipstick kiss mark, and then she flashed them another radiant smile.

Mace cleared his throat again. "Yeah, about that, what's the deal with these boxes? I'm not going to read this stuff without an explanation, and where's Ike? He told us to be here by nine," Mace complained.

"Oh, he's here," she answered. "He was sitting right where you are reading these files when I walked in at eight this morning. He's upstairs taking a shower right now."

"Taking a shower?" Mace protested. "He told us to be here by nine, or he might leave without us. Now you tell me he wants us to read all this crap while he takes a shower?" Mace's bully was trying to control the situation.

Kay didn't miss the sarcasm in his tone. "Oh, it's not crap, Mr. Spinella. You don't know how lucky you are that Ike is willing to take you under his wing and let you help him with this."

"Ike lives here?" Brick interrupted.

"Sometimes, he does, Mr. Hawthorne," she answered. "After you gentlemen left yesterday, a couple showed up at the reception desk with these boxes and asked to see Ike. He was on his way out the door, but he came back to see what they wanted. He met with them yesterday for about two hours and read most of the file last night. He finished it this morning. So I suggest you get busy if you don't want to be left behind." Her tone had turned from sweet to authoritative in a matter of seconds.

"So does Ike want us to help him with this case?" Brick asked, trying to break the tension. *Don't shoot us in the foot, Mace,* he thought.

"That depends on you," she answered.

"So what's it about?" Brick asked enthusiastically.

"Not sure. That's why Ike wants you to read it. All I know is there was an explosion, and the man got hurt. Bad. It happened in Waco. They've been through two or three lawyers that took the case and then dropped them, and they've been turned down by a bunch of other lawyers too. The lady told the receptionist that Ike was their last hope."

"That doesn't sound too good. Why would we want to waste our time on something that's already been turned down by a bunch of other lawyers?" Mace asked suspiciously. "There's probably not any money in it or else the other lawyers wouldn't have dropped it. I may be new at this, but I can smell a rat. What's Ike trying to pull?"

"That's all up to you. You don't have to do anything. You don't have to read it. You don't even have to be here." Kay had taken offense to Mace's remarks and tone. "Ike can find another drag rat like you anywhere, anytime. He doesn't need your help. He's helping you."

She topped off her coffee and walked to the same door she had entered, but right before she stepped through it, she turned around and smiled at Mace. She held the pose just long enough for the hem of her blue polka-dotted skirt to stop its rhythmic sweeping and come to rest once more at the top of her beautiful knees. Then she spun again and stepped through the door, and it closed behind her.

No sooner than the door clicked closed, it opened again. Kay stepped back in and looked Mace square in the eyes. She held a chrome-colored cube in the palm of her hand. It had three black buttons on the top of it. Kay pushed the button in the middle. A metallic, Stephen Hawking-sounding voice came out of the cube. "Fuck you. Eat shit," it said. Kay smiled. She spun around again, her skirt danced again, and the door closed behind her. This time, she was gone.

When Brick was confident she wasn't coming back in, he turned on Mace. "I can't believe you! You manage to shoot yourself in the foot and piss off that beautiful woman all at the same time. What the hell's the matter with you?"

"I'm just trying to protect us, buddy."

Behind the door, they heard the metallic, robotic, Stephen Hawking sound again. "Fuck you. Eat shit," it said.

They cringed and got quiet. Brick continued in a whisper, "Either we work this situation, or we don't. Either you play Ike for a patsy, or you don't. I don't care, but if we leave, I want it to be our decision. I don't want to get thrown out on our butts because of your mouth."

"I'm just trying…"

"You're just trying to control everything. Leave it alone. What do we have better to do right now anyway? Anything?"

"You know, you're starting to piss me off." Mace crossed his arms and glared at Brick.

"So. What are you going to do about it?" Brick answered and glared back.

"What are you going to do about it?" Mace snapped and glared all the more.

They sat in silence and stared at each other for a while. Then Brick reached for a handful of the papers in the box and started reading them. Almost immediately, Mace did the same. They read in silence for about twenty minutes, when Mace suddenly slammed the deposition he was reading on the table. "Drag rat? Where the hell did she come up with drag rat?"

Brick snickered. They shared a quick glance and went back to what they were reading.

After a while, Brick said, "At least we know what that Stephen Hawking voice is now."

"The yu-ne-verse is like a piece of spa-gat-tee," Mace said, imitating and misquoting Stephen Hawking.

They both laughed and went back to work.

Around a quarter till ten, Ike entered the room. "What do you boys think?" Ike asked, smiling and nodding his head toward the papers and files that were now scattered all over the table in front of Brick and Mace.

Brick laid down the bound deposition he was reading. "Looks like he got hurt pretty bad," Brick said.

"Yeah," Mace added, "and it looks like he's an arsonist too." Mace emphasized the word *arsonist* and waited for Ike's reaction.

"Yes, it kind of does, doesn't it?" Ike answered.

"Then why do you want to take this case?" Mace asked. "I mean...I don't care if he's an arsonist if you can win it, get him some money, get *us* some money—fine. But if you can't win it...and this one looks bad...I mean, hell, he had gasoline all over him at the hospital, then why get involved? I think that's probably why all the other lawyers dropped him."

"I think you're probably right," Ike answered. Mace was surprised Ike agreed with him.

Ike walked around the table to the back door, where a small, framed painting of some butterflies hung on the wall, but the butterflies were painted on a mirror, and a lot of the mirror had not been painted over. Ike looked past the butterflies into the mirror portion and began straightening his tie. "I put this here so I could straighten my tie and check my teeth before I leave," he said.

"That's smart!" Brick said enthusiastically. He suddenly felt a sense of kinship with Ike. Mace rolled his eyeballs.

"Hey, you're not wearing a Willie Nelson shirt today. What gives?" Brick said.

"Like I told you yesterday, wear a suit and tie, just in case."

"Just in case what?" Brick and Mace asked at the same time.

"You don't know?"

"No," they answered at the same time.

"Why does a lawyer ever wear a suit?"

"Why?" they both asked.

"Well, we're not going to a funeral," Ike answered with excitement. "We get to go to court today."

"We do?" Brick asked. He was excited about the idea of going to court with Ike. Maybe Ike was going to introduce them around.

"That's great," Mace said—and he meant it. He was excited about the prospect of getting to watch Ike in his element, to see him work. It might give him enough information to validate his low opinion of him.

"I'm sure glad to hear you fellers say that," Ike said, using a country drawl that was more pronounced than usual.

Mace was immediately apprehensive. He knew from his days as a rhino perfume salesman on the streets of Los Angeles that whenever anyone takes on an affectation, like a fake accent or a change in their voice, it usually means they are running a con of some sort. And just then, Ike sounded more country than usual. Something was up, Mace thought, and Mace was right.

"I remember my first time," Ike continued. "I was so nervous. I tripped over my own briefcase and fell on my face, right in front of the judge. He said, 'You don't have to prostrate yourself, Mr. Turner; a simple curtsy will do.'" Ike laughed, but the two young men watching him did not see the humor.

"What do you mean? What are you talking about, first time?" Mace interrupted.

"We're going to court. I called the clerk this morning and got us two courts at the same time. Two, two, two courts at once," Ike sang. "They had cancellations. It's a lot like scheduling a tennis court or getting concert tickets. If you check back on the day of, there's probably some cancellations, and you can get in. That's what Max Deale says anyway. We're going to court, boys."

"Two courts? What do you mean, two courts? I thought we were going to go watch you do court," Brick said.

"Two courts," Ike repeated. "Fortunately for us, they're both on the same floor, so I'll be able to go back and forth and see how you're doing. You've got Diaeta Pepsi, and Pretty Boy's got Wilfred Johnson."

"Yes, but...but...we haven't even talked to them yet," Brick said. All of a sudden, Brick felt a little tingly and weak. The thought that he might have to speak in front of strangers without any time to prepare made him feel faint and anxious.

"Doesn't matter. I've talked with them already. I'll tell you all about it on the way to the courthouse," Ike said.

"You mean now?" Mace asked. He couldn't believe it. "You're crazy!"

"That's me, crazy Ike," Ike quipped. "Haven't you boys ever been to the courthouse? You act like you've never seen the inside of the courthouse."

"We went a couple times during law school, but never on a case…just observers," Brick answered.

"I see. Then I guess I'll have to talk you through it. I'll run back and forth between the two of you. You can improvise, can't you?"

Mace cocked his head to the side, giving Ike a quizzical look. "You're shitting us, aren't you? This is a joke you play on the new guys, some sort of initiation. Right?" Mace was doing his best to make sense of the situation. It had to be a joke, an initiation for the newcomers. Mace looked around in vain for a hidden camera or some sign from Ike that it was all a joke. But nothing was forthcoming. Mace realized Ike was serious—crazy serious.

Ike ignored Mace's question and continued with what he was saying. "You learned courtroom procedure in law school, didn't you?"

"Well, sort of," Brick answered.

"Just follow my lead then," Ike said nonchalantly.

"You're crazy. This is malpractice. I'm not going," Mace said. He gripped the edge of the table like it was the throttle of a crashing airplane. The white of his knuckles made no secret of his anxiety. Ike took notice of Brick's and Mace's stressed mental state and decided it might be better to relax the tension a little rather than risk a mutiny.

"You can do it. Trust yourself," Ike said. His voice took on a calm and soothing tone. The cowboy accent was gone. "I have an hour or so to get you ready. Think about it. Wouldn't you love to have your first courtroom victories, in less than a month of being lawyers, and on near-hopeless cases? Wouldn't you love those bragging rights?"

Brick perked up again. "Hopeless cases? What do you mean, hopeless cases?"

"Yeah, what do you mean, hopeless case?" Mace chimed in.

"Figure of speech," Ike answered. "Mace, look at me. You've got a one-witness case. You'll have a verdict by five o'clock. It's a misdemeanor, so it's a six-person jury. Use a jury strike on the jurors that are related to cops, that date cops, or that have cop friends. Get rid of 'em. Get 'em off the jury panel. 'Cause if the jury believes the cop, case over; we lose. But if they doubt the cop, then we should probably win."

"Probably win?" Brick interrupted. "What do you mean, probably? If we show reasonable doubt, wouldn't we win? That's what they said in law school. Reasonable doubt."

"Wait a minute," Mace said and motioned for Brick to hold his question. "If we go with you and handle these cases, how do we win, and how much do we get paid?" Mace's inquiry was genuine. He had begun to calm a little, and the idea of a court victory did appeal to him, not to mention taking Ike for more money. It could be part of the plan. Take Ike for all they can.

"Tell 'em 'bout reasonable doubt," Ike answered.

"What?"

"Reasonable doubt...tell 'em about reasonable doubt. That's how you win. You've got to give 'em an alternate theory. Give 'em something that explains how the facts of your case could have happened without your client being guilty of anything. See what I mean?"

"You mean make something up, don't you?" The tone of Mace's question revealed his motive. His demeanor changed. He wasn't seeking knowledge to win the case anymore. He was back to his previous mission, one that his subconscious needed today more than it did a courtroom victory. His bully was back in control. He was out to get Ike, to catch him in any shortcoming he could so he could prove to Brick they didn't need this guy.

In spite of his own lack of a personal moral code, Mace now relished the thought of unearthing any moral flaw on Ike's part. He saw his chance to judge and criticize. "So by 'give them something,' you mean lie or make something up, something the jury can go off on to find her not guilty, even if she is guilty. That's what you're saying, right? 'Cause she did solicit a cop, you know? I read the report."

"No. I'm not saying to lie. Lying is something a *shyster* would do. If you want to know what I want you to do, ask yourself what would a *shyster* do, and then do the opposite." Ike was calm even though it was obvious to him, and obvious to Brick, that Mace was trying to provoke him. Ike didn't take the bait. "Just give the jury another way to look at the facts. It's all about perspective. Tell 'em a good story consistent with the indisputable facts. Not everybody needs to be in jail, and not every so-called crime is as serious as the tight asses in authority make it out to be. Just give the jury an excuse to cut a defendant loose, and sometimes they will."

There was that word again, *shyster.* Mace hated that word. And Ike managed to work it into every conversation. Instinctively, Mace wanted to blurt out a denial, that he was not a shyster, but he caught himself. *Bad strategy,* he thought. *If I deny it, he'll just call me a shyster again.* So Mace took the offensive and said, "So you're telling me you have no problem with getting a guilty person off?" Not that the idea bothered Mace, Mace just wanted to show Brick that Ike was as bad as he was, maybe worse.

"I have no problem with giving the jury another way to look at the facts. I have no problem with giving the jury a framework within which they can choose mercy over retribution. I have no problem with pleading for my client to the best of my ability—and then leaving the result to Divine Order." The words rolled from Ike like low, rumbling thunder. He assumed the role of an orator, an advocate. His presence filled the room.

When he finished speaking, Mace and Brick were momentarily mesmerized. Ike had their attention with the first "I have no problem" and had them fixated by the third "I have no problem."

Ike had used his "three points starting with the same phrase" technique on Mace, and it worked. It was one of Ike's favorite persuasive speaking tools: have three points, and start them all with the same words, such as "I have no problem with…I have no problem with…and I have no problem with." There was something magic about saying it three times that made people listen and made it stick.

And Ike had a way of punctuating and pounding each word of the common phrase so that a fresh, new neuron trail was laid down across the listener's gray matter like a trolley track leading back to the specific memory Ike wanted him or her to have. Ike had the ability to tell people something in a way that made them think they already believed it to be a fact, whether it was or not. He was good at that.

"Remember the story about the woman caught in adultery?" Ike continued.

Mace and Brick looked puzzled. They glanced at each other for a hint at what Ike was talking about. They didn't have a clue. They both shrugged.

"Haven't a clue," Mace said.

"Well, there was a woman who got caught committing adultery back during Jesus's time, and that was a crime back then—a crime for the woman, anyway— and the punishment was death." Ike looked sternly back and forth at Mace and Brick. "Do you think that was fair?" Ike asked. "Death? Death for adultery? And only for the woman?"

Brick thought for a minute. He looked pensive. "No, not me," Brick answered.

Ike looked at Mace and indicated he expected an answer.

"For adultery? No," Mace said reluctantly, and then muttered, "Unless it's my ex-girlfriend."

"But that was the law. And the law's the law, right?" Ike looked at Mace and waited for an answer.

"Yeah, but death, that's a little severe, I think, even for my ex," Mace said.

"But it was the law. Would you argue for the woman if you had been her lawyer? Would you try to get her off even if she was guilty?" Ike asked.

"Sure, I guess so," Mace answered.

"Sure. But how?" Brick asked. "If she's guilty, how do you do that?

"Give the jury another way to look at it. Give them a reason to show mercy," Ike said.

"So what happened with her?" Brick asked. Brick loved a good story.

"Yeah, I'll take the bait too; what happened to her?" Mace asked

"She was arrested and taken by her accusers, the Pharisees, to see Jesus. They hated Jesus, and they wanted to see if they could kill two birds with one stone...in other words, trick Jesus into going against the Law of Moses, get him to recommend mercy for this woman they were going to kill anyway. They tried to put Jesus between a rock and a hard place. If he said spare her then he was going against the law of Moses, and if he said stone her then the people would see he was as much a bastard as the Pharisees were."

"Between a rock and a hard place?" Brick asked.

"Sure. A no-win situation. If Jesus said don't kill her, then he was going against the law, and if he said kill her, then he was a heartless SOB like the Pharisees, and all his followers would see that. You understand that, don't you, Mace?"

"I guess so," Mace said, and then the light bulb went on his head, "OK, I understand the bumper sticker now. Don't be a Pharisee. Don't act like they did."

"Right...just wait until you have to deal with a few insurance adjusters. Then you'll really understand Pharisees."

"Not that I want to start attending Sunday school or anything, but I gotta know what happened to her," Brick said.

"Well, they told Jesus the evidence they had against her and they asked Jesus what they should do with her. Stone her to death, or not?

"The crowd was rambunctious. Some of them were yelling, 'Stone her. Stone her.' Then Jesus squatted down and started drawing or writing something in the sand with his finger, just sort of ignoring everybody. Everyone gathered around to see what he was doing. The tension was high. When the crowd got quiet, Jesus said, 'He who has no sin, let him cast the first stone.' Gradually, one by one, everybody dropped their rocks, and they left."

"Wow! That's pretty awesome. I usually don't like it when people start talking Jesus shit to me, but that's an awesome story," Brick said.

"Why didn't they just kill her anyway? I don't get it," Mace asked. "Why did they leave?"

"My thinking is when Jesus drew in the dirt, everybody saw something different. I think maybe each one of them might have seen their own secret, whatever it was, like they were watching a video or something, so they felt guilty themselves, and showed some mercy, at least that time. That's what I think."

"I see what you mean," Brick said. "Like you're saying, he gave them something else to look at. It didn't have anything to do with her case at all. It had to do with them, the Pharisees, right? He got them to let her go even though she broke their law. Interesting." Brick rubbed his chin, pondering the implications of the story.

Then Mace interjected, "So what you're saying is it's OK for you to get a guilty person off scot-free just because Jesus did it once." Mace wouldn't give up.

"Not just once. Jesus did that kind of stuff all the time. I believe he still does. I wouldn't be so quick to shortchange mercy if I were you, Mace. You may need it some day." Ike put the palms of both his hands on the table and leaned across into Mace's face.

Mace was silent. He was afraid for an instant Ike was referring to the bet. Ike's stare made him shiver, but then Ike straightened up, smiled, and went on talking.

"After the Pharisees left, Jesus told the lady to go on home, but don't sin anymore. And if you get a not guilty on Diaeta Pepsi, we'll take her home and tell her don't do anything like that anymore."

"Why?" Mace asked.

"Because Jesus may not be around to draw in the dirt for her next time. He expects folks to learn from their mistakes. So let's go to court and see if you can

138

get the jury to show some mercy...because the judge certainly isn't going to."

"I'm not ready for this trial yet." Mace protested.

"You read the file, didn't you?"

"Yes, but..."

"Well, that's the best you can do on a case like this. It's as ready as you can get it. Pick a jury, cross-examine the cop, and do a final argument."

"Yeah, but!"

Ike interrupted, "In your heart, you already know what to do. Any more preparation would be obsessing. And you don't want to obsess, do you? All you really need to do is listen. Really listen. Just shut up and listen to what people are saying instead of thinking about what you're going to say next. Most lawyers don't know how to do that. They don't know how to shut the fuck up. They are too worried about what to say next, so they never listen. If you really listen to people then you'll know what to say next. Whether it's a witness or a prospective juror, they'll pretty much tell you what you need to ask next, if you're really listening. Trust your gut, and go for it. Leap into the fog! Praise Jesus."

"Are you crazy?"

"Yep. Come on. Let's go." Ike tossed his keys to Brick. "You're driving."

"Wha..." Brick started to ask, but Ike interrupted.

"Come on, pansies, we're late," Ike said. He tossed half a cup of cold coffee down the sink and put his cup in the dishwasher. "Come on," he said. "Put your cups in the dishwasher, Kay's orders, grab the files, and let's go. Two, two, two courts at once."

With that, Ike left out the back door and headed across the parking lot toward his old Mercedes without even looking back. Mace and Brick hesitated but collected the files and then hurried behind him. They didn't like it, and they weren't happy, but what else did they have to do?

"This is fucking crazy," Mace said to Brick.

"I know. I know," Brick answered.

The drive to the courthouse was a straight shot down Guadalupe Street for about eight blocks, depending on how you count them, because not even the speed of light is a constant. It only took a few minutes. Along the way, Ike told them what he knew about both cases, which wasn't much, and it didn't give either of them any additional confidence.

Brick drove slowly past the courthouse, scanning for a parking spot, but there was none to be found. As usual, all the spots were full. Ike continued talking. Brick drove past West Tenth Street and coasted a block further down Guadalupe hoping he'd find one next to Wooldridge Square, a small, bowl-shaped park the size of a large city block across the street from the courthouse.

In the center of Wooldridge Square was a white, gazebo-style bandstand. The bandstand's graceful lines caught the shade of the large, stately oak trees nearby. It was a relic of gentler, slower times. Contrasting its antebellum appeal were several homeless men stretched out all around it, sleeping. They were wrapped up in dingy brown and gray blankets, even though the temperature was already approaching a hundred.

In days gone by, the little one-point-seven-acre, grassy, sloping park had been the hub of Austin's civic activity. Crowds gathered every weekend to hear the city's all-volunteer orchestra play from the glistening bandstand or listen to the candidates debate. In 1918, it is estimated that over ten thousand citizens crammed themselves into this natural little amphitheater for a community sing-along to show support for the troops during World War I. And it was from this very bandstand that Lyndon Johnson first announced his intention to seek the presidency of the United States.

But today the little grassy bowl was not so inviting. It had fallen into disrepair. The lights and the fountains no longer worked, and litter and crime were a problem. The houses and shops that once were within walking distance had been replaced during the building boom after World War II by big government buildings with small concrete parking lots. Finding a place to park had become a problem that nagged city officials nearly as much as the crime problem.

The land for the park was dedicated by city officials in 1839, but shortly thereafter, they changed their minds and decided to use it for a city dump instead. Back then, it was outside of the town, but today, like Scholz's Beer Garten, it was smack in the middle of it. People threw their trash there until the town grew up around it.

In 1909, Mayor Wooldridge decided it was time to do something. He had the property cleaned up, planted grass, and built the bandstand that still stands there—hence the name, Wooldridge Square. Sadly, by the mid-1990s, Wooldridge Square was taking on the characteristics of its former identity, a trash heap. It was unkept, and it was starting to look like a dump again.

After rolling past Wooldridge Square on Guadalupe and finding no place to park, Ike told Brick to make the block at West Ninth Street and come around by the south side of the courthouse on San Antonio Street. Brick grumbled under his breath. "There aren't any parking spaces back there. I looked." But he did what he was told.

They made the block and started up West Tenth Street toward the light at Guadalupe. Abruptly, an old pickup truck lurched out from a shaded space under an old oak tree adjacent to Wooldridge Square. It sped away, barely missing the right fender of the Mercedes. "There you go," Ike said, smiling. Brick whipped into the space and turned off the engine.

They got out of the car and were waiting to cross at the light. Mace took a couple steps into the street before he was jerked back by Ike's grip on his coat sleeve.

"Hey!" Mace protested.

"Wait for the light," Ike said. "You could have jurors watching you right now. Don't want to show 'em you don't follow the rules. They might hold it against your client."

The light changed, and they started across. Ike asked Brick, "Well, what did you think of that?"

"Oh, I've driven a Mercedes before. My dad has one. But he always has the newest one," Brick answered.

"Not the Mercedes—the parking space. What do you think about getting that parking space, right across the street from the courthouse and in the shade? Rock-star parking. Pretty good, huh?"

"I guess so."

"You guess so? What do you mean, you guess so? If you hadn't found a good spot, you'd be bitching about it till dark. You get rock-star parking, and you don't even notice. Where's the gratitude, boys?"

"Look, Ike, it's just a parking place…OK," Mace said. "We've got other things to worry about, thanks to you. Why are we doing this? This is crazy. And we're not boys."

"I agree with Mace," Brick said. "This is crazy."

"It's about gratitude," Ike said. "You think I'm the crazy one. You're goofy. I'm grateful for everything— the parking space, my old Mercedes, even you boys."

Mace curled his lip. Brick stared at the ground, lost in thought, but his thoughts were not on gratitude.

Chapter 6

DIAETA PEPSI

They made it through the metal detector inside the front door without incident and past the four sheriff's deputies working security detail. Ike led them into the elevator and pushed the button for the fourth floor. The motor groaned, and the cables popped. The rickety old elevator gave a little jerk and then proceeded slowly upward until it stopped. The doors hesitated and let out a sound of discomfort before finally deciding to open.

Ike and Mace stepped out of the elevator and into the hallway without looking back. But Brick did not move. He was frozen stiff against the back wall. He was pale and gray like cement. His eyes bulged large and round in a fixed gaze. Mace was the first to notice Brick wasn't with them. He turned just in time to see the gimpy old doors close again and Brick's panic-stricken face disappear behind them.

"Crap," Mace said, "he's freaking out. I'll go get him."

Mace had seen that look on Brick before. It was a condition the two of them sometimes shared but, fortunately, seldom at the same time.

"No, you don't. I'll get him. You've got stuff to do. Sit here. Don't move," Ike said. He snapped his finger and pointed toward a bench that resembled a church pew. It sat against the wall in the hallway right outside one of the courtroom doors. Mace grumbled something under his breath but sat where Ike had indicated.

"Don't move, or I'll get the bailiff to shoot you in the foot."

With that, Ike was gone. He bolted. His feet barely touched the floor as he practically flew down the three flights of stairs. He was waiting for Brick when the creaky elevator doors opened again. Ike stepped in with him.

Upstairs, Mace fumbled with the files in his lap and tried to concentrate, but he couldn't get it out of his head that Ike used the phrase "shoot you in the foot." Had Brick told Ike about his propensity to do just that? Or was it just another weird coincidence?

Brick looked blankly around the elevator. He seemed confused, like he had lost something. "Are we there yet?" he asked. "What happened to Mace?"

"He's waiting for us," Ike said. Once again, he pushed the button for the fourth floor. Once again, the elevator made its painful, arthritic journey upward. When the doors opened, Mace was sitting on the pew reading the police report on Diaeta Pepsi.

Brick stepped out of the elevator. Mace jumped to his feet. "What happened, dude?" He tried not to let it show, but his voice revealed his concern.

"What are you talking about?" Brick asked, with a look of confusion on his face. He was oblivious of anything that had happened.

Mace looked at his friend. He had witnessed Brick freak out before but never anything like this. This was the first time he had seen him so frightened and pale. A couple times in law school, maybe, he freaked over taking a test, but he had never lost his memory or forgotten where he was.

Those particular symptoms were reserved for Mace. Mace was the one prone to panic attacks. Mace was the one who had missed the first day of finals his first semester at the Carver-Washington Gospel School of Law because he had worked himself into such a frenzy and was so afraid of the exams he couldn't pull himself out of bed the morning they started. Fortunately, when he came to his senses the next day, he managed to convince his professors that he had come down with a twenty-four-hour virus and talked them into allowing him to take makeup tests the day after. And he passed. He even made good grades. But the ordeal was real and painful while it lasted, and it was only one in a long line of similar episodes.

"What are you talking about?" Brick repeated.

"Oh, nothing," Mace answered. He didn't want to cause Brick any more anxiety by bringing attention to his fugue. *That won't help matters any. He seems to be all right now. Why tell him he spaced out? That'll just make him obsess about how it happened and why it happened and make him worry it might happen again.*

Ike's voice interrupted Mace's train of thought. "You handled that good," he said to Mace and gave him a knowing wink that instantly made Mace feel uncomfortable. "Find anything new in that police report?" Ike asked.

"I don't know," Mace said, bringing his attention back to the papers in his lap, "but the more I read it, the more I don't like it. But I can't put my finger on what bothers me about it. Was it entrapment? Kinda looks like it might be entrapment. Could it be entrapment?" Mace asked.

"By golly, I think he's got it. Smells like entrapment to me. Might smell like entrapment to the jury too. Technically, legally, it's probably not, but if you convince the jury it was entrapment then it was entrapment. Like I said, the jury decides what the truth is. They are the ultimate deciders. Not the police. If it was up to the police, everybody would be guilty of something…except them."

Just then, the double doors next to where they were sitting were flung open. A herd of people spilled out into the hallway. There were at least thirty or forty of them. The hallway filled with echoing chatter. An elderly man and a young black woman sat down on the bench next to Mace. They didn't look at each other, but they looked at Ike and Mace. A lady with an umbrella and a Bible in her hand asked Ike if he knew where the ladies' room was. Ike directed her to an area around the corner from the stairs, smiling warmly and calling her ma'am.

"This is your jury," Ike whispered to Mace. "They're the ones the law says are Diaeta's peers. So be on your best behavior. They're watching everyone here, trying to figure out who's who and what the case is about. They're already making decisions about who they like and who they don't like…and they're already deciding subconsciously who they want to win."

"That's not what they taught us in law school, not the way it's supposed to work," Mace said.

"So?" Ike said.

"But they don't know anything about the case yet. They're supposed to keep an open mind till all the evidence is in. Right? That's the law, right?"

"Law school taught you some law—maybe. But it didn't teach you anything about people…Doesn't matter. Start winning them over now. Be your charming self."

Ike smiled and nodded approvingly at the two potential jurors sitting at the other end of the bench. They both smiled back. "This is his first trial," Ike said to them. "He's a little nervous."

"What'd you say that for?" Mace whispered at Ike.

They smiled again and glanced away.

Ike continued talking with Mace. "Winning them over. You know what Mark Twain said, don't you?" Ike didn't wait for him to answer. "Mark Twain said a court of law is where twelve impartial people decide who's got the best lawyer. The best lawyer—that's the one they like the most. You're going in there after a while and you're going to show 'em it's you. In this court, there's only six impartial people 'cause this is a misdemeanor,

148

not a felony…so you only got to convince six instead of twelve. Don't ask me why."

Being only minutes away from starting his first jury trial was surreal and disorienting, and Mace hadn't even met his client yet, which added to his angst. "Where's the client? I got to talk to the client. I'm not ready for this," Mace said. He felt his chest tighten. "I can't try a case without talking to the client first." Mace leaned over and cradled his pain.

Ike let him sit there with his chest flat on his knees until he realized Mace had stopped breathing. Ike sat up straight and drew a deep, loud breath that filled his lungs to capacity, inflating them like a large balloon. Then he slowly exhaled, making a soft, but audible, "ahhhhhh" sound as the warm CO_2 escaped through his windpipe and over his tongue. Ike's body visibly relaxed.

Without realizing what he was doing, Mace instinctively sat up and mimicked what Ike had just done. He drew a deep breath, expanded his chest to capacity, and then he let it out. "Ahhhhhh." He felt himself go limp along with the exhale. It was like when someone yawns because he or she saw someone else yawn. Mace calmed immediately. The deep breath signaled his mind and body to relax. The tightness in his chest loosened, and some color came back to his ashen face.

"You don't need to talk to Diaeta," Ike said. "Matter of fact, the better job you do getting her to keep her mouth shut, the better job you'll do."

"What?"

"You'll see. Just remember to breathe."

"But when do I meet her, I got to get her ready to testify."

Fear and dread pounded at Mace. His skin tingled, and he tensed again. "I don't want to do this. Why can't you wait? Why are you in such a damn hurry on this?" He wanted to leave, but the promise of more money compelled him to stay.

Ike drew another long breath and exhaled audibly. Again Mace mimicked him, and he immediately relaxed. He wasn't conscious of the deep breathing he was doing or the beneficial effect it was having on his body and his mind.

"You'll meet her when the guards bring her in the courtroom, right before jury selection starts. She's still in jail—been there six weeks already, just waiting for her trial date to come up. Six weeks. She's been in long enough to be released on her back time already—even if the jury convicts her. So relax. You can't make things any worse than it already is, no matter how much you screw it up. It's a win-win for you," Ike said. Then added, "Isn't that great? Even if you lose, you win."

"What? Are you saying she could just plead guilty and get out?"

"Yep."

"Then let's do that—plead her guilty—and let's get out of here. What's the problem with that? That's a good deal, right?"

"Not going to happen," Ike answered.

Brick was barely aware Ike and Mace were talking. They sounded far away, like they were in a long tunnel. Gradually, their voices got closer until they were sitting next to him again. Finally, Brick was back from the panic-induced fog and in the present moment, the here and now. He remembered Ike saying something about peers, and the word rang in his head. He couldn't resist joining the conversation so he interrupted, "Peers? What do you mean, peers?"

"A jury of her peers."

"Oh, now I get it—but why's she in jail if she hasn't been found guilty of anything yet?" Brick asked, remembering more of the conversation. "She's got a right to bail, doesn't she? I learned that much in law school. I did. Really," Brick said.

"She's in jail because she doesn't personally have the money to make bail," Ike answered. "And no one she knows wants to post bond for her. So she's got two choices. She can plead guilty and be sentenced to her back time, or she can sit in jail waiting for her turn at bat—her turn to go to trial. Sometimes it takes years to get to trial on a felony case. Six weeks is nothing by comparison. That's why so many people end up pleading guilty to stuff they didn't do, just so they can go ahead and get out. The judge sentences them to their back time and let's 'em go."

"That doesn't sound so bad," Mace said, still pleading his case for Diaeta to take a plea.

"Yeah, but nobody ever tells them about the collateral consequences. They'll have a final conviction on their record, and the next time they get arrested, the punishment is gonna be a lot stiffer, not to mention all the other consequences."

"So?" Mace said.

"It's not fair," Ike said. "And that's just one way the government wages war on poor people."

"War on poor people? Collateral what? What do you mean?" Brick asked. The conversation took his mind off the fear he had been feeling only a few moments earlier.

"Walk with me, and I'll tell you." Ike got up and started walking. Brick and Mace followed him around the corner, past two big, solid wood doors, and into an empty courtroom. Several of the potential jurors who had congregated around the door and the two on the bench watched them walk away. Ike nodded and smiled at each one and said "good morning" to the ones who made eye contact.

Once inside, Ike sat on the back bench, and Brick and Mace took their seats like they had done in the Brackenridge Hospital chapel, the first time they met Ike. Mace adjusted the papers in his hands, but he lost his grip, and they spilled in a cascade across the floor and underneath the benches.

"Damn it!" Mace said. "I need my fucking briefcase. How can I be a lawyer without a fucking briefcase?"

Mace looked up at Brick from the floor where he was crawling around on his hands and knees pathetically trying to retrieve the scattered papers. Then he shot Brick an angry glare and held it—because, the way he saw things, if Brick hadn't flashed the fucking fifty at the fucking nurse in the fucking hospital in front of the fucking cops, he'd still have his fucking briefcase and wouldn't be here with fucking Ike, about to try a fucking case he knew absolutely nothing about, for a client he hadn't even met.

"Watch your language," Ike said.

That did it. Like a rubber band that's stretched too far, Mace snapped.

"I didn't say anything. Calm down yourself!" Mace shouted. He didn't look up. He was still on the floor picking up papers. "I'm not doing anything." He complained even louder, still not looking up. "There's nobody in here, and I need my damn briefcase, and I'm sick of you bossing us around all the time." Mace pulled himself back onto the bench. His face pulsed red. He glared at Ike straight in the eyes. "And if you call me 'shyster' one more time, I'll deck you. So help me God, I'll deck you."

Brick grimaced like he had been smacked in the nose.

Mace bent over and snatched one last stray paper off the floor. He got back on the bench, this time not making eye contact with anyone. Brick anxiously looked away and anticipated Ike's comeback. He knew it would probably be bad. Ike might even hit Mace. Mace had been hit before. It could happen again.

Brick held his breath. He was afraid of what Mace might say or might do to make things even worse and mess up the lucky streak they had going so far with Ike. Brick still wanted to pay some bills—and buy some tuna. Every muscle in Brick's body tensed. Every muscle in Mace's body tensed too. He knew what he had done. And he knew what Brick thought about what he had done. They braced for whatever bad might come.

"I've got an extra briefcase you can have," Ike said, breaking the tension. "Just remind me when we get back to the office." Ike was calm and accommodating, as if he hadn't heard a word of Mace's tirade. Ike drew another deep breath and exhaled.

Obviously relieved, Brick's body loosened, and he took a deep breath, unconsciously following Ike's lead. Mace took a deep breath too. He was relieved too. He regretted what he had said, but once the bullet was fired and headed for his foot, there wasn't anything he could do to bring it back. He tried to hide his relief and embarrassment with a mock show of frustration at reorganizing his messed-up file papers. After a few seconds of uncomfortable silence, Ike said, "So, do you still want to know what I mean about the government waging war on poor people?"

"Sure," Brick said.

"Sure, why not?" Mace said, still not making eye contact with Ike. He was relieved, but he was baffled at why Ike had ignored his confrontational tone. He didn't mean to challenge Ike so hard. He didn't want a confrontation. He certainly didn't want a fight. He had been hit before, and that wasn't any fun. But, his emotions had overloaded his mouth—again—and he knew he usually had to pay a price for that habitual indulgence. But this time, instead of a showdown, he was offered a free briefcase.

"What I mean," Ike said, "is that the government makes it a crime to be poor. Think about it. A poor person actually gets punished more than a person who isn't poor, no matter what offense they're charged with.

If you've got money, you can get out of jail the same day you get arrested, most of the time. But a poor person is going to sit in jail and miss work and get behind on his bills, get behind on child support, maybe get fired, maybe get kicked out of his apartment."

Brick swallowed hard. The possibility of getting kicked out of his apartment was still a reality he could identify with.

"If you have money, you can hire your own lawyer, either have a jury trial and get a shot at a not-guilty verdict or work out the best deal possible on a plea bargain, usually just a fine and probation on a misdemeanor...if you have money.

"And fines are easier to pay if you're not poor. A hundred-dollar fine to a poor man can have a negative impact on his whole lifestyle for months, maybe longer, but a hundred dollars to a rich person is tip money...a green fee, lap-dance change." Ike paused and stared hard at Mace and Brick before continuing, "...or a week's worth of hydroponic pot."

Ike cocked his head to the side and gave the boys a look that made them both feel uncomfortable, like he knew for a fact they had smoked weed the night before, and the night before that, and the one before that. Why else would he say that? Brick blushed and looked down.

"They ought to fine a person a percentage of his income if they're gonna be fair about it," Ike went on. "That would make it more fair. Right? See how a guy who makes four hundred a week gets punished for speeding more than a guy who makes a thousand a week, or a thousand a day?

155

"If a purpose of the law is to teach a lesson and discourage repeat offenses, wouldn't that be fair? It would certainly slow down some of them damn BMWs. They should fine people on a sliding scale, a percentage of their income...unless they drive a BMW, then maybe it should be double.

"And if you have a good lawyer, and you demand a jury trial, chances are good the charges might get dropped...if it's not too serious an offense. Cops don't like to go to court if they don't have to. But if you're poor, and you're really not guilty, and you want a trial, chances are good you're going to sit in jail for months waiting for your turn, while some young prosecutor comes by your vermin-infested jail cell every day with his clipboard full of guilty plea forms, asking, 'Who wants to plead guilty to their back time?'

"It's a big temptation for anyone to just go ahead and plead guilty to something they didn't do just so they can get out of their dank cage, go back to work, try to make their car payment or pay their rent before they lose everything...or pay their child support before they get an arrest warrant put on them for not paying child support...or they'll plead guilty just to get back to their family or girlfriend.

"But pleading guilty to 'time served' is a final conviction. They never tell you that. People usually don't understand the dire consequences of a guilty plea. It means if they get arrested again, even for something they didn't do, the punishment is going to be stiffer for a second offense and even stiffer for a third. And they have the same temptation to plead guilty again

156

and again rather than exercise their God-given constitutional right to a jury trial like a person with money would get to do. Theoretically, a person could be branded a habitual criminal, with a record as long as my arm, and in actuality, they never committed a crime. Sad, ain't it?"

"Doesn't sound fair," Mace said. "But…"

"No, it's not," Brick added, looking more relaxed and alert.

"No, it's not," Ike continued. "Poor people don't have the same Bill of Rights that people with money have. It's the way the law is applied that makes it unfair. And another thing," Ike was starting to sound like a preacher, "they never tell you about the collateral consequences, what can happen to you even if you don't get arrested again."

"Collateral consequences?" Mace asked.

"It means you plead guilty to jumping a turnstile at the movie house, you go home, you think it's over with, and then you get a certified letter in the mail telling you to vacate your apartment because it's public housing, and they don't allow convicted criminals to live there.

"Or you're a single mother and you get caught shoplifting a five-dollar birthday present for your kid, you plead guilty, thinking it's over, and then you lose your right to get food stamps.

"Or you get fired from your job because the probation officer calls your boss checking up on you, telling him you're a convicted thief or you were convicted for narcotics when it was really just an ounce of weed.

"Or you get deported.

"Or you get a letter telling you your driver's license has been revoked because you pled guilty and paid an eighty-five-dollar fine for possession of a marijuana pipe, which goes on your record as narcotics parapher-nalia. It's just plain chickenshit is what it is."

"You can lose your driver's license for a marijuana pipe?" Brick asked. He didn't do a good job hiding his surprise and concern.

"Taking a fellow's driver's license because of a weed pipe is crazy. And then what? He can't go to work. He can't pay his child support. His kids go on welfare. And he goes back to jail. Don't get me started."

"So how is it you managed to get Ms. Pepsi a trial in just six weeks, if it usually takes months? I mean, couldn't we have waited some?" Mace asked.

"Yeah, *just* six weeks." Ike had a sarcastic tone. "Six weeks is a long time if it's you in there listening to the noise and racket every night and day, eating lousy food, having no choice in what you eat or drink or watch on TV or where you sleep or who you have to talk with. Six weeks is a long time if it's you listening to slamming steel doors echoing through cold concrete chambers night after night and the groans and moans and cries and farts of all sorts of miserable people filling the night air and keeping you awake…six weeks is a long time if it's you taking a dump in the open over a toilet with no seat with everybody watching…six weeks of John Wayne toi-let paper that your fingers poke through every time you try to wipe your ass."

"Eww! Gross!" Brick interrupted, turning up his nose and upper lip in a show of disgust at the thought of taking a dump in the open with people watching or his finger poking through toilet paper…while he wiped himself…while strangers watched.

"John Wayne toilet paper?" Mace asked.

"You never heard that before?" Ike asked rhetorically and then answered Mace before giving him a chance to respond. "John Wayne toilet paper—it doesn't take shit off of anybody." Both young men chuckled and committed the phrase to memory for use at a later time.

Ike went on. "But six weeks is fast for a jury trial around here, or anywhere actually. Real fast. I got her a trial in six weeks because I know how to work the system, how to watch for a cancellation and jump on it. Most of the people in jail who can't afford bail can't afford a lawyer either. It can take a couple weeks or more just to get 'em a lawyer appointed. And the court-appointed lawyers, even though most of them do the best they can, they're overworked and underpaid, so they're not running down to the clerk's office every day looking at the docket and trying to bump their defendant up the list."

"So you're not court appointed on this one?" Mace asked.

"No, I'm not. This is pro bono." Ike lied.

Brick chimed in again. "If she's too poor for bond and you're not court appointed, then why are you on her case?"

"Cause I know her mom, that's why."

"Pro bono?" Mace said. "That means you're doing this for free, right?" Mace was suddenly worried he wasn't going to get paid for this trial that he didn't want to do anyway.

"And the best way to avoid that awful jail," Ike continued without answering Mace's question, "is to avoid the police."

"Sure," Mace said, "but how do you do that?"

"For one thing, don't smoke weed in your car."

Brick and Mace gave each other a glance and then looked down.

"And don't drive if you've been drinking. It costs a lot less for a cab than it does for a DWI.

"And don't let anybody else smell you smoking. They can call the cops and, next thing you know, your door's kicked in."

"But how's a hypothetical person going to keep other hypothetical people from smelling their hypothetical smoke?" Mace asked.

"Use a toilet paper roll or a paper towel roll. Stuff it with dryer sheets, and exhale through that."

Just then, a wood-paneled door opened from the wall to the right of the judge's bench. A balding bailiff with a big potbelly, one that strained the buttons of his drab brown uniform, stepped through the open door and peered into the room. He furrowed his forehead at Ike and said, "The judge'll be here in a few minutes. He said go ahead and start setting up. The prisoner's being brought over now." With that, he closed the door and was gone.

"That's our cue," Ike said. "Let's move up front."

Mace gathered his papers and followed Ike to the table closest to the jury box. Ike told Mace to sit in the chair closest to the jury and Brick to sit in one of the chairs behind the counsel table, but inside the railing that separates the audience from "the bar," the place where all the action occurs.

"Sit here, right next to the jury. If anyone tries to make you get up, don't," Ike said.

"Isn't this our table?" Mace asked.

"No, it's the prosecutor's table—the one closest to the jury box is always the prosecutor's table—but he's late. Let's dick with him."

"But won't we get in trouble?"

"It's not a rule. It's just custom. Let's see what happens, throw him off his game."

"But…"

"Trust me."

Mace glanced from side to side, nervously. He had never been inside "the bar" before. His few visits to a courtroom had always been confined to the benches where the audience sits, known as the gallery. He never understood why it was called a gallery, unless it was because of all the portraits of previous judges that hung along the walls, mostly judges long dead, judges who had served on that particular court. *Maybe they call it the gallery because it's like an art gallery,* Mace thought.

"Why do they call that part of the courtroom the gallery?" Mace asked Ike.

"Because that's where the spectators sit," Ike answered matter-of-factly. "Now tell me, why do you think this was entrapment?"

"Well, because the cop approached her first, not vice versa. All she did was ask him if he wanted a date. She didn't ask him anything until he approached her."

"That's good. But the cop is going to testify that the word *date* is a code word prostitutes use that actually means 'do you want to have sex?' Did you know that?"

"No, I didn't know that."

"Good boy. I'm proud of you."

"But still, he approached her first," Mace said.

"That's right. And not everybody knows that 'date' means 'sex,' do they?"

"Right!" Mace said, getting Ike's point. "Not everybody knows that. But she probably knew it, right?"

"Maybe. I don't know. But the jury won't even hear that question because you're not putting her on the stand," Ike said.

"We're not?"

"No, you're not. I already told you it was going to be a one-witness case. Just the cop."

"But don't we have to tell our side?"

"Why? The government has the burden of proof, not the defendant. Innocent until proven guilty…ever hear that one before?"

"Yeah, but…"

"Trust me; you don't want to put her on the stand. It would be the worst thing you could do."

"But you told me in the car she didn't have any prior arrests. How are we going to get that in evidence if we don't put her on the witness stand?"

"Do you think the cop ran a records check on her when he arrested her?"

"Uh, probably, I guess."

"Do you think he found anything?"

"I don't know."

"Really? Under the name Diaeta Pepsi? You think that might be her real name, do you?"

"Uh...probably not."

"Then ask the cop," Ike said, "but only ask about prostitution, nothing else."

"I don't get it."

"You know he ran a records check on her. It's procedure. And you know they didn't find anything under Diaeta Pepsi."

"How do I know that?"

"Because I'm telling you so. But he's going to sneak it in that Diaeta Pepsi is obviously not her real name. It's an alias, and he'll try to get the jury to assume since she uses an alias that she is a prostitute."

"I figured that. But, how's that help me?" Mace asked.

"It doesn't. It helps her."

"How?"

"Do it like this," Ike continued. "You ran a record check when you arrested her, didn't you? And he'll say yes. And then you say, 'There wasn't one single, solitary arrest for prostitution, was there?'"

"OK." Mace wrinkled his brow, trying to follow the logic. "I see."

"Mr. Policeman," Ike continued, as though conducting the cross-examination, "when you ran that records check, you didn't find anything, under any name, anywhere, showing that my client has ever been arrested for prostitution, did you?"

Ike answered for the policeman. "Well, no, but Diaeta Pepsi isn't her real name.

"Well, you didn't find any arrest photos of her anywhere, did you, showing where she had ever been arrested for prostitution?"

"Well, no." Ike answered for the policeman again. "Because there's no index for photos that have the wrong name on them.

"But most of the prostitutes in this town are well know to the police, aren't they?

"Well, yes. I guess.

"But you didn't know Ms. Pepsi, did you?

"Uh, no.

"And neither did your policeman friends who helped you arrest her, did they?

"Uh, no.

"You take fingerprint impressions from people when you arrest them, don't you?

"Yes.

"And you ran her fingerprints through the system, didn't you?

"Uh, yes.

"And you didn't find any arrests for prostitution, did you?

"Uh, no.

"Nothing?" Ike asked the pretend cop again. Then he said, "Doesn't matter if he never answers you. Just look at the jury. They'll understand. Then ask him this, 'And isn't it a fact that her fingerprints didn't match any arrest records of any kind, anywhere, did they?'"

"Well, uh, no." Ike answered for the policeman again.

"You couldn't find anything, anywhere, showing that this young lady has ever been arrested for anything at all, could you?" Ike continued.

"Uh, no." Ike answered.

"No arrest record at all?

"Uh, no.

"See how I drug it out?" Ike said. "I could have just asked it once, but by limiting the first set of questions to only prostitution arrests and going from photos to fingerprints to showing she's had no arrests at all—see the difference? If you make it look like you're having to coax it out of him, it makes him look like he is being less than forthright. The jury won't trust him. And it drives the point home better. You get your evidence in, and your client doesn't have to get on the witness stand to do it. And besides, the jury is going to like you better than this cop anyway."

"So, Diaeta Pepsi is not a prostitute?"

"That's for the jury to decide."

"But…"

"Just go with it."

"I like that," Brick said from behind them.

"And if it looks like he's thinking too much about the question before he answers it, repeat it again before he can say anything, only this time say, 'Yes or no? It's a simple yes or no question. She didn't have any prior arrests for prostitution, did she?' Then follow up with, 'She didn't have any arrest record at all, did she?' You're doing cross-examination, so lead the hell out of him; that's your job. Don't let him say anything except yes or no to your questions. Got it?"

"I think so," Mace said.

"Good...You're going to do good. Don't worry about it. Just listen, and you'll know what to do. If you're really listening, the questions will come to you like magic. Lawyers who always worry about what to say next, they're not listening. They're more concerned about looking smart than they are about winning their case. It doesn't matter if you look like the dumbest guy in the room. What counts is winning your case. So just remember to breathe...and listen...and you'll do better than 90 percent of the lawyers who've been trying cases for years."

The courtroom was still empty except for Ike and Mace sitting at the counsel table and Brick, who was in a chair behind them. The panel of potential jurors had been excused for half an hour while the jail guards transported Diaeta from the county jail to the courtroom. Brick's hearing on Wilfred Johnson wasn't until three o'clock, so Ike told him to stay and watch the jury selection and opening statements.

The door in the wall behind the brown, wood-paneled judge's bench opened again. The chubby, turtle-looking bailiff popped his head inside again. "All rise!" he said. Then he stepped into the courtroom followed immediately by a man dressed in a black choir robe. It was the judge.

Ike rose to his feet and nudged Mace to stand up. Brick stood up too. The judge took his chair behind the elevated judge's desk, which is called the judge's bench for some reason. He scowled at Ike over his half-rim glasses.

"Be seated," the bailiff said.

Mace and Brick sat back down, but Ike continued standing.

The judge said to Ike, "Mr. Turner, what are we doing here? When my docket cleared, I planned to take this afternoon off, and you messed that up. Why are you messing up my afternoon, Mr. Turner? I've looked at this file. Your client is obviously guilty. She can plead to her back time. So why are you wasting my time, the jury's time, and a bunch of taxpayer money? Why, Mr. Turner?"

"Well, Judge..."

"Don't tell me about her constitutional rights, Mr. Turner. I've heard that speech from you before. There's something called practicality. And it's just not practical to ask a jury to listen to this case. They're not going to be happy with you making them sit through this, and they're going to lay the wood to your client on punishment, assuming you go to the jury for punishment...and if you don't, then I'm going to lay the wood to her and give her the max. You get my drift, Mr. Turner. So do you want me to get the prosecutor over here, and we can fill out the guilty plea papers and all go our merry ways?"

"We are ready to proceed..."

The judge interrupted. "I'm glad you've come to your senses, Mr. Turner."

"We're ready to proceed to jury trial, Your Honor."

The judge scowled at Ike again and slammed his Day-Timer shut. "It's your case, Mr. Turner. Mess it up however you want, but you're doing your client a disservice."

"Thank you, Your Honor. I will. But actually this is Mr. Spinella's case. I'm just here to help."

"That right, boy?" The judge frowned down at Mace.

"Yes, sir. I guess." Mace was caught off-guard and felt intimidated by the daunting figure leaning over the bench, condescending at him.

"Stand up when you talk to me, boy."

Mace jumped to his feet.

"Then why don't you plead her guilty and just get this over with?" the judge demanded. "You're not going to make any brownie points with me by hanging around with Ike Turner. So why don't you just plead her guilty, and let's all go home, and you find another job?"

Mace responded to the judge. He heard the words coming out of his mouth. The hammer cocked, the trigger pulled, the bullet fired, and there was no bringing it back. Again, it was like hearing someone else talking instead of himself, like being conscious of hearing a radio playing while you're half asleep.

"Because the government is waging war on poor people," Mace said. "If she was rich, we wouldn't be having this conversation."

The judge slammed his Day-Timer onto the bench and glared at Ike. "I can see he's one of yours. Just what we need—another liberal in the courthouse." He looked at his watch. "Court will resume in fifteen minutes. You better be ready, Mr. Spinella."

With that, the judge huffed and left the courtroom through the same door he had entered. The turtle-looking bailiff followed close behind. When the bailiff closed the door, he turned and winked at Ike, then he smiled.

Mace was terrified. His hands shook. The vibration of the closing door rattled a row of portraits of dead judges. Ike looked at Mace with an expression of amazement and admiration.

"Fuck, man. I guess I blew it. Fucking asshole. What came over me?" Mace said.

"Inspiration," Ike said. "That's what came over you—inspiration. I'm so proud of you, I could kiss you."

"Don't do that." Mace moved back a step.

"You handled him the only way you could. If you hadn't done what you did, he'd run over you the rest of your career. When a judge assumes the role of prosecutor, instead of being neutral, the whole court system is compromised. I'm proud of you. You acted like a hero, a real Davy Crockett."

Mace smiled at Ike, but the twitch in his lip showed he was nervous and revealed his residual anger toward the judge. Adrenaline coursed through his veins, and he felt it. And he sort of liked it. His lip twitched again.

"You did good. Trust me," Ike said. "But let's not talk in here. He's back in his office by now, and he has a reputation for listening in on the PA system."

Before Mace could say anything else, the door the judge left through was flung open with a loud crashing noise. The big brass doorknob slammed hard into the wall behind it. Portraits of the dead judges shook and wiggled. The judge bolted back into the room like he was shot from a cannon. He had a steamy, angry look on his face. He leaped the two steps to his chair, slammed his bottom down hard, spun around, and stared back and forth between Mace and Brick. No one said a word. Brick, Mace, and Ike were taken by complete surprise. The wrinkly necked bailiff entered next and closed the door behind him, trying not to show his bewilderment. The judge kept staring.

"Don't I know you from somewhere?" he asked. His tone was weaselly and accusing. He pointed his stubby, hairy finger at Mace and waited for an answer.

"I…don't…think…so," Mace said tentatively.

"Sure, I do. And I think I know your little friend there too," the judge growled, pointing at Brick.

Brick looked from side to side like he was planning an escape route. This judge was upset about something—mad—and it was scaring Brick. Ike's look was inquisitive. He had no clue what was going on, so he stood still and studied the situation.

"What kind of car did you drive to the courthouse this morning?" the judge asked. The flames of his inquisition licked in the direction of Brick and Mace as if his lips were the very gates of hell. His eyes bulged big and bloodshot, and his left eyebrow rose when he asked the question, accenting the sneer on his face.

Ike knew that look from this judge. He had experienced it before. It was his *tell*, a dead giveaway that this was the ultimate question, his "gotcha" question. How this question was answered would be the key to what happened next. Depending on how this question was answered, the course of the rest of the exchange, the rest of the day, would be set. A light went on in Ike's head. He repeated the judge's words to himself, "*What kind of car did you drive to the courthouse this morning?*" *This has something to do with their car,* Ike thought. *He's pissed about something they've done in that car, something he saw, something Mace did to him.*

"What kind of car, I asked you!" The judge was red with rage.

"I drive a…"

Ike interrupted him, "A black Mercedes. I saw them getting out of it myself, Your Honor."

"You sure about that, Mr. Turner? I'd hate to have to hold you in contempt for lying to this court."

"I'm absolutely sure, Your Honor. I saw them with my own eyes."

"You've never seen them in a piece-of-crap, light-blue Chevrolet?"

"I'm absolutely sure, Your Honor. I've known these young men for a while now, and I've never seen them in the car you're describing." Ike was relieved the judge hadn't asked him if it was a piece-of-crap, light-blue Ford. He could have tap-danced around it if he had to, but he was glad he didn't have to.

"If you'd like, Your Honor, come on outside. I'm sure Mr. Hawthorne will let you take that Mercedes I saw them in for a spin around the block. He was the one driving it when I saw them myself pull into a rock star parking spot this morning under a tree next to Wooldridge Square. I saw him put the key in his pocket myself. Then we all went through the metal detector together, and here we are in your pleasant company, Your Honor. Show him the key, Mr. Hawthorne."

"Cut the crap, Mr. Turner. And drop the 'Your Honor' crap every other phrase. I can tell you're being sarcastic."

"I apologize to the court. I was sincerely trying to hide that."

The judge narrowed his eyes at Ike with a menacing glare. He was having difficulty holding his rage. Brick and Mace sat frozen, frightened, taking in the spectacle. This was not the way either of them had ever dreamed their first day in court would be. They were both petrified that this judge had something on them and that they might end up spending some time in that awful jail Ike had described so vividly only a few minutes earlier. The judge kept staring. The silence was almost more than Mace could handle. Sweat beaded on his forehead. Mace couldn't think. He wanted to run.

"All right, then," the judge finally said. Then he looked at Mace and pointed his stubby finger again. "You look just like the punk that flicked his cigarette on the hood of my car the other day. And your friend here looks just like the punk who was in the car with you—him. You're lucky there's not a pale-faced little black boy, zombie-looking fella, in here, or I'd have you all arrested right now. Are we clear?"

"We're clear," Ike answered.

The judge started to leave the bench but sat back down and stared at Ike. "Seems to me your time would be better spent searching for your partner, Mr. Turner. I'm hearing rumors."

"Mr. Goldstein is fine, Your Honor. Next time I talk with him, I'll tell him you send your regards."

"Next time you talk to him, tell him to show his face if he knows what's good for you. People start to talk when someone hasn't been seen for over a year and someone else is spending his money."

"I'll deliver your message."

The judge got up from his oversized chair and started for the door. The bailiff called, "All rise," but before he could get the words out, the judge was already through the door. The rotund little bailiff smiled at Ike and raised his shoulders toward his ears like he was saying, "What was that all about?" Ike smiled back. Then the round bailiff with the bulging buttonholes pulled his head back out of the courtroom and closed the door behind him like a turtle pulling its head back into its shell.

"Whew," Mace exclaimed with a sigh of relief. He wiped the sweat from his face with the sleeve of his jacket.

"Shhhh," Ike whispered, "he's probably listening through the intercom system. Let's go to the men's room." Ike led the way to a restroom off the stairwell. When they were inside, Ike checked the stalls to make sure no one else was there. "Well, I'm glad I didn't have to lie," Ike said. "Good thing he doesn't know a Chevy from a Ford."

"Wow, man, that was close," Mace said.

"That was karma," Ike said. "I hope it taught you a lesson. You're gonna meet the same people again that you've done bad things to. Think about it. Anybody you offend today, even people you don't remember, might wind up on your jury next week...or worse, they might be your judge."

Mace knew what Ike was saying was true, but he felt defensive anyway. He wanted to explain. There was a reason he did what he did.

Ike knew what Mace was thinking. "Don't try to explain," he said. "We have work to do." Ike reached into his pocket, pulled out a quarter, and handed it to Brick. "Here, go downstairs, and call Kay. Tell her I said DO NOT let Marvin come over here. Tell her I'll explain it to him later."

Brick and Mace said it at the same time, "Marvin?"

"Yeah, Marvin. I was going to surprise you. Your little friend started working for me this morning. I was going to let him come over and watch some of your trial. But we can't let that judge see him now. We'd all be in jail."

"Was Marvin at the office this morning?" Brick asked.

"Yeah. He's working on the second floor. I didn't let him know until after he started this morning that you two are working for me too. I mean, working with me. He's still a little pissed. And he's still banged up. You're lucky that oleaginous judge didn't wait till this afternoon to realize he recognized you two."

"That what judge?" Mace asked.

"Smarmy," Ike answered.

"Yeah, I knew that," Mace said.

"Go make the call, Brick. Mace and I have a client to meet. Then come right back. Don't get lost."

Brick decided to forgo the cranky old elevator this time and headed down the stairs to the first-floor pay

174

phone. Mace and Ike went back to the courtroom and took their places at the counsel table.

Mace used the time to review his file on Diaeta Pepsi again. After a few minutes, he heard the clanking and rattling of chains behind a door on the far side of the wood-paneled courtroom, then the sound of someone inserting a key in the door. The door opened. In stepped two guards dressed in drab khaki…and Diaeta Pepsi. She was not at all what Mace was expecting.

Two armed guards led Diaeta shuffling across the room. Her forward motion was restricted by the leg irons on her ankles. She scooted her Travis County-issue flip-flops across the floor as best she could, dragging the weight of the chains with her. The spectacle produced an eerie sound. She stopped where Mace and Ike were sitting.

The guards unlocked the several padlocks inserted in the heavy chains around her ankles, wrists, and waist. Another chain ran from the handcuffs on her wrists through the chain around her waist and then through the shackles on her ankles. It was an intimidating sight, and it took a couple minutes to free her from it all. The overbearing contraption looked like it was designed for Hannibal Lecter, not some accused prostitute, but it was standard procedure, government at work.

Diaeta was a white girl, five foot two at the most, and she weighed at least a two-hundred and fifty pounds. She was short and fat. She had stringy, straight, over processed, orange and bleached-blond hair. She was dressed in a pair of white jeans that were a couple sizes too small and a man's white dress shirt that was a couple sizes too big. The tail hung out, and the sleeves hung long and unbuttoned. The disposable flip-flops with the county jail logo completed her ensemble. Her complexion was pale, and her face was full of pimples, some of them white-topped, swollen, and shaped like small volcanoes threatening to blow.

Mace stared in dismay. He was shocked and speechless. She was not what he was expecting.

"Not what you were expecting, is she?" Ike whispered into Mace's ear.

Mace shook his head, indicating no.

"What chu ponks mou-fin 'bout?" Diaeta asked in a shrill voice with the affected accent of an uneducated, black gangbanger. It was incongruous and disconcerting to anyone who heard her—a cognitive dissonance without the cognitive.

"No, she's not," Mace whispered, finally answering Ike. "Not at all."

"I axed you ponks a querstion," she said loudly.

"I know you did, Diaeta. We're talking about your case," Ike said.

"Well, dat bees good. Whose da junior?" she asked, nodding her head toward Mace.

"Diaeta, this is your lawyer, Mace Spinella. He's going to handle your jury trial. I'll be helping him out some."

Mace extended his hand to shake hands with Diaeta. She looked at it with disgust and curled her nose like he had buggers on his fingers.

"Lawd help me," she squealed. "He's still wet behind da ears, green as day come. How you spect me to win?

Damn it, Ike Tun-na? Just lock me up now. Throw da key away."

"Trust me, Geneva."

"Don't bees callin' me dat! Chu knows I don't likes to bees called dat."

"Have I ever let you down?"

"No, but dat bees sides da point."

"Don't worry. Mace is going to win."

"Wait a minute, Ike," Mace interrupted. "Don't be making promises you might not be able to keep."

"See dat," Diaeta said, "yo boy don't believe. He don't thank he can."

"He thinks he can," Ike said. "He just don't know it yet. Come. Sit here in the chair between me and Mace. Jury selection starts in about ten minutes."

"But…but," Mace said, looking pleadingly at Ike. The look on his face showed his apprehension and insecurity.

"Breathe," Ike said.

Chapter 7

DAN-DAN

Dan Danford had been a lawyer for six years. After attending law school at Texas Tech in Lubbock, he passed the bar on his first try and landed a job with the Travis County Attorney's Hot Check Division, prosecuting college students, welfare mothers, housepainters, and the like for the occasional small-amount hot check, less than two hundred dollars. He had interviewed for a job as a briefing attorney with the Texas Court of Appeals in Amarillo, a job more interesting and better for his career, and he even got a callback for the second round of interviews, but his new wife was from Austin, and she wanted to get back close to mom and dad. Besides, "who wouldn't rather live in Austin than in Amarillo?" she would ask him. So, against his better judgment, he withdrew his name from consideration and took the hot-check job.

He always resented that decision, and it left him feeling depressed, petty, and often in an angry mood toward his wife...and toward the defendants he prosecuted. By the time she filed for divorce, they had two small children, which meant that Dan would be paying out a large portion of his salary each and every month as court-ordered child support for many years to come—sixteen, to be exact.

So Dan settled into collecting bounced checks and decided to make the best of it, even though he hated it.

By the time a hot check gets turned over to the Hot Check Division, it has already been rejected by a bank due to insufficient funds and sent back to the merchant or vendor who originally took it for merchandise or services or cashed it. Then the bank charges a smorgasbord of various and multiple overdraft fees to the check writer's account, resulting in overdraft penalties being piled on, one on top of the other, sometimes totally obliterating a recent deposit that the check writer genuinely believed would be credited in time to cover the original check.

For some reason, still a mystery to physicists, checks clear faster than deposits. Make a deposit, and it may not clear for days because of some "administrative hold," which often results in a bounced check, unconscionable bank fees, closure of the account, a cascade of other checks bouncing, and then a frightening letter from the county attorney.

By the time a hot check hits the county attorney's office, the check writer is up to his or her neck in trouble and usually doesn't have any chance of getting out of it. The original bouncing check is the first domino to fall. In accordance with the fine print, which is never read, the bank legally steals any money that is left. Like being caught in quicksand, the check writer is going down unless someone on firmer ground throws him or her a lifeline. And that seldom happens.

One of Ike's biggest gripes was banks. He held them in low regard, like Jesus did the Pharisees. "We need banking reform, not tort reform," he would say as often as he could get anyone to listen. "If Congress doesn't pass some kind of meaningful banking reform laws, and soon, we are all on our way to another Great Depression."

If Ike still had their attention when he got past the Great Depression reference, he'd up the stakes. "Bankers are stealing us blind. Politicians are letting them get away with it. Mark my word, we're all going to wake up one morning to find our country broke and Wall Street bankers sipping cocktails in the Bahamas, and living off the hundred-million-dollar bonuses they took from the companies they ran into the ground. It's unpatriotic.

"A man with a gun can rob a bank, but a man with a bank can rob everybody," Ike would say. He was passionate about the subject.

An "average Joe" check writer can mess up one time and set off a chain reaction that can keep him or her broke and in debt for years to come. By the time the merchant turns the hot check over to the Hot Check Division, the trouble is just getting started. First comes the threatening letter from the county attorney's office, "You have thirty days from the date of this letter to pay the amount of the check, plus our handling fee, or criminal charges will be filed against you."

The handling fee is often more than the amount of the check that originally bounced. The county attorney's office gets to keep the handling fee. They rely on it for part of their budget, so there isn't much room for mercy or leeway. The hot-check writer thinks, "If I had that kind of money, the check wouldn't have bounced in the first place." Sometimes, because of address changes or whatever, the check writer doesn't even receive the warning letter until after the thirty days are up, if at all.

Then the county attorney files criminal charges, and another letter is sent fixing the ransom for freedom even higher: the amount of the check, plus the handling fee, plus a fine.

Try to imagine being the person in such a predicament. It is an anxious, desperate, and sad situation. Imagine wanting to pay but just not being able to.

Then one night, you're driving home, minding your own business, when some cop turns his overhead lights on and pulls you over for that busted taillight you intended get fixed, but the bank seized all your damn money when you bounced that lousy fifteen-dollar check. Then you're arrested on a dark street. Your car is impounded and hauled off by an expensive wrecker company that charges you a towing fee, plus a storage fee that costs you more every day than you pay for your apartment rent.

If you talk back, if you express your anger at the policeman, you might get tased. If you are overweight or have high blood pressure and you get tased, you might die. You are definitely put in handcuffs. They're tight. Your arms are squeezed painfully behind you. Then you're stuffed into the back of a police car that still has the last passenger's vomit on the seat.

You're taken to the jail, fingerprinted, photographed, and locked up with the depressing prospect of losing what little you have left and not knowing when or if you will ever get out. Then a few days later, you meet Mr. Danford holding a clipboard and asking if you want to plead guilty.

Over the years, Danford had heard every sob story, every excuse, and every plea. In the beginning, he cared, but it took an emotional toll on him. If he cared, there was still nothing he could do, except feel bad about what he had to do. Eventually it became easier not to listen, not to care. *If I listen, they'll want me to make an exception for them. If I make an exception for them, I have to make an exception for everyone. Fuck them. They shouldn't have gotten in trouble in the first place.* For Danford, like most prosecutors, compassion and common sense eventually went out the window.

About a year after the divorce, Dan Danford's boss promoted him to a second-chair position in misdemeanor court handling shoplifting, criminal trespass, driving while intoxicated, and prostitution cases. Dan appreciated the promotion, although he felt it was completely deserved and long over due.

He looked forward to the pay raise. It wasn't much, after taxes, but it was enough to get cable television and HBO installed in his efficiency apartment four blocks from the courthouse. The wife had gotten his half of the house. But even with the help of her parents, she was having a rough time making ends meet and wasn't sure how much longer she would be able to keep making the payments. All that weighed on Dan, but at least he had HBO. It was one of his only escapes.

Then he got the notice in the mail that his child support payments were being increased because of his recent promotion and minuscule pay hike. The increase in child support, plus taxes withheld, plus the required "voluntary" United Way contribution, and some kind of Child Support Division processing fee ate up all of Dan's pay raise. He begrudgingly canceled his Cablevision and HBO after the ninety-day introductory offer expired, reattached the rabbit ears, and adjusted the reception.

When the cable guy backed out of his parking space leaving Dan's apartment, he backed into Dan's car and broke the taillight. That's what Dan thinks happened, anyway, because the Cablevision man was there around the time it happened, but he didn't leave a note, and no one saw him do it. Now Dan keeps thinking he's got to get that taillight fixed, but right now he just doesn't have the money.

Dan pulled open the big wooden door and stepped into the courtroom. He had met Diaeta before when he tried to talk her into pleading guilty, so he wasn't as taken aback by her appearance as Mace had been. He looked at her with an expression of disgust. He sneered. She looked even fatter and uglier than he remembered. He walked to the counsel table reserved for the prosecutor, always the one closest to the jury box, but Ike and Mace were already sitting there.

"You're at my table," Dan said.

"Says who?" Ike answered.

"Get up."

"No."

"Get off my table."

"Where's it say this is your table? We were here first."

"It's always the prosecutor's table, the one closest to the jury box."

"Says who?"

Dan was exasperated. He walked to the other table and dropped his three-inch-thick file folder from the height of his shoulder. It landed on the table with a loud wham.

Diaeta's head jerked around toward the sound. Danford looked at her and sneered again.

"What chu looking at?" she barked at him.

"Tell your idiot client," he stressed the word *idiot*, "not to talk to me," Danford said. "It's bad enough you stole my table and you're wasting my time and a jury's time on…"

"Don't chu be calling me no idget, you idget!" Diaeta interrupted. "I tell you…"

Ike placed his hand on Diaeta's shoulder near her neck and gave her a quick squeeze with his fingers, like a pinch, and she got quiet, but she was still writhing in anger, blinking her eyes and twitching her lips. Ike pinched her again with his thumb and the tips of his fingers, but this time he made a barely audible "shhhh" sound between his lips and teeth. She settled down and sat calmly, but she was still breathing hard.

Mace didn't notice. It was all he could do not to spring from his chair and bolt from the room. He didn't want to do this trial. He didn't like Ike. He didn't like Diaeta at all. He didn't want to embarrass himself in front of a bunch of strangers who were all going to go out and tell all their friends how stupid he was. And he didn't give a damn what Ike Turner thought about him. But something deep inside his soul kept him glued to his seat, weighted down, like an anvil in his lap.

Ike smiled at Danford and, in a slow drawl, said, "She's got a constitutional right, don't she, Dan?"

Ike didn't use any profanity and didn't mean anything other than exactly what he said, but Dan was edgier than usual that day, and he felt like Ike's tone implied profanity. And Dan didn't appreciate being cussed at one bit, whether the cussing was explicit or implied. He didn't like it. And he didn't like Ike taking his table. That table had always been his table. It's the way things work. *The prosecutor always gets the table closest to the jury box. It doesn't have to be written anywhere. It's just the way it is.*

"She may have a right to a goddamn jury trial, but that doesn't mean she should goddamn get one," Dan snapped back. "She's guilty, and you damn fucking know it, Ike Turner."

Dan was shaking mad in spite of doing his best to control himself. If he had been asked about it under oath, he would have sworn, and would have honestly believed, that Ike cussed at him first. Ike had a talent for polarizing people that way; either they loved him and thought every word out of his mouth was angel poetry, or they hated him and thought he was an arrogant, profanity-spewing dick-head.

Ike wasn't shaken by Dan's tirade. He smiled and said, "Guilty? Isn't that for the jury to decide, Dan-Dan?" His demeanor was still calm and his speech still slow.

Dan Danford hated it when anyone called him Dan-Dan. It made him feel like he was being talked down to, like he was a child. His father had called him Dan-Dan. His father was an alcoholic who abandoned the family when Dan was only eight. He hated his father—what he could remember of him anyway. And he hated Ike Turner even more now for calling him Dan-Dan.

"Unless she pleads guilty, which she should have already done," Dan snapped back. "You're giving your client bad advice."

"Because I won't make her sign one of those forms on your clipboard?"

"Precisely!" Dan almost shouted the word. He stared icily at Ike and didn't say anything else. He just stared like a kid playing that staring game, but Dan couldn't concentrate. He wondered why he had chosen to use the word *precisely*. It sounded funny when he heard himself say it. It made him sound prissy. He hated himself right then. Dan judged and criticized himself harshly in that flash of an instant. It was enough of a distraction to make him lose concentration and glance away. And he hated himself for that too.

Ike smiled again.

Diaeta moved her eyeballs back and forth, watching the exchange between Ike and Dan like it was a tennis match.

"You really think we're going to lose this case, don't you, Dan?"

"I'm sure of it."

"You think the jury's gonna come back guilty, don't you?"

"I sure do."

"Care to place a hundred-dollar wager on it?" Ike asked. He said it loud, loud enough to be heard all over the room, loud enough that the judge might have heard it, even without his intercom system.

Dan was taken aback momentarily, but he composed himself and quickly ran a couple scenarios in his head. If he actually had a hundred dollars, he would take Ike's stupid bet on the spot. It was a sure thing he was going to win a guilty verdict on this awful-looking excuse for a prostitute. He had read the police report, had talked with the arresting officer, a good-looking, clean-cut guy, and he had seen and talked with Diaeta Pepsi. There was no way in his mind that a jury was going to let her go, not under any circumstances. Even her name pissed him off. It sounded like a prostitute's street name to him, and he thought it would sound that way to a jury too.

As far as Dan was concerned, all he needed to do to win was point at her and say, "This is Diaeta Pepsi. She is charged with prostitution. I rest my case." It was that open-and-shut to him. And when she took the stand in her own defense, which she would certainly have to do, then the jury would get to hear that Ebonics street talk and that crazy accent, and that would clinch it for him. But he didn't have the money, and besides, it is usually unethical for a lawyer to bet on the outcome of one of his trials.

"I'm not going to bet you, Ike," Dan responded.

"Why not? You afraid you might lose, Dan-Dan?" Ike said, double thumbing his chest where suspenders would have been if he were wearing any.

Mace felt uncomfortable with what he was hearing. It was too reminiscent of Ike's bet with him the day before. It gave him a disorienting feeling. Was Ike doing this to screw with him and remind him of yesterday's bet? Or was Ike just screwing with Danford? Or did this crazy bastard bet with everybody? *Maybe he makes bets with everybody. Maybe he makes so many bets he can't remember them all. Maybe he forgot about my bet.*

"I'm not going to lose," Danford said.

"Then bet with me. I bet you a hundred dollars she's not convicted. I bet you a hundred dollars you lose, lose, lose."

"I'm not going to lose," Dan repeated coldly.

"What's the matter then? Don't you have the money?" Ike goaded him. "Hell, you're a lawyer; you're bound to have a hundred lousy bucks on you. Do I need to tell your boss to give you a raise? Just say the word, and I'll go over there right now and tell him to give you a little raise so you can afford to make a lousy hundred-dollar bet with me."

"I've got a hundred dollars on me right now," Dan lied. "But I'm not going to bet with you." Dan didn't want to lie, but Ike pushed his buttons. Ike made him feel ashamed that he was a lawyer and didn't even have a hundred dollars to his name. He felt inadequate, a failure. So he lied. *One little lie. What could it hurt? Besides, this kooky asshole deserves to be lied to,* Dan thought. *Rude bastard. It's none of his business how much money I have.*

"Tell you what," Ike said. "I'll give Mace here two crisp one-hundred-dollar bills. He'll hold 'em till after the trial. You give him your one hundred to hold. If you win, then you get my two hundred plus your one hundred back, and if I win, I get your one hundred. How's that? You win two hundred for betting one hundred on a case you can't lose."

Dan was tempted. He could use two hundred dollars right now. He could get his Cablevision turned back on, at least for a while. Or he could get his busted taillight fixed and pay a bill or two. And he'd buy himself a couple Manhattans after work, the good ones, Gentleman Jack or Maker's Mark with a splash of vermouth, chilled, in a big martini glass, with two cherries, the kind with the stems still on them.

But what if something went wrong? He couldn't afford to lose a hundred dollars. He couldn't afford to lose any money. He didn't have it. He'd be caught in a lie if he lost. He couldn't afford for that to happen either. His honesty and adherence to the rules was all he had going for him right now. It was about the only thing left that gave him any self-esteem. Even though he told himself Ike deserved to be lied to, which gave him some comfort, he wouldn't want anyone to ever find out he had lied or that he was broke.

Before Dan could turn him down again, Ike said, "Tell you what, bet me a hundred dollars you win this case, and I won't even try it. I'll let Mace here try it. I won't say a word. Most I'll do is whisper in his ear now and then, but I won't say a word to the jury. I promise. This would be Mace's very first jury trial. You've never tried a case before, have you, Mace?"

"Uh, no," Mace answered. He was embarrassed Ike pointed that out—again. *Sorry bastard.* It was bad enough he might have to try this loser case in front of strangers who would go away thinking he was stupid, but now Ike was making things even worse by embarrassing him in front of the prosecutor.

"Haven't tried a case, and I bet this is your first time ever in court, too, isn't it?" Ike asked.

Mace's face flashed red. *I hate Ike. Why is he doing this to me? Why is he embarrassing me?* "First time ever," Mace answered.

"And you graduated in the bottom of your class, didn't you?" Ike asked.

"What chu doing, Ike Tun-na? Is you done gone crazy?" Diaeta snapped.

Ike grabbed Diaeta with the tips of his fingers again, gave her a little pinch between the neck and shoulder, and made a "shuuu" sound. Diaeta got quiet. Mace and Dan didn't notice. Mace leaned forward, ready to stand up and walk out of there, never to come back. Ike put his hand on Mace's shoulder and pushed him back

190

in his chair, then he leaned over and whispered into Mace's ear.

"Am I embarrassing you in front of Diaeta Pepsi and poor ol' starving Dan-Dan Danford? You know who you are...and you know you can win this case, no matter what they think of you and no matter what anyone says about you, including me. Am I right?"

"I guess so," Mace said. He was uncharacteristically at a loss for anything else to say. Then Ike straightened up and addressed Mace out loud so everyone else could hear too.

"How long you been a lawyer, Mace?" Ike asked.

"Just over two weeks." Mace answered.

"Just over two weeks, and he's never tried a case. What are you afraid of, Dan? It's a bird's nest on the ground...like finding money in the parking lot. This boy ain't got a chance."

Ike turned his head toward Mace and gave him a big, exaggerated wink. Then he turned back to Dan and gave Dan a big thumbs-up sign. Mace was more confused than before. He didn't know what to think, except that he couldn't stand Ike. Dan felt the same way.

Mace and Diaeta started talking at the same time. Mace said something like, "But you said I'd win," and Diaeta was protesting something like, "Ain't no honky greenhorn baby lawya gonna..."

Ike pinched them both between the neck and shoulder and made the "shuuu" sound again. They got quiet and looked down. Diaeta's face relaxed, and she half smiled. She looked at Ike and Dan, peacefully awaiting the next round to begin. Mace was still confused. He was too afraid to fight but too panicked to flee. He was frozen stiff like a scared little rabbit, paralyzed and shaking under the shadowy wings of a circling hawk. He was stuck to the seat of his chair, too frightened to leave, but he sure wanted to.

"Come on, Dan-Dan, what do you have to lose?" Ike goaded. "A greenhorn, honky, baby lawyer up against a seasoned prosecutor like you, and defending a client the likes of Diaeta Pepsi. How can you lose?"

Ike sensed Mace and Diaeta were about to say something again, so he lowered his brow and looked at them hard. They both got quiet.

"If I lose this bet, Dan, I'll pay you two hundred dollars cash today. If you lose, pay me a hundred dollars. Write me a check. I'm in no big hurry. I might even wait a week or two to cash it. I like you, Dan. Say it's a bet," Ike taunted. "Come on. Say it's a bet."

Dan weighed the possibilities. He couldn't see how he could lose. He quickly reconsidered the evidence. He looked at Mace. He looked at Diaeta Pepsi. Maybe the rumors he had heard about Ike going a little crazy after his partner Goldstein went missing were true. Crazy or not, two hundred dollars would help out a lot right now. *I don't have to show him any money up front, and by five o'clock today, I'll be two hundred dollars richer, which is two hundred more than I have right now, and I'll have two Manhattans sitting in front of me.*

"So you're not going to say a word during the whole trial?" Dan asked Ike.

"Nope."

"And he's going to try the whole case by himself?"

"Yep."

"No tricks."

"Nope."

"I don't know why you are doing this, Ike, but if you keep insisting, I may have no choice but to take you up on your bet."

Right then, Ike knew Dan had taken the bait, and the hook was in his lip. "*I may have no choice*," Ike repeated the words in his head and smiled.

Dan was casting himself in the role of the hero with no choice, and Ike knew it. *If I have no choice, then how can it be wrong?* Ike sensed what Dan was thinking. All he had to do, according to Dan, was keep insisting.

"I insist then. I insist," Ike said. "I insist you take my money. You have no choice."

"OK, then." Dan pondered a second longer, and then he sealed the deal—and his fate. "It's a bet," he said, smiling. And why not smile? He had no choice. Besides, he needed the crazy fool's money.

"This is good; you won't be sorry," Ike said.

"What do you mean, I won't be sorry? What is it with you, Ike? Do you just like giving your money away?"

"I do. I do," Ike said, and then he added, "but I like to win too."

Something in Ike's voice or facial expression made Dan feel uneasy. A small twinge in his gut tried to warn him on a deep visceral level that he should back out of this bet right now. But he didn't listen to that voice in his gut, and he didn't back out. His choice was made.

The main door to the courtroom opened, and Brick stepped inside, talking loudly as he walked. "It's all OK. I got a hold of Kay, and she told Mar…" He stopped dead in his tracks, and his voice trailed off as he saw Diaeta for the first time. Then he noticed Danford. Then he noticed Mace, and Mace was putting off strange vibrations. The mood in the room hit Brick, and he sensed something had been going on. "What's going on?" he asked.

"Just Ike making *another* bet," Mace said sarcastically, trying to redeem himself in his own mind for being such a scared little rabbit a few moments earlier. But as soon as the words left his lips, especially the word *another*, he knew he had messed up. He certainly didn't want to remind Ike about the bet the two of them had made the day before, the bet about the cussing, the bet Mace had lost, and about Ike's money that they had already spent on the rent.

"Oh," Brick answered. "What kind of bet?"

Ike put his arm around Brick's shoulder, pulled him close to his face, and whispered in his ear. "Don't be talking about Marvin in here. Remember, this place is bugged. If that judge figures out it was Mace that flicked that cigarette on his car then we're all going to jail." Then he turned back to Danford and extended his hand. "Shake on it," he said.

"OK, Ike, I'll shake on it, but you're going to lose."

The two men shook hands.

The instant their hands parted, the door between the courtroom and the judge's chambers opened, and the pudgy bailiff stepped in. "All rise,"

he said. Ike, Danford, and Brick were already standing. Mace jumped to his feet. Ike leaned over and
poked Diaeta in the back, and she stood up. The
judge entered wearing his black robe and took his
seat behind the big, elevated judge's desk at the
front of the room. "Be seated," the bailiff said, and
they all sat down.

The judge rustled a stack of papers in his hand and
then shook them toward Ike. "Mr. Turner, I have some
questions about your client's identity."

"Yes, sir."

"I do not believe that her real name is Diaeta Pepsi,
yet apparently she's never been arrested or finger-
printed under any other name, and apparently she had
no driver's license or other ID in her possession when
she was arrested. Mr. Turner, do you know what your
client's real name is?"

"I can't say, Your Honor."

"You can't say, or you won't say?" The judge glared
at Ike over the rim of his glasses. Steam seemed to roll
from his hairy nostrils.

Ike sensed a familiar trap. He had been down a
similar road once before with a different judge, a slimy
little federal judge up in Dallas. He knew this judge was
trying to set him up for a contempt of court charge too.
*If I answer the question with "I won't," then he'll find that my
refusal to answer is "willful," and he'll hold me in contempt,
and he'll lock me up for a few hours, or days, and they'll pressure Mace to plead Diaeta guilty.*

"I'm ordering you, Mr. Turner. If you know her
legal name, I'm ordering you to tell me."

Ike knew when a judge orders someone to do something, he plans to hold the person in contempt if they don't do it, if they don't obey his order to the letter. An order by the judge is a prerequisite for most contempt charges except for the ones having to do with disrespectful behavior that happens in the courtroom, usually directed toward the judge or opposing counsel. But the judge's order has to be on the record, taken down and transcribed by the court reporter, and so far none of this exchange was on the record. Ike took some comfort in that. Then the sound of the judge's voice interrupted Ike's thought.

"Mr. Bailiff, will you ask the court reporter to come in please?"

Crap! Ike thought.

A couple minutes later, an elderly court reporter waddled in, sat herself down behind her desk near the witness stand, and added a stack of paper to her court reporting machine. Her fingers began to move over the rectangular black keys, and like magic, everything everyone said was written down verbatim and put into the official record—for all eternity.

"Once again, I'm ordering you, Mr. Turner, if you know your client's legal name, I'm ordering you to tell me."

"May I confer with my co-counsel, Your Honor?"

"Make it quick."

Brick and Mace glanced at each other with stunned looks. They were worried about what was going on, but they both felt a sense of pride over being called "co-counsel." It was their first time. Ike leaned in where Mace was sitting next to Diaeta, and he motioned for

Brick to come over. Brick rolled his chair into the huddle, and Ike whispered to them.

"Watch this, and learn. He's going to try to hold me in contempt. This will be educational for you guys. But if he throws me in jail, call Kay. She'll know who to contact and what to do."

"Jail," Mace said in a loud whisper. "You can't go to jail! You have to be here. I can't do this by myself. Just tell him her name."

Mace glanced toward the door that went to the hallway, that leads to the stairwell, that leads to the bottom floor, that leads to the sidewalk and out of there forever.

"What's your answer, Mr. Turner? For the last time, I'm ordering you to tell me the legal name of your client. I am ordering you to tell it to me now."

The court reporter's fingers worked feverishly, keeping up with the judge's mouth, snatching each word from the air and pressing them, one after the other, onto the paper.

Ike took a deep breath. "One more moment please, Your Honor."

"Well, hurry it up."

Ike leaned back in and whispered to Mace and Brick. "Don't ever tell a judge you won't do something. Tell him you can't and then give him a good reason why you can't. And be polite. Remember, the court reporter is writing down everything you say. But she can't pick up voice tone or facial expression, so you can say a lot of things between the lines, things that won't get written down. Know what I mean?"

Mace and Brick nodded in the affirmative.

"And never, ever use an obscene gesture. It's too easy for a judge to describe that for the record. Everybody knows what shooting the bird is. Flipping someone off. Giving 'em the finger. That'll put you in jail for sure. It's better done with your voice tone, not by projecting your middle finger. Shoot him your expression, your voice tone, not the finger."

Ike was sounding like a college professor.

"Mr. Turner!" The judge boomed. Brick and Mace jumped in their chairs. "You've had enough time, Mr. Turner. Now, for the last time, I'm ordering you to tell me the name of your client."

Ike drew a deep breath, centered himself, and exhaled slowly before answering. His tone was slow and measured. "I can't, Your Honor. I sincerely wish that I could...but I can't. I most certainly would if I could... but I can't. Please understand, I am not conceding that I even know my client's name, but, hypothetically, if I did, I would tell you her name if I could...but I can't... Your Honor."

The judge narrowed his eyes. "What did you just say? You can't, or you won't, Mr. Turner?"

Ike didn't have to think about the answer. "I can't, Your Honor."

"Then why does the cat have your tongue, Mr. Turner? Why is it that you are refusing to obey an order of this court?"

Ike knew this trap. There was that word again: "refusing." Ike never said he was refusing. He said he couldn't. He never used the word *refuse* or any derivation thereof, but the judge was now asking him why he was "refusing." If Ike's answer begin with the word *because*, he would be admitting by implication that he refused.

"I am not refusing, Your Honor." Ike stayed cool.

"Then why are you not answering my question?"

"I can't, Your Honor."

"And why is that?"

"I can't because, if I did know my client's legal name, which I am not conceding that I do, I would have learned it during the course of attorney-client protected conversations, conversations that this court knows I am bound by duty and by law to keep confidential."

The judge narrowed his eyes and glared even harder.

"Furthermore," Ike continued, "if an attorney can be punished by contempt of court, threatened with jail, for refusing to divulge a constitutionally protected conversation with his client, then not only is the attorney harmed, but the client is harmed as well...because her constitutionally protected right has forever been violated. Once a protected and confidential communication has been divulged, it can never be undone. That bell cannot be unrung. The toothpaste is out of the tube. The cat is out of the bag. And the harm is compounded further by the chilling effect that a contempt-of-court finding would have, not only on the attorney and client directly affected, but also on others similarly situated."

Ike paused, drew another deep breath, and began again. The judge frowned even more.

"I cannot answer because it would violate my client's constitutional rights. It would have a chilling effect on her constitutional right to effective assistance of counsel...because I cannot adequately or effectively represent her if I am worried that this court is going to lock me up for doing my job. And, as I said, it would have a chilling effect upon the rights of other defendants similarly situated. I have no doubt that if this court, or any court, ever handed down such a ruling that the ACLU and the Texas Criminal Defense Lawyers Association would be filing briefs and calling press conferences on the courthouse steps before the day was over."

The court reporter's fingers struck the large black keys on her machine, memorializing every word that had been said so later a reviewing court could determine whether the judge had made the correct ruling or not.

Sometimes it is the threat of being reversed by a higher court that causes a judge to check his bias and emotions and enter the correct and proper ruling. Sometimes it is because of the possibility of adverse press coverage. And sometimes it is simply because some of them are decent human beings who try to follow the law.

When Ike mentioned press conferences, it hit a chord with the judge. He didn't want any negative press. He had been there before and didn't want to go there again. The idea of the American Civil Liberties Union didn't concern him much. In Texas, it was usually good press for a judge to go against the ACLU, but the Texas Criminal Defense Lawyers Association was another matter. By banding together in an association, the criminal defense lawyers had become more powerful than any of them could ever be standing alone. They no longer had to face daunting situations like this by themselves.

The members of the Texas Criminal Defense Lawyers Association come to each other's aid when one of them is being picked on by a petty tyrant judge or when there is a danger that bad precedent is about to be established. The TCDLA, as it is known, keeps volunteer lawyers on standby to file briefs and to intervene with writs of habeas corpus in the event of just such a situation as Ike was facing now, and the judge knew it, and he knew that Ike was an active and respected member. And he knew that Kay kept their emergency phone number in her wallet. He also knew if he offended Ike and the TCDLA badly enough by actually putting Ike in jail, they might even recruit and finance an opponent to run against him in the next election.

Thank God this judge is elected and not appointed, Ike thought.

After chewing on his pen for a while, the judge glared at Ike and then at Diaeta. "What about it, ma'am? What is your name? What does your birth certificate say your name is?"

"I'm instructing my client not to..." Ike said, but before he could finish his sentence, Diaeta was talking.

"Burf ticket? What chu mean, burf ticket? I ant got no burf ticket."

"What was your name when you were born?"

"I'm instructing my client not to…"

"What was my name when I was borned? Is you crazy? I don't member nothing dat fa back!"

Frustrated he was getting nowhere with Diaeta, the judge narrowed his eyes at Ike, and said to him in a threatening voice, "I'll take this matter under advisement, Mr. Turner. After the verdict, I want you to stick around. We've got some unfinished business. Jury selection will start in ten minutes."

He got up and left the room before the bailiff could say "All rise."

"Jury selection in ten minutes," Ike said to Mace. "Let's get ready."

The thirty-minute break the judge gave the jury panel had turned into nearly an hour. That's the way court time works.

"But the judge…he said he had unfinished business with you. What's that mean?" Mace asked.

"He said 'after the verdict,' so we'll worry about that after the verdict. We've got other stuff to do right now. One thought at a time, boys, one thought at a time."

When it was time, the jury panel filed into the room and were seated by the bailiff in order of the numbers on the jury summons notices that they had all received in the mail. This took about five minutes.

Ike drew a chart with twenty-four squares on it, three rows of squares with eight squares per row. Each row represented eight potential jurors, and each square represented where they were seated in the courtroom. Ike matched each potential juror to the juror information sheet they were required to fill out earlier that morning when they were impanelled with a larger group of jurors who had been sent to other courtrooms for other trials.

As Ike matched a potential juror to his or her information sheet, he handed it to Mace who wrote the names down in their respective squares on the chart. Ike explained to Mace that they were going to use the chart to make notes on. "I'll put anything important they say in their square. Then later when we're deciding which ones to use strikes on, we can put a face to them. Otherwise, we'll get 'em confused with each other."

When Mace finished writing the last name in the twenty-fourth square, he handed the chart to Ike.

Ike handed it to Brick along with a sheet of paper, a ruler, and a black felt-tip pen. "Here, Brick, make a copy of this. Mace can use it to help him remember their names, and I'll use the other one to make notes on. You got that, Mace?"

"Yeah, I got that. But I still don't know what I'm supposed to say."

Ike reached into his inside jacket pocket and pulled out a folded piece of yellow legal pad paper. "Here, I wrote out some notes for you. This is all you need to know. Single out a few folks on the back row, ad-lib with them, and just see where it goes," Ike said, handing Mace the folded paper. "This is all you need to know, really."

"Ad-lib? What do you mean, ad-lib?"

"Start with somebody on the back row, and work your way forward. By the time you get to the front row, you'll have it figured out."

"But…" Mace said.

Brick interrupted, "Why start on the back row?"

"Because the people on the back row probably aren't going to be on the jury. So if you accidentally piss one off, no big deal."

"Why won't the people on the back row be on the jury?" Brick asked.

"Because in this trial, like I told you, it's a misdemeanor and not a felony. There are only going to be six people on this jury. And they'll be the first six in the order they've just been seated, unless we use our three strikes or Danford uses his three strikes on them."

"I see," Brick said, but his expression signaled some uncertainty.

"See," Ike continued, "if none of them are excused for cause, and assuming we don't strike any of the same people that Danford strikes, then we'll have our jury out of the first twelve people. Six on the jury, plus our three strikes, plus Danford's three strikes, equals twelve."

While Brick and Ike discussed the general makeup of a jury, Danford was busy reading through his notes and making marks on the margins with a pencil that he was pressing way too hard against the paper. The lead broke.

Diaeta Pepsi listened to Ike with uncharacteristic interest. Mace frantically looked at the notations Ike had scrawled on the yellow piece of paper. He kept flipping it over from side to side. All that was written on it were three words, all in capital letters, one word on top of the other. All it said was:

BE
BOP
BYRD

"What is this crap?" Mace said. "I can't make sense of this. I can't read your damn writing. I don't know what this means. This is no help." Mace was exasperated, and it showed.

The stress was getting to him. He had been at the brink of freaking out a couple other times today but managed to pull himself back together. But time was running out, and he still didn't know what his first word would be when it was his turn to stand up and talk.

On the ride over, Ike told Mace it would be as easy as selling perfume. But this was absolutely nothing like selling perfume. Selling knockoff perfume to strangers on the street and in office buildings was hard, but this was impossible. Fortunately, Ike had already explained that Danford had to talk first, but that wasn't much comfort for Mace right now. Time was running out.

"What don't you understand?" Ike asked.

"Bop!" Mace said. He almost shouted the word and made a popping sound at the end of it. "Bop," he repeated, "Be bop byrd—that's all the hell it says on here. What the hell is this, a fucking fifties' rock song?"

"Not bop," Ike answered calmly. "B-O-P."

"B-O-P. What the hell is B-O-P?" Mace asked, pronouncing each letter in an accentuated, sarcastic tone.

"Burden of proof," Ike said. "It's one of the most important concepts in our American criminal justice system. Burden of proof—who's got the burden of proof, and how much proof does it take? Our law says the government has the burden of proof, and they have to prove their case beyond a reasonable doubt. Burden of proof, B-O-P. Their burden of proof is beyond a reasonable doubt. Beyond a reasonable doubt, B-Y-R-D. Get it? B-Y is for beyond. R-D stands for reasonable doubt."

"Reasonable doubt…I got that. Reasonable doubt," Mace said.

"Yes, but people have different ideas about what reasonable doubt means. Some people think it means the government has to bring in a lot of evidence. They believe the government should have to exclude every other reasonable hypothesis or explanation for the defendant's behavior, or else the government hasn't proven its case.

"Other people think that reasonable doubt means she must have done it because the police arrested her for it. They think if she wasn't guilty, she wouldn't be here. There's a big disparity in what folks believe on the topic of how much evidence the government has to bring, B-E stands for bring evidence, before they can find someone guilty beyond, B-Y, a reasonable doubt, R-D. See, B-E stands for bring evidence. B-O-P stands for burden of proof, and B-Y-R-D stands for beyond a reasonable doubt."

"OK. I see. OK. So what you're saying, I think, is it's my job to find the people who need a lot of evidence presented to them before they'd be willing to vote 'guilty' and then get those people on the jury," Mace said. He was a little calmer than before.

"Not exactly, but close," Ike answered. Then, pausing between phrases for emphasis, he said, "Your real job...is to identify the folks...that would convict someone of a crime...on little evidence. Then do everything you can...to keep those people...off the jury. It's not really jury selection...it's juror elimination. You get them talking...and then close the sale."

"Close the sale," Mace repeated under his breath, "close the sale."

"Just like when you sold perfume."

"It's not like selling perfume."

"Yeah, it is. You're a rhino. You told me so yourself. You never take no for an answer."

"I was a rhino. I'm a shark now...and don't say shyster." Mace glared at Ike.

"Sharks have dead eyes. You don't want to be no shark. Just keep 'em talking until you get what you want. It's not important what *you* say. What's important is what you can get *them* to say. If you don't want a person on the jury, get 'em talking. Establish on the record that they're biased in some way. Then the judge has to take them off the panel or risk a reversal on appeal. So get out there and act like you're selling perfume again. Same thing, only different. Trust me."

"Trust me's just another way to say fuck you."

"No, it's not."

"I don't know how to do that. How the hell do I show they're biased?"

"Well, the first thing is don't ask 'em that question. It just tips 'em off where you're headed. Who's going to admit they can't be fair? Instead, ask them something like, 'How much evidence do you need to convict—a little or a lot?' The fact that she was arrested will be enough evidence for some of them, really. You want the ones who will require the state to B a lot of E before they would call someone guilty BYRD, beyond a reasonable doubt."

"Guilty byrd." Brick snickered the words.

"I get it," Mace said. "The government has to B-E— bring evidence—B-O-P—because they have the burden of proof, in order to find her guilty B-Y-R-D—beyond a reasonable doubt. BE BOP BYRD."

"That's it," Ike said. "Oh, and remember this. Almost everybody wants off jury duty, so tell them how to get off this jury."

"How?" Mace interrupted.

"Tell them to talk a lot," Ike said. "Tell them, if you talk, you probably walk. If you have nothing to say, you probably stay."

Most of the jury panelists sat in their assigned seats and stared straight ahead, sometimes making eye contact with Mace or with Danford, both of whom would glance away nervously. Neither of them realized that the jurors were probably as nervous as they were, as nervous as Danford was anyway. Probably none of them were as nervous as Mace. Ike smiled and made notes and little marks and abbreviations on his jury list. The symbols made sense to Ike, but they looked like hieroglyphics to Mace.

The bailiff entered the room and shouted his "all rise" command. Everyone stood up for the judge to enter and then everyone sat back down when the judge sat down. The judge started reading something to the jury panel, but Mace was too nervous to listen. He was still worried about what he was going to say. When the judge finished reading the general instructions, he turned the floor over to Mr. Danford, who stood from his table and walked to the podium that the bailiff had placed in front of the rail that separates the gallery, the place where the audience sits, from the bar, the place where the lawyers sit.

"Ladies and gentlemen," Danford began, "my name is Dan Danford. I work for the Travis County Attorney's Office. We're all here today because the defendant, Diaeta Pepsi," he pointed at her when he called her name and curled his lip with a look of disgust, "yes, you heard me right, Diaeta Pepsi, was arrested for prostitution, and she refuses to plead guilty because she has a constitutional right to drag us all in here and make us give her a trial. So that's why..."

Ike whispered "object" and jabbed Mace hard in his ribs, hard enough to leave a bruise.

Mace jumped to his feet. "Objection!" he shouted. Pain throbbed in his side. The pain was all that was on his mind, until he heard the judge angrily shout, "Sustained! You know better than that, Mr. Danford!"

Mace immediately forgot about the pain. His mouth dropped open, and he sat back down in his chair. He never expected the judge to sustain his objection. In fact, he didn't even know what he was objecting to. Ike, on the other hand, knew that judges don't like to have their cases reversed by a higher court, not even this judge, and Danford had clearly overstepped the bounds of proper jury selection.

The judge stared daggers through Danford for a full five seconds. Then, with a more cordial expression on his face, he said to the jury panel, "The panel is instructed to disregard everything Mr. Danford said after 'My name is Dan Danford. I work for the Travis County Attorney's Office.' Do you understand me? Disregard everything else that he said."

Then the judge turned his attention back to Danford. "Mr. Danford, you and I have some unfinished business after these proceedings are over. I want you and Mr. Turner to both stick around."

Danford wished it was five o'clock already. He wished it bad. He wanted a drink, and he wanted it now. He didn't think he needed a drink; he just wanted a drink, but he wanted it bad. Maybe two. Probably two. At least.

Dan had never considered himself an alcoholic, not even close. He hadn't been a regular drinker until after Karen left him. He hardly ever drank alone, not much anyway. He knew better than that, but he wasn't able go to the neighborhood bars for fear of running into someone he had prosecuted, and he couldn't often afford to drink at the pricey downtown clubs, so he gradually became accustomed to relying on the generosity of other people—criminal defense lawyers.

He wanted it to hurry up and be five o'clock so he could just get the hell out of there and head down to the Cedar Door, a local lawyer hangout. There, he would pretend to be friendly with some slimy criminal defense lawyer, it didn't matter which one, any slimy criminal defense lawyer, as long as he was flashing around a gold credit card and buying drinks for the county prosecutors who happened to come in, and a lot of them did. Dan had been going there for a few months now, only since his Cablevision got shut off and the loneliness of his small, pathetic apartment with its bent rabbit ears and terrible TV reception had started closing in on him.

Drinks at the Cedar Door seemed to help—a little— even though he often woke up feeling more anxious and depressed than the day before. Sucking up to the competition made him feel like a whore and a failure. Sometimes he hated himself for that. He hated feeling beholden, compromised, belittled…but not as much as he hated Diaeta Pepsi right now…and Ike Turner.

Dan needed to relax. He didn't know why he messed up and said what he did to the jury panel. He knew he had stepped over the line the instant he said it. But he couldn't help himself. He was still upset with that smartass Ike Turner. He knew he shouldn't have made that bet. That fucking Ike Turner was trying to get him off his game. *That's why he took my table. I shouldn't let him get to me. What if I lose that bet? I'm not going to lose. But I never thought I'd be in trouble with this judge either.*

"Attorneys approach the bench," the judge said and motioned Danford, Ike, and Mace to come forward. The court reporter got up from her chair and stood next to the judge, balancing her stenograph machine on the side of his desk. The judge leaned over to the three attorneys and looked sternly at Mace, who was the only lawyer leaning with his elbows on the desk. "Get your elbows off my desk," he growled. Mace jumped back. Ike and Dan had been in this courtroom before and knew better than to lean on the judge's desk. It was one of this judge's many pet peeves.

The members of the jury panel watched with curiosity what was going on at the bench, but they couldn't hear what was being said.

"Gentlemen," he continued, "I believe Mr. Danford has tainted this jury panel by his improper appeal for them to be prejudiced against this defendant because of her insistence on exercising her constitutional right to a trial by a jury of her peers." He glanced in Diaeta's direction and smirked when he said the word *peers*. "If you want to ask for a mistrial, Mr. Turner, I'll grant it."

"All right!" Mace said triumphantly under his breath, feeling a surge of relief and joy.

"No, thank you, Your Honor," Ike said, shattering Mace's newfound tranquility. "We've worked hard to get ready for this trial, and we are ready. Mr. Spinella is chomping at the bit for his first courtroom victory. My client is here ready to go to trial, and she's expecting to go home today. Let me remind the court that she is still incarcerated."

"I'll tell you what," the judge said, "we will reset this case for next week. Then I'm sure Mr. Danford will agree to let her plead to her back time, and she can go home—a guaranteed result, win/win."

"So that the record is perfectly clear," Ike said, glancing at the court reporter to make sure she was getting everything down, "the defendant waives any objection she might have to Mr. Danford's earlier remarks, and she hereby makes her demand for a speedy trial. This trial."

The judge looked at Ike over the top of his spectacles. Trying to sound conciliatory, he still came off condescending. "If it's the additional jail time you don't like, Mr. Turner, I'm sure that Mr. Danford would be willing to let her plead to her back time right now. That would be good for him after the way he got things off to a bad start today, and that would be good for you and your client. She can have a sure thing right now, and she'll get to go home right now instead of getting the book thrown at her after you lose."

"No, thank you, Your Honor. We're ready to pick the jury," Ike answered.

Mace was crushed. His way out of this bad situation had been blocked by that know-it-all, smartass, crazy Ike Turner. Dan was crushed too. He wanted this trial to be over. He wanted it to be five o'clock—bad. In his thoughts, he was already on his way to the Cedar Door.

"Have it your way, Mr. Turner. Mr. Danford, you may proceed, but watch your step this time," the judge said.

Chapter 8

VOIR DIRE IS A FRENCH WORD

Dan did a pretty good job of jury selection. It wasn't great, but it was OK. He composed himself fairly well and launched straight into the cookie-cutter opening remarks he had done enough times before to almost know the whole routine by heart. He told the panel what a great civic duty they were doing. He thanked them. Then he thanked them again. He droned on and on. He told them that this is the part of the trial that is called *voir dire*, as if they cared, and he told them what voir dire means.

"Voir dire is a French word that means to speak the truth." Blah, blah, blah. Dan continued talking.

He told them that this was a prostitution case. He told them that Diaeta Pepsi had been arrested for prostitution by an undercover policeman and that she had been officially charged with the crime of prostitution by a duly elected justice of the peace. And then he read the jury panelists' names off the list, one by one, stopping dramatically to make eye contact with each potential juror as he called his or her name, and he asked them one by one if each could be "a fair and impartial juror" in this case. Blah. Blah. Blah. Ike rolled his eyes and sighed.

Of course, none of them said no. Who in their right mind is going to admit to being unfair, biased, and prejudiced? Not once during the two years Dan had been doing this canned voir dire had anyone ever raised a hand to that question. Yet he asked it every time, just to fill up space. It's no wonder jurors get pissed off about their jury service. People want to be entertained, and they don't want their time wasted with a bunch of senseless questions, but Dan persisted, case after case.

After about half an hour, he sat down. He was not able, or he simply did not try, to get any of the potential jurors excused for cause by the judge. And he hadn't learned much information about them either. He would exercise his preemptory strikes the same way he always did—strike the ones on the front row who didn't smile at him when he introduced himself in the beginning.

Normally jury selection is when a lawyer tries to stack the deck a little bit in his or her side's favor by selectively and strategically thinning the herd. With surgical precision, the lawyer zeros in on a single panelist who, for some reason or the other, the lawyer prefers not to be on the jury: maybe it is the way the person answered one of his or her questions, or maybe the lawyer just doesn't like the panelist's zip code.

Like a cheetah separating its potential prey from the rest of the herd, the savvy lawyer separates the undesirable panelist from the rest of his peers and directs the good citizen down the slippery slope toward juror disqualification.

The job of a good trial lawyer is to identify the personality types he or she does not want on the jury, figure out who those people are, and get as many of them as possible off the list and out of consideration. The lawyer tries to get rid of the most obvious and objectionable ones with a "challenge for cause" and save his or her preemptory strikes, the strikes he or she can use for any reason, for the panelists closer to the middle of the road, the ones he or she doesn't like but can't get disqualified on legal grounds. A really good lawyer can wind up with a jury seated in the box that is already leaning in his or her favor because of subtle biases generally associated with one's profession, religion, political beliefs, organizational and associational memberships...and even zip codes.

A story has been handed down from one generation of trial lawyers to the next about a rich Texas oilman who had a son attending Texas A&M, the state agricultural and mechanical college. (Some Aggies are offended by that description of their beloved university.) One day, the oilman's son was caught red-handed, so to speak, in the ag barn receiving oral sex from a sheep. The young man was arrested on the spot and charged with the crime of bestiality. The father wanted the best criminal defense attorney he could possibly find for his son, so he asked his personal attorney if he had any recommendations.

He had two. He said one lawyer was an expert at final argument and always won his cases because of his impassioned final plea to the jury. He said the other was an expert at jury selection, and after he picked the jury, he could relax because he knew he already had it won. Obviously, the father chose the lawyer who was the jury selection expert, reasoning that he would prefer to win the case sooner as opposed to later.

When it came time for the trial, the lawyer worked his magic, and after the jury was in the box, the prosecutor got up to give his opening statement. He pointed his accusing finger at the frightened and embarrassed young defendant and said, "Ladies and gentlemen of the jury, we will prove to you that this degenerate defendant allowed, encouraged, and enticed an innocent sheep to lick him upon his genitals in order to satisfy his own sexual gratification."

It is reported that one of the jurors leaned over to another and said in a loud whisper that all could hear, "A good sheep will do that sometimes, ya know."

There is great value in picking the right jury, and it requires a great deal of talent. Mr. Danford did not possess that talent—not yet, anyway.

After Mr. Danford finished and sat down, the judge called a fifteen-minute recess and informed the jury panel that Mr. Spinella would speak to them when they returned from break.

The bailiff called out, "All rise." Everyone stood up, and the judge left the room. Everyone stood up except

Mace. He just sat there, pale in the face, staring blankly at the floor. His hands gripped one another so tightly that his fingers were a ghostly white. Mace was becoming dizzy and disoriented. His breathing was fast and shallow.

He had no awareness of what he was doing and certainly no awareness that he was doing it to himself. He just knew he was about to pass out. And he felt that same icky, skin-crawling, clammy feeling that he felt that time in law school when he freaked out and went missing before exams.

People started leaving the courtroom, milling around and talking. Mace was still fixated on the same spot on the floor about three feet in front of him. His skin was a pasty white, and little beads of perspiration ringed his forehead.

Ike saw what was happening with Mace and instantly understood what he was going through. He moved over and stood right up beside him and draped his hand on Mace's shoulder. Ike drew a deep breath and then exhaled with an audible sigh through his mouth. He relaxed his shoulders and neck. He shut out the commotion and noise and energy and everything else that was going on around him. It felt to Ike like he was walking through a large, empty house, in the middle of the night...turning off the lights...one switch at a time...letting the darkness in...one room at a time, until everything went black...quiet.

Ike was in his space. It was a dark, vast, and timeless space, a space pregnant with possibility, poised, and ready. The first time Ike found his way into this "space" was quite by accident, when he was a small child. Ever since, he visited it fairly often. It was his laboratory, a place for his ideas to incubate. It was his place of silence and his place from which oratory sprang. It was the womb of his creativity and inspiration. It was a place of potential miracles. It was within.

Ike opened his eyes and put his hand more firmly on Mace's shoulder. He drew in a deep breath, inhaling until his lungs were completely full. With his eyelids relaxed into half-closed slits, Ike visualized in his mind that the incoming breath was filling and stretching each fiber of every muscle of his whole body, opening up his cells, and relaxing his DNA. He held a vivid mental image of individual DNA double-helix strands suspended in space. He envisioned them loosening, stretching, unwinding their spiral form, absorbing energy and light. All this took two or three seconds.

Then Ike exhaled again, slowly and completely. As he exhaled, he visualized himself relaxing even more. Again he saw individual spiraled DNA strands in the vast universe of his body relaxing, opening up, unwinding, illuminated with energy and light. They were golden.

The outside world disappeared for Ike. While he exhaled, a thought exploded within his silent place and took the form of a prayer for Mace.

It wasn't a typical prayer. It was a gentle prayer. It wasn't a prayer like a sledgehammer, the kind the TV preachers pray. It was a prayer like a feather. It didn't begin with a greeting to any deity. It contained no plea. It didn't attempt to strike any bargains. It didn't have a formal ending, and Ike didn't even say amen.

Ike's prayer was simply to visualize Mace standing in the courtroom confident, persuasive, and with a happy, satisfied, and victorious look on his face. Ike conjured up the experience in his own mind and body and allowed himself to feel the joy that Mace would feel after hearing a not-guilty verdict announced. And Ike imagined Diaeta free and reunited with her mother. Then he allowed a feeling of gratitude to wash over him. He smiled and, under his breath, he said, "Thank you."

All this took about three more seconds, and no one knew except for Ike. He didn't bow his head or assume any pious posture or mutter any audible words or do any other thing that would bring attention to himself. To the rest of the world, if anyone had been watching, he merely put his hand on Mace's shoulder, breathed in and then breathed out. Mace wasn't conscious that Ike was standing next to him or had touched him. Mace sat and stared blankly ahead, his heart beating faster and faster, his stare growing more distant.

But the instant Ike completed his exhale and removed his hand from Mace's shoulder, as if by instinct, Mace drew a deep breath as well. The air filled his chest and lungs and energized his brain with a fresh and much-needed supply of oxygenated blood. He was like a drowning man gasping for breath. The inhale was so deep and his lungs so full of air that his shoulders quivered and his head and ribcage shook in a little convulsion. The little quiver and shake came at the part of the breath where Mace had stopped inhaling, but he wasn't exhaling yet either, the "twilight of the breath," that powerful space between the inhale and the exhale.

"Come with me," Ike said firmly. He grabbed Mace by the coat collar and lifted him out of his chair. He pulled Mace, stumbling, past several people, through the double wooden doors, out of the courtroom, into the hallway, around the corner, then a few feet past the water fountain to a door. The door had a sign dimly painted on it that said "BROOM CLOSET." The whole trip from the counsel table to the broom closet took about ten seconds. Ike looked both ways. Then he jiggled the doorknob. It was locked. He jerked it up and then down with a quick motion of his wrist. The door popped open on the first try.

"It's all in the wrist," Ike said. Then he stepped inside. He pulled Mace behind him with one hand and closed the door shut with the other. The smoky glass panel rattled when the heavy old wooden door made contact with the frame. A second later, the doorknob made a clicking sound, and it was locked.

"It's locked," Ike said. Then he flipped on the light switch.

Under normal circumstances, Mace would have already been complaining, but this time he was speechless. It happened so fast. He couldn't quite comprehend yet that he had been pulled stumbling out of the courtroom and halfway down a courthouse hallway by the collar of his coat, that he had witnessed a breaking and entering, and, oddest of all, that no one had seemed to notice.

Later that night, after the dust and smoke of battle had settled and cleared, Mace would find himself relaxed into the familiar indentations in his couch, surrounded by the unmistakable odor of marijuana, reflecting on the odd events of the day and remembering how he teased Brick and made fun of him after Ike had done nearly the same thing to him at the hospital. Mace will chuckle. But when Brick asks, "What's so funny?" Mace will keep it to himself and just say, "Oh… nothing."

Chapter 9

OUT OF THE CLOSET

Mace glanced around the small, dim room behind the door labeled "BROOM CLOSET." It measured about ten by ten. There was a bookcase covering the entire back wall. It was half filled with rusty coffee cans, miscellaneous janitorial supplies, and a pile of dusty rags. Everything in the room was covered with cobwebs.

There were no windows in the little room. The only light came from one flickering bulb that dangled in a rusty fixture overhead. Against a wall were a couple push brooms and a big mop bucket on wheels with a metal contraption affixed to it that was once used for squeezing water out of wet mops. One sad-looking, old mop rested its head in the squeezing part of the apparatus. It hadn't seen water in at least a decade.

Across from the mop bucket, up against another wall, sat an old wooden teacher's desk and a wooden reporter's chair. Flung across the back of the old chair was a pink, white, and red Mexican blanket. Mace never noticed, but sitting on the desk was a monthly, tear-off calendar displaying the page for September 1986.

"What the..." Mace started but was interrupted.

"Shhhhh," Ike said, gripping his fingers and thumb gently on Mace's shoulder near his neck. "Sit in this chair, and listen to me. We only have five minutes, and you want to win this trial, don't you?"

Mace hesitantly did as he was told and showed his displeasure by feigning pain where Ike had grabbed his shoulder. Ike ignored him and picked up a metal pail from the corner, turned it upside down, and sat on it, facing Mace.

"Put your arms on the armrest."

With a sigh, Mace complied.

"Support your back against the back of the chair, and put your feet flat on the floor," Ike said.

Mace slid the soles of his shoes back and forth a couple of times on the dusty concrete.

"Take a breath."

Mace took a breath. Then he felt the odd sensation of his spine spontaneously lengthening. The feeling initiated from the soles of his feet and traveled up his inner thighs and through his psoas muscles, the two large muscles that connect the pelvis to the lumbar region of the spine. He instinctively stretched his vertebral column against the back of the chair in an upward direction. He could feel increased space between the vertebra and ligaments in his back. Blood rushed in, energizing and calming. It felt good.

"Inhale again," Ike said.

Mace inhaled, and blood rushed to his head. A thousand needles danced on his scalp. His eyeballs ached. Then they relaxed. It felt good.

"Exhale."

He did. And as he exhaled, his mind raced. He wondered what this strange and dusty little room was all about. How did Ike know about it? How did he unlock the door? Why did Ike drag him in here? What was going to happen next? What about the trial? His eyes opened and darted around the room.

"Close your eyes, and take another deep breath. Shut off the inner dialogue. Relax," Ike said calmly.

Mace did. The electric sensation of the dancing needles left his scalp. He relaxed. It felt good.

"Exhale slowly."

He did.

Ike spoke softly and rhythmically. "Now take another deep breath...and exhale tension."

Mace followed Ike's instruction, and when he exhaled, he felt noticeably lighter and could feel tension leaving his body.

"Breathe slowly...through your nose...and relax your shoulders," Ike said.

Mace breathed slowly through his nose and relaxed his shoulders. When he did, Ike noticed Mace's shoulders loosen from where they had been fixed up around the top of his neck, and both shoulders dropped two or three inches down his spine away from his ears. Ike smiled when he saw it. Mace smiled too. He knew he felt better, but he didn't know why.

"Take another deep breath…and when you exhale, take off the burdens of your life and lay them aside," Ike said.

The hypnotic sound of Ike's voice was comforting, and low, like a loving mother humming a lullaby to her baby. For an instant, Mace's mind took him back to a time when he had felt comforted, a time when he was a small boy, cradled in his mother's warm arms. More tension left his body. He relaxed. He smiled. It felt good.

Mace took another deep breath, and when he exhaled, he felt a physical sensation like the burdens of his life drifting away, like sand through his fingers, out of his body, into the limitless void. He sighed heavily with relief. It felt good.

He took another deep breath. Mace felt peace, a warm, comfortable, cozy peace. He was four years old again, wrapped in his favorite blanket—the brown one with the red and blue cowboys on it, still warm after his mother took it from the clothes dryer and put it around his chilly little arms. It felt good. He felt good.

But then Mace got an awareness in his conscious mind that he was feeling good and experiencing peace. He started waking up. He sensed the unfamiliarity of feeling good and being at peace. In a strange way, it frightened him. He liked the new peaceful feeling, but he already feared losing it. He wanted to hold onto it.

Then he remembered where he was, and fear pulled at him to come out of the peaceful place and return to the dark little room, and the trial, and Diaeta Pepsi, and Mrs. Chen, and Brick, and the car, and the bills, *and I wish I had my fucking briefcase.*

"Take another deep breath," Ike said.

On cue, Mace took another deep breath and allowed himself to relax back into the warm and secure world he had been in a second earlier. Fear disappeared.

"Another breath," Ike said, "and while you exhale… relax your neck. Let go of any resistance and tension. Let go of struggle. Let go of control. Be present in this moment."

Mace breathed slowly in and out, and as he did, he became more and more relaxed. He wished he could stay in that relaxed and peaceful place forever. It felt so good…sort of like smoking pot after a hard day. *I wish I had some pot,* he thought.

"Take another deep breath," Ike said, interrupting Mace's thought. "Breathe slowly in and out…and as you breathe…relax all your muscles…sending oxygen and blood coursing into them."

In his mind's eye, Mace saw his muscles relax and bright red blood flowing through them, energizing them. It felt good. He smiled again.

"Let go of the burdens of this trial...let go of the idea that you have to please anyone. Lay them aside."

The burdens of the trial...Ike's statement jolted Mace into remembering the trial again, and the strange little room, and the people in the hall, and Danford, and the judge, and Ike...and he frowned.

"Breathe slowly through your nose...relax and let go...let go of every thought. Thoughts and fears have no power over you." Ike's voice was calm and soothing.

Mace relaxed again. He breathed. He let go of his thoughts.

"Relax your facial muscles...and let go of any tension in your jaw."

Mace smiled. He relaxed his jaw. He breathed. He smiled again.

"Relax your eyes and your forehead. Take another deep breath, relax and quiet your mind." Ike paused a moment, then he continued. "It feels good to relax and quiet yourself...to be present in the moment... present in your body...and in your mind." He paused again. "You are ready to trust your intelligence and your instincts."

Mace drew another deep breath, exhaled, and smiled. He was at peace. At that instant, he had little present awareness or recollection of where he was or how he had gotten there. He breathed softly through his nose. His shoulders, face, and neck relaxed more. His eyelids quivered as tension melted away.

"You are ready to trust your intelligence and your feelings," Ike repeated. "You are ready."

Ike heard the sound of people talking in the hallway. A shadowy figure approached and leaned its body against the door. The glass panel creaked under the pressure of the shadow's weight. The door handle strained and made a metallic pop, but the door did not move. Laughter and muffled words oozed around and through the cracks above and below the doorframe, but Mace didn't notice. Mace continued breathing in and out and smiling.

"Exhale tension, and inhale energy," Ike said. "You relax…you let go…you smile."

Mace's body moved up and down slightly with each inhale and exhale, and he smiled again…a soft, gentle smile, like the smile of a Buddha statue.

The shadow in the hallway peeled its backside off the door, walked away, and disappeared like a cloud floating past the moon.

Ike continued encouraging Mace to relax, center, and locate his inner power.

"Exhale fear and limiting thoughts," Ike said. "Now inhale courage, confidence, and determination."

Mace felt a surge of courage, confidence, and determination fill his body and mind. A look of determination crossed his face. It felt good. He felt courageous and self-confident. He took another deep breath and exhaled through his nose.

Then Ike spoke to Mace in the first person.

"I exhale, and I let go of all my worries," he said. "Worrying has never changed anything. Worrying has never helped me."

Mace breathed through his nose and repeated in his mind what Ike said. *I exhale, and I let go of all my worries. They have never changed anything or helped me.*

Ike continued, "I inhale flexibility, trust, and freedom. I exhale rigidity, fear, and resistance."

Silently, Mace repeated the words. *I inhale flexibility, trust, and freedom. I exhale rigidity, fear, and resistance.*

"I am relaxed, open, and present to this moment."

Mace repeated the words in his head, *I am relaxed, open, and present to this moment.*

"I inhale," Ike said.

I inhale, Mace thought.

"I exhale," Ike said.

I exhale, Mace thought.

"I am ready," Ike said.

I am ready, Mace thought.

"Say it out loud," Ike said.

"I am ready," Mace answered.

"Say thank you," Ike said.

And Mace said, "Thank you."

Ike waited a few seconds and then told Mace to open his eyes. Mace opened his eyes.

"We only have a couple more minutes," Ike said, "so listen well. I'll answer your questions later."

"OK," Mace said. He was still in a semihypnotic state. His eyes were half closed. His eyelids made little slits, and he strained to peek through them.

"Remember that little piece of paper I gave you? When you get in a tight spot, go back to it."

Mace looked perplexed.

"It's in your back pocket."

"I know where it is, but I don't know what to do with it."

"You'll know when you need it."

"But what do I do till then?"

"Be present. Look at them. Not the squirrelly way Dan looked at them...not too long either. Don't stare. Just look at 'em, and imagine they are children."

"Children?"

"Inside, they're all like children. Some are frightened children, some are bullies, some are naive and clueless. But some are wonder children. You want the wonder children. Dan wants the scared bullies."

"OK," Mace answered, but Ike could tell he didn't understand.

"Evaluate their energy. Ask yourself if they are wonder children or scared bullies. Your gut will know."

"How can I tell if my gut knows?"

"One thing you can do is imagine they have wings."

"Wings?"

"Wings. Imagine their wings. What do they look like? Wonder children have happier wings than bullies. You'll be surprised how good you get at it if you practice."

"Right?" Mace said skeptically. "So, do you see wings on me?"

"Why do you think I saved your asses at the hospital?"

Mace thought about the wings a second, but such a thing was too far outside his paradigm, so he changed the subject. He wouldn't do that today. Maybe some other time.

"But what do I say?

"Say the same things you said and do the same things you did when you were figuring out who would buy your perfume and who wouldn't.

"Listen to them. And listen to your gut. Shut off your internal mental dialogue, that blah blah blah that's always going on in your head. Shut it off, and just listen to the jurors and follow your gut. Your gut will tell you what to say and do. That's being present.

"Ask questions, and ask whatever you want. If Danford objects, so what. If the judge sustains him, so what. Be ballsy. Act like you are selling that knockoff perfume door-to-door and in parking lots again. That took guts. That took balls."

"Yeah, we were rhinos."

"And have fun," Ike continued. "And smile. Don't forget to smile. It doesn't cost you anything, and it's worth a lot. A smile is lubrication for any social situation. It's like oil in your car. You wouldn't drive your car without oil in it, would you? Well, maybe you would—bad example—but don't forget to smile in there. It puts them at ease. It'll help relax you too. One smile relaxes your whole body from your skin all the way to your muscles and bones.

"And don't react personally to anything they say. Just smile. And remember, it's not about you. That way you won't get your feelings hurt if one of them comes back at you with anger or cynicism, and a few might. Some people are just that way."

"Yeah. I've noticed."

"And stay calm. Laugh at yourself. It gives you a great advantage if you can laugh at yourself. It keeps you from being tempted to play their game or match their energy or dance to their music. When you can laugh at yourself, you call the tune. You get to dance to your music, not theirs."

"OK," Mace said, trying to take it all in and remember.

"If any of the jurors come at you with a negative comment, let it bounce off and then ask, calmly and assertively, with an approving smile, 'Who else feels the way *Mr. So-and-so* feels?'"

"You're saying if somebody disses me, I ought to encourage the others to diss me too?" Mace asked. He was perplexed by Ike's statement. He had always been one to stand up for himself and not take any shit, like that John Wayne toilet paper.

"Yes. That's a good way to put it. Don't try to make any of them like your case. Just find one of them who says something that lets you know you don't want that person on your jury and then ask who else feels that way. Who agrees? Get them to raise their hands. Say 'Tell me more.' Then you'll find out who you don't want on your jury. It's great. What *they* say is a lot more important than what *you* say. The best question you can ask is 'Tell me more.'"

"Sounds a little hard," Mace said.

"It's not hard. It's easy. Most lawyers think it's hard, so they make it hard. All you have to do is get to know that jury panel." Ike paused a beat and then continued. "Most people don't know that caprice is a more powerful motivator than reason, most of the time. So don't try to reason with them at this point in the trial. Instead, just find out what they've got knee-jerk reactions about. The best question is always 'Tell me more.'"

"Caprice? What's that?" Mace asked.

"It's the inclination that a lot of folks have to do things on impulse, by knee-jerk reaction, without even thinking. Habitual responses are just part of human nature." Ike said.

"Oh."

"It would be caprice, impulse, if a juror voted to find Diaeta guilty. Caprice instead of reason. Because there is going to be reasonable doubt in this case."

Ike threw in the "reasonable doubt" prediction and kept talking, without looking for any response from Mace. Mace didn't consciously pick up on it, but subconsciously he accepted it, and the Universe began to conspire with Mace's mind to figure out a way to make it happen. Reasonable doubt. Not guilty.

"It's caprice to shell out fifty bucks to a punk in a parking lot for a bottle of cheap perfume that smells like WD-40. That's caprice, not reason. Get it?

"Most people are asleep. They operate from prior programing, habitual thinking, not from reason. They'll tell you it's reason, but it's not."

"Oh," Mace said. His face flushed a little from embarrassment. *He must have checked us out, or he wouldn't know what the perfume smelled like.*

"Some folks already have their subconscious minds made up that a defendant is guilty—just because he's been arrrested, he's already guilty—and you're not going to change their minds, no matter what you say or do. Those are the ones you want to get rid of."

"Yeah, but how do I find out if they already have their minds made up? Danford didn't do such a good job, did he?"

"Ask them," Ike said. It's that simple. It's on the paper in your back pocket. Ask, 'Who already thinks she's guilty?' And then say, 'Nothing I could ever do or say would change your mind, would it?' Make them feel that anything they say is OK and it's safe to say it, because it is.

"Make them raise their hands. I'll write their names down for you, and you can ask each one some follow-up questions. Don't take notes. I'll do that for you. Everyone will notice that you're staying calm and assertive and that you're enjoying what you're doing, and they'll fall in step with you. They won't be able to help it. You're right; Danford didn't do that. You'll establish yourself as the leader of the flock, their shepherd."

"Shepherd?" Mace asked.

"Let me put it this way. Ever hear of Cesar Milan?"

"No."

"Well, you will…quite a guy, a dog trainer. They call him a dog whisperer. Just stay calm and assertive. That's what Cesar Milan says to do with dogs. People are the same way. The group will come to see you as their pack leader.

"People need a leader the same as a pack of dogs do. They'll pick the one they trust the most to be their leader. And since I don't get to say anything, they're gonna pick you. They'll trust the one that's calm and assertive, the one who appears to know what he is doing, even if he doesn't. Remember Reagan? So trust your feelings, and act like you know what you're doing even if you don't. And smile."

"I'll try."

"Do or do not. There is no try," Ike said. He was quoting Yoda from *Star Wars*, but Mace didn't get the reference.

"OK, I'll do it. I'll trust my feelings. I'm ready," Mace said with newfound courage and conviction.

"And let the force be with you."

"I wish you hadn't said that. You had me till then," Mace said.

"Yeah, well, it's time to go."

Ike stood up, and Mace followed his lead. "Wipe the dust off your pants," Ike said.

Mace brushed the chalky dust from his butt, and they left the broom closet without anyone seeing them. Ike closed the door behind them, and a metallic click signaled it was locked again.

"Don't tell anyone about this room," Ike said. "Not anyone."

"Not even Brick?" Mace asked.

"Especially not Brick. This is my room, and I don't want anyone else finding out about it."

Chapter 10

MUSTARD SEED

When they rounded the corner, Brick was pacing back and forth in front of the courtroom door. "Where you guys been?" he asked nervously. "The judge sent me to find you. He's been waiting at least ten minutes—and he's pissed. The jury panel's already in there."

Ike opened the door. He and Mace entered the courtroom, followed closely by Brick. The room was freaky quiet. The judge stared at them over the top of his glasses. Ike motioned for Brick to take a seat in one of the chairs just inside the railing. Ike and Mace took their chairs at the counsel table. All eyes were on them.

"I'm glad you two finally decided to grace us with your presence," the judge said sarcastically. "Mr. Spinella, you may begin your voir dire."

Ike grabbed Mace's arm, leaned in close, and whispered in his ear, "Remember, when you don't know what to say, just take a deep breath, exhale completely, and smile. Something will come to you."

Mace was about to whisper something back to Ike, when the judge shouted, "If you girls are through chatting, the rest of us would like to get started!"

Mace was startled. "Thank you, Your Honor," was all he could think to say. A few of the panelists snickered. One attractive blond woman gave the judge a disgusted look. Ike took notice, quickly located her name on the seating chart, and put a star by it with his red pen.

Mace stood from his chair at the counsel table and stared blankly down at the file he had been studying for the past couple of days. His heart pounded in his chest. He glanced at Ike. Ike smiled back with a look of full confidence and trust. Mace looked at the judge. The judge frowned. Mace reached for his file, but Ike pulled it to his end of the table before Mace could grab it. Mace remembered what Ike had told him about not taking the file to the podium. "You don't need a crutch," Ike had said. "Just use the seating chart."

Mace walked to the podium. He felt naked. Every step felt like his feet weighed two hundred pounds. *This must be how it feels to walk to the gallows*, Mace thought. "Help me, God," he whispered.

That was only the second or third time Mace had prayed in his entire life, depending on how you count them. The only time he prayed before, sort of, was that time in the hospital chapel.

"Help me, God" wasn't much of a prayer by some people's standards, but it was a good prayer. It was concise, sincere, and it was heartfelt. This time, Mace's prayer was said to something bigger than Mace—something other than Mace. It was said to God, whatever that word means, because "God" is relative too.

God will never be more to you than you believe Him to be, nor will He ever be less. If you believe in a vengeful god, He is vengeful. If you believe in a loving god, He is loving.

Wars and much suffering would be avoided if everyone would make the choice to surrender the 'little bully' ego, and begin the process of growing into the realization that there is One Universal God, seen differently by every person, limited only by the exercise of our individual will, and by what we choose to believe or not believe.

God is relative to the volume of one's spiritual vessel, the level of one's consciousness and the openness of one's heart. One's perception of God is relative to one's faith and to one's ability to comprehend the Truth of God, which is unchanging...yesterday, today, and forever. It is man's capacity to comprehend and understand the Truth of God that changes, commensurate with the growth of one's consciousness.

The brief contact Mace made in the hospital chapel with something other than himself, the feeling he pushed back down and forgot about, had been stirring his subconscious. And even though Mace believed he had no belief, he had nonetheless planted a little seed of faith.

Having enough faith to say a prayer is some faith, even if you don't realize what you are doing. The little seed Mace planted was as small as a mustard seed, which is a very small seed, but it has the potential to grow into a tree, and it can happen fast—the faith of a mustard seed.

Some of the panelists smiled at Mace. Others stared ahead, showing no emotion at all. One old man sat with his arms crossed and looked angry. One young woman was reading the romance novel she had been reading all through Danford's voir dire.

Mace gripped the sides of the podium. Silence. It seemed to last forever. He had no idea what to say or how to begin. Danford had begun by introducing everybody, including Ike and Mace and even Diaeta. So if he started with that, he would only be repeating what Danford had already said. That wouldn't be good.

So Mace surrendered to the situation and to the flow that was beginning to stir within him. He closed his eyes, drew a deep breath, exhaled slowly, opened his eyes, smiled, and then reached for the folded piece of paper in his back pocket. He looked at it. BE BOP BYRD. It hadn't changed. That's all it said. BE BOP BYRD. Then Mace remembered the phrase "burden of proof."

"How many of you already think my client is guilty?" Mace asked, remembering Ike's suggestion. But nobody said anything; nobody raised a hand. Mace's eyes darted around the room from person to person. No one gave any response. Mace stood there, dumbfounded. He glanced at the paper again. Burden of proof.

Mace looked at Ike as if pleading for help. Ike smiled with a look that showed Mace he had all the trust and faith in the world in him, then Ike smiled at the jury panel and looked at a couple of them in particular, the attractive blond lady and the angry-looking old man. Ike's smile gave Mace a momentary sense of confidence. He took another deep breath and exhaled. *I exhale fear and insecurity, and I inhale confidence and courage.* Then, without realizing what he was doing, he smiled and said the first thing that came to his mind.

"Oh, come on," Mace said cajolingly. "You heard Mr. Danford say that my client, Diaeta Pepsi, was arrested for prostitution. How many of you heard him say that? Raise your hands." Mace raised his own hand as he said it, and everyone on the panel raised his or her hand, too, except for the young lady reading the romance novel, but when she saw everyone else raising hands, she raised hers. Ike made a note of it.

"And how many of you heard him say that a duly elected justice of the peace had filed the prostitution charges against her? Raise your hand," Mace said, raising his hand high in the air. They all raised their hands. Mace was on a roll. It felt good.

"And how many of you heard him say her name is Diaeta Pepsi?" They all raised their hands before he even asked them to. A few of them grinned. Mace rolled on. "And have any of you in your whole life ever heard of anybody named Diaeta Pepsi?" Mace shook his head no as he asked the question. No one responded. "I didn't think so," Mace said. "Sounds like a prostitute's name, doesn't it?" Mace shook his head up and down in agreement as he said it, and several of the panelists did the same. Ike made quick notes on the seating chart.

Danford jumped to his feet. "Objection, Your Honor!"

"What's your legal objection?" the judge asked.

"Well…it…it," Dan stammered a little, "…it… sounds like he's trying to convict his own client."

"Overruled," the judge said.

Mace's expression signaled that he had no clue what had just happened or what he should do next.

"That means I didn't agree with him, Mr. Spinella. In my courtroom, a lawyer can convict his own client all he wants to. So you just continue from where you left off," the judge said.

I won one, Mace thought triumphantly. He smiled. But his smile quickly vanished when his thoughts became, *Continue where you left off? Oh, crap! What was I talking about? Where was I? What was I saying? How can I be so stupid? Shit! Shit! Shi…*

His confidence left him as fast as it had come. He thought his memory had left him too. Then, about halfway through the third "Shit!" in what normally would have been a series of seven "shits," the memory of something Ike had said shot its way up from a submerged and stagnant crevice in Mace's brain and exploded into a thought.

Like a flower finds its full expression in the light of day, the memory of Ike's advice blossomed in Mace's awareness. *"When you don't know what to say, take a deep breath. Inhale…exhale…and say the first thing that comes to mind."* Or something like that. That was close enough. And that's what Mace did.

He inhaled completely. Then he exhaled the warm, spent breath from his nostrils. He looked up from the podium at the jury panel and smiled. He didn't realize it, but his prayer had been answered—again. Then he started to speak.

"Let's talk about the burden of proof in a criminal case. How many of you already think she's guilty? I mean, she was arrested, so she must be guilty of something, right?" Mace said, raising his own hand. About ten people raised their hands along with him. Ike hastily made notes.

"Objection, Your Honor!" Danford shouted, jumping to his feet.

"Move things along," the judge said. "But watch your step, Mr. Spinella, or you'll be starting this thing over again." He glanced down at his wristwatch, still hoping for an excuse to declare a mistrial and maybe make his tee time. But it was too late. "Carry on," he said.

"How many of you already think she is guilty? Raise your hands," Mace said, raising his own hand and bracing for Danford's objection. The same ten people raised their hands again.

Mace waited a beat, but Danford's objection did not come. Dan was thinking about that drink again. So Mace continued where he left off.

"Keep your hands up so that my…" he wanted to say 'my assistant' so badly, but he knew this was not the time nor the place to be razzing Ike. *That would be shooting myself in the foot for sure.* Mace wanted to win. He did not want to shoot himself in the foot this time.

Mace looked at Brick and saw a look of admiration on his face, something Mace had not seen in a long, long time. He looked at Diaeta. She was scribbling aimlessly on a piece of paper. He looked at Ike. Ike smiled reassuringly. Mace knew what he had to say.

"Keep your hands up...so my friend and co-counsel, Mr. Turner, can write down your names." Mace overcame his temptation.

They kept their hands up until Ike had made notations by their names on the seating chart. Then one by one they lowered their hands as Ike signaled to each one with a smile and a nod of his head that he had recorded their responses. Then Ike signaled to Mace it was time to continue.

Neither the pretty blonde, nor the old man with his arms crossed, nor the girl reading the romance novel had raised their hands. Either they didn't think she was guilty just because she had been arrested, or they didn't want to answer. Now it was Mace's time to say something again.

Like you are selling perfume, he repeated to himself, remembering Ike's advice. *Like selling perfume. If I was selling perfume, this would be the time to close the deal. Get them off the jury...that's what I need to do.*

From the corner of his eye, Mace saw Ike lean toward him and place the seating chart on the podium in front of him. The word *NO* was written in red ink on each square corresponding to the ten people who had raised their hands. Mace knew what to do. Close the deal.

"Mister," Mace drew out the word as he looked at the first name on the chart with the word *NO* written on it, "...Cummings...Mr. Cummings, what you are saying by raising your hand is that you have your mind made up already that Ms. Pepsi is guilty as charged. I'm right, aren't I?"

"Well...?" Mr. Cummings said, but the word had a question mark attached to the end of it.

Mace knew in his gut what that question mark meant. He knew what equivocation was. Mace may not have known what the word *equivocation* meant, but he certainly knew what it was. It was a deal killer. That's what it was, and he sensed equivocation in Mr. Cummings' voice. He was equivocating, and that meant he was going to talk himself into changing his mind if Mace didn't stop him from talking, and quick. If that happened with this first juror then it could set a bad pattern, start a chain reaction, and screw things up with the other nine. *Damn*, Mace thought, *I wish I'd started with someone easier. I should have started on the back row. Damn.*

But Mace was fast. He interrupted Mr. Cummings before he could utter another equivocal word.

"And you are in good company. I mean, nine other people here already agree with you. And I want you to know that I appreciate your honesty and candor and the honesty and candor of the other nine who raised their hands too. And Ms. Pepsi and the judge and Mr. Danford appreciate your honesty as well. It takes real guts to say something that other people might disagree with. But that is what makes our American system great. Isn't that right?" Mace was on a roll.

Ike was so proud. Mace made a good save. Not only had he assured Mr. Cummings that he was not alone, that he was a part of a group, but Mace made him feel like his opinion was OK and even approved of by the judge, the defendant, the prosecutor, the state of Texas, and the United States of America.

Mace continued. "And you look like the kind of man who would stick to his convictions. You are, aren't you, Mr. Cummings?"

"Well…" There was no question mark this time. "Yes, I am."

"And you strike me as the kind of strong individual that wouldn't let anybody force you to change your mind if you have a sincere belief and conviction about something. And that's the way you are, aren't you, Mr. Cummings?"

Mace was finding his rhythm. The knockoff perfume salesman in him was coming back. He was figuring out that the same techniques that worked for him when he was hawking junk perfume on the streets of LA also worked for him in a court of law.

Hot dog! Now I'm cooking with gas, he thought, a better use of the phrase than what Brick had done. Then he went in for the kill. "I couldn't change your mind, could I, Mr. Cummings?"

"No, sir, you couldn't."

"No matter how hard I tried."

"That's right."

"And the harder I tried, the stronger you would hold to your convictions and beliefs that Diaeta Pepsi is a prostitute, wouldn't you?"

"I'm afraid so."

"No reason to be afraid of expressing that belief, Mr. Cummings. I believe everyone here respects you for it. And since you just told me there's no way I can change your mind, I can't imagine that you'd let Mr. Danford get back up here and say anything that would change your mind either, would you, Mr. Cummings?"

Earlier, Ike had cautioned Mace that if he was close to getting a juror excused for cause, the judge was going to give Mr. Danford a shot at "rehabilitating" that juror, meaning bringing the juror back in line with questions like "But you could be fair, couldn't you? You could set your personal feelings aside, couldn't you? You could follow the judge's instructions, couldn't you? You could reach a verdict based just on the evidence, couldn't you?"

Mace went on before Cummings could answer. "You wouldn't let Mr. Danford change your beliefs, would you?"

"No, sir, I wouldn't."

"And you wouldn't even let the judge here change your mind, would you?"

"No, sir, I'm afraid I wouldn't. Uh, I mean, I wouldn't."

"No matter what evidence you hear in this courtroom, you already know in your heart that she's guilty, guilty, guilty, don't you?"

"Yes, sir, I do."

"And you couldn't set your belief aside…ever, could you?

"No, sir, I couldn't."

"Even if the judge told you it's the law that you are supposed to set your personal feelings aside, you wouldn't do that, would you?"

"No, sir, I wouldn't."

"Even if the judge told you that the government has the burden of proof here and Diaeta Pepsi doesn't have to prove anything, you'd still hold firm to your belief that she's guilty, guilty, guilty, wouldn't you?"

"I would."

"'Cause you believe in your heart she's really, really guilty."

"Yes, sir, I do."

Mace and Mr. Cummings had worked themselves to a climax.

Danford sat dumbfounded. He had never heard a voir dire like this one. He started to object a couple of times. He even stood up once and uttered part of the word *objection*. "Ob...j...j..." he said, but then he changed his mind and sat back down. It sounded to him like Mace was doing everything he could to convict his own client.

Dan thought Mace should be trying to turn the jury to his way of thinking, trying to convince them he had a defense to present and then get a commitment from them that they would keep an open mind until after all the evidence was heard. But Mace wasn't doing that. *This case may be easier than I thought. Fuck that stupid bet. I'm going to win.* Dan had no clue what was happening to him.

While Mace spoke, Ike took the notes they would use later while arguing with the judge over which of the potential jurors ought to be excused. When Mace thought he had done enough on Mr. Cummings, he glanced at Ike. Ike nodded, indicating he was satisfied, and Mace moved on to the next square with a "NO" written in it.

"Mrs. Sampson, you raised your hand a while ago when Mr. Cummings and several others raised their hands. You heard the questions I asked Mr. Cummings. I assume that when you have a belief or conviction about something, you hold that belief or conviction just as strongly as Mr. Cummings holds his beliefs and convictions. I am right about that, aren't I?"

"I would imagine," she said.

Mace looked in Ike's direction for a signal. He figured he had done enough on this one too. Ike wrinkled his brow and nodded toward Mrs. Sampson, signaling he needed to continue.

Mace took the cue, understanding he hadn't closed the deal yet. *OK*, he thought, *how do I get her from "I imagine" to "Yes, I think she's guilty?"*

"A while ago when I asked who already believed she was guilty, you raised your hand, didn't you?"

Actually, Mace had not asked the panel any such thing. He asked, "How many of you already *think* she is guilty?" There is a big difference between thinking something and actually believing it. If a man is pushing a wheelbarrow across a tightrope suspended between two tall buildings, you might *think* he can make it to the other side; you might even place a bet on it. But you don't really *believe* he can do it unless you are willing to climb into that wheelbarrow while he pushes *you* across. That's true belief.

But Danford hadn't been listening close enough. His mind was on that drink he wanted, so he didn't object. He just sat silent and let Mace bridge the gap with Mrs. Sampson between thinking something and believing it...and she didn't pick up on the difference between the two either; neither had Mr. Cummings. Most people wouldn't.

"Well, that's right. I did," she said.

Without knowing it, Mace had unwittingly taken advantage of another flaw in human nature—that most people will not change their opinions once they have expressed them, even if their opinions were formed with little or no facts or forethought.

People don't like to change their minds. It feels too much like admitting they were wrong. Like one of Brick's law professors said to him after Brick had jumped to a stupid conclusion during a class discussion, "It's easy to express an opinion, Mr. Hawthorne, when you are not burdened with a knowledge of the facts."

Once a person has expressed an opinion, even if it has no basis in fact, he or she tends to cling to it, like the jaws of a pit bull clamped to a pull rope. Try to get them off it, and all you do is make them mad. Unless you can get the person to think they connected all the dots and came to the conclusion alone, you are not going to get the person to change his or her mind. People are just that stubborn—generally.

Danford was about to learn that lesson when it was his turn to talk again. He would not be able to rehabilitate the jurors Mace had set up for disqualification because once they said out loud that they *believed* Diaeta was guilty, there was no turning them back.

Mace questioned Mrs. Sampson until Ike signaled he was satisfied.

The skills Mace learned during the years he was selling cheap crap to people who didn't want it and couldn't afford it were finally finding their purpose. His rhino attitude and training were making their transition into the courtroom. Never quit, never give up, never take no for an answer.

By the time Mace finished voir dire, seven of the ten people who raised their hands were legally disqualified. Not even the judge could disagree, and Danford wasn't able to dissuade them. But three of the ten were still on the panel.

Sometimes it just works out that way. Some people don't know what they believe. They equivocate. They agree with the last person who speaks. They are outliers from the norm. But people like that are usually followers. They go with the flow, go along to get along, bend like a reed in the wind. But that can present a problem for the defense attorney since the prosecutor always gets to speak last. Should a criminal defense lawyer use his valuable preemptory strikes to get rid of them or take a chance and leave them on the jury? Thankfully for Mace, he had Ike to help him make those decisions.

Dan's unsuccessful and bumbling attempt to rehabilitate the seven and get them to change their minds got him nowhere. The judge finally put a stop to it and recessed the panel for fifteen minutes so he could go to his private bathroom for a smoke. The lawyers went to their respective corners and decided who to strike.

The judge didn't give a damn whether the lawyers had time to make it to the men's room or not. *Let them pee their pants.* All he cared about was getting this miserable defendant a quick guilty verdict so he could beat the traffic home. He had already missed his tee time at the Austin Country Club and a free golf game courtesy of a Clark, Thomas & Winters lawyer who had a civil case going to trial in his courtroom next month. *Maybe another time...fucking Ike Turner. I hate that liberal, commie bastard...and his little doggie too.* He was referring to Mace.

Dan Danford sat scratching his head, mulling over the list and trying to remember who hadn't smiled at him so he could strike them. Mace, Brick, and Ike huddled on the opposite side of the courtroom.

"I definitely think we should strike the old man, the one who kept his arms crossed," Mace said.

"Why's that?" Ike asked.

"'Cause he kept his arms crossed."

"What else?"

"Uh, he looked grumpy."

"I look grumpy, too, but I'd vote not guilty."

"That's what they taught us in law school," Brick said. "And our old boss told us that too. Rhonda Ramsey was the best salesman ever. She told us when somebody crosses their arms while you're talking to them, they're not listening, they're shutting you out. Move on to someone else 'cause they're not going to buy."

"That's good advice," Ike said, "but this guy didn't cross his arms while you were talking to him. His arms were already crossed. They were crossed while Danford was talking to him too. Did you notice the way he walks?"

"No," Brick answered.

"No," Mace said. "What's walking got to do with it?"

"He's got back trouble. He's in pain. It hurts him just to sit there. That's why he keeps his arms crossed," Ike said.

"So why don't we just let him go? Put him out of his misery," Mace said.

"'Cause I think he's on your side. His eyes twinkled some when you were talking. He thinks you're funny. He rolled his eyes a few times when Danford was talking. Thought he was wasting time, especially all that 'can you be a fair and impartial juror' bullshit. Over and over again. So boring, made me want to scream. Him too. He hated Dan's snotty 'voir dire is a French word' bullshit too. And even though he's in pain, his wings were happy. We're keeping him. And he'll appreciate you for trying this case quick and getting him out of here today."

"But…"

"No butts. *Derriere*. It's a French word. We're keeping him."

"Wings?" Brick asked.

"Later," Ike said.

"OK, then," Mace said, "but if we lose, it'll be your fault now. I don't like him. I'm not taking responsibility." Mace's little bully was acting out again, trying to take control.

"So what's new? Just pretend you like him. He's going to be on your jury, and you don't want him sensing you don't like him."

"OK, then, but I'm not taking responsibility," Mace said.

"I know you're not taking responsibility, unless we win—and then you'll take all of it."

"Will not."

"Will too," Ike said.

"How do you know he's gonna be on the jury? How do you know Danford won't strike him?" Brick asked.

"Because his pain makes him look all mean and conservative. Makes him look like a grumpy law-and-order type. Danford's not going to use a strike on him. Besides, he's on the second row. Dan'll run out of strikes before he gets that far on the list, even if he wanted to strike him. Danford's going to strike the music teacher on the front row first, and then he's going to strike the Methodist preacher."

"Awah, I like the music teacher," Brick said. "Why's he going to strike the music teacher?"

"For the same reasons you like her. She's intelligent. She's open-minded. She's a music teacher—right-brain stuff. And she didn't smile at his bullshit. She's not going to be on the jury. Trust me."

"There he goes with that 'trust me' stuff again," Mace said.

"Then who do we strike first?" Brick asked. "I know, I know. It's the girl with the romance novel. She wasn't paying attention to anything."

"No. Not her either. She'll go along with the majority, however they vote. Remember when she didn't raise her hand until she saw everyone else doing it?"

"What about the pretty blonde then? We've got to have some scenery," Mace said. "I'm not striking her."

"You're right. We're not. And neither is Danford. She'll be on the jury."

"How do you know that?" Brick asked.

"Danford won't strike her for the same reason Mace won't."

"Why's that?"

"'Cause she's pretty, and because we don't know much about her. Danford wants some scenery too."

"So why are you willing to take a chance with her, if we don't know anything about her?" Mace asked.

"She showed her colors when the judge jumped on me and you and called us 'you girls.' She got mad at him. She's been rooting for us ever since...and you're right...she's pretty."

It only took a few minutes for Ike to convince the boys to strike the three jurors Mace hadn't been able to get rid of for legal cause, the ones who expressed doubt about holding the state to its burden of proof, B-O-P, guilty beyond a reasonable doubt.

The bailiff walked to their table and picked up the list. Then he picked up Danford's and took both lists behind the door to the judge's chamber.

In his chambers, the judge compared the two lists. There were no double strikes. Neither the prosecution nor defense had used a strike on the same person. Unbeknownst to the panelists milling around in the hallway outside the big double doors, the process was over. The six people who would soon be sitting in the jury box holding the fate of Diaeta Pepsi in their hands had been determined.

Chapter 11

STEMS AND SEEDS

After jury selection, the next phase of a criminal trial is opening statements—one from the prosecution and then one from the defense. After opening statements, the prosecution calls its first witness. Then the defense lawyer cross-examines that witness. Then the prosecution calls their next witness. Then cross-examination. And on it goes until the prosecution rests its case. After that the defense gets to call witnesses, if they have any, and the prosecutor gets to cross-examine them. This is called the evidentiary phase. Sometimes the evidentiary phase lasts for an hour or less. Sometimes it can drag on ridiculously for months, like the OJ Simpson trial that was still playing out in another state.

It was August 1995. Diaeta Pepsi would have a verdict before they would finish with even one witness in the OJ Simpson trial in Los Angeles. The OJ Simpson trial had been going on since November 1994. The trial was expected to go a few more months. It was billed as "the trial of the century"—not likely, but it's a catchy title.

Ike loved talking about the OJ Simpson trial. He told everyone who would listen, "If I were the prosecutor, I'd have gotten a guilty verdict in two weeks. When I was a young lawyer working for DA Vic Feazell in Waco, he wouldn't of let Marcia Clark try traffic tickets in our office. She could fuck up an anvil. Mark my word, she's going to let that guilty bastard go free."

Marcia Clark was the lead prosecutor in the OJ Simpson trial in Los Angeles. Vic Feazell had been the district attorney in Waco, ninety miles up IH-35 from Austin. DA Vic Feazell gave Ike his first job out of Baylor Law School. Ike made his first enemy there too, an assistant DA named Snappy Reese. Ike moved to Austin and went in with Goldstein after Vic Feazell left the DA's office and Snappy Reese got appointed to take his place.

A couple months after Diaeta Pepsi's verdict, Marcia Clark would prove Ike's prediction correct. OJ would go free. When asked about it, Ike would shake his head and say, "Marcia, Marcia, Marcia," a reference to a character in an old TV show called *The Brady Bunch.*

The judge finished his cigarette break and told the bailiff to "bring 'em all back in." Everyone obeyed the stand-up-sit-down, genuflect routine they had all become accustomed to. The judge read off the names of the six chosen jurors who would decide Diaeta's fate, and they took their seats in the jury box. The judge began reading aloud the rest of the general jury instructions the same way he had done hundreds of times before.

Ike grabbed Brick by the lapel and pulled him up from his chair. "Come on, you're going with me," he whispered.

"Going where?"

"Time for court."

"This is court."

"Your court."

"What do you mean?" Brick asked.

"Yeah, what do you mean?" Mace asked.

"Brick has a court appearance too. Remember? Stems and seeds."

"You can't leave. I don't know what's coming next," Mace said.

"Opening statement. It's a snap."

"But…"

"No butts. Derriere. Remember? It's a French word like voir dire. Just tell 'em what's in your back pocket."

With that, Ike gave a little jerk to Brick's jacket, and they were both out of the courtroom before Mace could catch his composure. The judge kept reading and didn't notice.

The other courtroom was around a corner. Ike and Brick walked at a fast pace down the hallway. Ike threw open the big wooden door and stepped inside. Brick followed. The plaid-shirted man from Scholz's was already there, along with Mr. Wilfred Johnson and his dreadlocks.

"Hey, Tripper," Ike said.

"Hey, Ike.

"You guys ready to get started?"

Tripper and Johnson nodded yes. Johnson looked nervous. Tripper looked even more nervous.

"OK, Wilfred, you sit up here at the counsel table with Brick. I'll be sitting behind you with Mr. Tripper."

"But," Brick said.

Ike interrupted him. "No butts. Derriere, Pierre. Just say your line, and do your stunt."

"What?"

"Stems and seeds. That's all you say besides 'we're ready, Your Honor.' And say it in that order, stems and seeds, not seeds and stems. Got it?"

"But…"

Ike interrupted, "Don't make me say that French word again."

Brick started to respond, but just as he was getting his first word out, the door to the courtroom flew open and a woman stepped in. She was the hottest, most beautiful woman Brick had ever seen. To Brick, her energy filled the room like angel light. She didn't hesitate. She didn't look around. She sashayed straight to the prosecutor's table without a glance to either side. Brick's jaw dropped and his eyes popped.

When she got to the table, the edge of it met her hip creases. She leaned into the table and stretched over it in an exaggerated way with her arms outstretched in front of her. Then she laid a thick file folder on the far side of the table. The movement caused her skirt to stretch and hike up a little, accenting the shape of her sculptured butt, which was squeezed like a ripe sausage into the tight khaki business suit she was wearing.

As she stood back up, she let her perfectly manicured fingernails drag lightly and gracefully across the file folder and then across the top of the table. The graceful bow of her slender arm had the look of art, sacred geometry, and Brick's heart pounded at the sight of her.

Brick admired her bright, sexy pink nail polish. His breath got fast and shallow. His stare fixated on her butt. Then she sat down, as if she knew she was depriving him of the pleasure of gawking.

She crossed her perfectly shaped legs, dislodged one of her cream-colored high-heel pumps, and bounced it dangling precariously on the tip of her toe. She was oblivious to everyone else's presence. Brick was speechless. Ike, Tripper, and Wilfred Johnson watched in silence and reverence.

It seemed like a long time had passed, but it was only a few extremely entertaining, sensual, slow-motion seconds. Einstein was right. Like everything else, time is relative. It depends on what you are doing.

Brick whispered to Ike, "You can't say 'no butts' about that."

"Beware the kitten's claws," Ike said.

"What?"

"Sit down," Ike said, nodding toward the other counsel table.

"Hi, Candice. It's a pleasure seeing your lovely face again," Ike said.

"Hello, Mr. Turner." Her tone was cold and businesslike. She glanced in the direction of Brick, Tripper, and Wilfred Johnson, but didn't say anything. She didn't even nod in recognition of their presence. She continued bouncing her shoe on her toe.

"Candy, Candy, don't be so cold. Have I done anything to offend you yet today?"

"Not yet, *Ike*." She punctuated the word *Ike* with a snarly emphasis. She didn't like Ike calling her *Candy*. "But it's still early," she added.

"Candy, Candy, Candy," Ike said.

"It's Ms. Kennedy to you, sir. I'm an officer of the court."

"Yes, ma'am," Ike said, and saluted her.

She didn't like that either.

The bailiff entered the room and said, "All rise," and everybody did. The judge walked in wearing the expected black judicial robe, but blue jeans and desert boots were visible below the bottom hem. The judge sat down, and the bailiff said, "You may be seated." Everybody did.

The judge bore a striking resemblance to David Carradine, the former star of the 1970s television series *Kung Fu*. He even had the shaggy haircut and the same "I'm all used up" facial expression. He looked so much like Carradine that some of his friends, including Ike, called him Kung Fu when he wasn't sitting on the bench.

Judge Davis didn't mind the reference. He had been an avid fan of the *Kung Fu* television series, and he liked Carradine as an actor even though Carradine's career was on the skids recently, mostly because of drugs and alcohol.

As of late, Carradine only appeared in low-budget, independent films like the one presently being shot in Austin, called *Monster Hunter*, about a deranged FBI agent on the trail of a psycho killer known only as "The Postman" because he'd leave a postage stamp affixed to the foreheads of his victims. Carradine played the deranged FBI agent. He could have played the deranged psycho killer postman too. He was often typecast as a deranged something.

Carradine's half brother, Michael Bowen, was playing the role of the deranged psycho killer this time. Years later, Michael Bowen would become famous playing the deranged psycho bad guy, Uncle Jack, in the popular TV series *Breaking Bad.*

For the past few days, Judge Davis had been thinking about leaving early so he could go out to the movie location and try to get Carradine's autograph and maybe even get a picture taken with him. Neither Carradine nor Judge Davis had any idea that in a few years David Carradine's movie career would skyrocket thanks to his starring role as the title character Bill, in Quinton Tarantino's movies *Kill Bill* and *Kill Bill II,* also starring the lovely and kick-ass Uma Thurman.

In years to come, Judge Davis's nickname would gradually change from "Kung Fu" to "Bill" as the popularity of the two *Bill* movies and the Bill character grew. But after Carradine's untimely and embarrassing death, both nicknames would cease to be used.

"Is the state ready?" the judge asked. His voice and mannerisms were mellow, a sharp contrast from the court Ike and Brick had just left, the court Mace was still in.

"The state is ready, Your Honor," Candice Kennedy said, snapping to attention and flashing the judge a Vaseline-shiny smile.

"Is the defense ready?" the judge asked, looking at Brick.

"Er, uh, yes, we're ready, I guess, Your Honor, sir," Brick said.

Candice smirked and gave Brick a glance of utter contempt. Brick smiled. Candice's lip curled like Billy Idol's. Brick was thrilled she looked at him. Her display of contempt didn't register on Brick at all. He was too turned on. His brain was in his pants. He was behaving the way he didn't like for Mace to behave.

"Ms. Kennedy, you may proceed."

"Thank you, Your Honor. Mr. Wilfred Jack Johnson is charged…"

"Joonson," Wilfred Johnson interrupted, but no one paid him any mind.

Ms. Kennedy continued, "…with felony possession of a controlled substance with intent to deliver, to whit, marijuana. I believe from discussions with Mr. Johnson's prior attorney…"

"Joonson," he interrupted again.

"OK, Mr. *Joonson*, point taken. Now hold it down," the judge said, but not in a demeaning or angry manner. He was mellow, and he pronounced *Joonson* with a Jamaican accent almost as good as Mr. Johnson's.

"I believe from discussions with *his* prior attorney," she continued, "that *he* is prepared to plead

265

guilty to this offense. Furthermore, Your Honor, *he* is a resident alien of the United States and is therefore subject to deportation upon conviction of this offense. The state would request that *he* be held without bail and be remanded to the custody of Immigration and Naturalization pending deportation proceedings."

She said it with all the vinegar and stiffness she could muster and without saying Johnson's name again.

"Is that right, Mr. Joonson?" Judge Davis asked. "Are you ready to plead guilty to this offense like the prosecutor said?"

"No, Your Honor, I'm not," Johnson answered.

"But Ms. Kennedy said she worked out a plea with your prior attorney?"

"That is right, Your Honor. That is why he is my *prior* attorney." He emphasized the word *prior*.

"I see. So, Mr. Hawthorne, are you his *present* attorney?" the judge asked.

"Uh, yes, sir."

Candice smirked at Brick again. It was a well-rehearsed look of contempt. This time, Brick didn't notice. He was too nervous.

"Why shouldn't he plead guilty, Mr. Hawthorne? Are you smarter than Mr. Joonson's prior attorney?" Judge Davis said, while smiling at Ike.

Brick looked confused. He didn't know what to say. He glanced at Ike for help. Ike gave Brick a stern stare and nodded, first toward him and then toward the judge, urging him on.

Then it came to him. "What are stems and seeds, Your Honor?" Brick said it like he was answering a *Jeopardy* question just as the buzzer was going off.

"What did you say?" the judge asked. His eyebrow arched.

"Stems and seeds, Judge. That's all I've got. Stems and seeds."

"Stems and seeds, huh?"

"Yes, sir, stems and seeds." Brick looked nervously back at Ike.

"What do you have to say about that, Ms. Kennedy?" the judge asked.

Ms. Kennedy was taken aback. "What do you mean, Your Honor?"

"Well, stems and seeds, Ms. Kennedy."

Her stare was blank. Her mind searched for a meaning to the judge's perplexing question.

"How much was the total weight of this marijuana that Mr. Joonson was arrested with?"

"Let me see, Your Honor." She searched her file. "Four point two ounces, Your Honor."

"Four point two ounces? You know that anything under four ounces is a misdemeanor, don't you?" Judge Davis asked.

"Well, yes, sir, but…"

"Actually, anything a hair less than four ounces, even stephen, is a misdemeanor, isn't it, Ms. Kennedy?" His tone seemed to have taken on a condemning quality.

"I think so, Your Honor."

"Bet you've never seen one of those before, have you? Four ounces, even stephen. Never seen a lab report like that before, have you, Ms. Kennedy?" He didn't wait for an answer. "Four ounces, even stephen? You'd think that somewhere out there someone has been arrested with exactly four ounces, don't you think? But in all my years on the bench, and as a prosecutor before that, I've never seen a lab report that says four ounces exactly. Have you, Ms. Kennedy?"

"Well, uh, er, no. I don't think so. Not exactly, Your Honor."

Brick snickered. Candice's "Well, uh, er, no," made him laugh, but he tried to choke it back.

The judge shot Brick a steely look. "You may be smart, but that's no excuse for disrespect toward opposing counsel." The judge's tone was admonishing.

Brick's chest immediately swelled, and his face flushed red with excitement. The judge had called him smart, and in front of Candice. He was so proud. Then Judge Davis turned his attention back to Ms. Kennedy.

"Did the lab separate out the stems and seeds before they weighed it?"

"I...I don't know, Your Honor. I doubt it."

"Then how do you know it's a felony amount, four ounces or more, if you didn't take out the stems and seeds?"

"But..."

"The law is clear, in my opinion. The weight of the substance has to be of a usable quantity. Nobody smokes stems or seeds, so that part shouldn't be counted as a usable quantity, should it, Ms. Kennedy? Get my point?"

"But," she said.

"You don't smoke the stems and seeds, do you, Ms. Kennedy?"

"No, Your Honor, but…"

"Get my point?"

"For the record, Your Honor, I don't smoke marijuana at all. I never have."

"Duly noted," he said, making a gesture like he was writing it down.

"Thank you, Your Honor."

"Mr. Joonson, the government says that you had four point two ounces of marijuana…a felony. How much of that four point two ounces do you think, in your opinion, was stems and seeds? Would it have been over two-tenths of an ounce?"

"Oh, more than that, Your Honor. It was not the best weed I have seen. Plenty of stems and seeds. Big stems. Lots of seeds."

"Your Honor, I object," Ms. Kennedy interrupted, "he's no expert. He doesn't know how much of an ounce of marijuana is stems and seeds."

"Been smoking long, Mr. Joonson?" the judge asked.

"Since I was a wee child at my mother's knee, Your Honor."

"You know the difference between Austin hydro, Jamaican, Acapulco Gold, and Mexican dirt weed?"

"I most certainly do, Your Honor."

"Have you manicured marijuana before? Cleaned it?"

"Oh yes, Your Honor. For years and years, almost daily, for my dear mother."

The line of questioning was making Brick nervous. He didn't know where the judge was going. He didn't like hearing his client confessing to crimes. He glanced back at Ike, who seemed to be enjoying the show. *This can't be right*, he thought. He squirmed in his seat. "I object," Brick finally said.

"Overruled. I find the defendant to be qualified as an expert on this subject, and the court adopts his opinion that there was more than two-tenths of an ounce of stems and seeds in that four point two ounces of weed."

"But, intent to deliver, Your Honor. If he's found guilty of less than four ounces, it's not a felony, and the presumption of intent to deliver goes out the window."

"You think I don't know that, Ms. Kennedy? You think maybe the state overcharging here could be part of my concern?"

"But…"

"Pipe down, Ms. Kennedy."

"Mr. Joonson, were you going to sell any of that weed?"

"Oh no, sir, Your Honor. Not very good weed. That barely be a couple months' supply for me."

Judge Davis addressed Mr. Tripper, who was taking it all in wide-eyed. "Are you Mr. Tripper?" he asked.

"Yes, sir, Your…Your…Your Honor."

"I see your commercials all the time. And I see from the file that you posted bond for the defendant. Does he work for you?"

"Ye...ye...yes, sir." Tripper squeezed out the words as best he could.

"Do you want him back? Do you plan to keep him on?"

"Ye...ye...yes, sir. He's one...one of my b...b...best."

"How much back time do you have, Mr. Joonson?"

`"In jail, Your Honor, forty-seven days."

"Forty-seven days? Why so long before you got bonded out?"

"That's another reason he is my former attorney, Your Honor."

"OK, then. Mr. Hawthorne," Judge Davis continued, "will your client plead guilty to a misdemeanor, less than four?"

Brick looked at Ike. Ike nodded yes, but before Brick could respond, Mr. Johnson said, "Yes, I will, Your Honor."

"Then it is the finding of this court that you are guilty of the class A misdemeanor offense of possession of marijuana under four ounces and that you are sentenced to your back time, plus a thousand-dollar fine. You can afford that, can't you, Mr. Joonson?"

"Objection, Your Honor. This is a travesty," Ms. Kennedy screeched.

"Overruled."

"I object too," Brick shouted. "My client has a job. He is eligible for probation. We demand a presentence investigation for probation."

"You won, Mr. Hawthorne. It's time to shut up," Judge Davis said.

"But…"

"You want to be on probation, Mr. Joonson?"

"No, sir, Your Honor. I can't pee in no cup."

"Court adjourned then." The judge got up and walked out.

"All rise," the bailiff said. But it was too late. The judge was already out the door and on his way to get that autograph he had been wanting.

Candice Kennedy fumed. She stood with her arms crossed tight against her heaving breasts and patted her foot angrily up and down on the floor. It made a loud clicking sound. Her nostrils flared. Her eyes tightened.

She wasn't accustomed to losing. She had not become one of Travis County's youngest female prosecutors by losing. And she knew the judge was wrong on the law, but it was his call, his discretion. There was nothing she could do. She was helpless, and she hated that feeling.

Wilfred Johnson patted Brick on the back several times. "Way to go, tiger," he said. Tripper shook Ike's hand and smiled. The mood was festive.

Candice exploded. "How dare you celebrate! I hope you are all pleased with yourselves, setting this dope-smoking, drug-pushing criminal free, back on our streets, corrupting our children, ruining our country, destroying our neighborhoods." Her eyes were flames. She glared at Brick and then at Ike, pointing a shaky finger at one and then the other. "I hope you're happy."

It looked like she was going to say something else, but she stopped herself, grabbed her file, and headed for the door. Her shoes clicked fast and rhythmically on the marble floor. All four men stared at her rounded khaki ass as it swayed to the beat. They couldn't help themselves.

"We're happy. OK. But don't get upset, Candice. I'm just doing my job," Brick called after her.

Without turning around, she flung her right hand over her left shoulder, shot him the finger, and yelled, "Fuck you, you little asshole!"

Brick's eyes widened in surprise. Ike, Tripper, and Johnson laughed out loud.

"Let's get out of here before she calls Immigration and makes something up. She's a vindictive little…person," Ike said. "Mace might need our help by now."

"Did you hear him?" Brick asked. "He said I was smart. Did you hear him say that?" Brick was caught up in the victory, the excitement…and Candice. He did a little happy dance. He wasn't thinking about Mace right then.

"I'll explain that later," Ike said. "Come on, *you little asshole.* You want to walk with me this time, or do I drag you by the collar?"

"I'll walk," Brick said, but he was thinking something else. *Explain what? He said I was smart. Nothing to explain? I'm smart.*

273

Chapter 12

ALL SHE HAD

Tripper and Johnson followed Ike and Brick to the courtroom Mace was still in. They wanted to see more courtroom excitement. When they slipped into their seats in the gallery, Danford was taking his seat after delivering his ho-hum opening statement. He told them again what "the state" intended to prove, that Diaeta was a prostitute.

"Does the defense wish to give an opening statement?" the judge asked, looking at Mace.

Mace didn't know what he was going to say, but he knew he needed to say something.

"Well?" the judge asked.

"Yes, Your Honor, I believe I will."

"You have fifteen minutes."

Mace rose from his chair and walked to the jury box. His heart pounded, but he had more resolve and more confidence than earlier when he was doing voir dire. Experience is a good teacher. He glanced at Brick and Ike. Then he noticed Tripper grinning from ear to ear and the dreadlocked Jamaican sitting next to him looking all goggle-eyed and attentive. "Go get 'em," Johnson whispered under his breath just loud enough for Tripper, Ike, and Brick to hear.

Mace noticed a rickety old easel with a flip pad on it leaning against the wall next to the judge's bench. He walked over and pulled it to the center of the room in front of the jury box. It clattered and shook as he pulled it.

On the court reporter's table was a coffee cup stuffed full of pens, pencils, and Magic Markers. "May I borrow one of these?" Mace asked the court reporter. She nodded, communicating her consent, without saying a word or removing her hands from the stenograph machine.

Mace selected a black Magic Marker. Then he pulled the folded paper from his back pocket and wrote the three words on the flip pad, all in capital letters: BE BOP BYRD, one underneath the other. He looked curiously at the words and then he looked curiously at the jury.

He took a deep breath and began. "Mr. Danford told you what they have to prove. And I agree with him. They have to prove it, every bit of it. We don't have to prove anything. That's what these words are about," he said, pointing to the chart. His voice was calm. His pace was slow, and his tone was low.

"B-E," he continued. "They have to *bring* you the *evidence.* Not speculation, not maybe, but real evidence. Not what some policeman thinks she might have done, but real evidence. That's the law. Why? Because they have the B-O-P—*burden of proof.* Why?

Because this is America. We have a constitution. And that's what the Constitution says. That's what sets us apart from dictatorships and lawless countries where people can be dragged in off the streets and put in jail on suspicion. But people in America are presumed innocent. That's the law, unless the government brings the evidence, B-E, because they have the B-O-P, burden of proof.

"We don't have any requirement on us to prove anything. We don't have to prove she's innocent. They have to prove she is guilty. We don't have to B-E, bring any evidence. We can just keep quiet if we want to and see if they can B-E to reach their B-O-P." Mace emphasized each letter, pointing at the flip chart.

"And what is their burden? It's B-Y-R-D, *beyond a reasonable doubt.* So it's not enough for them to bring evidence, B-E, that she *might* have done it. They have to bring evidence that she *did* do it, *beyond a reasonable doubt.* And you are reasonable people. You told me during jury selection that you are. And all I am asking you to do is be good Americans and abide by our Constitution and make the government bring evidence beyond a reasonable doubt."

That was all Mace could think of. He glanced at Ike. Ike smiled approvingly. Mace started to sit down, but then he had a thought, something he had learned at one of the Carver-Washington Gospel School of Law's required preaching classes. Make a rhyme.

"Bring," he said. "It rhymes with spring. And unless you are willing to spring forth and find her guilty when they are finished, then you have a reasonable doubt."

Danford was squirming, wanting to object and mess up Mace's flow, but he couldn't think of one until then. He jumped to his feet. "Objection!"

"Sustained," the judge said.

"Whatever," Mace said. Then he told the jury thank you, and he sat down.

The blond lady juror giggled. She already liked Mace and disliked the judge. It was lucky for Mace the judge didn't hear him. But the court reporter did, and one of her eyebrows arched up as she typed it.

Brick was amazed by Mace's performance. Ike was pleased. Tripper and Johnson enjoyed the show. Ike whispered to Brick, "Short and to the point. I liked it."

Johnson whispered to Tripper, "This is better than TV, boss."

The judge said to Danford, "Call your first witness."

Danford said, "The state calls Detective Martin Kelinski."

Detective Kelinski took the stand. He was a handsome young man, early thirtysomething, full head of brown hair, a chiseled face like a movie star, and he was trim and fit. He wore plain clothes, not a uniform, and was dressed in designer jeans, a nice dress shirt, and cowboy boots.

Under questioning from Dan Danford, Detective Kelinski recounted the events surrounding the arrest of Diaeta Pepsi. He was working vice that day and had been assigned to the antiprostitution squad. He signed out a vehicle from the police garage, a red Ford pickup truck, an F-150. He was cruising an area just west of the University of Texas campus near Guadalupe Street. He had not made any arrests yet that day. He saw a suspicious-looking woman standing on the corner. He pulled his truck over to the curb and rolled down the window. The woman, now known as Diaeta Pepsi, approached the window and asked him if he wanted a date. *Date* is street language for a hookup with a prostitute.

Detective Kelinski testified that he said, "Sure, how much?" to which Diaeta Pepsi responded, "Forty bucks." Detective Kelinski testified that he said, "OK, get in." Diaeta Pepsi got in. He drove down the block and around the corner to where other policemen were waiting, and they arrested her. When she heard she was under arrest, she began screaming. No money ever exchanged hands. That was the extent of it.

"Pass the witness," Dan Danford said, all cocky and self-satisfied.

He was pleased with how the testimony had unfolded. Kelinski was a good witness. No way that crazy son-of-a-bitch Ike Turner would win that stupid bet now.

It was Mace's turn. He recalled what Ike had told him about cross-examination. *"Get to the point, and only ask leading questions. 'Leading the witness' is not a valid objection to cross-examination. You're supposed to lead on cross."*

Mace began by asking the questions Ike had fed him about Diaeta never being fingerprinted or booked or arrested for anything—ever—not prostitution, not anything. He did a pretty good job reciting the questions

278

from memory, and Kelinski did a pretty good job of answering just as Ike had predicted.

Now what? We didn't talk about anything else. What do I ask next? Mace waited for his next thought.

"Ask a question, or pass the witness," the judge said.

"Uh…no money ever exchanged hands, did it?" Mace asked.

"No."

"And sex was never mentioned, was it?"

"No," Kelinski answered, but then he continued, "but I knew what she was talking about."

Mace was stumped. He wasn't expecting the nonresponsive answer. *What do I do now?*

"But no money ever exchanged hands, did it?" Mace asked again.

"Objection," Danford shouted. "Asked and answered."

"Sustained," the judge said. "Move along, Mr. Spinella."

Mace looked at his notes.

"Move along, I said, or pass the witness."

Mace looked at his notes again, but still no thought came. So he decided to follow Ike's advice. *Why not?*

He took a deep breath, exhaled, and got ready to say the first thing that came into his head. His body relaxed, a thought was born, and it sped down the pathway from his brain to his mouth.

"A while ago, you said you knew what she was talking about when she asked you if you wanted a date, correct?" Mace asked.

"Yes, I did say that. I know what she was talking about." Kelinski smiled at the jury.

"You're telling the jury you were able to read what was in her mind?"

"Well, no, but I knew what she was talking about."

"So you're telling the jury you could read her thoughts?

"No, not exactly."

"You admit you are not a mind reader, correct?"

"No, I'm not a mind reader." The tone of Kelinski's response had a scornful connotation to it.

"You admit you don't know what she was thinking?"

"Correct. I didn't know *exactly* what she was thinking."

"I thought you said you were not a mind reader?"

"I'm not."

"Then you didn't know what she was thinking *at all*, did you?"

Mace was in the zone. He felt it. The questions were coming to him easily, without effort. For Mace to be in the place he was now, it required that he give up his ego, his need to control things, and experience a sense of surrender to something bigger than himself, that something he had experienced when his little prayers had been answered.

For right now, for this moment, Mace was able to do that. Like Simon Peter, he was walking on water as long as he could resist looking at his own feet, looking to his own power.

Kelinski looked at Danford for help. He didn't know where the questioning was going. He didn't want to mess things up by saying the wrong thing. Danford shrugged his shoulders. He didn't know where it was going either. The old man in pain and the blond lady noticed Kelinski was looking to Dan for help.

"I guess not," Kelinski answered.

"You guess not," Mace repeated. "For all you know, she might have thought that *you* were a prostitute?"

"I doubt that," the detective answered. He nervously looked toward Danford again. Danford ignored his glance this time.

"There are male prostitutes working in Austin, aren't there?"

"Well…yes."

"But you didn't care about busting male prostitutes, did you? You were just looking to bust some women?"

Danford objected. The judge sustained his objection. The blond lady on the jury looked at Ike and signaled her displeasure with what she interpreted as the policeman's sexist attitude.

Mace was not daunted. He was inspired. He didn't know where all the ideas were coming from, but he liked the magical feeling of watching it all happen. He had caught a glimpse of the unicorn, but didn't know it.

Mace continued, "Well, you've never arrested a male prostitute, have you?" Mace was just guessing, shooting in the dark. But it paid off.

"No, not me personally, no."

"But you admit there are male prostitutes in this town?"

"Yes, but…"

"You answered my question." Mace cut him off before he could get out the rest of his nonresponsive answer. A nonresponsive answer is when the witness answers a question that has not been asked. Ike had warned Mace that cops are good at that.

"You pulled over to the curb, didn't you?" Mace asked.

"Yes," Kelinski answered.

Not only was Mace still asking leading questions, but he was breaking the questions down to one element at a time. That's good lawyering.

"She didn't flag you down, did she?"

"No."

"If she had, you would have put that in your report, wouldn't you?"

"That's right."

Mace knew it wasn't in the report. He had read the report. Several times. And he knew the question he asked was not for the information it would elicit, but for repeating and buttressing the fact that Kelinski pulled over to the curb and Diaeta had not flagged him down.

"It wasn't in your report because she didn't flag you down?"

"That's correct."

"But it was in your report that you just pulled over to the curb?"

"Yes."

"She didn't ask you to?"

"No."

"And you rolled down your window?"

"Yes."

"She didn't make you?"

"No."

"She didn't ask you to?"

"No."

"So you saw her, you pulled to the curb, you rolled your window down, and all this time, she hadn't done anything yet?"

Mace had taken the elements of his previous questions and combined them into a summary question. It was effective. The man in pain nodded his head up and down. The blond lady scribbled notes.

Danford needed that drink now. Within one hour, he had gone from *"I'd like to have a drink"* to *"I need a drink."*

"That's what my report says."

"I bet you smiled at her too?"

"I don't remember."

"You're a good-looking man, wouldn't you agree?" Mace continued.

"I wouldn't know about that."

The whole room knew Kelinski's answer was disingenuous. He carried himself like a man who knows he's good-looking. You could tell by the way he used his walk he was a woman's man...no time to talk. He embodied the Bee Gees' lyric from *Staying Alive* almost as well as John Travolta did.

"So you're an ugly guy that women are not attracted to, is that what you're saying?" Mace asked.

"I wouldn't say that either."

"So, women *are* attracted to you?"

Kelinski looked at Danford. Danford objected. "Irrelevant."

"What's the relevancy here, Mr. Spinella?" the judge asked.

Mace glanced toward Ike for direction. Ike nodded and winked, encouraging him to unload on them.

He did.

"Your Honor, my client was arrested for prostitution by this man, who admits that no money ever exchanged hands and sex was never mentioned. He admits that he approached her first. He admits he is not a mind reader. And he's a good-looking man who admits that male prostitution is a problem in Austin, Texas, just like in that eighties' movie, *American Gigolo*, starring Richard Gere, screenplay by Paul Schrader."

A couple of the jurors snickered out loud. Ike made a notation of who they were.

"How is this jury to know that my client didn't think it was him that was the prostitute unless I can question him about it? That's what beyond a reasonable doubt is all about. B-Y-R-D."

The judge reluctantly overruled Danford's objection and added, "I will give you some leeway, Mr. Spinella, but wrap it up."

Mace was emboldened by the judge's ruling and went right back to where he had left off.

"So, women *are* attracted to you?"

"I don't know," was his answer.

The blond lady rolled her eyes. She knew he was lying. She knew his type. She knew that he knew he was hot. He was the very sort of good-looking man she, herself, would be attracted to, but had learned not to be, because he was the kind of jerk who never calls you back after he gets what he wants. Her psychological transference was working in Mace's favor.

Mace pushed on. "You don't have any trouble finding a date for the weekend, do you?"

Kelinski was getting frustrated. "I guess not. I don't know," he answered. "Usually not."

"You would never ask anyone out on a date who looks like that, would you?" Mace asked, pointing at Diaeta. Kelinski looked at Diaeta. Involuntarily, his lip curled up a little under his nose. Diaeta looked at him and smiled.

For the first time, Mace noticed that Diaeta's teeth were white and perfect.

"No, I wouldn't," Kelinski answered.

"And you wouldn't pay forty dollars for her, either, would you?"

"That's besides the point."

"Well, look at her. That's exactly the point," Mace retorted. He knew he didn't have to press for an answer. The damage was done. By now, some of the jurors were probably thinking Diaeta had been thinking Kelinski was the prostitute. Mace hoped so anyway.

Kelinski stammered.

"I pass the witness," Mace said.

Kelinski breathed a sigh of relief and started to stand up and leave the witness box, but then the judge asked, "Any follow-up questions, Mr. Danford?" Kelinski sat back down.

Danford looked at his notes. He tried to think of a question. Kelinski was good-looking. He couldn't counter that. Diaeta was homely, downright ugly. He couldn't counter that. There are a few male prostitutes, escorts, in Austin. He couldn't counter that either. The judge sat patiently while Danford thumbed through the pages on his yellow legal pad without asking a question. After a while, the judge said, "Mr. Danford, either ask a question, or I'll excuse the witness."

"She asked you for a date, didn't she?" Danford finally asked, but before he finished the last word, Ike leaned over the rail and poked Mace hard with his writing pen.

Mace jumped up and said, "Objection!" He didn't know what he was objecting to, but he knew that's what Ike wanted him to do. He got the point.

"Sustained," the judge said. "Don't lead the witness, Mr. Danford."

"What did she say to you?" Danford continued.

"She said, 'Do you want a date?'"

"Then what happened?"

"I said, 'How much?'"

"And what'd she say?"

"She said, 'Forty dollars.'"

Danford was satisfied. He looked smugly at the jury and passed the witness back to Mace. "No more questions. Pass the witness," Danford said.

Mace snapped out his first question before the echo of Danford passing the witness had subsided. He was energized. It was all falling into place for him. He remembered a document Ike had pointed to in the file back at the office saying in a nonchalant way, "Well, would you look at that." Mace had looked, but hadn't realized the significance yet.

"You asked how much?" Mace said.

"Yes, I did. And she said forty dollars."

"And since you're not a mind reader, forty dollars might have been how much she was willing to *pay you?*"

"Pay me?"

"Yes, what she was willing to pay you for a little warmth and human companionship."

"I don't think so. Certainly not."

Mace walked to the court reporter's table, where the official court file on Diaeta Pepsi was lying. He looked quickly through the file. He didn't see what he was looking for. He looked again. It wasn't there.

He glanced at his feet, so to speak. He got afraid. He felt panic coming. His chest tightened, and his head got lighter. But this time, instead of a panic attack, he took a deep breath. He exhaled, relaxed, and looked again. There it was. He removed it from the file and walked to the witness stand.

"Detective Kelinski, you booked Diaeta Pepsi into the jail after you arrested her, didn't you?" Ike was so proud that Mace was still asking leading questions.

"Yes. I did."

"And when someone is booked, a booking card is filled out, isn't it?"

"Yes."

Mace handed the booking card to the witness. "This is the booking card for Diaeta Pepsi, isn't it?"

"Yes, it is."

"And this is your handwriting, isn't it?"

"Yes."

"And this is an itemized list of her personal property, in your handwriting, that was taken from her when she was booked into jail, isn't that right?"

"Yes."

He was inspired. He had no idea where the questions were coming from. But he was loving it. He was going with the flow and was conscious that all he needed to do was continue doing just that. The magic was happening. He was riding the unicorn. *Go with the flow. Don't take control.* He could hear himself thinking at the same time he listened to himself talk, *"Just say your lines, and do your stunt."*

Mace stood right up against the witness box and stuck the booking card under Kelinski's face. He turned and looked at the jury without glancing at Kelinski while he asked his next question. Mace didn't want to miss the jury's reaction to the answer. Mace knew that how they responded emotionally to the next answer or two could determine the outcome of the case.

"How much money did Diaeta Pepsi have on her when she was arrested and booked into jail?"

It took only a second or two for Kelinski to locate the figure, focus on it, and transfer the data from his eyes to his brain, but it seemed like five minutes to him. He swallowed hard. His throat creaked when he answered.

"Forty dollars," he said.

Two of the jurors immediately snapped to the significance, the blond lady and, oddly enough, the young woman who had been reading the romance novel during jury selection. Their eyebrows shot up, and they both had aha expressions, like they had just solved the puzzle: *Diaeta thought Kelinski was a prostitute, and she offered him all the money she had.* That's what they thought, and somehow Mace knew it, like he knew the man in pain was processing the information too. His wheels were spinning, and Mace knew when they stopped, the man in pain would believe it too, or at least give Diaeta the benefit of the doubt. That was enough for Mace. He knew he was on the right track. He had never felt so confident and yet so vulnerable at the same time.

Kelinski quickly added, "It was probably money she got from her previous trick."

Mace was quick. "You don't have any evidence of that, do you?" Mace pointed to the flip chart still leaning against the wall. The jury's gaze followed his finger, and they looked at it too. "You don't have any E. Evidence," Mace continued. "You can't B-E, bring evidence. Even though you know you have the B-O-P, burden of proof. And it's B-Y-R-D, beyond a reasonable…"

"Mr. Spinella, do you have a question in there? Final argument isn't until later," the judge admonished.

"Yes, sir, I do," Mace responded. "You don't have any evidence of that baseless allegation, do you, Detective Kelinski?"

He hesitated. "Well, no."

"And you already said you are not a mind reader, right?"

Kelinski shook his head in agreement.

"So you're guessing?"

Kelinski just sat there.

"Like you guessed her into jail for the past six weeks waiting for this trial?"

"Objection," Danford shouted.

But before the judge could say anything, Mace said, "I pass the witness."

Danford wanted to ask more questions, but he didn't want to give Mace another crack at this witness. Besides, he figured he could make up for it when Diaeta got on the stand. He had to. The memory of the bet got heavier by the moment.

"Do you have any further questions?" the judge asked.

Danford thought for a second longer and answered, "No, Your Honor."

"You may step down."

"May I be excused?" Kelinski asked the judge.

"Yes, you may."

Kelinski climbed out of the witness stand and quickly left the room without a glance toward Danford or the jury. He knew he had been screwed.

Chapter 13

CAN YOU IMAGINE THAT?

Ike's Mercedes turned right off Fifteenth Street onto Hartford Lane, a beautiful, tree lined street rowed with stately and well-maintained old mansions. The street was once in the new-rich neighborhood out on the edge of town. Now it was the old-rich neighborhood just minutes from the bustling business center of downtown Austin and a block from Loop 1, a freeway that connects Barton Creek Mall in the south with the Arboretum shopping area in the north. Brick was driving. Ike didn't want to take a chance the judge might see them leaving with anyone driving other than Brick.

"Turn in here," Ike said.

Brick maneuvered the car onto a gated driveway. It was blocked by an elaborate ironwork privacy gate. On the other side of the gate, a circular drive led up to the house and then around to an exit gate. The entry gate was at the north end of the property and the exit gate at the south end. A long brick-walled fence ran along the front of the property line, connecting the two gates.

A huge, white, three-story Southern mansion filled most of the oversized lot. It had white colonial-style columns, each so big that two grown men couldn't reach around them and touch fingertips. The scene was reminiscent of something out of *Gone With the Wind.*

Brick's dad and new wife lived in a fancy house, but it was nothing like this.

"Push the button," Ike said, pointing to a speaker box on a pole.

Brick rolled down the car window on the old Mercedes. It was nothing like their old Ford. The electric motor hummed softly, and the window came down with a purr. Ike's car might have been old, but it was perfectly maintained. Brick pushed the button on the speaker box. A few seconds later, someone answered.

"Yes, may I help you?" an inquisitive voice in the box asked with the genteel drawl of a Southern lady.

Ike leaned over Brick and answered, "It's Ike. I'm here with Geneva."

"Oh, thank God," she said excitedly. "Thank God."

The gates parted. Brick drove through and followed the circular driveway up to the house. He parked by the front steps. A woman in her late forties or early fifties, in a flowery summer dress, ran out of the front door, both hands waving in the air. She waited on the porch for the car to come to a stop.

"Oh, Geneva. Oh, Geneva, darling."

Ike got out of the car and stopped her at the bottom step. "She's still Diaeta," he said.

The woman's face dropped. Brick watched from the car. Mace watched from the back seat with Diaeta.

Diaeta looked at her lap and didn't say anything.

Ike and the woman helped Diaeta from the car and walked her into the house.

"Alfred!" the woman yelled at a man trimming the hedges along the front fence. "Get her to her room. Give her some of her pills, and fix her something to eat."

Ike walked with the woman to the front door and talked with her there. Brick and Mace watched but couldn't hear what they were saying.

They could see some of the furniture in the house through the open door. It looked expensive, oiled wood, fancy lamps, overstuffed chairs, and a huge crystal chandelier.

Outside, on the far end of the house, was a swimming pool cabana. The reflection of the sun on the water glistened and danced on the cabana wall.

"Can you believe this shit?" Mace said. "Pro bono, my ass."

Ike reached out to shake hands with the woman. She gave him a hug instead and kissed him on the cheek. Ike pointed toward Mace. She smiled and waved at him, then blew him a kiss. Ike got back in the car and said, "Let's go."

Brick followed the driveway to the exit gate. As they approached, the gate opened gracefully like a pair of giant butterfly wings. Then the Mercedes was back on Hartford Lane headed for the office. No one said anything for a few minutes.

After a couple blocks, Mace blurted out, "Pro bono, my ass."

"You ought to be thanking me," Ike said. "You learned a lot, didn't you? If you'd known she was rich, you'd have been more nervous than you were. You mighta asked her to marry you."

"Eww!" Brick said.

"How'd you know I'd win?" Mace asked.

"I didn't. I told you even if you lost, we'd win. Remember?"

"Sort of. Maybe. Not really."

"Sure, you do. If we'd lost, I'd have had her doctors over there tonight getting her moved to a private psychiatric hospital. She's been in one before. But her mom wanted to keep this under wraps. They're an old Austin family. Pride, ya know.

"Geneva was a cute little thing when she was a kid, a debutante, junior cotillion, all that crap. Smart as a whip. But a little disturbed, especially after her mom had her locked up that year for skipping school. I almost didn't recognize her."

"Cute little thing? You mean she wasn't fat and pimply?" Mace said.

"Shut up, Mace. That's not nice," Brick said.

"No, she wasn't. And didn't talk like that either. Was actually kind of pretty 'til ninth or tenth grade… about the time mama sent her to the psych hospital. I disagreed with that decision, but nobody asked me."

"So she wasn't guilty, for real?" Mace asked.

"'Course not. Mental problems. Some drugs too. Mom tries to handle it at home now with medication. That's why the gates, and Alfred. Sometimes she gets out. This was her first arrest though. Never been finger-printed before. That was lucky.

"When her mom asked me to find her, it took a while. She'd never used the name Diaeta Pepsi before. And like I said, I didn't recognize her at first. She's changed a lot."

"When you found her in jail, why didn't you just go get her out?"

"I was going to, but her mom didn't want a prostitution arrest on her record. Like I said, family pride. Old money here. Didn't want her real name found out. And you can't bond someone out who doesn't have an ID or an address. So I decided to just try it under the name she was using, Diaeta Pepsi. They didn't know who she was, and she did an excellent job sticking with her delusion and not breaking character."

"I'll say," Brick said.

"But you fucking lied to me," Mace said. "There's no way you could have known I'd win."

Mace had slipped back into his old behavior patterns and old ways of thinking. He had dismounted the unicorn. The magic was gone, and the spell that comes after, dissipated.

"But you learned a lot, didn't you? You should be thanking me, *you goddamn greenhorn, wet behind da ears, honky lawya.*" Ike was doing the best Diaeta imitation he could. Brick snickered.

"Shut up," Mace said.

"You shut up," Brick said.

"Damn, I was good in there, wasn't I?" Mace said.

"What difference does it make?" Ike said. "You're not accepting any responsibility, remember?"

"Yeah, well, I think I will now, now that I won."

They were silent for a few blocks except for the occasional snicker from Brick and then Ike.

They were almost back to the office when Ike said, "I forgot something. Turn the car around. Get on MoPac, and head north. I gotta cash this check before the bank closes." He held Danford's check between his thumbs and forefingers and popped it the same way Brick had popped the fifty-dollar bill at Brackenridge.

"But you told him you'd wait a couple weeks," Mace said. "I heard you. I was there."

"I did? Hum? I don't remember it that way," Ike said.

Brick and Mace made eye contact in the rearview mirror but didn't say anything.

When they got back to the intersection with Hartford Lane, the Mercedes turned off Windsor Street, veered onto a curved ramp, and merged with the other traffic going north on MoPac.

MoPac, as the locals call it, is an in-city four-lane freeway that runs north and south along the west side of central Austin, almost parallel to IH-35. It's called MoPac because it was built along the right-of-way of the Missouri Pacific Railroad. The tracks actually occupy the highway median between West Eighth Street and Northland Drive. At night, the headlights of an approaching train look like they're coming right at you. The official name of the freeway is Loop 1, and most of the signs say Loop 1, but locals insist on calling it MoPac, which can create confusion for visitors asking directions.

They took the exit at Northland Drive, turned left, and in a couple minutes were in the parking lot of the bank.

"Don't use the drive-through," Ike said. "I want to go inside. I know the manager. She'll process this for me right now and make the call tonight. Wait here."

After a few minutes, Ike was back in the car still holding the check in his hand. He showed it to Brick and Mace. It was stamped in red ink: "Insufficient Funds."

"Damn thing bounced," Ike said. "Can you imagine that? Let's go to the office."

The Mercedes pulled into the parking lot at 1800 Guadalupe. Brick turned the engine off. No one said a word on the ride back. Brick and Mace were both thinking about Mace's bet with Ike. The way Ike was handling Danford's bet, and the check, and the bank, gave them a sense of impending doom. Brick was hoping Mace wouldn't shoot himself in the foot again.

"Let's go in and talk," Ike said.

Brick and Mace had never been in Ike's private office before. It was on the second floor. It was big. It was furnished with antiques and bronze sculptures and overstuffed leather chairs and couches. His desk was huge and cluttered. In the middle of the clutter was a little sign that read: "A Cluttered Desk is the Mark of Genius."

One wall was windows. Two walls were decorated with framed original paintings by AD Greer and Pal

Fried. The last wall was filled with framed photos of Ike with different presidents and senators and other politicians, each one individually inscribed and autographed. There were two from Texas Attorney General Jim Mattox, two from Governor Anne Richards, one from President Bill Clinton, one from Agriculture Commissioner Jim Hightower, one from Julian Bond, and many others. Each was personalized in its own way: "*Ike, Keep up the good fight. To Ike, I'm glad you're on our side. Keep doing the Lord's work. To my friend Ike Turner.*"

Also proudly displayed was a framed letter from former Louisiana Governor Edwin Edwards that said, "*To Ike Turner, the only man I know who distrusts the government as much as I do.*" Governor Edwards was presently serving a life sentence in federal prison on charges Ike thought were probably trumped up.

Brick and Mace looked around Ike's office with envious admiration. They took mental note of every photo and object. They thought Ike's office was cool. Each of them coveted it for himself.

There were a couple photos of Ike with Willie Nelson and there was a photo of Albert Einstein inscribed, "*To Ike—Thanks for all the great ideas. Albert –1947.* The handwriting on the Einstein photo looked suspiciously like Ike's.

"Good job today, boys," Ike said.

"I was good, wasn't I?" Mace said.

Brick chimed in, "The judge said I was smart."

"About that," Ike said.

"About what?" Brick said defensively. "He said I was smart."

"But you need to know the rest of the story."

"Rest of the story? Don't ruin it for me. What?"

"Here's the rest of the story. Kung Fu Davis and I were in law school together. Same study group. We called him Kung Fu even then because he looks so much like David Carradine. He made good grades. All the time. Smarter than me even. Our senior year, he wrote an article for the *Baylor Law Review* and called it "Stems and Seeds." It was basically about what he was saying today. It made sense. I thought it was good. I helped him edit it. The *Law Review* committee refused to publish it. Said it was good, but too controversial for Baylor. 'It may be right, but it's too controversial,' they said. Pissed him off.

They tried to get him to write another article, but he refused. Then the legislature changed the law a few years later and closed that little loophole. But Kung Fu never got over it and he still thinks that should be the law. So, you had an inside advantage today. It wasn't just your brilliant argument."

"You had to take it away from me," Brick said.

Ike perceived Brick needed a little approval from a male authority figure right then, something he never got from his dad.

"You are smart," Ike said. "You had to know how to take advantage of your advantage, and you did."

"Oh, get a room," Mace said. "You guys make me sick."

"Got something on your mind?" Ike said.

"Yeah, you lied to me. You pushed me into that crazy trial with that crazy woman, and you lied to me."

299

"About what?"

"Pro bono."

"Is that all? So what? You get paid the same, either way."

"Then pay me."

"I don't owe you anything," Ike said. "You owe me five hundred. You lost the bet."

Brick gasped. Mace almost gasped.

"I didn't lose the bet. You can't B-E, bring evidence, that I lost the bet," Mace said.

"I'm not going to pay you any more money on this. We had a deal. But I will give you that briefcase I promised you." Ike reached under his desk and pulled out a briefcase. "Here, take this one."

Mace's eyes got wide. Brick's eyes got wide. Brick's jaw dropped open...again.

It was Mace's briefcase. The one with the past-due bills and the marijuana cigarettes in it. The one that wasn't where it was supposed to be next to the mirror that Brick installed by the door so it wouldn't miss him whenever he walked by.

"Holy fucking shit," Mace said. "Fuck, fuck, fuck, fuck, fuck, fuck, fuck. You've got my fucking briefcase."

"Marvin," Ike yelled, "how many times did Mace say 'fuck' just now?"

Marvin stepped into Ike's office from the hall where he had been standing and listening.

"Seven, Mr. Ike. Seven times in a row, like he always does. Seven 'fucks' in a row."

"Seven 'fucks' in a row. Like he always does," Ike said. "Thank you, Marvin."

"Yes, sir, seven times. Seven 'fucks' in a row."

"Rather compulsive? Wouldn't you say? Compulsive, compulsive, compulsive, compulsive, compulsive, compulsive…wait for it—compulsive." Ike said, grinning at Mace.

"Yes, sir, I'd say. Compulsive," Marvin said.

"And Brick?" Ike asked. "That's what he did last night when he realized his briefcase wasn't where it was supposed to be. He said 'fuck' seven compulsive times. Isn't that right?"

Brick looked down.

"I take your downward glance as confirmation that Mace lost the bet last night."

Neither Mace nor Brick said anything. Brick looked at his shoes. The jig was up. They looked like dogs caught in the act of digging through the kitchen trash can. Guilty.

Ike leaned back in his overstuffed chair, put his hands behind his head, propped his feet on the desk, and crossed his legs at the ankle. "Be sure your sins will find you out," Ike said, using his preacher voice.

Mace felt a surge of embarrassment because he was caught, but he couldn't admit to himself he felt embarrassed because that would be the same as admitting he had done something wrong. So he stayed in denial, got mad instead, and took it out on everyone around him.

"I don't need this shit," Mace said. "You lied to me. You fucking lied to me." His pace got faster, his volume got louder, and his face got redder. "And you lied to Brick. You made him think you were all psychic and everything. But all you did was ransack my briefcase.

That's how you knew we were past due on our bills and we smoke pot. You used what you found in that briefcase against us. You manipulated us."

Mace turned and glared at Marvin. "And you. I can't believe you. After all I've done for you. You're just a little snitch. A snitch. And you know what snitches get, don't you?"

"Britches?" Ike said, interrupting.

"No, they get…"

Ike interrupted him again, "Ditches? Riches?"

"No."

"Bitches?" Ike said.

"No, damn it!"

"I know, witches?" Brick chimed in.

"No, damn it! They get…"

"Sandwiches?" Brick said. "I could use a sandwich." Brick was enjoying the momentary levity—and he was hungry too.

"No, they get stitches, damn it! Stitches!" Mace had worked himself into a frenzy. "Snitches get stitches!"

Marvin's eyes were big, and he was turning white again. Mace's bully always scared Marvin. He already had a sore neck thanks to Mace and Brick. Stitches were one of the last things he wanted, but Mace looked mad enough to give him a few.

"Oh, stitches," Ike said. "Now I get it."

"You're just a con man," Mace said. "You don't know shit."

"But our couch," Brick said, "he knew about our couch…and my mom. I told you you'd get caught."

"Shut up," Mace said. He grabbed the briefcase off the desk and opened it. The past-due bills were there, but the pot was gone. "How'd you get it?"

"You left it in the emergency room the night the cops were chasing Pretty Boy here. I saw it when I left. You didn't want them to find it, did you?" Ike was still reared back in his chair with his boots propped on the desk, grinning like he thought the whole exchange was funny.

"Where's my pot?"

"Ate it."

"I'm out of here. Come on, Brick."

"Give me a minute," Brick said.

"I'll wait by the car. If you're more than five, I start walking."

Mace stormed out and slammed the door hard behind him.

Kay's voice came from down the hall, "Watch it, asshole." Then came a belated metallic "Fuck you. Eat shit."

Brick, Ike, and Marvin sat in silence for a few beats. Brick was stunned. His victory celebration was stolen. His hope for paying the bills, gone. His hope for regular income, vanished. His trust in Ike, shaken.

"What now?" Brick asked.

"That's up to you," Ike said.

"I have to stick with him."

"I know."

Brick looked at the floor.

Ike reached into his pocket and pulled out a wad of cash. He counted out five hundred dollars. "This is for you. My bet was with Mace, not you. You did a good job today."

"I can't accept this."

"You don't have a choice."

"Let me talk to him."

"OK. But I'm meeting with the clients tonight, the man and woman on the explosion case. If he's not there, you're not in on the case."

"Let me take him home. I'll come back and meet with you and the clients. We can work this out."

"The woman doesn't want to meet with you. She made that clear when I mentioned your name."

"But why? What did I do? What's her name?"

"Jill. Jill Junior."

"She's a junior?"

"Her last name is Junior. From Waco."

"Never heard of her. Never been to Waco. What did she say I did?"

"She didn't. I didn't ask. She seemed adamant."

"Please let me come. I promise, I've never met this woman. She must have me confused with somebody else."

"She was pretty clear about it. Said your name, Brick Hawthorne. How many Brick Hawthornes are there?"

"Must be more than one because I'd remember a woman named Junior. Please let me come. Mace gets like this. He'll come around. I want to help on the case. I've already read most of the paperwork."

"No."

"Please. Please. Please."

"Well, that's a real compelling argument," Ike said wearily. "How can I say no to that? But if you get in there and she says a word about it, you leave. Got it?"

"I will. I promise."

"Drive Mace home. Get your ass straight back here. No dillydallying. Our meeting starts in fifteen minutes. With traffic, you'll be an hour late."

Ike tossed his car key to Marvin. "Take the Mercedes. Go to Scholz's. Jill and Carl are probably already there. You remember what they look like from last night, right?"

Marvin nodded.

"Tell the guy behind the bar you're there to pick up Ike's church-meeting special. He'll know what you're talking about. I'll get Kay to call it in. Tell Jill and Carl we've been in court all day. Ask them to follow you back here. We'll meet in the kitchen. Don't mention Brick."

"Will do, boss," Marvin said. He was happy the scene with Mace was over, and he was happy to be of help.

Chapter 14

CARL JUNIOR

The old clunker rattled into the parking lot at Casa Grande. It was noisier than usual, like metal hitting on metal. Mrs. Chen stuck her head out of her upstairs apartment to see what all the racket was about. It was only Brick and Mace, so she closed the door. It was too hot to come out and gawk. Her nosiness would have to wait for a cooler day.

"I can't believe you're going back to that asshole," Mace said.

"And I can't believe you lost it like you did. You're always pulling this shit, Mace. I'm tired of it. I don't know how much more I can take. Seriously."

"'I don't know how much more I can take. Seriously,'" Mace said, mocking Brick. "What's that lying son of a bitch got that you'd risk our friendship for?"

"Where do I start? Duh? Like a real case to work on. Like rent. Like groceries. Gas. Weed. I can't believe you. Tuna. Get out. I'm already late."

"I may not be here when you get back," Mace said.

"So be it. Where you going to go? I'm calling your bluff."

"Ro-sham-bo?" Mace said.

"Not this time. This is too important, and you're too wrong."

"But it's the rule."

"No."

"Fine then," Mace said. He got out and slammed the car door, but he didn't move. He stayed where he stood, looking at Brick through the open car window, hoping he would change his mind.

Only one time before had Mace seen Brick this upset at him. It was that time Brick threw him and his two trash bags full of possessions out into the hall and told him he never wanted to see him again. But that was LA. He had friends in LA who would take him in. He didn't have any friends in Austin. He'd been too busy with law school. And the few friends he had made, he had managed to run off—like Marvin.

Brick yelled at Mace, "You better calm down and think about things. Do some of that breathing shit Ike showed you or something."

"Fuck you," Mace yelled.

Brick never mentioned the five hundred dollars in his pocket, almost six hundred counting what was left from yesterday. He didn't know if he would.

It took Brick right at an hour to get from the office to Casa Grande and back to the office. He parked next to Ike's old Mercedes. He took a deep breath to relax himself and entered the kitchen through the back door, hoping he wouldn't recognize this Jill woman, or her him.

They were seated around the table finishing up plates of lean barbecue brisket, sausage links, potato salad, beans, and pickles. Half a loaf of bread and two half-empty plastic containers of barbecue sauce sat in the middle of the table. The remainder of Ike's church-meeting special was spread out on the countertop.

Everything was there for a traditional Texas barbecue dinner except the sliced raw onion. Ike didn't like the taste of raw onion, and he didn't like smelling it on other people's breath. And as long as he was paying the bill, there wasn't going to be any. He even had a code word with the workers at Scholz's that meant "no onions." It was "church-meeting special."

Everybody looked up when Brick walked in.

"Fix yourself a plate. You know where the drinks are. Pull that chair over, and sit by me," Ike said. He didn't call Brick by name, and there was no hint of recognition from the only female at the table other than Kay. Brick glanced in her direction, then glanced away. He didn't remember ever seeing her before.

"Carl, Jill, this is one of my lawyers. He's going to be working on your case with me."

Brick extended his hand to Carl but quickly withdrew it when he noticed Carl's hands on the table. They didn't have any fingers. Brick's cheeks flashed red, and he stammered a couple words of apology.

"That's OK," Carl said.

Jill smiled, a little embarrassed. There was something vaguely familiar about her. She cut a piece of brisket, put it on a fork, and extended it to Carl's mouth. He took it, chewed, and swallowed. Then Carl reached for a glass, squeezed it between both palms, carefully lifted it to his mouth, and drank. Brick put his plate on the table next to Ike and sat down. Kay got up, grabbed a Diet Dr. Pepper from the refrigerator, popped the top, and set it in front of Brick.

"Thank you, Kay," Brick said.

"You're welcome. You've had a long day."

"We were talking about the night of the explosion," Ike said. "It was the day before Jill's birthday. Carl closed up a little early that night so he could run by Target and pick up a present. On the way home, he decided to swing back by the store because he couldn't remember if he put the push broom away after sweeping the sidewalk earlier that day. When he pulled in, he saw it leaning against the wall. He left the headlights shining on it and got out to unlock the door. He was blown backward by the blast and trapped under the rubble. He hit his head and his back real hard. He tried to move but couldn't. The last thing he remembers was the pain, screaming, and a smell like bacon frying."

Ike took a drink from his soda can. "Did I get that right, Carl?"

"Yes, sir."

"What do you remember next?"

"Waking up in the hospital. They told me I was unconscious for five days. I think the bacon smell was from my fingers burning off."

Carl wiped tears from his eyes with his sleeve. Jill put her arm around him. He composed himself and continued.

"They told me if it weren't for that piece of tin that blew off the awning and landed on me, I would have died. But my hands were sticking out in the fire. The tin got so hot it burned me all over my chest and my legs and this one on my face."

He put the part of his hand where his fingers used to be up to a scarred area on his cheek about the size of a credit card.

"I begged them to let me die. Please just let me die.

"I was on morphine, but it still hurt so much I cried and screamed whenever I woke up. They knocked me out for a couple more days. The first thing I said whenever I came to was 'please let me die, please just let me die.'"

The mood was heavy. Brick was dumbstruck with sadness. He couldn't have said a word even if he could have thought of something to say. Kay was misty-eyed. She reached for a clean napkin from the chicken napkin holder and dabbed her nose.

"I'm a proud man, Mr. Turner. I was a Marine, Special Ops. I could always take care of myself. I didn't want to be a cripple having to depend on other people to take care of me—being a burden."

Jill comforted Carl with her arm around him. She was small framed and looked to be several years younger than Carl, maybe midtwenties at the most. Brick recalled Ike referring to her as a woman, but to Brick she looked more like a girl, a weary girl.

Brick saw the tiredness on her face, and he sensed her fatigue. She was naturally pretty, even with tear-puffed eyes and no lipstick or makeup. Her inner beauty defied the veil of her present situation. In her face, Brick saw the unmistakable expression of a really good person, the kind of person he would never want to con, or lie to, or take advantage of.

Brick wondered how long they had been married and what a burden all this must be on their relationship. *I would be so sad,* Brick thought. He genuinely liked her.

Carl lifted the glass between his palms and took another drink.

"Tell us what you remember next, Carl?" Ike asked.

"Mainly just coming in and out of consciousness. It got to where I was staying awake longer. Nurses and doctors checking my hands. That was before the worst of the debridement started—scrubbing the dead skin and tissue off. It hurt really bad."

"We can talk about the debridement later," Ike said. "Tell us about the men in your room."

Carl was relieved. He didn't want to talk about the debridement. Talking about it made him cry. He didn't want to cry anymore today. Crying didn't fit the image of who he had been, who he still wanted to be.

"One day, I woke up, and there were two men in my room. They asked me questions about the explosion. I was drowsy. Still on morphine. I told 'em what I could remember. But I don't remember what all they asked me."

"Do you remember anything you told them?"

311

"Basically what I just said, you know. That I smelled gas right before I got to the door. I was about to put the key in the door when I got a strong whiff of it. That's all I remember, except the smell of my hands burning and me not being able to move.

"But when I said gas, one of them said, 'Gasoline, huh?' And I said, 'No, natural gas.' And he said, 'Well, that's funny because the fire marshal's report and the emergency room records say you had gasoline all over your belt and on your jeans when they brought you in.'"

"Did they say anything else about that?" Ike asked.

"I don't remember. I was still woozy. I remember a badge. They said they were ATF. I passed out while they were there. I don't remember them leaving."

Jill stared at the floor.

Carl said, "One of them told me it would be good for me if I left things alone. Then the other one said I should let things lie."

"Interesting," Ike said. "So what happened next?"

"At first, it was one doctor visit after another. That took all our time. Then about eight or nine weeks after I was out of the hospital, Jill drove me over to the gas company offices, downtown Waco. I wanted to see the gas line transmission maps to see if there were any gas lines around my store because my store was all electric, no gas.

"They kept putting me off. Telling me to come back later, next week, next month. I went back four more times. The last time, I said I'll just sit here till the manager comes out and tells me why I'm not being allowed to look at the utility maps. They're supposed to be public records.

"About ten minutes later, their security guards show up. They tell me to leave and not come back. I say no, I'd rather wait. So they picked me up by the arms, dragged me out the door, and threw me on the sidewalk. Skinned up my knees and elbows pretty good. They just stood there glaring down at me and wouldn't help me up."

Kay gasped audibly.

"I wish I'd been there," Brick said, puffing up, forgetting for a second that his muscles were only for show.

Carl continued. "Jill saw what was happening from the car. She ran over and helped me get up. They said, 'If either of you come back, you'll be arrested for criminal trespass.' I hired my first lawyer after that.

"He wrote 'em a letter saying he wanted to see the maps. A few days later, he called me and resigned from my case. Wouldn't give a reason. Just said he couldn't help. We've had five lawyers in all, six if you count the two brothers that worked on it together. They filed the lawsuit for me."

"Tell us how that went," Ike said.

"The gas company took my deposition right off the bat. Their lawyer got right up in my face and said I committed arson. He said I burned down my own store, got myself hurt doing it, and I'm trying to profit from wrongdoing. He asked about gas cans and past-due bills. He said they have a witness who claims I took my personal pictures off the wall a couple days before the explosion, and that's what arsonists do.

"But it's not true, Mr. Turner. Everything was there, the family pictures on the wall, business records, everything. It all burned up. He asked me how I got gasoline on my pants and belt. I said I didn't have gasoline on my pants and belt. He called me a liar and said he'd see me in prison."

"Prison?" Kay said.

"Prison?" Brick said.

"He was really nasty," Jill said, "to both of us. Said they have evidence and lab reports, and they already talked to the DA."

"The DA? Whoa," Brick said. He remembered parts of Carl's deposition he had read earlier that day—it seemed like a month ago now—and Mace's take on it. Mace already thought Carl was an arsonist. And he remembered the fire marshal's report, and some pictures, one with a burned-up, five-gallon gas can lying in the debris.

"Whoa," Brick said again.

"Help us, Mr. Turner," Jill said. "You're our last hope."

"Whoa," Brick repeated, trying to take it all in. It was sad. She seemed sweet, and beautiful, and in need of rescue, but six lawyers already gave up. Six lawyers think he's an arsonist. And Mace too. Seven counting Mace. "Whoa."

"How did you get my name?" Ike asked.

"The Campbell brothers," Carl said. "My last set of lawyers."

"Ronnie and Donnie, I was in Baylor Law with them," Ike said.

"Yes, sir. They said you're the only lawyer that might be crazy enough to take my case. They didn't mean it in a bad way. They said you can build lemonade stands and I should call you right away because they were withdrawing from my case."

Jill interrupted, "When life throws lemons at Ike Turner, he builds lemonade stands. That's what they said. Please help us, Mr. Turner; we have nowhere else to turn. The medical bills are in the hundreds of thousands and still coming in. I can't open them anymore. Carl lost his business. He can't work. He can't take care of himself. We're at the end of our rope. Please help us."

The only one crazy enough? Whoa, Brick thought. *Maybe Mace was right for once. Maybe Ike is crazy. ATF. DA. Shit.*

"I had to drop out of Baylor," Jill continued. "I was starting my senior year. I had a scholarship—and a job. Now I live with my brother and take care of him full time. Don't get me wrong. I'm not complaining. Carl resigned from the military early to help Dad run the store after Mom died, so I could stay in school. Then Dad died.

"Carl did his part and sacrificed for Dad and for me. Now I can do my part for him. I'm all he has. But the world keeps going by outside, Mr. Turner, and we keep getting deeper in debt. We're out of options. Will you take our case? We don't know where to turn, Mr. Turner. Please, if you can, help us."

"Whoa," Brick said. He missed the part about her dropping out of Baylor and Carl being her brother, not her husband. That part was still bouncing around in his ear canals and hadn't found a landing spot in his brain yet. "Whoa."

"Let me do a little investigating. I want to see what the DA has first and talk with a couple of my experts. Then I'll let you know," Ike said.

Carl lowered his head. He thought he was being rejected—again. *I knew Ike Turner wasn't going to take my case.* Another wasted time baring his soul. Another wasted trip. Wasted, like his life. Wasted, like Jill's life. *Why didn't they just let me die?*

"Either you believe us, or you don't, Mr. Turner," Jill said. "If Carl is telling the truth then your experts will find what you need for them to find. And if Carl is telling the truth then the DA doesn't really have a case. You're going to spend your money on the experts anyway, whether you're working on the case or just investigating it. It's your call, Mr. Turner, but don't make us drive back to Waco not knowing. Please."

She glanced at Carl, who was motionless, expressionless; his shoulders slumped, and his head hung.

Ike sensed the depth of Carl's despair and realized Jill's concern. Carl would interpret a delay to mean another no. Jill was afraid a suicide might happen before Ike made his decision.

"You're right," Ike said. "I believe you. I'm ready to get started."

At the same time Brick heard Ike agreeing to take the case, the words *Baylor* and *brother* finally registered in his conscious mind. He sat straight up in his chair. He stared at Jill. *Oh my God. This is the girl from Taco Bell.*

The one Mace wants to stand in the rain for. Oh my God. She was wearing a Baylor T-shirt at Taco Bell—Baylor. She dropped out of Baylor. Oh my God.

Brick leaned over and looked under the table. He remembered Mace commenting on her red toenails. Sure enough, she was wearing flip-flops and had red toenails. This was her, all right.

Oh my God. I gave Mace my business card. That's why she didn't want to see Brick Hawthorne. She thinks Mace is me. Oh my God. And they've had six lawyers. That's why she said, "That's all I need is another worthless damn shyster lawyer." Oh my God.

"Thank you, Mr. Turner," Jill said, wiping the tears.

"Thank you, Mr. Turner," Carl said. He wiped a tear with his sleeve and promised himself, again, that this was the last time...today.

And she's not married. This is her brother. Whoa. And Mace missed this. Oh my God.

"Call me Ike," Ike said. Then he pulled a wad of cash from his pocket and peeled off two hundred dollars in twenties and slid it across the table to Jill. "Here, take this. Everybody's tired. Stay another night in the motel, and come by in the morning after breakfast, say ten. Kay will have the contract ready for you."

"We can't take your money, Mr. Turner," Jill said.

"Call me Ike."

"We can't take it, *Mr.* Ike."

"You don't have a choice," Ike said. "Kay, log this two hundred as our first case expense on *Carl Junior vs. Central Texas Gas Company.*"

Vic Feazell

"Yes, sir," Kay said. She smiled. Kay was happy Ike was taking their case. She had read the depositions too. She knew it was going to be a very difficult case. But she also knew Ike had won several cases that other lawyers had turned down. And she had personally seen Ike take the lemons that life had thrown at people and make enough lemonade to build a lemonade stand. He did that for her once. That was part of the reason she loved him and would forever be loyal.

"I'll get this money back from you, Jill, after we win the case. And if we don't win, you don't owe me anything. The same goes for court costs, depositions, expert fees, travel expenses, whatever. You pay me back all my expenses after we win, and I get 40 percent of the gross recovery on contingent fee for my time and my staff's time and for risking the expense money."

"OK," Jill said. She smiled a smile of relief.

"And if we don't win, you don't owe me anything. No expenses back. Nothing."

"Thank you, Mr. Turner," Carl said. "I mean Ike, Mr. Ike."

They talked for a little longer and then Kay, Marvin, Carl, and Jill left through the back door.

After Ike heard their cars leave the parking lot, he said to Brick, "Well, I guess she didn't recognize you, whatever you did to her."

"Oh my God," Brick said. "She had me confused with Mace. He gave her one of my business cards."

"I should have known," Ike said. "Come on. Let's leave."

Ike stood on the landing while locking the office door. Brick walked to the old Ford. He was thinking about how much fun it was going to be telling Mace about meeting the girl from Taco Bell. Maybe that would be enough to get him to come back—if Ike would have him back.

It wasn't quite dark yet. Birds chirped in the trees that lined the parking lot. The sound of traffic had died down. The evening was calm and still.

Brick opened the car door and dropped the weight of his body, exhausted, onto the seat. That was all it took.

Without warning, a loud *ka-pow*, like a gunshot, shattered the peaceful scene. Feathers and leaves rustled as dozens of startled birds took flight from their perches. Panicked, Brick leaped from the car, trying to see where the noise had come from. It echoed in his head. Then Brick saw Ike's body lying prone across the top of the steps.

Chapter 15

OH, NOTHING

Judge Davis made it to the set in time to watch the movie crew do a few takes of a disturbing scene with Mr. David Carradine himself. Judge Davis couldn't believe his luck. Maybe he'd get that autograph after all. Carradine was doing a lengthy, crazy, wild-eyed monologue while flogging himself across the back with a makeshift cat-o'-nine-tails.

Between each take, the makeup/prop lady added more fake blood to his fake wounds. It was an independent, nonunion movie. Otherwise, there would have been at least one person from the makeup department and at least one more from the prop department working on Mr. Carradine.

Sometimes the rules are so confusing about what makeup is and what props are that it can hold up production for days while union officials argue over whether the trail dust on a cowboy is a prop or makeup. Union rules.

This day's filming was taking place at an old motel on South Congress Avenue. It was usually frequented by prostitutes, but today the whole place was rented out by the movie production company. Judge Davis introduced himself around and was made to feel welcome by everyone except the sound guy, who kept shushing at him, even when the camera wasn't on. Judge Davis was impressed. He had no idea it took so many people to shoot a scene, even a nonunion scene.

Dale Dudley, a popular Austin radio personality and part-time actor, was playing the serial killer's crazy younger brother who had a habit of sticking loose change and toy soldiers up his rectum. He told the judge this was a skeleton crew because of the tight location. He said there were usually a lot more people on a movie set. He said they were shooting on 16 millimeter Kodak film stock, with plans to blow it up to 35 millimeter, whatever that meant.

It was hot, real hot. The little motel room had at least ten people crammed inside. There was no air conditioning. A row of hot, bright lights, installed that morning on poles near the ceiling, glared down on the actor.

Carradine was sweating profusely, but he never complained. He seemed to be enjoying himself. Someone brought him water and touched up his makeup and fake blood at every break.

Ten or more people were doing things outside. Some peered through the open window. A few crew members, production assistants, they call them, had pried the window open earlier in the day trying to get some fresh air into the room. They had to leave the air conditioner turned off because the noise it made messed things up for the sound guy.

Judge Davis loved it when the assistant director yelled "action" and "cut." It was a dream come true.

After the last cut was called, Carradine got up from the floor and started dusting himself off. A lady wiped sweat from his body with a towel while another lady removed some of his makeup and fake blood. Production assistants started packing up the equipment. Judge Davis knew this was the time to get his courage up to ask for that autograph and see if someone would take a photo of him with Carradine. He had his camera with him, just in case.

About then, Carradine noticed Judge Davis in the crowd. "Hey, you," he yelled.

"Me?" Judge Davis asked.

"Yeah, you. Anybody ever tell you that you look like me?"

"All the time," Judge Davis said.

Carradine smiled. "Stick around if you can."

"OK."

Carradine located his wife, Marina, a beautiful lady with nice big breasts and a small part in the movie. He spoke with her for a moment and then strolled to where Judge Davis was still standing, waiting, watching everything.

"Wife wants to go to the mall. Dillard's. Needs panty hose. I'm too beat. Can you give me a ride back to the Four Seasons?"

"Sure thing," the judge said.

They drove down Congress Avenue. The capitol building loomed in the distance and grew larger as they got closer. Judge Davis prepared to turn right on

First Street and go a couple more blocks to San Jacinto, where he would drop David Carradine off at the Four Seasons. He still hadn't asked for the autograph and photograph he wanted.

They were almost there before Carradine figured out from their conversation that Judge Davis wasn't part of the production crew. Carradine thought that was a hoot, and he belly laughed when he found out he was being chauffeured by a state district judge.

Carradine took a quick shower and met Judge Davis in the lobby bar. They shared a plate of angus sliders and some wasabi-crusted peanuts. Davis had a scotch, and Carradine drank water. Davis didn't notice Carradine was only drinking water until after he ordered his second scotch.

The judge was drinking Balvenie, the twelve-year-old version, not as expensive as the thirty-year-old version but still pricey. He was celebrating, but when he noticed Carradine was drinking water, he ordered a Diet Dr. Pepper and didn't touch his second scotch.

They talked for a couple hours until Marina showed up. She sat with them awhile and then ushered David to his room for some much-needed rest. Judge Davis paid the check.

When Judge Davis left for home, he had his autograph and at least ten photos of himself and Carradine together, thanks to one of the friendly cocktail waitresses. He even got one of himself, David, and Marina sitting together. That photo would eventually hang on the wall in his judge's chambers and, in the years to come, he and Marina would correspond by email until well after David's death.

———

Grandma was happy to get Marvin's call. She always loved it when her little Marvin came to Waco to visit her. Before Marvin hung up the phone, Grandma said, "You be sure and tell Mr. Ike I said thank you for calling me back the other night and checking on you in the hospital. I bent his ear about everything going on with you and them two young lawyers. And tell him I'm gonna make a chocolate meringue pie just for him. It's his favorite, you know."

"I'll tell him, Grandma," Marvin said.

Marvin's uncle Kevin, his mother's brother, picked Marvin up after work and drove him the ninety miles north. They planned to stay the weekend. Uncle Kevin could tell Marvin had something on his mind, just like the last time they made this drive and the time before that. He waited, but Marvin never said what it was, and Kevin wasn't one to push.

Marvin wanted to tell Uncle Kevin, but he couldn't bring himself to do it. Grandma was the only person in the family who knew—and she still loved him. But Grandma loved Marvin unconditionally. She was open-minded and was liberal before there was a word for liberal. But Uncle Kevin—who knows? They had never talked about things like that before.

Uncle Kevin had been like a dad to Marvin, and Marvin loved him. His biological father left before

Marvin was born—crack. Uncle Kevin stepped in and helped his little sister raise her baby boy.

Marvin was looking forward to telling Grandma about Mr. Ike taking the case for the man who got blown up at the convenience store in Waco. Grandma remembered that night. The explosion rattled her house, and the live news coverage interrupted her favorite TV show, *Dallas*. Marvin was hoping since Grandma lived in Waco, Ike might let him work on the case some. At least he'd have a place to stay so he wouldn't add to the expense of the case. Grandma always enjoyed having Marvin stay with her, and she'd certainly enjoy seeing Ike.

Grandma already knew Ike from his days as a law student at Baylor and his time as a McLennan County assistant DA. Before she got on Social Security, she was a cook at one of Ike's favorite hamburger joints over on Clifton Street; not the best part of town, but worth going there for the burgers and barbecue.

On the ride to Waco, Marvin told Uncle Kevin about Mr. Ike taking Carl Junior's case, but he didn't mention the other thing he had on his mind.

———

Dan Danford never made it to the Cedar Door that night. After the verdict was read, the smarmy judge told Dan and Ike they could leave, "but don't pull any monkey business in my court again, or I'll hold you both in contempt."

Dan handed his hundred-dollar hot check to Ike and then walked home with his head hung low. He had a six-pack in the refrigerator and told himself he'd drink three tonight and save the other three for tomorrow. Then the phone rang. He answered it. It was the bank.

Dan sat alone, staring at the wall. As the sun went down, he drank the other three beers, with no TV.

He hated Ike Turner, he hated Mace, he hated Diaeta Pepsi, he hated the judge, he hated the jury, and he hated his boss, but the thing he loathed most of all was his own existence.

The phone rang again, but Dan didn't answer this time. He let it go to the machine. "This is Dan. I'm not here. Leave a message and I'll call you back." When Dan heard the voice on the other end, he threw an empty beer bottle, and it shattered against the wall.

———

Mace didn't pack and leave that night, but he didn't practice any breathing exercises either. Instead, he sat on the couch all by himself, smoking pot, the last of it, and wondering why Brick was taking so long to get home. Each moment that dragged by without the sound of Brick's feet coming up the steps caused a feeling of insecurity to grow in him. Was he coming back? Had Ike offered him a place to stay, something better?

He knew Brick was pissed. Really pissed. He couldn't remember another time when Brick had flat refused to ro-sham-bo. It was their rule, their arbitor, ro-sham-bo. But not this time.

Mace knew he'd misbehaved. He knew he had regressed into destructive and infantile behavior patterns. He may not have known what the phrase "destructive and infantile behavior" meant, but he certainly knew what it was…and he was doing it.

His temper was a problem. He recognized that. His tantrums and his sick need to control things had never gotten him anywhere. It never did him any good. And he always ended up regretting what he said.

Mace was experiencing a catastrophe, of sorts. But the upside of a catastrophe is that it can be a door to a higher level of consciousness and understanding. The painful life lessons we place ourselves in can become our greatest teachers…if we will humble ourselves… and look within. Otherwise, the painful experience is suffered, but wasted.

Gradually, Mace was chipping away at the protective shell that sourounded him, the shell he had created, the shell that can only be cracked from the inside. He was beginning to experience a degree of self awareness, which was a new feeling for Mace. He thought about his childish and immature responses to situations he couldn't control. He thought about mistakes he had made and the people he had hurt.

After experiencing such a wonderful and improbable victory in the courtroom that very afternoon, a victory he should be celebrating and reveling in, Mace had managed to shoot himself in the foot instead. As he sat in silence, he gradually became aware of a recurring pattern in his life, the pattern of almost making it and then messing things up. Sure, Brick was a whiner, but maybe he was right. And now Mace sat alone with no one to share his victory.

Mace knew Ike was the reason for the win. He wouldn't have known where to start without Ike, but he still felt resentment toward him and didn't know why. Mace knew Brick was his biggest supporter and his only friend, but he didn't really respect Brick's opinion and never wanted to follow his advice. He didn't know why that was either.

He sensed it had been his momentary surrender to something bigger than himself, something other than himself, that made the courtroom victory possible. But his old defense mechanisms were hard to shake, and they kept kicking back in, even when he didn't want them to.

It seemed whenever he managed to surrender his old self and die to his self-destructive attitudes and behaviors, they would somehow resurrect stronger than ever. And sometimes it took him quite a while to figure out he was on autopilot and not in control of his mind and mouth.

His life was fucked up, and he felt powerless about it. He sensed that surrender was the key. The seed was already planted in his subconscious, and it was finding root, but it needed nourishment.

For a time in the courtroom, he had managed to surrender himself by faith, and faith took control, but as soon as the excitement ended, he let fear sneak back in. Like Peter, he lost his faith, looked at his feet, and started to sink.

Mace hadn't figured out that when fear enters your house, faith leaves through the back door. And he had no idea that if he would let faith back in, then fear would leave. It was his choice. Like light and dark, faith and fear do not coexist. The switch was his to flip—if he could figure out he was in the dark.

Mace didn't blame Brick for being angry with him, but at the same time, he was having trouble not being angry at Brick. He vacillated between wanting to pack and leave and wanting to stay and make things right.

He knew the right thing to do, but his diseased ego resisted him doing it. He kept going back and forth between *I don't need this shit* and *I must be full of shit.*

His internal dialogue and the internal battle raged on. Fear versus faith. Faith versus fear. Light versus dark. Scared bully versus the world.

He was starting to feel afraid that Brick wasn't coming back, that fucking Ike had offered him something better or was letting him live in one of the rooms in the office building he had heard about but hadn't seen yet, the ones with a kitchen and a shower.

He opened the door and looked at the parking lot. No old Ford. No Brick. Maybe he had overdone it this time. Maybe Brick wasn't coming back. *Fuck, fuck, fuck, fuck, fuck, fuck, fuck.*

Mace was going through his own fire that day, and he was suffering—but suffering can bring awareness. Sometimes our worst struggles are our best teachers.

———

Brick watched as Ike picked himself up from the landing where instinct had thrown him flat to his belly with his arms outstretched in front of him. It looked like he was holding an object with both hands. Brick thought he saw Ike replace a handgun between his belt and the small of his back, but he wasn't sure. Twilight was fast setting in.

Ike dusted himself off and walked to Brick's crippled car. It was leaning sideways, and the driver's side bumper was on the ground. The fender rested heavy on the tire.

"That was loud," Ike said. "Looks like your suspension's broke."

"I thought somebody shot at us," Brick said, pacing nervously and looking from side to side.

"Me too."

Ike wrestled with the squeaky hood and finally got it raised. "Yep. Look at that. Your A-frame's broken right in two. This shouldn't have happened. How long since you *really* had this thing inspected?"

"Uh, I don't know."

"Look at this. You don't even have a shock absorber on this side. What happened to it?"

"I don't know."

"The spring's broke too."

Brick didn't say anything.

"How long since this hood's been raised?" Ike asked.

"I don't know that either."

"Let me guess. Mace takes care of the car."

Brick didn't say anything. He felt downhearted. The noise of the car's suspension breaking and the bumper hitting the pavement still rang in his ears.

He thought about the young mechanic Mace pressured and then bribed to put the inspection sticker on the windshield last year, and the year before that. "This is the last time," he had said. "I'm not doing this next year. Don't even ask. You have to get this thing fixed."

Brick felt like his life had fallen apart, in a split second, just like the car. He didn't understand it hadn't happened all at once; it had been coming for quite a while.

He kept pacing, looking at the damage, and wondering how he was going to get home, or find work, or pay the rent. He was wondering if Mace was at home or if he had already packed and left.

"I'm glad it didn't happen while you were driving. That would have been bad," Ike said.

"Yes, it would," Brick answered.

"You could be dead," Ike said.

"I wish."

A lot of people live on the brink of disaster and ruin, just one broken pipe, one stay in the hospital, one unexpected little emergency away from losing what little they have. This was Brick's emergency. It wasn't anything like what happened to Carl, but it was big to Brick.

With nearly six hundred dollars in his pocket, he thought he was seeing some daylight, that things were getting better. Now that hope was gone. Six hundred wasn't enough for a car. Even if he could find a car for six hundred, he'd have to show proof of liability insurance to buy it. Their liability insurance had lapsed nearly a year ago. And he still needed to buy groceries, weed, gas, and finish paying Mrs. Chen.

"This thing ain't worth fixing," Ike said.

"I was afraid of that."

"At least it went out with a bang."

"No kidding there."

"But you still got all your fingers."

"Yep. That's true."

"And you still got your law license, so far anyway."

"So far."

Brick knew what Ike was referring to—nearly getting arrested at the hospital.

"Can you give me a ride home?" Brick asked. He was depressed, and it showed.

"I guess so—but I can do you one better if you're up for it."

"One better? Up for what?" Ike's question concerned Brick and made him feel a little uneasy. He remembered Mace razzing him about Ike being gay. *That's all I need right now.* And he was a bit concerned about that gun, too, if it was a gun.

"Do you want to work on Carl's case with me? You didn't seem too keen on it in the kitchen."

Brick felt relieved. "Well, yeah, I guess so, but he's been turned down by six lawyers. And the ATF, the DA, and the fire marshal's office all think he's an arsonist. I was kind of surprised you took it."

"Yeah, me too. But my gut told me to believe him. And I like his little sister. She's got spunk. You want to work on it or not?"

"Sure. Why not? Make me a proposition," Brick said. As soon as he heard himself say *proposition*, he wished he had chosen another word.

"Work on this case. I'll give you some direction and guidance along the way. It'll be a long process, though. At least a couple years," Ike said.

"OK, but how do I get by till then? Ya know? How do I pay the bills? How do I get around, come to work? Maybe I should find a job. I don't know what to do."

"I'll throw you enough cases to keep you going. I've got another weed case against Candice Kennedy you can have."

That got Brick's attention. The idea of going another round with Candice—"beware the kitten's claws"—got him momentarily excited.

"And I'll give you a few percentage points of my 40 percent of Carl's case when you win."

"I guess I don't have a choice. But how am I going to get to work?" Brick kept looking at the old Ford and shaking his head in disbelief.

"Follow me," Ike said. He walked toward the back corner of the parking lot where the old carriage house sat. Ike took a big key from his back pocket—it looked like a jail key—and opened the huge padlock that hung from the carriage house doors.

Brick helped Ike slide the doors open. Ike flipped on the light switch inside.

"Wow," Brick said.

"I was planning on driving this one tonight anyway. Gotta pick my fiancée up at the airport." Ike smiled real big when he said the word fiancé.

"Wow," Brick said.

———

At a stoplight on his way to the airport, Ike reached for the big black car phone and dialed a number. No answer. He left a message.

"Doesn't feel so good, does it? Give me a call, Dan-Dan."

———

Mace was sprawled on the couch, snoring, when the sound of Brick's key unlocking the door nudged him awake.

"Wake up," Brick said.

"I'm awake. I'm awake."

On the coffee table in front of Mace was an empty beer can, an empty bag of potato chips, the empty bong, and a totally empty plastic sandwich bag that once contained the meager remains of their marijuana supply. Mace stretched and yawned, trying to clear the cobwebs from his brain. He saw the empty marijuana bag and quickly stuffed it into the empty potato chip bag, but it was too late. Brick had already seen it.

"Dude, I'm glad you're home," Mace said.

"Yep."

"What time is it? I must have fallen asleep."

Brick looked at his watch. "Eleven-thirty."

Then he looked at the empty potato chip bag with the empty weed bag inside. He frowned and shook his head disapprovingly at Mace.

"Sorry about the weed, man. I was so depressed and…"

Brick's frown turned into a smile. "That's OK. Look what I've got." He reached into his jacket pocket and pulled out a clear bag with two fat joints in it and shook them in front of Mace's face.

Mace grinned, and his eyes widened. "Where'd you get that?"

"Ike gave it to me. It's the weed from your briefcase."

"Dude! Why'd he do that? I mean, I'm glad and all, but that doesn't seem like Ike. Unless…"

"Settle down. He thought you might need it tonight."

"Really?"

"Yeah. He said he knew you had a hard day and he'd rather you smoke this than drink alcohol. He's really not that bad."

He's really not that bad. Mace started to say something sarcastic, but he thought the better of it, caught it, and pulled it back in. It took some effort, but he did it—and the awareness that he had controlled his tongue made him feel good, and rightfully so.

The self-reflection he experienced on the couch— waiting alone, and wondering if Brick was coming home—had scared him into the realization that his demeaning and judgmental attitudes had always been a hindrance and had never done anything for him, except get him into trouble. He had taken an inventory of himself and noticed how often pride and willfulness controlled his life.

When pride and willfulness are finally identified and surrendered, true character development and spiritual transformation can take place. That's what was happening with Mace.

The ordeal of the past couple days...being broke...feeling hopeless...being alone...being afraid Brick wasn't coming back...and smoking up all of the weed, had actually resulted in a positive outcome for Mace.

Contrary to government propaganda, marijuana isn't bad. And neither is it just about laughing, getting the munchies, or having good sex. It's more about context and the consciousness level of the person using it.

Marijuana may not be right for everyone, but it certainly isn't wrong for everyone. Government financed lies and propaganda have mislead the public into believing marijuana is harmful. It's not.

Scientific studies have shown marijuana is a cure for cancer and that it helps with Alzheimer's, autism, Crohn's disease, glaucoma, migraines, seizures, and even restless leg syndrome, to name a few.

And it certainly isn't a gateway drug any more than coffee is. You can ask Willie Nelson about that.

Sometimes marijuans is used as an entheogen, a pathway to spiritual understanding and higher consciousness. Rastafarians have used it as a spiritual sacrament and in their reasoning sessions for decades. Indians of the Hindu faith have used it for centuries. And in the Holy Bible, the book of Genesis, chapter one, verses eleven and twelve, God Himself says that on the third day of history, He gave the Earth marijuana, and it was good. Seriously, it says that. He gave the Earth "the herb that yields seed," and "God saw that it was good." He didn't say "the herb that yields seed, *except for marijuana.*"

Some Christian fundamentalists may want to argue, but that is what the Bible says. Their friends who ascribe to the literal interpretation of the Bible should set them straight. Marijuana is *literally* an "herb that yields seed." There's no way around it. Marijuana is natural. It requires no processing, manufacturing, fermentation, or distillation. Just drop a seed on the ground, and it grows. And God says it's good.

At the right time and in the right place, marijuana can be the catalyst to usher in a catharsis, similar to the way a good, insightful cry can purge the soul of negative emotions. Mace had experienced a catharsis, of sorts, an emotional purification and an intellectual clarification of who he had been, who he was, and who he wanted to be. He had been a rhino; he thought he was a shark, but he wanted to be more. He sensed there was more to life, and he wanted it. He was evolving. He just didn't know it yet.

"Really?" Mace said again, and he smiled.

"Yeah. Ike said it wouldn't cure your pain, but it might help it a little."

Pain, what pain? Mace almost said defensively, but then he remembered. He was in pain, a lot of it. He had come face-to-face with the realization that his sick need to control things was the source of many of his mistakes and much of his suffering.

"Want to light one up?" Brick asked.

"Does the pope shit in the woods?" Mace said with a smile. He welcomed the relief. He sat on the edge of the couch, pulled a Bic lighter from his pocket, and handed it to Brick.

Brick took one of the joints from the bag. He was about to light it when he stopped, handed it to Mace, and said, "Here, you go first."

"Oh, man," Mace said. "You're the best."

"Nothing you wouldn't do for me."

They smiled at each other, remembering when Mace had done the same thing for Brick just the other night. Mace lit the joint, took a long drag, and passed the joint to Brick. Brick took his familiar place on the couch and sucked air through and around the little hand-rolled fatty. He exhaled right after Mace did. Smoke filled the room.

Mace watched the smoke as it tumbled through the air. "Next time we should remember to do that exhaling through a toilet paper roll stuffed with dryer sheets trick Ike told us about," he said.

They nodded in agreement and then took another drag. Brick tapped the flame out and laid it into the jawbone-shaped ashtray.

"Let's finish this later. We need to talk," Brick said.

"Oh, dear. I knew it. This was too good to be true. Ike giving us weed. You."

"It's not…"

"I know I fucked up. I'm sorry. I wish I could take it all back. I wish I could make it up. Give me another chance." The memory of the emotional suffering that day flooded his mind. And that was a good thing. Suffering caused by our mistakes can be our growing pains. The real tragedy of suffering is when we fail to learn the lesson. Mace was learning his.

"It's…"

"Please. I'll try harder. I'll even make up with Ike, if you want me to, if he'll let me…"

Brick had never seen Mace so contrite, so apologetic, not even that time Brick threw him out. He waited nearly three months then, had to go looking for Mace, and still didn't get an apology, and he certainly never witnessed Mace trying to behave any better. Brick didn't know it, but Mace's time on the couch that night, his emotional tug-of-war, the battle between fear and faith, had done some good and had given him a degree of insight and perspective.

"I'll look for a job. Really. Even a lousy job, anything. I promise. I'll pay Ike back. I'll pay my part of the rent. I'll get a checking account. I'll pay for my own shirts. Just give me a chance," Mace said.

"OK," Brick said.

"OK?"

"Yes, OK."

"I don't get it," Mace said.

339

"I'll give you another chance. And you don't even have to look for a job unless you just want to. Ike said he'd give you another chance too."

"But I fucked up so bad. Maybe I should look for a job."

"You'll want to go back after I tell you the rest of it."

"The rest of what?"

Brick told Mace about meeting the girl from Taco Bell, that her name was Jill and she was the sister to the guy on the explosion case. Mace wanted to get up right then and go find her, but Brick talked him out of it.

"Settle down, dude. She thinks your name is Brick Hawthorne because you gave her my business card, remember? Haven't seen you around these parts before, remember? She doesn't want anything to do with Brick Hawthorne—I mean you."

Mace was beside himself with excitement. The love of his life had been found, and she was right under his nose. *I could have seen her tonight if I hadn't been such a dick to Ike. Damn.*

"Ike wants both of us to work on Carl Junior's case."

"You mean the love of my life turns out to be the sister of an arsonist on a case we can't possibly win? Oh, well. Whatever, man. I don't care. I'm chilled. But how am I going to work on Carl's case if Jill doesn't want to see me?"

Mace enjoyed the way the sound of her name felt rolling off of his tongue. "Jill," he said again.

"That's what I asked Ike, and he said, 'Don't worry. We'll get there.'"

"He always says we'll get there. What the hell does that mean, we'll get there?"

340

"I guess we'll find out when we get there. Do we have anything better to do?"

"Guess not."

"So do you want to help on Carl's case or not? I already told Ike I would. I didn't have a choice."

"Of course I will. I don't have choice either," Mace said.

"That's what Ike said you'd say."

"That fucker. I think he enjoys putting people in that situation, where they don't have a choice."

"Hum," Brick said, rubbing his fingers on his chin, thinking about it.

"That's what he did to Danford too, about his bet. He told Danford, 'You have no choice.'"

"Really?"

"Really."

"Wonder what he's got planned for Danford?"

"Don't think I want to know. Don't care."

"Yeah, me neither."

Then Brick told Mace about the car breaking apart and the loud noise that sounded like a gunshot, and Ike falling flat to his stomach, and it looking like he had a gun.

"Dude, I told you that guy was some kind of crook," Mace said. Then he quickly added, "Never mind. I didn't say that. I'm sorry. I'm trying. I'm really trying. It's hard, but I'm trying. How did you get home? What are we going to do for a car now?"

"That's the weird part," Brick said.

"Weirder than everything else we've seen? Weirder than playing Rambo and pulling a gun?"

"Well, sort of. I'm not sure it was a gun. It could have been that big key."

"What big key?"

"The key he opened the carriage house with. You know that building in the back corner of the parking lot? He calls that a carriage house."

"OK."

"Anyway, inside that carriage house was a brand spanking new, shiny, black Mercedes sedan, S-500, with gray leather upholstery, and it had an antenna on top and a car phone in it. No shit. He has a brand-new Mercedes with a car phone."

"No way."

"Way. And it's bigger than the one my dad drives."

"I want a hit."

"Me too."

Brick picked up what was left of the first joint, lit it, took a drag, and passed it to Mace. Mace took a long drag and then snuffed out the three-quarter-inch roach on the empty beer can.

A roach is what's left of a marijuana cigarette after it's been mostly smoked. It's probably called that because the paper turns brown, and it looks a little bit like a roach—not a flattering name, but descriptive. Mace laid the roach in the ashtray in case they needed it later. It might have some weed left in it. They only had one joint left, and then it would all be gone.

Brick exhaled as he talked. Puffs of smoke punctuated some of his words. "He said he gets a new one every four years. I think he's richer than he lets on, the way he throws money around. He even gave two hundred to Carl and Jill."

"Remember what the judge said about Ike spending money and his partner, Goldstein, and stuff?"

"Yeah. I hope not."

"So I wonder why he's driving us around in that old car when he has a brand-new one in the garage?"

"Carriage house."

"Whatever."

"I asked him that. He said he doesn't drive the new one while he's in trial and at least a week before. He doesn't want any jurors seeing him in it."

"Why not? Seems like good advertising."

"I asked him that. He said he didn't want any peers to see him in it and hold it against his client. Says people get jealous about fancy cars."

"I didn't think of that."

"Then he tossed me the key to his old Mercedes and said, 'Use it.'"

"No shit?"

"No shit. It's outside right now. He said he'd charge us two hundred a month for the extra insurance, but we got to take care of it—and no smoking in it."

"We ain't got two hundred a month. All we got is the change from that hundred."

"No. Ike paid me five more."

"Five hundred?"

"Yep, for Wilfred Johnson. Said his bet was with you, not with me."

"I told you so. I told you he didn't like me. Listen to me, man, I think he's coming on to you. He wants me out of the picture. Why else would he do that?"

Mace couldn't help himself. Relapse comes easily if you're not diligent every moment.

It takes more than having a catharsis to change one's character at depth. You have to carry the memory of the catharsis with you hour by hour, day by day. And when you realize you are off track, you have to get back on.

The catharsis experience helps you understand the reasons you should change. And it helps you understand the things you need to change about yourself. But, the catharsis must turn into a *decision* to change— a way of life. Sometimes the process takes place in a single leap. Most of the time it is a step-by-step journey.

"No, he does like you. He told me so," Brick said.

In an instant, Mace considered it and got back on path. In that synapse of opportunity, he overcame impulse and made a decision to change, at least this time. "You're right. I know you're right," Mace said. He had suffered enough tonight.

Mace, one. Relapse, zero.

"Really. He thinks you're funny. He said tell you to come back and work on Carl Junior's case. See Jill. He just has a few *conditions*."

Brick got things a little wrong. Ike hadn't really said he thought Mace was funny. He said he thought Mace was acting goofy. There's a difference.

"Why does he think I'd want to come back? I mean I screwed up so bad."

"Because I told him about you seeing Jill at the Taco Bell and going all stupid and saying, 'I'd stand out in the rain all day hoping she might walk by, and she's my drug, man.'"

"You asshole. You didn't tell him about 'haven't seen you around these parts before,' did you?"

"No," Brick lied.

"OK then. Go on."

"Let's light up."

"Good idea."

Brick took the last joint from the plastic bag and lit it. He took a long, slow drag, held his breath, and passed it to Mace. Mace did the same. They exhaled. "Ahhh." Smoke filled the room. They sat for a while in the quiet. Then a memory stirred.

"Conditions?" Mace said. "What conditions?"

"What are you talking about?"

"A while ago, you said Ike would take me back, but there were conditions. What conditions?"

"Oh, that." Brick said. He reached into his back pocket, pulled out a folded piece of legal paper, and handed it to Mace.

"Oh, dear," Mace said. He opened the piece of paper and looked at the three words Ike had written in the middle of the page. All it said was:

TALC

LENT

PACT

"Not this shit again. What does this mean?" Mace asked.

"He said you have to carry that piece of paper in your back pocket all the time. That's one of the conditions."

"This is bullshit," Mace said. Then he remembered saying the same thing about BE BOP BYRD. And BE BOP BYRD hadn't turned out to be bullshit after all. It was a big help. It had been his road map for winning the case. "Never mind," Mace added, "but what does it mean? I have to know what this means before I can agree to it. Right?"

"Ike said it was simple."

"That part sounds good. Simple. I like that. Simple."

"But it's not easy," Brick added.

"What?"

"It's simple but not easy."

"I heard you, but what does that mean?"

"Beats me."

"TALC," Mace said musingly. "Do I sweat too much? Does he want me to put on talc powder? What's the deal? I don't get it. What does that mean?"

"TALC. It means think about less cussing. T-A-L-C. Think about less cussing."

"Think about less cussing? If he wants me to stop cussing, I can't do that."

"He said you'd say that."

"And?"

"He just wants you to think about it. He didn't say you had to stop. Just think about it."

"But you cuss. So does Ike."

346

"Not as much as you do."

"OK. I can do that. I can think about it. If all I have to do is think about it, I can do that. OK, what's the next one? LENT. I'm not even Catholic. I don't know what that means. What does it mean?"

"I don't know."

"Well, think."

"I really don't know. He said he'd tell you the other two conditions later. He just told me the first one."

"That fucker."

"But he said they were simple," Brick said.

"But not easy. What the hell does that mean—not easy?"

"Well, you just called him a fucker, didn't you? So, thinking about cussing less must not be easy for you, or you wouldn't have called him a fucker after he just made it a condition that you think about cussing less."

"Fuck you."

"See what I mean."

Mace thought about it. "OK, I see what you mean. I'll think about it. I'll probably still cuss, but I'll think about it first. If that's his condition, I can do that. Think about less cussing. TALC. I can do that. I'll start tomorrow."

"OK. Great. Problem solved."

They stared at the ceiling for a spell.

"What else?" Mace finally said.

"That's all I can think of except I never got to congratulate you on the great job you did today. I was some impressed."

"Thanks, man. Me too."

"I thought the judge was going to have a hissy fit when he couldn't find you and Ike. He sent the bailiff looking for you. It was tense, man."

"You think that was tense? You should have seen me in that fucking broom closet with Ike and all his hypnosis shit."

"Broom closet?"

"Yeah, right down from the courtroom. It's written on the door: BROOM CLOSET. He jerked the handle, and we were in. He called it *his* room. Looked like no one had been in there for years. Dust. Cobwebs. Freaky."

"Hmmm," Brick said. He took another hit off the joint and passed it to Mace. Smoke filled the room. The familiar smell of burning marijuana brought comfort to them both. Brick lost himself for a while in a pleasant fantasy about pulling Candice Kennedy into that broom closet and them having their way with each other. He smiled.

Mace was tired. He laid his head on the back of the couch and thought about the events of the day. *Had it only been a day?*

He recalled Ike yanking him from his chair, dragging him out the door, down the hall, and into that broom closet, without anyone even noticing—the same way he had done Brick at the hospital. Mace remembered the unmerciful teasing he had given Brick about it, only to have it happen to him.

Karma, Ike would call it. Mace chuckled.

"What's so funny?" Brick asked.

"Oh...nothing."

"No, I heard you laugh. What's so funny?"

"We'll get there."

———

Ike steered his new Mercedes past the "FULL" sign and onto the crowded parking lot at the Robert Mueller Municipal Airport. He drove straight to the front row and coasted effortlessly into the only vacant spot on the lot, the one closest to the entrance. Was it a miracle or just a lucky break?

At the stop light, after talking to Dan's machine, Ike had taken a moment to visualize that spot. Now he was parked in it. Miracle or coincidence? The question never crossed Ike's mind.

He walked to the gate where he checked the arrival time on the overhead screen. The plane had just landed. He watched through the concourse window as it taxied in.

While standing there, he inhaled, exhaled, and entered his private place. All mind activity ceased. Then a prayer took form from the void and came into being, a prayer for Brick and Mace, a prayer that Divine Intelligence would manifest in them.

End of Book One

POSTSCRIPT

There are only two ways to live your life. One is as though nothing is a miracle. The other is as if everything is. –Albert Einstein

Rhinos Sharks & Unicorns is a story about the hero's journey.

Heroes do not incubate in a vacuum. They owe their existence to all the heroes who came before them, those who helped to clear the path and mark the way. They owe a debt that cannot be repaid with money or goods but only with service, the service of heroism itself, because the collective goal and purpose of all heroes, whether they know it or not, is to make the world a better place. And the world does get better because of the mere presence of heroes and their heroic thoughts and deeds.

Some heroes are born heroes. From the cradle, they are aware that they possess a higher purpose, a destiny. The desire burns within these born heroes to be all they are intended to be. They set out upon their quests as soon as they possibly can to discover their destiny and fulfill their heroic potential. They are satisfied with nothing less than accomplishing great feats against insurmountable odds for the betterment of mankind, and they raise the collective consciousness of us all by their mere presence and their examples of generosity, gratitude, and service.

Then there are the reluctant heroes. These heroes have no idea they are heroes at all. They stumble blindly from day to day thinking only of their own personal survival and comfort. They are not concerned with their destiny, with raising their consciousness, or with changing their own lives, much less the lives of others. They lack any awareness that they have the divine spark of a hero within.

They are like Moses of the Old Testament, an undisputed hero in his later life, who for many years was totally content tending his father-in-law's sheep in the desert, spiritually asleep until his encounter with the burning bush, the catalyst that changed his life and began his well-known journey.

Whether the hero is born a hero or is a reluctant hero, there is a spark of nobility that resides within him or her, and it is that spark that ultimately ignites the soul and sets the hero ablaze, placing him or her upon the path of the hero's journey.

The spark of nobility may manifest itself in different forms and quantities. It may be a spark that, upon recognition, instantly explodes into a mighty flame, spontaneously igniting an eternal conflagration of the soul that is Truth, and Enlightenment.

Or it may take the form of a dim, sleeping ember awaiting fulfillment of its potential until someone or something from outside applies muscle to the bellows, pumping fresh air through the window of the soul, thus becoming the catalyst that nourishes the tiny flame so the miracle of the hero's journey can begin.

Such was the situation with Moses and his life-changing discourse with the burning bush. Had it not been for the catalyst of the burning bush, Moses may have been satisfied finishing out his years leading a herd of sheep from watering hole to watering hole rather than leading a new nation across the dry floor of the Red Sea, out of bondage, and into a new world.

But whether the igniting spark within the hero's bosom begins as a roaring flame or a dull ember, its nature is the same. It is Divine Nobility bearing witness that the hero is one with the One.

It is not difficult to recognize nobility when it manifests in the familiar and expected attributes of high-mindedness, honesty, and right thinking. But the spark of nobility can also be found in the simple attribute of being honest and candid about who you really are— even if it starts as nothing more than awareness of the fact you are a scoundrel.

The beginning of awareness is the beginning of the hero's journey. Awareness is the lamp oil that feeds the flame, eventually illuminating a greater awareness— awareness that the spark of Divine Nobility residing within the hero also resides within each and every one of us.

Rhinos Sharks & Unicorns is a story about all of us. We all possess the hero's potential—no exceptions.

APOLOGIES

I wish to apologize to the city of Austin. It's not hot all the time, and it does rain—occasionally.

I want to apologize to the Basement Law School, the first Texas state law school for black students. It was my inspiration for the Carver-Washington Gospel School of Law.

I apologize to Marina Anderson Carradine. I know she and David were not married until 1998, but 1995 fit the story better. However, she does have a nice set. No apologies there.

I apologize to the movie *Monster Hunter*. I know *Monster Hunter* was not filmed until 1999, but 1995 fit the story better.

I apologize to Travis County. I know that in 1995, criminal trials were held in the newer Blackwell-Thurman Criminal Courthouse just west of the Heman Marion Sweatt Civil Courthouse. I just wanted to write about the squeaky old elevator in the civil courthouse.

PROPS AND KUDOS

Praise and honor to Heman Marion Sweatt (nickname Bill), the NAACP, WJ Durham, Thurgood Marshall, the Travis County Commissioner's Court, and the district judges of Travis County for helping to right a wrong. *Austin really is the heart of Texas.*

Kudos to the city of Austin for finally cleaning up Wooldridge Square.

Thanks to *Rhinos, The Movie* for serving as the prequel to this story and thanks to my friends, Adam Warren and Chad Nell, for making *Rhinos* with me and for encouraging me to write this book.

THREE BOOKS

This is the first book of a three-book series: *The Hero's Journey, The Journey Continues*, and *Endings and Beginnings*.

Read the other two books to find out what Marvin's secret is; if Mace and Jill get together; what becomes of the broom closet and why was it there; what became of Ike's partner, Goldstein; what happens on Carl Junior's case; what becomes of Dan-Dan; why Ike and Snappy Reese are enemies; what Kay's background is and why she loves Ike; how the Carver-Washington Gospel School of Law got its name; if Brick and Candice Kennedy get together; if Diaeta Pepsi comes back into the picture; if Marvin's grandma and his uncle Kevin play into the story; more about the "gun" Brick saw Ike with; and what obstacles Brick and Mace will face along the Path to Enlightenment.

ACKNOWLEDGMENTS

I want to thank the following people: my wife, Cecelia, for her emotional and intellectual support; my son, Gregory, for proofreading and being an insightful sounding board; my friend and legal assistant, Jonathon Zemek, for proofreading and for his encouragement and insight; my friend David Pittard for proofreading and for his helpful comments; Jeff Breckenridge at Ellis Graphics for the awesome cover art and design; my dad, Fred, for teaching me to appreciate a good story; my friends and mentors, Gilles and Liliane Desjardins, for helping me learn how to Practice the Presence; Emmet Fox, David Hawkins and Anthony De Mello for helping me learn how to live; my friend Gary Richardson for being my legal mentor and my champion; and my friends Adam Warren and Chad Nell for being sounding boards, for helping me come up with the story line, and for helping create the characters Brick Hawthorne and Mace Spinella.

AUTHOR'S NOTE

Come visit Austin. You'll have a great time. But please don't move here. You won't like it. Austin used to be a great place to live, but it got too crowded because of all the tourists who came and stayed. Nearly five thousand people move here every month. The traffic sucks. Locals have started calling Loop 1 "SloPac" instead of MoPac. We're running out of water. Rent and property values are through the roof. So, welcome to Austin, but please go back home, if you can.

May the light of Love and Wisdom illuminate your Path.